CW00819415

URGE TO KILL

JJ FRANKLIN

Earth *Tiger*

Published by
Earth *Tiger*
11 Pampas Close,
Stratford-upon-Avon,
England,
CV37 0TN
01789-267245

Email: brenda308@btinternet.com

Website: www.BMLittlewood.com

Copyright © JJ Franklin 2011

JJ Franklin has asserted her right under the Copyright, Design and Patents Act of 1988 to be identified as the author of this work.

ISBN 978-0-9571935-0-5

Copyright © JJ Franklin 2011

This novel is entirely a work of fiction. The names, characters, and incidents portrayed in it are the work of the author's imagination. Any resemblance to actual persons, living or dead, is entirely coincidental.

All rights reserved. No part of this publication may be reproduced, stored in a retrieval system, or transmitted in any form, by any means, electronic, mechanical, photocopying, recording, or otherwise, without the prior permission of the author.

ACKNOWLEDGEMENTS

Without the help of the following people, I doubt that this book would have been completed. A big thank you goes to Gemma Williams, who gave such excellent advice and encouragement and to Maureen Hill, for her editing and help through countless drafts.

Thank you to all my family and friends for being so encouraging and supportive during the long process, especially Janet Williams and Diane Franklin.

Special thanks go Cathy Whittaker and the members of The Stratford Scribes Writing Group, who listened to my early chapters and gave me helpful and constructive comments.

I would also like to thank The Arvon Foundation for the opportunity to work with top writers. They gave excellent tutoring and helped me find the courage to write this book.

The Hilary Johnson Authors' Advisory Service set me on the right track and helped me to believe in myself.

Thanks go to De Montfort University's 'Writing for Television' MA programme for instilling a sense of professionalism in me.

Last but not least, Robert McKee and his story structure seminars, for inspiring me and for giving me an understanding of how story works.

CHAPTER 1

He chose her from the robed figures waiting in the perfumed atrium. Engrossed in the celebrity gossip magazines, no one noticed the white-suited therapist approach her. No one watched as she followed him obediently to the treatment room.

As he walked behind her down the white corridor, he assessed her figure, congratulating himself that she would be perfect for his purpose.

He held open the door for her to pass into the relaxing oasis, allowing the mingled scents of essential oils to drift out into the corridor.

She turned to appraise him, certain of her well-maintained beauty.

'I thought it would be a lady therapist?' she said, her voice rising in a question.

'Don't worry. We'll soon have you relaxed.' He treated her to a shy smile. 'Unless of course, you would prefer…?'

She shrugged. 'It doesn't really matter.'

He closed the door behind him, and turned to watch as she moved to stand beside the therapy couch.

Taking two steps towards her, he brought up his hands as if to help her remove her robe. Her neck was warm and soft and yielded easily to his hands.

She looked surprised, flung out her arms, her long painted nails clawing at the couch as if it could give her support against his sudden assault. He smiled, relentlessly increasing the pressure, unprepared for how easy it was. Her mouth opened as if to scream but turned instead into an ugly gape through lack of air.

Before real panic could reach her eyes, she was dead. Suffering was not part of his plan.

Releasing his hands, he caught her as she sagged to the floor and lifted her gently onto the couch. When he pulled her robe open, he discovered she was naked beneath. This was good since her firm flesh did not interest him, and having to remove her underwear would just cause delay.

She was his and he was free to make any statement he wanted with her lifeless body. Now she would become the perfect expression of his pain.

He turned away from her and went to the heating panel, where he had hidden everything he needed. From the pile of clothing, he selected the little-girl knickers printed with pictures of a fairy-tale princess. Luckily, obese little girls liked to pretend they were princesses too. He lifted her limp, painted feet and inserted them into the knickers. It was no trouble to tug them up to her waist.

Next, he shook out the pink party dress with its deeper satin sash, and carefully sitting her up, he placed it over her head. Her head slipped onto his chest and, for a moment, he indulged in the great sense of power this gave him. His fingers began to tremble as he straightened the dress and fastened the matching bow in her hair. He was aware that time was of the essence and that he might be discovered at any moment.

Then he stood back to admire his handiwork. She looked perfect, just like a child going to a party. In his excitement, he had forgotten the finishing touches, so he added these, carefully placing each one for maximum effect. Until, completely satisfied, he recorded the scene on his mobile phone.

After quickly changing into his own robe, he folded the borrowed therapist suit and her robe under a towel and left the room, dropping the whole bundle into the full linen trolley at the end of the corridor, before strolling nonchalantly away. Mission accomplished in less than three minutes.

CHAPTER 2

Matt wiped the steam from the bathroom mirror and adjusted his tie. It seemed funny sharing his space with anyone since, apart from a mate or two staying to celebrate the occasional rugby win, this small flat had been his home for six years, ever since he had made Detective Inspector. It was here he did his best thinking when embroiled in a difficult case.

Now he had a wife. Matt was still amazed at how easy it had been to realise that Eppie was meant to be his life-long companion. If he tried to analyse the attraction in true detective fashion, he knew he would never be able to work it out. It went beyond cerebral thinking and was something much more primitive and essential.

Eppie wasn't beautiful, whatever that was; she was unique, the sort of woman anyone would immediately notice when she walked into a room. She didn't give up; she could, in fact, be downright fierce, as he had found out when they first met.

He had been attracted to her from that moment, even though she had just beaten him to a rare parking place on Jury Street, and what's more, she had left the tail end of her car sticking out into the oncoming traffic. 'Don't tell me you're going to leave it like that?' he had shouted from his open window.

She had turned in surprise. Matt thought she looked out of place in the medieval market town of Warwick. She certainly wasn't dressed for a rainy, English summer day, the sort of day that made him want to turn on the central heating. The red cotton top had a Mexican look to it. Plus, she was getting soaked, and the thin material was beginning to cling, allowing her black bra to show through.

The woman turned in surprise. 'Oh. Sorry, only be a minute,' she said turning her back and striding off into the newsagent's shop.

Matt experienced a mixture of annoyance and intrigue. He wasn't used to being ignored, especially when he was pointing out a matter of public safety. He put on his hazard lights and got out. This woman needed sorting out. Taking a walk around her car, he was disgusted to find that she hadn't even locked it. How stupid could people be?

At least she was true to her word and came out of the shop within a minute, tearing the wrapping from a cheap umbrella. As she flipped it open, she stopped, shocked to see him. 'Still here?' she asked, almost poking him in the eye. 'I'm going now, so you can have this space. You're blocking traffic there,' she said, nodding towards his car.

Matt felt the blood rising to his head. How dare she accuse him of causing an obstruction?

'Excuse me,' she said, trying to get past Matt to the door of her car.

Matt stood his ground debating with himself whether to get heavy and bring out his warrant card. She had stopped in front of him, a bundle of energy, brown eyes beginning to spark as he stood looking down at her.

'I want to get into my car, so please move—now.'

She was obviously used to getting her own way, but so was he. 'Can I point out that your car is parked in a dangerous position?'

'And who are you? The traffic police?' she snapped taking a half step forward. 'Get out of my way.'

Matt had no doubt she would physically try to push him aside if he didn't move. What an attitude. He admired her for it and suddenly saw how funny it must look, this pint-size woman squaring up to his six-foot-one. A smile crept into his eyes.

She picked up on this immediately. 'It's not funny. I have a thousand things to do: get the dry cleaning, pick up Dad and ring the agent. And this bloody rain. I thought it was supposed to be summer here.' She frowned at him as if she held him personally responsible.

Matt felt his smile widen. 'I'll move only if you promise to have dinner with me.' He felt like an idiot as soon as the words were out. She would think him some kind of pervert. He watched a range of emotions cross her face to end with the faintest echo of his smile. She was beginning to see the funny side too. Matt pressed home his advantage. 'When you have time, of course.'

'OK,' she said, smiling up at him.

It had been as simple as that: dinner the following night in a small bistro in Kenilworth with the food hardly tasted as they laughed together. For now, he was just happy to accept that he was the luckiest man on Earth. Well, except maybe for having McRay as a boss.

He could hear Eppie clanking about in the small kitchen and hoped she wasn't going to be the sort of wife who felt it her duty to fill him with greasy bacon and eggs in the morning. Matt moved across the small living room, stopping only to remove the bridal garter from one of his rugby trophies.

He came up behind Eppie and slipped his arms around her. She put down the coffee pot and turned into his arms, standing on tiptoes to reach up and kiss him. Matt loved her damp, fresh-from-the-shower smell. Eppie and hot coffee, it couldn't get much better than this.

Eppie turned away to pour the coffee, hot and strong, reminiscent of the lazy mornings of their honeymoon in Italy. Matt took a sip and watched her as she put some bread in the toaster before reaching into the warming oven to retrieve two steaming plates.

'The bacon was just about at its use-by date, and there's no black pudding, but I'll get organised for tomorrow.'

Matt couldn't stop his look of disgust as Eppie placed the hot plate in front of him. The sight of bacon, eggs, baked beans, and fried bread brought back memories that made his stomach churn.

'Oh.'

He saw the disappointment on Eppie's face and tried to soften the blow.

'Love the bacon. But the rest...'

'I'm sorry. I should have asked.' Eppie picked up his plate and turned back to the oven.

Feeling like a heel, Matt jumped up and went to her, slipping his arms around her waist from behind and nuzzling his face into her neck. He felt her relax in his arms as she turned towards him.

He kissed her—a long, deep kiss fusing them together and arousing the passion in both of them. Matt felt for the tie on her robe and eagerly pushed it aside to caress her body.

Afterwards, he reassured himself that everyday things like cooked breakfasts didn't matter as long as they loved each other.

Matt watched as Eppie put some fresh bread in the toaster before scraping his uneaten breakfast in the bin. 'It was at scout camp. I won't tell you what they did. Ever since then...'

'Must have been pretty dire.'

'You don't want to know.'

'Anyway, I don't want my man to become fat and flabby.' She aimed a playful punch at Matt's middle, which he dodged with ease, grasping her wrists and pulling her towards him again.

When Matt released her to rescue the burning toast, he was sure she had something on her mind.

'I thought I'd start looking for a job,' she said, still with her back towards him.

Matt, in honeymoon mood, had been hoping to keep Eppie all to himself for a little longer. He played for time. 'No hurry is there? We have no round-the-world yachtsmen here in Warwick.' Their express courtship had ruled out thinking of long-term plans, other than the urgent need to be together.

'No, but working for Dad has given me all sorts of skills, like planning, organising, sports injuries, cooking, massage...'

Matt laughed at her eagerness and cut her off midstream. 'All skills you can use on me.'

'So you want to keep me locked up and all for yourself?' Eppie mocked him.

CHAPTER 2

Matt drew her into his arms again. 'You bet.'

When he left the flat, Matt prayed that the criminals on his patch had been on their best behaviour. All he wanted to do was get back to Eppie. He had felt a bit heartless, leaving her there alone in the flat. Also, he couldn't wait to take on his old role of tour guide and show her the delights of the area. Except maybe his favourite, Kenilworth Castle, as he would always associate the castle with Jo.

Although in ruins, Kenilworth Castle had always drawn him with its sense of peace, as if the red sandstone walls had infused only the happy memories of those who lived there. Among them all, Matt liked to imagine John of Gaunt riding in on his charger to receive a seductive welcome from his mistress, Katherine Swynford.

After the bombshell of his grandfather's suspension, Matt had gone there seeking comfort and trying to digest how such a thing could happen to the best village bobby in England. Granddad was Matt's hero and could do no wrong, so a charge of corruption just couldn't be true. Matt could make no sense of it then, but he had made enough of his own mistakes since to realise that nothing was ever completely black and white.

CHAPTER 3

Lisa was calling his name as he ambled back to the Atrium. Pleading a call of nature, he apologised for keeping her waiting.

'No matter, but we had best get started on your massage. Got them packed in back to back this morning.'

He followed her to the therapy room, just three doors down from where his *statement* lay waiting to be discovered, thinking of how Lisa's morning was going to be delightfully disrupted.

Trying to relax was difficult as he waited for sounds that his efforts had been discovered.

'You are very tense today, Mr Draper.'

'Work I'm afraid. Just need your magic fingers.' He let her rub the essential oils into his back while his mind drifted back to what had sparked his endeavour.

He knew exactly when it had resurfaced, this urge to kill. Margaret, his sister, had placed her new baby in his Mother's arms, and he watched that old face relax into a rare smile, evoking agonizing memories of Mother with Lizzie.

The child gurgled and flailed its chubby arms in the air, as certain of its inherent power as all females. The unbroken bond between mother, daughter, and granddaughter left him excluded and alone again.

In danger of letting his jealousy show, Clive walked to the large bay windows and pretended an interest in the tree surgeon attending to next door's overgrown oak, grateful that all those years at St. Stephen's had taught him self control.

Then, with his hatred concealed, he felt able to join Mother and Margaret for a cup of tea and endure their conversation about what Margaret could expect, based on what she had been like as an infant.

'She really is the most beautiful baby in the world.' Mother put her cup down and peered again into the carrycot while Margaret preened as if she had just painted the Mona Lisa.

Little Emily interrupted their tea, screwing up her face, and preparing to let the world know who was boss.

'If only she would sleep through the night.'

'She will, just give her time. I used to stroke your head, like this.' Mother reached into the cot and began gently stroking Emily's head. *'Rock a bye baby in the tree tops.'*

Clive felt himself squirming as she sang the forgotten lullaby, while Emily, knowing she now had control, was quietening.

Had Mother ever smiled at him in that way? Had she ever loved him?

He blamed Elizabeth or Lizzie, as she now preferred, for after she arrived, although just a toddler himself, he had no chance of holding Mother's attention and, instead, was expected to give way to the new screaming bundle of pink. When he had tried to scramble onto Mummy's lap, she had spoken sharply and pushed him to the floor.

'Go away and play Clive. You are a big boy now, not a baby.'

He wasn't allowed to have a cuddle or a song; those things were for the new sister, while he was expected to become like his father, a thought which horrified him, even then, despite inheriting his tall, straight military frame.

When Clive's anger had exploded, and he had thrown his ball at the puking thing, enthroned in its lace basket, he had been promptly removed to his father's unfamiliar, musty study.

Father's booming voice, from somewhere high above him, filled the whole room, releasing showers of dust from the books and making him tremble.

'What have you got to say for yourself, Clive?'

He didn't have the words to scream that he just wanted some love and a cuddle from Mummy. But Mummy now only sang to and loved the new one.

Father sat down, bringing his face nearer, but Clive daren't look at him. He reached out and put his hands on Clive's shoulders, drawing him closer so that he could smell his tobacco breath on his face.

'This won't do. You have a new sister now. Time for you to grow up. Become Daddy's little man.'

Clive kept looking down at his shoes, not knowing what to say. His favourite word of the moment was *'No,'* but he didn't think saying it with a stamp of his foot would gain release.

'Your job now is to help me look after your sisters. You would like that wouldn't you?'

'No.' It had stumbled out and Clive waited in dread silence for the reaction. Suddenly, he found himself lifted up. The impulse was to struggle and cry for Mummy but he was too scared.

'Well, Clive, one day you will become a soldier like Daddy and just like these little fellows.'

He shifted Clive to one side and opened a glass door to take out a small model soldier.

'Here, you can hold him.'

He forced the brightly coloured little fellow into Clive's chubby hand. Clive looked down at it in disgust and threw it to the floor. Then he was lowered, crying, even before the sharp blow hit him across the back of the legs.

That dark, claustrophobic study haunted him, as did the model soldiers, arrayed in their battalions behind the glass-fronted cabinet. Although they were his father's pride and joy, they did not fascinate Clive. He wanted to jump up and down on them, see their silly uniforms and weapons broken to pieces and trampled into the carpet, but he never dared.

Instead, he made a pact to do the opposite of what his father wanted, even though he kept trying, in his brusque, inadequate way, to turn Clive into a worthy miniature of himself.

CHAPTER 3

Abandoned to the strange alien world beyond the nursery, Clive quickly learnt that it was best to hide his real feelings and began to encourage the people around him into believing that he was conforming to their plans.

By the time he was eight, Clive was an expert at playing the game. On the surface, he gave what was required of him while at the same time gaining satisfaction from the small, malicious tricks he played on his sisters. He had perfected his look of innocence and concern so that nothing could touch him. This stood him in good stead when, later that year, he was sent away to St Stephen's to learn how to become like his father.

St Stephen's was Father's old school, and many of the alumni had become distinguished military men. It highlighted activities such as self-defence and martial arts. To Clive's surprise, he excelled in these, mainly, he was sure, because he didn't like being hurt, and so had to be better than his opponents.

Father seemed pleased with Clive's progress and started calling him 'my good man' which left him feeling as if he had gained entrance, by default, into some strange male club.

As he continued to excel in martial arts, father took it as a sign that he would continue the family tradition of military service. However, Clive knew Father was going to be disappointed.

When the time came, he took great delight in informing Father of his intentions. Although he took the news like the soldier he was, Clive saw the bitter disappointment etched on his face and enjoyed the moment, regarding it as payback for all the hours forced to spend in his study.

This family of females had never needed him, although, of course, they had made the right noises at the appropriate times such as graduation, birthdays, and Christmas. It wasn't until two years ago, after his father's death, that they realised his usefulness. Mother was frail and couldn't stay on her own.

Before she had become pregnant, Margaret went abroad to exciting places like China and Peru with her husband and didn't want to give up that freedom to care for Mother, while Lizzie was doing yet another degree and couldn't, or wouldn't, be tied down.

When the invitation to dinner came, Clive soon realised what they had in mind. He had his own house with plenty of room for dear Mother. At first, he was appalled at the thought of this cold, grey haired, elderly stranger called Mother sharing his smart minimalist house, even if, as was pointed out to him, it was near the surgery and across from the park. To Clive she was his mother in name only, having closed her heart to him all those years ago.

Slowly, he began to see some of the advantages. Mother couldn't walk very far and, even with the help of a housekeeper during the day, she would be reliant on him for everything. He could control everything she did, just as she had once controlled him. He began to look forward to her stay.

Mother had settled in well and seemed to enjoy living with Clive. His sisters congratulated him on how well he cared for her. He was sure they were afraid that he would give up and land them with the opportunity. For once in his life, he had Mother's exclusive attention, and he made the most of it, sitting her down to dinner opposite him and making her listen to every detail of his day at work. Well, not every detail, as his thoughts and feelings about Ben were as yet undefined and too delicate, only suitable for when he was alone and daydreaming.

Overall, Clive relished his control, which he mooted as in Mother's best interests of course. She didn't go out if he was busy because it was too cold or raining, or that visit to a friend had to be put off because there were a lot of viruses about. Margaret and Lizzie began to praise Clive as some kind of saint, and he accepted this as his payment to keep the status quo.

Then Emily, Margaret's daughter, arrived, to take away his power. Clive watched as Mother became obsessed with the creature. Every conversation was about Emily, so the details of Clive's day became unimportant, easily dismissed by the latest gurgle from dear Emily.

Now at last, Clive was taking his revenge. Soon the world would understand his pain, his anger. He gave himself up to Lisa's nimble fingers, knowing he could do nothing until his endeavour surfaced.

CHAPTER 4

Matt pushed open the door to CID, a surprised look already etched on his face knowing that the lads would have prepared some sort of welcome back.

He hadn't quite expected the efforts the team had made and, as a hail of confetti hit him full in the face, thrown with great vigour by Sam of course, he caught sight of the huge banner spread from one side of the office to the other. *"DI Turrell—Booked at Last,"* it proclaimed.

Matt sighed at the pathetic attempt at humour. He was more than happy to be 'booked' to the delectable Eppie. In fact, he still couldn't quite believe his luck in attracting the most wonderful woman in the world, just when he had begun thinking maybe he would end up as one of those sad middle-aged men married to the job.

Sam stood on a desk shaking the rest of the multi coloured bits of paper purposefully over Matt's head. The grey serviceable carpet squares were covered, and as he moved forward through the congratulatory pats on the back, Matt wondered what McRay would say.

Detective Chief Inspector McRay had always been a grumpy sort of man, but since his wife had left him, and who could blame her, he had turned into even more of a growling bear who spent most of the day locked in the lair of his office. The door to the lair flew open.

'What bloody tomfoolery is this then? Isn't it bad enough that another good man has gone and got himself snared by some designing female?'

The team was suddenly changed back into something resembling a working CID team as each scattered to their appointed place. No one dared risk arguing with McRay.

'You,' he spat in Matt's direction. 'Suspicious death—place where silly women go to waste their husbands' money. Health spa place out at Heath Stone End. Take Sam and DC Meadows.' With a last glare around, he stalked back into his office and banged the door shut.

The team relaxed. Fluff whipped her jacket from the back of her chair and moved towards the door eager to get started on the case and out of McRay's orbit. Not that Fluff was the sort to cave in over some boorish middle-aged man whose wife finally had the sense to leave him, but she was used to keeping the peace. In less than two minutes, Matt was back in command and the job took over.

Matt chanced a glance at Fluff as she walked beside him down the corridor. He had often wondered if she had felt hurt or let down when their brief affair hadn't continued. It had started at the traditional celebration for the end of a particularly long and difficult case. The inevitable over indulgence of spirits had continued into the early morning and into Fluff's bed. Matt regretted the affair, not only because he received a fierce lecture from McRay about compromising his position as DI, but also Matt realised it wasn't fair to Fluff.

That was eighteen months ago and, although Matt had let her down as best as he could and they both laughed over how silly they had been, putting it down to the stress and alcohol, he sensed that she still held a faint hope that one day they might get together.

Despite the nickname of Fluff, Detective Constable Jane Meadows was one of the brightest officers in the team. It was unfortunate that she had worn one of those fluffy jackets, which were all the fashion, on her first day. The team gave her a thorough roasting before accepting her as one of their own and adorning her with the honour of a nickname.

Fluff broke the silence first, and he realised she was trying to ease the slight awkwardness between them. 'So, how was it then? I want to see all the photos.'

'I don't think we took many.' He and Eppie had spent most of the time just being with each other, walking, touching, eating, and loving, too engrossed in each other to think of anything else or of recording the setting of their deepening love. He quickly heard how this might sound and tried to back track. 'Much too lazy.'

There was silence between them until Fluff laughed as if it didn't matter. 'Oh well, that's what honeymoons, holidays, are all about isn't it?'

Matt was glad when they had reached his car and the moment passed. It would be easier now they had a job to concentrate on. They worked well together and Matt had full confidence in his team. Fluff's intuitive instinct to spot when the smallest thing was out of place, especially when a witness was lying, was a great asset.

Detective Sergeant Sam Withers performed his usual trick and shot into the back seat of the car at the last moment, closing the door just as Matt backed out of his appointed parking place. Another perk of making DI and one that Matt really appreciated as it cut out all that scrabbling for the left-over places on the forecourt and the danger of becoming one of the unlucky losers forced to park in the rear yard.

Sam broke into his thoughts. 'Hawkes were bloody hopeless last Saturday. Glad you are back for next week or Morris's lot will wipe us out for sure and take the cup.'

For the first time in his adult life Matt knew he didn't want to turn out to a wet, muddy pitch on Saturday to get sweaty and bruised. He would rather be with Eppie, but he also knew that he wouldn't be able to walk away from the team now that the season had started; only an injury or work would allow him to do that. He was spared from thinking about it as the traffic through Leamington became busy, and he had to concentrate to get them safely down the Parade and out towards Warwick.

The magnificent Warwick Castle dominated the town, and it always reminded Matt of the summers he spent working as a tourist guide as he slogged his way through A-levels.

That final summer was difficult as he tried to decide between following his love for history or of becoming a policeman like Granddad. Dad was pushing him to go to university, while Granddad quietly trusted him to make his own decisions.

Dad had tried to use Granddad's suspension as a lever to get Matt to do as he thought best. Matt still held an unspoken resentment towards him for that. However, in the end, it was as if Matt had made the decision many years before when he had listened, rapt, to Granddad's tales of his life in the force.

Matt knew that his Granddad was innocent, and his loyalty paid off a year later when Granddad was cleared. When he returned to work, he seemed to have lost his pride in the force and died just four months later—but not before he knew Matt had decided to follow in his footsteps.

Sam and Fluff's voices brought him back to the present as they spoke in unison.

'On the left, overlooking the River Avon, we have the magnificent Warwick Castle. The first fortification here was built by Ethel...?' They both laughed at the usual sticking point.

Matt joined them, used to their teasing about what used to be his running commentary when they first got together as a team. 'Ethelfleda,' he supplied, not for the first time.

'Sister of Edward the elder.' Fluff and Sam added in a chorus, making Matt laugh.

CHAPTER 5

Although Lisa had only just begun her massage, Clive felt as if they had been enclosed in the room for hours. Every sense was straining, waiting for the discovery of his work. He knew he needed to relax, to occupy his mind. He turned his thoughts to Ben and smiled.

One evening Clive had arrived home to find his pristine living room had suffered a pink explosion. Baby items, ranging from a carry cot to nappy bags, clothing, bottles, and several other items he couldn't even recognise filled the room. His space, the very centre of his universe, had been violated so that he hardly recognised it.

'Oh, Clive, please say you don't mind,' Mother greeted him. 'I told Margaret that we would love to have dear little Emily for the evening.'

Clive stood in the doorway and took a deep breath, aware that he couldn't show the fury that was boiling up inside him at this invasion. He allowed the breath to escape slowly through his mouth before managing a shaky reply. 'But I know nothing about taking care of an infant, Mother.'

Mother had anticipated this.

'You do not need to worry, Clive. Mrs Sinclair is going to stay on for the evening, just until Mummy and Daddy come back from the theatre.'

He squirmed as Mother placed her forefinger playfully on Emily's nose. The baby gurgled back and Clive's fingers itched to place his hands around that tiny neck as they had once itched to encircle Lizzie's. It would be so easy to squeeze the marauder's life away.

Blazing with fury, he searched for a way out. 'Sorry, but I have to return to the office tonight,' he said, trying hard to keep his voice calm.

Mother looked up at him as if she couldn't believe that he could pass on this opportunity to hold and play with his precious niece. Clive felt the need to elaborate. 'We have a problem with one of our major clients. Therefore, you can have her all to yourself, Mother.'

'Please, Clive, you do know better. She has a name. Haven't you, my little darling?' mother corrected, giving Emily a loving look. In return, Emily waved her little arms with renewed vigour, as if she was thoroughly enjoying his discomfort.

Clive accepted the rebuke with a quick 'Sorry,' before turning to escape from the room. Trying to make sense of the murderous thoughts whirling around his head, he stood in the hallway for a moment, before picking up his briefcase from the hall table and stumbling out to take a gulp of the clean air.

As he left his home to the ravages of Emily that night, he felt bewildered and angry. Why hadn't he seen this coming? How could she invade and take over the very centre of his space? Having Mother there was different since he had the control. However, it was too much for this thing to demand that all circulate around her like planets around a sun, there in his pale, understated living room with all her filthy baggage.

With no escape route planned, Clive headed on automatic pilot to the office. As he slid the silver BMW into its appointed place, he was surprised to find the office lights were on. Guessing it must be the cleaning staff, he hoped they had finished in his office.

Crossing beyond the tasteful reception area with its curved desk and potted plants, Clive took the lift to the office. As the doors opened, he was shocked to find Ben facing him. The last of his anger vanished, replaced with a tingle of excitement, which left him unable to speak.

With his dark curly hair and ready smile, Ben had an indefinable essence about him, making Clive's heart thump as if it were trying to burst out and declare itself. He had felt the attraction from the start, even though in many ways they were complete opposites.

Ben was cheerful, open, outgoing, and American. Always ready to help and inclined to be untidy, immediate. Whereas Clive was compulsively neat, and although he could easily charm when it was necessary, he made sure his inner self was never exposed.

'Hello.' The voice sounded unlike his own.

'Hi. Just finishing that contract.' Ben seemed almost as shocked as Clive but he was still able to produce that wide grin.

As Ben stood aside for him to leave the lift, he fought to say something intelligent. 'Forgot my mobile,' he mumbled, feeling like an awkward teen.

'I'll wait on and go down with you.'

Clive nodded and made a show of going into his office to open and shut desk drawers. As he made his way back to the lift, he was thinking about how he could prolong this chance meeting. Ben saved him the trouble.

'Fancy a drink or will you have to get back?'

'No. That would be good.' He hoped he hadn't sounded too eager, for the thought of sitting across from Ben sharing a casual drink had been just one of his fantasies over the last few months. Now that it was all happening, he felt unready, out of control, yet he knew he must seize the opportunity.

Ben led the way to a cosy looking pub, The Brown Horse, just off the Parade. It didn't look like the type of place he would take Mother. It was obvious Ben had been here before as he pointed out a small corner table set against the far wall where the lighting was low and comfortable.

'There's a space. Grab a seat, and I'll get a round in? What's your poison? Real ale?'

Clive nodded. He didn't mind drinking Mother's bath water just as long as he could sit here quietly with Ben, although he hadn't the slightest idea what he wanted to say or even how to say it.

He made his way through the office workers reviving themselves before the drive home to the table Ben had pointed out, settling himself with his back to the wall to watch Ben as he waited at the bar. When Ben turned to flash him a smile, Clive felt something jerk in the region of his heart. Was this love? Love for someone else was alien to him. Could he allow such an unaccustomed feeling to enter his life? Clive had never thought of himself as gay, either, but maybe this strange exhilaration meant he was.

Feeling confused, he was still searching for topics of conversation when Ben returned with the drinks. Luckily, Ben, like most Americans, wasn't so tongue tied, and as he responded he felt himself relax.

Ben placed the pints on the table while he put the jingle of change in his pocket. Clive quickly slid a bar mat under each glass and Ben laughed as he sat down opposite.

'Obsessional.' He shook his head sadly.

He realised how it looked and quickly covered his tracks. 'Living with Mother, I'm afraid.' Clive made sure that, after taking a large, nervous gulp of his drink, he replaced the glass firmly on the table, even if it did go against his instincts.

'They sometimes have a group on here. A folksy, pop sort of mix.'

'Are they any good?' Clive was trying to sound like he understood the kind of event Ben was describing.

'Not bad. The lead is a character, should have been a stand-up. He picks on someone in the crowd and, as long as it's not you, it's wild.'

He could see from Ben's face that he enjoyed that sort of evening and knew he would be willing to endure all just to be with him. 'So, when are they on again?'

'Won't be till next year now. They've gone on tour...Ireland I think.' Ben downed the rest of his pint. 'I'll let you know, if you like?'

'Yes, I'd like that,' he said, surprised to find Ben's glass already empty. 'Another?'

'Sure,' Ben said

It was after that second pint that Clive began to enjoy himself. That was until a hen party of ten strong—the intended bride complete with tiara and fairy wings—claimed the table next to them.

The women were noisy, drunk, and fully expected the rest of the people in the bar to accept, without a complaint, their stupid behaviour and loudness. Clive could see that most of the male patrons had decided to grin and bear it, except one or two of the older men at the bar who finished their drinks and left. The women clientele were all smiles and one or two even began cooing about the coming marriage in a similar way to how Mother and Margaret cooed over Emily.

They tried to carry on with their conversation and ignore the party until one of them, the one with mousy blonde hair that reminded Clive of Lizzie's before she had dyed it that ridiculous shade of red, staggered towards Ben and flung her arms around him dumping herself onto his lap, much to the great amusement of her friends.

One of the group called out, 'you planning to be next then, Tassie?'

As she ran her fingers through Ben's hair, Clive's hands were hot with the desire to choke the life out of her. He could see that Ben was trying to be gracious and remained smiling but also that he was getting more and more embarrassed at the vulgar comments and suggestions from the other girls as they egged Tassie on. Tassie's hand was now sliding up Ben's inner thigh.

Unable to stand it any longer, he stood ready to leave. 'Shall we get out of here?'

Ben seemed grateful for the interference, as it spurred him into action. As he jumped up to follow Clive, the slut slipped onto the floor where she sat in an ungraceful, ugly position with her legs wide open, laughing while her mates screamed with laughter amid their caterwauling.

As they reached the fresh air, Clive found that he was shaking with anger, devastated that his chance to get to know Ben lay in ruins, thanks to those women. Were females always going to ruin his life? He stood wondering if he was brave enough to suggest they adjourn to a different venue when Ben interrupted his thoughts.

'Think I'll head home. You?'

Clive tried to keep the bitter disappointment out of his voice. 'Yes. There's a programme I want to see.'

With a brief, 'See you tomorrow then,' Ben was gone, leaving Clive standing alone and oblivious to the people passing by and going over and over in his head every word that had been spoken between them. He found he couldn't clutch onto any promise of real interest or desire from Ben.

Walking back to his car, his anger grew. Who knew what would have happened if those disgusting girls hadn't taken over? Maybe he was being naive and it was nothing more than two colleagues meeting up for a drink after work. The fantasy and need were all on his side. Ben had probably been glad of a chance to escape. Clive's Mother had already proven he was unlovable, so why would anyone else be willing to give it a try?

It wasn't until he was driving home that he realised there was nothing to stop him allowing his hands the expression they were craving. He squeezed the steering wheel hard and felt the strength in his grip.

In Mr Argyle's unarmed combat class, they had touched on the theory of killing silently and quickly, not that they were allowed to put the knowledge into practice, but Clive could still recall every detail. Plus, he knew he could further his education via the ever-helpful Internet.

He felt excited by the power he could have over life and death. However, if he gave in to his impulse to harm any of his family, he knew he would be an immediate suspect. Clive had seen too many TV programmes not to know that was how it worked. However, if he chose a stranger, he could remain completely unsuspected with no motive at all.

Clive began to see the possibilities and problems his plan entailed and realised that he would have to work out the details with great care if he wanted to succeed. It would be a shame to waste his time on a simple murder. He wanted everyone to understand his pain. If he were never to have love, then instead, he would have his revenge.

As he negotiated his way through the crowds of revellers setting out to get drunk, pictures began to form in his mind. Clive knew getting the right clothes would be essential and difficult. He needed to ensure nothing could be traced back to him.

With a flush of excitement, Clive realised that he was planning more than one murder. He would rival Jack the Ripper and become a celebrity in the newspaper headlines.

By the time he pulled into his driveway, he had made his basic plans and felt so cheered he was able to enter his invaded home and smile briefly on young Emily. She would never find out that her arrival in the world had become the catalyst for a chain of unsolved murders.

Margaret and Tom arrived soon afterwards and whisked their precious daughter away, together with all her clutter, and Clive found he could even join Mother in a bedtime cup of cocoa while all the time running over his plans.

Under Lisa's expert attention, he had almost drifted off to sleep, so that when the expected scream came it startled him as well as Lisa. She gasped and left him to open the door. A male voice drifted in, his words belying the panic in his voice.

'Everything is under control. Please…please just carry on with your treatments.'

Lisa returned. 'Probably someone trying it on. Some of them do, given half the chance. And young Katie seems to pick 'em all.'

Clive murmured something in reply while forcing himself to remain calm. Once the police arrived, he would need all his wits about him.

CHAPTER 6

Heath Stone Manor had come on the market ten years ago following the death of old Mr Ronald Moor, the last of a long and unexceptional line. Matt had learnt the history of the Manor during his guide training and had been surprised to hear that it had been a resting place for Royalist troops during the Civil War.

The Manor became a conference centre for a few years until bought by a consortium of businessmen who poured in money to turn it into a prestigious health spa. It was the place to get fit, or at least, to be seen in.

Matt manoeuvred the sweeping drive, which meandered through the well-kept and attractive grounds. Coming out of the last bend, they faced the warm Cotswold stone building, standing firm and solid amidst the trees. Matt was glad to see that the refit had not altered the imposing front. He had warm memories of attending a police conference here when he had just made it into CID.

As a new young Detective Constable he was at the stage when anything was possible, believing, like a knight of old that he would rid the world of the corrupt and evil. Matt smiled at the memory and at how time and experience had taught him that the battle was on going and would last forever. All he could hope for was to make some difference to his own little area, to give his best, and to encourage others to do the same, like Granddad.

He had felt encouraged back then as older, wiser heads had taken him seriously, knowing that his idealistic streak would soon be tempered with the reality of day-to-day police work and limitations of what they could do.

There had been other encouragements at that conference, and Matt wondered if DC Jenny Hadden ever thought of those moonlit walks in the grounds and their brief but passionate coupling. He had heard down the grapevine that she also had made DI a year after him.

Matt pulled himself back to the present as he drew up at the front entrance. Two patrol cars were already there, and Matt nodded to the uniformed policeman now stationed at the entrance.

As he stepped into the cool interior, it was obvious that this was where the refit had taken over. From the shining marble floors and pillars to the bright airiness of Reception with its ceiling skylights, it was clear that the original building had been gutted. The only thing that remained was the magnificent seventeenth-century staircase that flowed gracefully down into the lobby on the left. Matt supposed it gave the guests a sense of class, of a timeless elegance. Plus, it allowed another few quid to be added to the cost of membership.

The manager came forward to introduce himself as Daniel Smith. He looked very young and nervous. Matt tried the calm authoritative approach, reassuring the poor man that everything was now in hand.

'DI Turrell, Mr Smith. We'll take care of everything now. Can you tell me who found the body?'

'Katie…Miss Taylor. However, she is terribly upset, Inspector. The head receptionist is trying to calm her down.'

'Right. We'll leave Miss Taylor for now. If you would take me to the crime scene, Mr Smith.'

Mr Smith hesitated before pointing a feeble hand towards a green sign marked *Treatment Rooms*.

Matt helped Mr Smith overcome his initial reluctance to lead the way by placing a gentle, yet firm, hand under Mr Smith's elbow while encouraging him to move in that direction with him.

The victim appeared completely relaxed but then Matt supposed she would. The soft lights and low mood music were set to enhance an escape from the stresses of the outside world. Except that maybe she was just a little too relaxed. The limp arm drooping over the side of the couch was too casual; the lips gaped in that unattractive way of a politician at question time.

Matt moved forward in a useless reflex action to check the carotid pulse. There was no doubt that she was dead, although at first glance there were no obvious marks, but he decided it would be best to leave Slim, the Police Surgeon, to his area of expertise in figuring out how she died.

Matt turned to usher the shocked manager out while calling for Sam.

Before he closed the door to preserve any evidence, Matt stood and tried to take in all the details. He looked at a young, pretty woman, even in death. Though it was obvious she was a woman, the bows in her hair, her pink party dress, and white ankle socks said she was a little girl. On her right side was one of those cloth dolls, and she looked as if she was cradling it. Across her lap lay a large yellow and orange lollipop.

Matt felt a shiver at the odd mix of images. It was almost as if they had the copper's nightmare to deal with—a child murder. Except this was no innocent child but a young woman, he would guess around twenty-two and with everything to live for.

Sam arrived at his side, and Matt stood aside to let him see the body.

'Bloody hell, Guv. That's downright creepy.'

'Yes.' Matt shut the door firmly and signalled a uniformed PC to stand guard outside. 'We need to get the team and Slim here fast. Let's clear this corridor now.'

Fluff joined them. 'There's a small café, just off to the left at the end of this corridor, Guv.'

Trust Fluff to be one step ahead. 'Good.' Matt looked at the ashen-faced manager. 'We will need somewhere to question the guests from this corridor. The café would be ideal.'

The manager, who seemed incapable of speech, nodded his consent. Matt knew it would be best to give the man something constructive to do. 'I need you to make sure that the rest of the guests stay calm. It would be advisable to say there has been an incident, nothing more at this stage.'

Mr Smith nodded, already edging away, eager to get away from the scene of death.

Fluff referred to her notebook. 'Checked on Katie, Guv. The deceased was her nine-thirty appointment. She's still in a state. I'd say it's best to leave her to have another cup of tea. Head receptionist is with her. She seems pretty sensible.'

'Thanks, Fluff. Let's get through this lot then—especially those who would have been waiting in the atrium for a nine-thirty appointment. They should have seen something.'

Matt helped Sam and Fluff usher the mixture of horrified yet curious guests and staff along the corridor and into the café, knocking at doors on the way to alert and move guests who were in the middle of various treatments. He thought grimly that if they came here for relaxation and escape from the worries of the world then a juggernaut had just crashed in on them.

As Matt followed the last of the guests and staff making their way to the café, he noticed that Fluff had started taking down the names of the mostly robed guests.

The café was a pleasant place, the wicker chairs with their bright autumn colours made vibrant in the light from the glass roof. The staff busied themselves to provide the startled guests with complimentary drinks from the health food bar. Matt wondered if carrot and orange juice would really help with the shock of finding that there was a body just a few feet away from where they had been enjoying their relaxing massage.

Putting on his most official voice, he took control. 'Hello, everyone. My name is Detective Inspector Turrell, and this is Detective Sergeant Withers. Over there is Detective Constable Jane Meadows.'

He pointed to Fluff who was helping an elderly woman in a white robe. Too many white robes he thought—makes escape easy.

'We will try to make this as quick and easy for you as possible. However, before you can leave this area, we do need to speak to each one of you briefly. There has been an incident in one of the rooms along this corridor.' Matt indicated the long corridor to his right and noticed that Sam was already busy sealing it off with the crime scene tape.

'We need to know where each one of you was at the time of the incident, and to make sure we have your personal details. Then you will be able to return to your rooms or another part of the spa.'

Matt estimated there were at least twelve guests and several staff, which meant allowing about three minutes each, speed dating came to mind, to collect the vital information from each guest and highlight those who needed further investigation. He estimated around twenty minutes to clear this room. By then, Forensics and Slim should be well entrenched and the important information would start feeding in. Then maybe Katie would be able to string two words together.

The team were efficient and worked fast, calming and reassuring the guests as they recorded their names, addresses, and room numbers, while reminding them they were to stay in the health club until given permission to leave. Day guests were told they would be able to leave as soon as their addresses had been checked.

No one had noticed anything out of the ordinary, but given the mixture of staff uniforms, from white-suited therapists, blue-suited maintenance men, to red-topped serving staff, not to mention the white-robed guests, Matt guessed it would have been easy for the murderer to slip in unnoticed. Whether the murderer had slipped out again or remained within this innocuous group was another matter.

As the last of the staff and guests left the café, Matt checked with Sam and Fluff.

'Well, all my lot seem innocent. Maybe too innocent,' Matt sighed. He knew this wasn't going to be easy.

'Nothing to set off that famous quiver then, boss?'

'No. How about you, Sam?'

'Not much. One young lady…'

'Oh, here we go,' added Fluff

'Hey, I can't help that I drew the short straw can I?' Sam appealed to Matt.

Matt ignored the usual bantering. 'So what aroused your suspicions about this young lady?'

Fluff shook her head at the word aroused. Sam merely grinned at her and carried on.

'Miss Tania Belcott gave me the wrong area code for where she said she lived. It's probably nerves, but I've marked her down to see again.'

'I bet you have.'

'Fluff?' Matt cut in, eager to know if they had any leads.

'Two. A Clive Draper who is a day guest. He mentioned a murder. Thought it was worth following up, since we haven't told any of the guests it was murder yet. Second is a cocky little git who started work as a therapist a week ago. Only thing is, he doesn't seem to remember where he worked last. A possible I would say.'

'Good. Sam, have another go at these three. Fluff, could you see if we are likely to get any sense out of Katie yet.'

Matt was impressed as always with his team. True these first queries were probably nothing and would be put down to a combination of nerves and rumour, but it showed that their antennae were in full working order.

Matt didn't have much time for conjecture as the pathologist, Slim, caught up with him. Slim always had a sad look on his face. Matt used to think it was in deference to all the victims he had to examine, but at one Christmas party Slim turned up with his wife and elder daughter, all of whom had that same hangdog look, which sent everyone scurrying for another drink.

'I'd say that the cause of death was manual compression of the vagal nerves.' Matt looked blank, and Slim added, 'The jugular vein together with the carotid arteries. Stops the heart. Loss of consciousness would have occurred very quickly.'

'Time?'

'Not long ago. I'd say nine a.m. the very earliest.'

'Any sign of sexual activity?'

'No, I don't think so. Tell you for certain later. But I can say that he dressed her in that odd way post mortem.'

'He?'

'Well, it would take some strength to apply that much pressure. Could be a woman, but more likely you're looking for a man.'

At least it was a blessing that she died quickly. Matt found the worst murder cases, aside from those of children, were when the victim had been tortured before death, like Gracie, who was always there in his memory, prompting him not to let anyone else down.

Gracie was only sixteen. She was a bright spark of a girl with many friends, looking forward to the future, until the monster he should have stopped took her life.

Matt was one of the first to see her. She looked at peace but her naked body, carelessly tossed in a ditch, told him all he needed to know of what her last hours had been like. She had fought hard for her life and lost out to Fraser, the pervert who had simply used her for his own pleasure.

CHAPTER 7

After Matt had left, Eppie took her breakfast from the warming oven to discover she had lost her appetite. She was starting to realise that she and Matt knew nothing about each other. Dad had always loved a good, hearty breakfast—said that was how a sailor should start the day—good ballast if the seas were rough.

And she had known immediately that Matt hadn't even thought about her working. However, if he expected her to stay cooped up in this tiny dismal flat with nothing to do, then he didn't know her very well.

Eppie wiped down the dark granite worktops and all the cold stainless steel, thinking that even the morning sun couldn't bring any warmth into this kitchen. She knew it was unfashionable but to Eppie, a kitchen should be a warm, inviting place, the hub of a house, like Grandma's warm, cosy kitchen with its promise of treats still hot from the oven. Matt's tiny kitchen did not delight her at all.

Finishing in the kitchen, Eppie walked around the flat wondering what she could change in this male space with its neat order and dull masculine colours. Even the trophies crowded onto the mantelpiece left no room for as much as a photo. For her, it needed something to liven it up, and she had the urge to rush out and buy some multi-coloured cushions and scatter them carelessly about.

For the first time since her marriage, Eppie felt a sense of loss for the lifestyle she had given up. Working with Dad had brought her a new challenge every day. Pete Featherstone was a famous yachtsman, so most people had heard of him. Eppie's job had been to smooth the way, deal with officials and clear the way for Dad and the Mary Lee to berth to take on essential supplies and sometimes much-needed repairs.

Meeting Matt was as sudden as it was inconvenient. One moment she was cursing the inconsiderate man who blocked the way to her car, and in the next, as he smiled, she fell in love.

Dad had given his blessing, and it was obvious that he liked Matt.

'I can't leave you in the lurch, Dad.'

'Rubbish. One more trip and I'm done. Matt has saved me having to pay someone to take you off my hands.'

'Dad!' Eppie laughed while attacking him with a washing up sponge.

Just six weeks later, she and Matt were married in a short but lovely ceremony at Braebeck Grange, a stately home that made a killing in arranging marriages. Wanting Eppie to have the best, Dad had paid for everything. Nothing had been left out.

Well, except for the absence of Mother who said she couldn't leave her latest husband during the social season in Argentina. Not that Eppie counted this as much of a loss, and it was compensated for by the welcome sight of Mo and Amy, two old schoolmates from college.

Eppie knew this sense of not belonging would pass and refusing to dwell on it, she kicked herself into resolute action. She found what she wanted in one of her, as yet, unpacked suitcases.

She decided it would go on the mantelpiece, but now, as she stood looking at all Matt's rugby trophies, she hesitated as to where to place it. Having no space of her own brought back vivid memories of staying at Aunt Sandra's. There, Eppie couldn't make even a corner of Cousin Natalie's bedroom her own. But Eppie had no intention of running away this time.

Which one would Matt miss the least she wondered after trying for the fourth time to move the trophies along to accommodate the photo of her smiling and proud Dad. It was taken after a particularly difficult leg of a race, when he and the Mary Lee had been battered and badly damaged by fierce storms.

She remembered how relieved she had been as the Mary Lee limped into port.

'There's my girl,' he said as he jumped ashore to enclose her in a bear hug.

'Oh, I'm so glad to see you, Dad.' Eppie was trying to keep the tears from her eyes.

'Hey, none of that. You should know by now that you can't get rid of me that easily. Come on, let's face the music,' he chided as he led her towards the eager crowd of reporters.

One of the TV crew thrust a brimming pint into his hands, and she'd stepped back to capture the moment as he'd gratefully swallowed it down.

The picture deserved a place in the flat, her flat. Eppie made her decision and, removing the smallest, plainest trophy, she relegated it to the bookcase before realigning the others so that her Dad could grin down at her from the middle of the mantelpiece.

Standing back to admire her work, she felt better and the momentary panic had passed. She could live here, at least for a while, and make it a shared space. When she had a job, they could save towards buying a house.

With a sigh, Eppie returned to the classified section of the local paper and began circling the possibilities. Many of the positions would leave her bored to tears, and she decided the only antidote would be to work with people.

It was then that an advert for a receptionist at Heath Stone Manor Health Spa caught her eye, and she quickly marked this while reaching for the phone.

CHAPTER 8

Clive had fully given into Lisa's ministrations when the knock came, followed by a brisk order that they all gather as quickly as possible in the café at the end of the corridor.

He moved as bid with the other guests while pulling the white fluffy robe around him and making sure he looked surprised and anxious. A bossy young woman, part of the police team, shepherded everyone towards the health food café with its basket chairs and soft colourful cushions. Clive hesitated at the café entrance and reached out to grasp her hand.

'Is there a fire?' he said, making sure he sounded concerned.

'My DI will explain in a moment, Sir,' she replied before returning to hurry the rest of the guests along. 'If you could all find a seat please, the Inspector will be with you shortly. We'll try not to keep you very long.' She moved away to direct other guests. 'There are two seats over here, Madam.'

He sank obediently into the nearest chair and felt his heart rate steadying; the inner glow of satisfaction began to spread through his body. It was an effort to keep a broad smile from his face, but he forced his muscles to obey him and kept the concerned mask in place. Clive looked around to see which of his immediate neighbours it might be best to engage in worried and speculative conversation.

To his left was a grey-haired, anxious looking woman, and he decided she would be the easiest. He didn't want to put in too much effort, but instead wanted to relive what he had done, savouring the temporary soothing of twenty-nine years of hurt and anger.

He agreed with the grey-haired woman about how awful it all was while thinking secretly that it wasn't awful but a wonderful kind of poetry. Yes, that is what it was, poetic justice. Clive felt no sorrow for the pseudo victim; no doubt she was set to go through life in a spoilt and cosseted manner, ruining any chance of happiness for the men or boys around her.

'Don't worry—It will be alright now that the police are here.' The old lady laid a caring hand on his arm, and he forced himself back to the present, time enough later to enjoy his endeavours when the immediate danger had passed.

Clive smiled at the old lady. 'I heard someone say there had been a murder, so I was just so upset at the thought of…you know,' he stuttered.

There was carrot juice on offer and he realised he was thirsty, not that this small cup of weak and boring juice was ever going to satisfy either his physical thirst or his growing appetite to kill again.

The woman detective had started writing down names, and Clive began preparing what he would say. He had to let them know he was only a day guest, and that he needed to get home before Mother's carer left. This should put him at the top of their list for release once they knew where they could find him.

Later, as Clive stood in Reception with the other day guests waiting for permission to leave, he berated himself for being so stupid. That young woman detective was no fool and had spotted his error straight away. He had mentioned the word *murder*.

As soon as he had said it, he knew it was a mistake. Clive watched as she put a star next to his name and told him briskly to wait. Eventually, the detective sergeant re-interviewed him. He had been brisk and business like.

'Mr Draper.'

'Yes, Officer.'

'Detective Sergeant Withers. Would you just run through how you first became aware of the incident?'

Interesting official line—*the Incident*. For a moment, he wanted to reach across the table and scream the truth into the man's stupid face. There was a dead girl lying in that room and he had killed her. Instead, Clive took a breath and pretended to think.

'I was with Lisa. There was a scream. Lisa went to the door and I heard someone, a man, say everything was under control. Then Lisa came back and started to massage me again. She said something about someone trying it on and how it was always Katie that seemed to get the men like that.' He shook his head as if disgusted at the thought of such men.

'When interviewed by DC Meadows, you stated...' the Sergeant paused to read his notes. '*I feel very upset at the thought that someone has been murdered.*'

He looked up at him, waiting for an explanation. Clive gave him a puzzled look, forcing him to continue.

'What made you believe that someone had been murdered, Mr Draper?'

'Oh,' Clive nodded as if suddenly understanding his problem. 'The elderly lady next to me was getting very upset and I was trying to calm her down. She kept saying it must be a murder as soon as the yellow tape went up.' He gave the Sergeant a smile. 'She probably watches too much TV, just like my Mother. I'm so sorry, Detective, if I have caused a problem. I'm afraid I just repeated what she, everyone, was saying.'

His explanation seemed to satisfy the Sergeant. Clive doubted if the old dear would say different if they asked her, as the murmurings had begun among the guests detained in the café as soon as the crime scene tape had been put in place. It forced him to realise just how very careful he would have to be. This was no game, but a battle of wits with the police.

This little team, although not Scotland Yard, were well led by DI Turrell. Clive decided he didn't like this tall detective who walked with such easy, purposeful strides. He looked like a sportsman of some sort as he moved and held himself in a way that suggested he was always ready for action. Or maybe it was that sense of easy authority in the way he directed his staff or the obvious esteem in which they held him. There was the sense of a well-ordered team of which the DI was an easy and natural leader.

There was something about the DI that reminded him of Philip Spencer-Blake, the head boy who had tried to give Clive a hard time at school. But he had managed to get his own back. He smiled at the thought of Spencer-Blake's disgrace after he had been caught with a small amount of banned substance. True, the Spencer-Blakes had managed to pull enough strings to avoid the disgrace of dear Philip being expelled, but he had been thoroughly pleased with the results of his actions after the arrogant lad had lost his cherished position.

Clive was aware that this authoritative DI Turrell was his enemy, and therefore, it was vital that he became fully aware of how the man worked. History had been one of his favourite subjects at St Stephen's, and he remembered Mr Thompson stressing, during an exploration of World War Two, that often the difference between winning and losing was to know your enemy. Clive intended to win.

CHAPTER 9

U sually, when Matt was on a case, everything else had to take a
back seat, but what of Eppie? Even now, as the team began to
work methodically through the rest of the guests, he found himself
thinking of her and wondering what she was doing.

Tonight's cosy dinner would be out for sure, and he realised
that he had better warn her in case she was planning to go to any
trouble for their first dinner together in the flat.

As she answered, Matt was a little surprised from the background
hubbub that Eppie seemed to be in the middle of a noisy crowd.
He wanted to ask where she was, but pulled himself back hoping
that she would tell him without him having to pry. He took refuge
in the fact that he was busy and had to keep it brief.

'Sorry, Eppie, but I won't be able to make it home very early or
even at all.'

'I heard about your case. Look don't worry, I'll leave something
out in case you make it.'

Her reply puzzled him. He could hear the excitement in her
voice and several questions arose. Where had she heard about the
case? Had the news hounds got hold of the details already? Why
did she sound excited? And where was she? Matt reviewed them
all and came up with the limp, 'It sounds noisy your end?' in the
hopes that she would fill him in. He was disappointed and her
reply only added to the questions.

'Everyone is talking about the murder. Must go. Tell you all my news when you get home. Oh, and love you.'

Matt could hardly give a return assurance in front of the team and had to make do with a pathetic, 'Same here,' before ending the call.

Still puzzled, he sent a uniformed PC to communicate with headquarters to check if there was a press release. It would be unusual for this to happen without the officer in charge being consulted, but McRay was turning into a liability and could have contravened this rule.

Jason, Head of Forensics, brought Matt out of his reverie.

'The bastard almost certainly wore gloves, Matt.'

Matt strained to hear what Jason had to say through the wad of chewing gum moving rhythmically about his mouth. Jason said it helped him concentrate, but Matt always found it a distraction.

'Too careful for his own good. I don't think we'll get anything in there, but we'll have a go anyway.' Jason paused to chew while Matt waited. 'Someone's been at the heating panel recently so that's where he could have stored his props. We might get lucky. Best I can do.'

Matt agreed. This wasn't a suddenly impulsive crime of passion, where the perpetrator got carried away and careless, but one of careful planning. Matt was sure this killer wanted to say something, to make a statement. He didn't need profiler Professor Derek Meredith to tell him that this killer would kill again and again, unless they stopped him, or her, although his instinct told him that he was looking for a man. Of course, given that the premises had more than a few female massagers who would need strong hands for their work, he thought he had better keep an open mind.

'Thanks, Jason.'

Before he had time to move, Fluff came up.

'Young Katie has calmed down a bit. Handled right she might be able to string two words together.'

Matt guessed this was Fluff's way of saying she wanted to conduct the interview, and he was happy to leave the questioning to her.

'OK. Let's do it.'

Passing the crime scene tape Sam had optimistically put in place, he followed Fluff along another airy, light corridor. It was lined with a multitude of green plants all in white containers with pebble arrangements neatly interspaced with glass cases showing the enticing, must have, wares of the gift shop.

As they entered the manager's office, a pretty, dark-haired young woman, who looked as if she had been crying, jumped up as if desperate to escape. Her white uniform looked crumpled and had a tea stain down the left side. Several used cups, a bottle of water, and a wine glass littered the small table beside her.

As Matt held the door open for the older woman to leave, he learnt she was Mrs Trowbridge, the head receptionist. Matt thanked her and said they would catch up with her later. She gave a gracious nod of her elegantly coiffured head and left. Here was someone who took murder in her stride, Matt thought.

Matt realised he would be accused of being sexist, but he had to admit that this was the time when Fluff came into her own, and he was more than glad that she was on his team. He didn't think it was just because she was female, more that she had, and he tried recalling some past police lecture, *empathy*—that was the word.

Fluff moved forward, taking a seat and encouraging Katie to sit beside her.

Matt took a seat to the side, content to let Fluff handle the whole interview.

'Katie, I know how awful this must be for you. However, if we are going to catch the person who did this to Miss Metcalfe, then we need you to tell us exactly what you saw. It could give us a vital clue.'

Katie cleared her throat. 'I went to the Atrium—to collect Miss Metcalfe. I called her name about three times, but no one answered. So I went to Reception just to check it was right. Sandi said...said...'

Fluff broke in to stop Katie from breaking down again. 'Katie. Look at me, Katie.' She waited until Katie looked up. 'You are doing so well. What you have to say could really help us.'

Matt watched as Katie fought back her tears.

'Sandi remembered her especially because...because the massage had been booked by her mother—for a birthday treat.'

The last words came out in a sudden rush, as if Katie didn't want to think about the people involved. Not Amy or her mother who lived in Leeds. Matt thought grimly that Amy's mother would just about now be hearing how her birthday treat had ended.

'How many people were waiting in the Atrium, Katie?'

'It was fairly quiet being Monday. I would think about eight, maybe ten.'

'So what did you do then?'

'I went to...to the storeroom, to get some oils and things. I thought I would give her five minutes, then check again.' Katie's voice was beginning to quiver and she looked down into her lap.

'Katie, I know this next bit is going to be difficult for you, but I need you to be brave for just a little longer. Do you think you can do that?'

Katie looked up at Fluff. 'I'll try.'

'Great. Now, as you left the Atrium and walked along the corridor to the storeroom, did you see anyone?'

There was silence in the room as Katie tried to recall her walk towards making her gruesome discovery. Matt knew that a witness could become amnesic around such horror.

'Just think about the first few steps,' Fluff prompted her.

'After I passed the guests who were waiting, I turned left into the corridor. Moira was just going into her room with a client. She does heated stones. Then I passed the end of my corridor...The storeroom is on the right...just a bit farther up.'

Katie tapered off and Matt couldn't help injecting. 'And?'

Fluff gave him a sharp look and flapped her hand at him warning him not to interfere before turning back to Katie.

'You passed your corridor?'

'Someone passed me. Oh God, what if it was him?'

'So the person you passed was a man?'

Matt felt like shaking Katie but stayed still. Katie nodded.

'Would you recognise this person again, Katie?'

'No. I wasn't really looking.'

'But you're sure it was a man. What was he wearing?'

'White. A white robe.'

Another white robe, just like all the others. He would be free to mingle in amongst all the other guests. The murderer had chosen well, Matt thought.

'I know you weren't looking, Katie, but did you get an impression that this man was tall or short?'

'Tall, about that much taller than me.' Katie indicated the difference with her hand.

Matt estimated that Katie was five-one, which meant that the man was around the six-foot mark. Matt stood. 'So about my height?'

Katie, now much quieter, looked at Fluff almost as if she was asking permission to answer his question. Fluff nodded encouragement.

'Yes.'

'Thank you, Katie.' It was a shame that Katie hadn't been able to give them any specific information. Once she had opened the door to the horror inside, she had run straight to Mrs Trowbridge who, unable to make out what Katie was saying, had sent for the manager.

Before Katie could begin to deteriorate back into a tearful helplessness, Matt suggested that it might be a good idea if he return her to Mrs Trowbridge's care with the suggestion that the good lady arrange for a taxi home.

Glad at the thought of getting out of the room, Katie dried her eyes and allowed Matt to lead her to the front desk where Mrs Trowbridge gathered her in behind the reception desk like a mother duck collecting one of her wayward chicks.

As Matt left the desk, Sam caught up with him

'OK to let the day guests leave, Guv? One or two are becoming a right pain. I've checked all the addresses and re-interviewed those we highlighted. Sam referred to his notes. 'Clive Draper,' he read, flipping over the pages of his notebook. 'If you remember he was noted because he had mentioned the word *murder*. Well, he says the old lady next to him told him, and I think it's possible or highly likely that such a rumour would spread through the crowd. What with all us lot clomping about, the police tape, et cetera. It's what they see on *Midsomer Murders*, and they put two and two together and make five pretty fast, or in this case four.'

'Let them go, Sam, but make sure they know we might need to see them again. And impress on them to ring us if they remember anything, no matter how small.'

'Will do.'

'What about the others who were highlighted?'

'Well, Miss Belcott, who gave the wrong area code, has only just moved here from Norwich, so I think I'm inclined to believe her.'

'And she's very pretty,' Matt teased.

'Well, yes. She does have a lovely smile and those sky blue eyes—wow. But of course that wouldn't affect me at all. You know me, Guv, not at all.'

Matt grinned, glad that they were able to relieve the grim realities of dealing with the murder case with some harmless banter. That was all it was, harmless banter, and although it might seem cruel and uncaring to anyone from the outside, it helped the team keep the victim and those affected one step away, essential if they weren't to be dragged down into the agony of feelings that shut out the details and clouded the facts.

Before Sam left to tell the anxious knot of day guests they were free to go, he turned back to Matt. 'Oh, and I've put Mr Williams in Mrs Trowbridge's office. Something right dodgy going on there.'

'Right, we'll see him together. Give me a minute.'

As Matt turned to head back to the manager's office, he was shocked to see Eppie sitting and talking to two of the guests they had interviewed in the café. What was she doing here? The phone call made sense now. He was overwhelmed with a rush of fear. The murderer could still be on the scene. Eppie, his Eppie, could be sitting there talking to the killer. Anger took over, leaving him so shaken that for a moment he couldn't move. It was then that Eppie looked up and saw him.

'Matt,' she called jumping up and moving towards him before he could stop her.

Matt knew that he needed to keep all his concentration on the job. He couldn't have Eppie on the scene. This was an entirely new feeling worrying about another person, and he didn't like it at all. He grasped her arm roughly and led her to a quiet corner.

'What on earth are you doing here?' he demanded. 'I can't have and don't want you around while I'm working on a case.' As she shook her arm free, Matt could see that his words were like a blow to Eppie. She was quick to recover, moving a step backwards before replying with dignity.

'I'm here for a job interview. What did you think? That I'm following you around like a lost kitten?'

Matt felt embarrassed and stupid but pride kept him from admitting this. 'Well, go home. You might compromise my investigation.'

'That's downright stupid. How could I possibly do that?'

Matt could now see the same fiery glint in Eppie's eyes that had been there on the day they first met and realised he would have to calm things down quickly. 'Because with a murderer running around, I don't need to worry about you.' He was relieved when Eppie smiled and thought she had seen the sense of what he was saying until she reached up to kiss him on the cheek.

'That's OK then because I can look after myself,' she replied over her shoulder as she walked away. 'And besides, it might be good to have someone on the inside.'

Touching the side of her nose with the tip of her finger, she gave him a grin before walking back to Reception, leaving Matt angry and undecided. Should he go after her and demand that she obey him? He couldn't recall there had been anything in the wedding ceremony about *obeying*, but wasn't it what a wife was supposed to do? However, even if he had the right, it was obvious that Eppie would just laugh at him, and he could hardly march into Reception and cause a domestic scene.

While he stood in a quandary his mind was made up for him by the arrival of Fluff who had finished writing up her notes from the therapist's interview and then of Jason who also wanted a word with him. He gave in and tried to concentrate his mind on the job.

CHAPTER 10

It was sheer luck that, when the skinny young detective came to tell the group of day guests they could leave, Clive was chatting to Sandi, the receptionist, filling her in on what had been going on. He watched the other guests scurry away, no doubt to seek solace from loved ones and friends for the dreadful ordeal they had been through, while he remained.

It was then that he noticed the bossy Inspector Turrell with a young woman. At first, they appeared to be arguing, and although he couldn't hear what they were saying, the Inspector looked angry, even when the girl reached up to kiss him.

Intrigued, he decided to take his time glancing through the treatment brochure while at the same time taking it all in. Was she a girlfriend or his significant other? It was obvious he didn't want her here, and Clive guessed a working detective wouldn't want his love life clogging up a murder scene. She, however, seemed perfectly happy and was now chatting to three of the guests interviewed with him in the café, including the old lady.

Realising that it might be to his advantage to learn a little more about the girl, he decided that Mother could wait for her shopping trip and ordered a cappuccino at the small coffee bar. He made sure he chose a table by the door so that he could observe her while he decided how to use the knowledge to his advantage.

Clive watched her as she chatted with the guests. She seemed to have an easy rapport with all ages. The guests would be talking of their experience, and he guessed they would feel better for having unloaded their feelings. *Maybe I should stroll across and join them*, he thought.

But, if this woman knew his name, was able to recognise him, would that be a good thing? It might not be to his advantage, depending of course on what use he found for her. She could be a very potent weapon against DI Turrell and would be a suitable subject for his next statement. The thought excited him and he began to imagine how it would devastate the Inspector.

However, she might be more useful to him alive, at least for a while. If he found out more about her, then he would learn more about the Inspector. Having made his decision, he finished his cappuccino and strode across the foyer towards the group.

The old lady offered an easy introduction and he bent towards her putting his hand solicitously on her arm.

'How are you feeling now?'

'Oh fine, thank you. It certainly wasn't a pleasant experience. But the police were very kind weren't they?'

This gave Clive the opening he needed and he nodded towards the young woman. 'Not to everyone.' She seemed upset that anyone had witnessed her interaction so he allowed concern for committing a possible social faux pas to cross his face. 'Oh, so sorry. I couldn't help noticing.'

The group were all looking towards the woman, who seemed a little embarrassed by their attention.

'He is just someone I know.'

'So you're not the chief suspect then?'

'Not guilty. I'm hoping to get a job here.'

This was interesting. Clive needed to know more.

'What job will you be doing, my dear?' the old lady asked.

Clive could have kissed her for asking the exact question he had in mind.

'Receptionist. They need someone urgently, due to sickness.'

'Well, they have the kindest receptionists here and I'm sure you will just fit right in,' the old lady said and patted the woman's hand.

'She's right.' He decided to be bold and offered his hand to the old lady. 'Clive Draper. Mrs...?'

'Mrs Cox.'

'I wondered if you needed a lift home. I know how Mother would feel if she been caught up in something like this.' Although giving his full attention to Mrs Cox, from the corner of his eye he saw the Inspector's woman smile. He had established his kindness and had moved a step towards earning her trust.

'That's very kind of you, Dear, but I've called my daughter. She should be here shortly.'

Clive's smile was genuine. 'If you are sure?' Mrs Cox nodded and smiled. For a moment he felt at a loss on how to prolong the conversation so he stood as if to leave, then he leant towards the Inspector's woman holding out his hand. 'Good luck with the job...Miss?'

'Featherstone, Eppie. Oh no...it's Turrell. I've just got married.'

'How lovely. I wish you so much happiness, my dear.'

He let Mrs Cox gush before carrying on, deciding to ignore the obvious connection to DI Turrell. That maiden name was ringing bells with him. 'Featherstone? Seems familiar.' He looked suitably puzzled hoping that she would enlighten him.

'Probably Pete Featherstone, my dad. He's a yachtsman and always in the news, usually for getting blown off course or capsizing.'

'That's it. I used to follow all the news bulletins.' Clive sat down next to her trying to think of something intelligent to say about yachting. 'It always seems very dangerous.'

'It is unless you know what you are doing, and even then...'

'Wasn't he in that race where everyone had to be rescued? The big storm?' He sought to remember the news reports of a few years back.

'Yes. But he was one of the lucky ones and ended up helping to bring in some of the other boats.'

'You must be very proud of him.'

'I am.'

He noticed a sense of sadness. 'But you miss him?'

'Sometimes. But I'm with Matt now.'

'For better or for worse?'

Eppie smiled at that and the sadness lifted. 'Probably worse for a few days until all of this is wrapped up. He's upset just because I'm here.'

'It will just be the stress of the case.'

'I would give him something nice to eat when he gets home, my dear,' Mrs Cox interjected, 'and it will all be forgotten. That's what I used to do when my Alf was out of sorts.'

'I'll give that a try,' Eppie laughed.

Mrs Cox had served her usefulness and Clive wished her daughter would come and whisk her away so he could have Eppie to himself. However, he smiled at her to keep up his caring persona. Eppie was quiet and he guessed she was wondering what meal she could prepare to ease her husband's anger. He needed to get back into conversation with her, so he ventured a question. 'What are his favourites?'

'I haven't really cooked for him yet, but we both enjoyed the Italian food we had on holiday.'

Fate was indeed handing him Mrs Turrell on a plate. It couldn't be more perfect. 'Then you need Rossini's delicatessen. You are sure to find everything he likes there.'

She jumped at the idea, and so he began giving directions before pausing, as if struck by an idea. 'Look, why don't you follow me? I've been promising Mother for ages that I would pick up some of the ham she likes.'

'Well, I haven't been interviewed yet. Plus, I don't want to take you out of your way.'

'You won't be and I was about to have a light lunch, so you don't need to worry about the time.'

'Well, if you are sure?'

'It will be my pleasure.' Even as he said it, he realised what a stroke of luck this was. It felt as if the gods were supporting him. He couldn't lose.

Clive left Eppie and Mrs Cox and went back to the coffee bar, knowing he had better look at the early lunch menu, otherwise he couldn't justify remaining at the small table while the other tables around him were beginning to fill up. Ordering a salad from the lite bite section and another cappuccino, he settled back to wait.

Mrs Cox went off with her daughter, giving a friendly wave as she did. Then it wasn't long before the head receptionist, who reminded him of a stately galleon, came to collect Eppie. The two of them disappeared into the offices behind the reception desk.

While he was idly picking at the boring salad, the Inspector strode up to the reception desk. Clive watched as his eyes went to where Eppie had been sitting and saw him turn away as he realised she wasn't there. Neither relief nor disappointment registered on the DI's face, but Clive guessed he would always try to keep his feelings under control in a work situation. It said something for the extent of his anger that he had lost his temper before.

Well, the inspector was going to have a lot more to contend with by the time Clive had finished with him.

CHAPTER 11

Matt forced himself to concentrate on what Jason was saying although his mind kept slipping back to Eppie. Jason handed Matt an evidence bag and inside was something Matt would have never expected, a small toy soldier in what at first glance appeared to be a uniform from around the Napoleon period. He glanced up in surprise at Jason.

'Where?' Matt asked. Jason didn't seem shocked at the find, but then he had been in forensics for nearly thirty years and had seen everything a few times over.

'Folds of the dress,' he replied laconically, chewing.

'Doll, lollypop, and now a toy soldier. What the hell is going on here?'

'Damned if I know. The professor is bound to have a theory though,' Jason grinned.

'I'll bet he will.' Matt nodded, fully aware that he would be forced to listen to the team's profiler. Everyone knew he disliked working with the man, who always acted as if he was superior and cleverer than anyone else.

'I would say, looking at the dust pattern, that the murderer hid his props behind the heating panel at least two days ago.'

'So he's a planner.'

'With access.'

'And almost certainly wore gloves.' Matt sighed thinking of the difficulties this gave the team. 'What about the door?'

'Don't think he is the sort to slip up, but we've dusted, just in case.'

'We'll have to eliminate the staff.'

Jason shifted his gum to one side. 'Already started with the maintenance department. Surprising how many men it takes to keep these places going.'

'Good. Let me know how it goes. I can spare a constable or two if necessary.'

Jason shook his head. Matt knew he much preferred to work with his own team whenever possible. 'Got that lady…'

Matt raised his eyebrows in question.

'Big lady, posh hair do—head receptionist or something. She's checking if they've had any outside company doing work in the therapy rooms recently.'

Matt handed the evidence bag back to Jason. He would find out everything he could about the soldier down to the last detail of where and when it was made.

'I'll let you have the details as soon as I can, Matt.'

'Thanks.' Matt left Jason to make his way back to Reception intending to speak to Mrs Trowbridge.

There was no sign of Eppie or Mrs Trowbridge, although that estimable lady had left him a sealed envelope. He opened it as he walked back to her office where Sam was waiting with the therapist, Stuart Williams, who couldn't seem to remember where he had worked before.

There was silence as Matt entered the room. Sam had his sheepdog-cornering look fixed on a young man, who was good looking except for his intense sullen look. Sam kept his gaze fixed as Matt sat down beside him, while the young man hitched himself up like a condemned man hoping for a lenient judge.

Sam spoke without looking at Matt, his eyes on the therapist. 'This is Stuart Williams, Guv. Employed one week and can't seem to remember where he last worked. My guess is that he has been a bad boy back there and doesn't want his reputation to catch up with him.'

Matt took a moment to read the contents of the envelope before he looked up and spoke to Stuart. 'Well, Mr Williams, does

Fairfield Health and Sports club ring any bells?' For a moment, Stuart's eyes flickered as he realised he couldn't hide any more, and that he would have to tell the truth. Matt watched the turmoil in him and saw the change, as he had seen many times before, when the suspect becomes almost aggressive in their own defence and quite willing to send their own Grandma down the line if it would save their skins.

'OK, OK, I'll tell you what happened.' Stuart held up his hands almost like a supplicant.

Matt waited, watching as Stuart formed the best way to present the story in his head.

'She was a client, and well, you're not supposed, supposed to fancy them, are you?'

Matt nodded for him to continue, making sure that his face showed none of the disgust he was feeling.

'Except that it's bloody difficult sometimes, when they act like that,' Stuart continued.

Matt refused to give him the encouragement he was looking for and instead waited. Stuart looked from Matt to Sam before stumbling on.

'They...she...are always flirting and acting...you know. And it was damned hard at times not to want to...well, you know.'

'So you couldn't control yourself with the clients?' Matt asked.

'Not all of them. I mean more than half are old bags you wouldn't want to touch. Unless you were getting paid to of course.'

'So it was just the young, pretty ones,' Sam threw in.

Stuart did not seem to realise that he was backing himself into a corner. 'They were up for it. Said I was fit.' Stuart flexed his muscles as he enjoyed the memory.

'Until?' Matt questioned.

There was silence from Stuart. He knew he was going down a one-way alley. 'Till this silly cow starts making a fuss, saying I molested her. I reckon she makes a habit of it. Probably wanted money. Anyhow, I wasn't stopping around there to be taken for a ride.'

Matt sighed and stood up. 'Take a full statement, Sam. Then check with Sussex Police; see if they need Mr Williams to answer any other charges. I've got more important things to do.' Matt turned at the door. 'Oh, and you may want to come clean with the management here before we have to do it for you.' Matt was pleased to see that trapped look had returned to Stuart's face before he closed the door behind him.

CHAPTER 12

The timing was perfect. Having just finished his uninteresting salad, Clive was contemplating investing in an unaccustomed dessert, when he saw Mrs Turrell come from behind Reception accompanied by the matron-like woman. Both women seemed pleased and shook hands, as if they were sealing a deal. It looked good.

The thought excited him, and he began to imagine all sorts of possibilities. With the DI's wife working on reception, it would give him the chance to build up some sort of rapport with her, as he had done with Sandi.

Clive already had Sandi eating out of his hand, so he saw no reason why this spirited young lady would be immune. He would become her confidant and friend, only while she was at work of course. She would be lonely with her new husband tied up in this dreadful murder case. And Clive planned to keep him busy for a long time yet. If he played his cards right, this girl would provide him with valuable information about DI Turrell. 'Know your enemy' would be his motto, and the DI's wife would become his special agent.

Having perfected the role of a caring, almost saintly son, women trusted Clive; they saw him as a 'new man.' They liked to feel they understood his burden, and he patiently listened to their advice.

He practised his charm on the women in the office, and he knew any of the single girls would jump at the chance to go out

with him, if asked, but he was adept at keeping them at bay, apart
that is from dear Anne.

He watched as Eppie took a quick detour to glance down the
corridor to the right, guessing she wanted to tell her good news to
the DI. There was only minor disappointment on her face as she
came towards him. Clive stood, as trained, as she approached.

'Good news?'

'Yes. I start tomorrow.'

'That's quick.'

'Yes. One on sick leave and another on maternity.'

'Well done. Would you like lunch or a coffee to celebrate?'

'No. But thank you. I have a lot to do if I'm going to appease
the angry husband.'

So the DI would arrive home to her news, and Clive was sure he
wouldn't be happy. 'Ah yes, the delicatessen. It's not far.'

As he led the way out of the building towards the car park, he
realised having Mrs Turrell follow him meant that she would know
his car. This would put him at a disadvantage for the next part of
his plan. But there again, Clive reasoned, if Mother and Margaret
were anything to go by, women hardly noticed cars as long as they
were clean and in working order.

When they reached Rossini's delicatessen and bakery, she
parked her car next to his in the small parking lot. Inside she
seemed delighted and Clive guessed she would be here for a while.
He watched her as he ordered some ham for Mother.

'This is just perfect. I feel like I am still on honeymoon.'

'Will you be able to find your way home from here?'

'I think so. I just carry straight on along the main road.'

'Right. Well, I will leave you to it then. And good luck with your
husband.'

She laughed and raised a hand in thanks, too caught up in
deciding on what to buy to pay him much attention.

Before getting into his car, Clive made a mental note of her
licence plate, and then he drove out of the parking lot and out
onto the road, parking several cars away.

After seven long minutes, he watched her come out, loaded with bags and looking rather pleased. Waiting for her to place the bags carefully in the back of the car, Clive wondered what Ben's favourite foods were, and if he liked to cook.

He had always been glad to leave the cooking to someone else. Mrs Sinclair was a good cook on a fairly plain and simple level who could, if given enough notice, rise to almost gourmet levels for special occasions like Mother's birthday. It would be lovely to invite Ben to the house, but not with Mother installed. Yet another disadvantage of having her living with him.

Clive wrenched himself out of these daydreams and started the car as Eppie pulled out into the traffic, managing to manoeuvre himself so that there were just two cars between them. For once, he was glad that most cars on the road were silver, like his, as it made it less likely she would spot him.

The small three-storey block of flats, Miranda Court, was on the outskirts of town in a leafy area on the Kenilworth side of Leamington Spa. He guessed the block had been built about twenty years ago.

As Mrs Turrell pulled into the resident's car park, he wondered what to do next. Should he follow her into the building to see which flat she lived in? If he did, she might see him, and he certainly didn't want that.

He hesitated as she struggled with the door code and the heavy bags until she entered the lobby, before deciding that discovering which flat she and the Inspector lived in could wait until he had the cover of darkness.

All the information he had gathered today about the DI made him vulnerable and gave Clive the advantage. He felt confident that he could outwit him, even with his smart little team around him.

Time to start planning his next move, one designed to show the DI and that clever little constable who was boss. Still kicking himself for the mistake, Clive vowed he would make the young lady pay. He was beginning to enjoy this intrigue. Maybe he should follow the constable home next. The more he knew about the team the better.

By the time he arrived home, it was too late to fit in Mother's shopping trip, and he knew she was cross the minute he walked in and heard her sharp, brittle voice telling Mrs Sinclair.

'No thank you. I do not want a tray on my lap. I will wait for my son, although goodness knows where he has got to. He knows very well he had an arrangement to take me shopping.'

Clive braved the living room making sure that he had a worried, apologetic look on his face, to accusing looks from Mother and Mrs Sinclair, who had her coat on ready to leave. Playing up the ordeal of being on the scene of a murder, not to mention being questioned by the police, he sank into his favourite chair with the air of one at last reaching a safe haven. Once he had their attention, he began to explain himself.

'I've had a very harrowing experience.'

'Oh dear. What on earth happened Mr Draper?'

'I can't even bear thinking about it.'

'Oh dear.'

'For goodness sake, Clive, stop shilly-shallying and tell us what happened.'

'I'll try.'

'Clive.' Mother never had an ounce of sympathy. Well, not where he was concerned anyway. She had set her face determinedly against his tears at Father's hands believing that was the way to raise a man.

'There was a murder. At the spa.' He watched as his news hit home. Whatever they were expecting it wasn't this. Maybe they thought Clive had been involved in a car accident on the way home. But a murder, now that was worthy of even his Mother's attention and he relished the word.

'A murder,' he repeated, enjoying the sound.

'Oh my goodness.'

Mrs Sinclair dropped into the nearest chair and unbuttoned her coat as shock sent a hot flush soaring upwards, turning her neck and face a beetroot colour. But Clive wasn't going to let her take the attention from him. Mother was made of sterner stuff and barely glanced in Mrs Sinclair's direction.

'So who was murdered?'

'I heard someone say it was a young girl. She was in one of the treatment rooms, practically next door to me.'

'But I thought you were going to the gym?'

Too late, he realised that his pride had outstripped the need for caution. His dear Mother was always as sharp as a tack.

'Lisa was just giving that pulled muscle a quick massage.' Mother accepted the lie although she took a second more than necessary before her eyes left his face.

'Margery—get a glass of wine for Clive. And have one yourself—you look like you need it.'

Clive cursed himself for embellishing the story and kept everything factual as he described how they were herded into the café, ordered about and questioned by Inspector Turrell.

By the time he had finished, they were feeling suitably sorry for him, and Mrs Sinclair had poured him a glass of his favourite red wine. Now, as they finished clucking over him, he wanted to be on his own. He was sure his exploits of today would receive attention from both the local and national press, and he couldn't wait to see his publicity.

Pretending concern for keeping her so late, and thanking her profusely for staying with Mother, he hurried Mrs Sinclair to the door. It was a relief when the door closed behind her. Clive headed straight into the kitchen, calling to Mother on the way.

'Won't be long now, Mother.' Mother said something in reply but by then he was halfway down the flagged hallway and into the modern, black and white kitchen. Ignoring the steaming casserole, he turned to the small television, thankful he had purchased it to keep Mrs Sinclair happy.

He was delighted to find the murder mentioned on both the local news and the national news. The rush of power and excitement reminded him of the time he won the cup for unarmed combat. He had enjoyed seeing all those nondescript faces looking up at him and clapping. Soon, the whole nation would come to realise how important, how powerful he was. No one would beat him now.

One young reporter was inclined to be lurid and called it 'The Baby Doll' murder, which he didn't like. Nor did he like the solid reassuring tones of the local police superintendent who vowed that his force was doing everything they could to catch whoever committed this heinous crime and, while the public should continue to take normal precautions, there was no need to panic. His rather pompous tone made Clive determined to prove him wrong, and he began to plan his next statement.

He knew that it would be prudent to place his next message in a different location, but he wanted to throw down a personal challenge to DI Turrell. The Inspector would look such a fool when another murder took place right under his nose, where no one would expect it, back at the health spa.

Clive began to think of ways he could undermine the Inspector. Maybe he would start by sending him a small token, and, thanks to the new Mrs Turrell, he could send it straight to their home. It made him smile, as he imagined how this would worry and distract the DI from the case.

Looking forward to the DI's downfall, he reviewed his plans as he carried the meal through to the dining room. Mother annoyingly wanted to keep talking about his experience.

'Did you say the Inspector's name was Turrell?'

'Yes. Why?'

'That was the man who was responsible for getting little Gracie killed. You remember—Joan Harrison's granddaughter.'

She had his attention back. He remembered it now. Inspector Turrell had arrested the wrong man, leaving the real murderer to kill again. 'Yes, I do remember. Let's hope he does better on this case.'

'He should have been disciplined.'

Clive half-heartedly agreed with her while wondering how this past mistake had affected the Inspector. Either it would make him more determined to solve a case, or he would become over anxious and miss vital evidence. Not that Clive intended to leave any for him. There was little chance that he would be caught.

As Mother chatted on, he allowed his mind to run through the plans for his next statement. He knew where to place it as, having often walked around the grounds of Heath Stone Spa, he had come upon the perfect spot.

It was a wooden contraption with two seats facing each other, which swung back and forth depending on the input from whoever was seated there. Although rather a shame that the occupant wouldn't be in a position to start the swing, once he had placed her there, he could give a little push just to start it off.

The swing was situated at the end of a small pond, which had been widened out from a small stream. There was a little wooden bridge, more for show than need, which led to the putting green and the smoker's tent.

The smoker's tent was a popular place as Clive had found after wandering in there by accident one day. He hadn't stayed long, as the six ardent smokers, although at first eager to claim him as one of their own, were just as eager to close ranks on the outsider without a cigarette in his mouth, and who seemed in no hurry to light up.

Before he strolled away, he noticed the several statuesque vases filled with colourful flowers at intervals around the tent, placed there no doubt to give an illusion of health and beauty to those who were so intent on destroying themselves. Similar vases were dotted around the health spa, and although they looked like expensive ceramic creations, he had found on investigation that they had a small hollow centre. A perfect hiding place for his props.

His next problem would be to find a suitable subject and then to get her into the appointed position. Clive could hardly carry her out through the main entrance in full view of everybody, nor could he walk out chatting with her, as that would take him straight to the top of the suspect list.

The added problem was that most guests only stayed a few days, with the odd exception, like Mrs Potterton who, according to the waiter, came for two months every year and sat regally alone in the dining room at her chosen and favourite table. She was too old to fit in with his plans, and Clive laughed at the ludicrous thought of her in one of his party dresses.

This left him with two options: it would either have to be a staff member, or he would have to bring the girl in from the outside. He ruled out the latter, as that would be too fraught with problems, which could lead to discovery. A staff member it had to be then and in this mostly female culture, there was an abundance to choose from. His own masseuse, Lisa, was young and pretty, but maybe just a little too plump for the purpose, and her demise would put him under suspicion.

Of course, the new Mrs Turrell almost fitted the bill but her somewhat elfin looks did not quite suit his plans. Plus, she would be more use to him alive as a pathway to her husband. He decided he could afford to keep the options open, for the moment.

Mother twittered on but he was only half listening.

'Clive. Are you listening to me?'

'Yes, Mother.'

'Don't lie, Clive, it is unbecoming of a gentleman. I was asking if you would have to be a witness.'

'I wouldn't think so. There were a lot of other people about.'

'Yes, but the police would recognise an intelligent man. One who would notice anything amiss. And I shall expect you to do your civic duty if called upon, Clive.'

He almost laughed aloud and part of him wanted to tell her that her dutiful son was a murderer. How would her social niceties deal with that? No, maybe one day, when she was dying perhaps, he would take his time and enjoy it. Not today, he had too much to do. Today he pacified her because he needed her to play a role in his next outing. 'Of course, Mother,' he acquiesced to her demand.

The deed would have to be done under the hours of darkness, leaving him with a problem, since on the odd occasion, like this morning when he had taken a day owing to him, his sessions at the spa were fitted in straight after work on the nights when Mrs Sinclair could stay that bit longer with Mother. Sometimes, he went there on Saturday mornings, but for this task, darkness was going to be his biggest ally.

Although the autumn nights were now drawing in, he would need to dispatch his next victim later in the evening when it was fully dark and when most of the guests would be happy to stay cosy and warm indoors, and out of his way.

Clive would need a legitimate reason to be at the health spa during the evening. Last year he had tried to persuade Mother that the occasional massage might help the blood flow in her legs, in the vain hope that it might stop her constant grumbling in the mornings.

Although she hadn't taken to the idea then, he decided to revise the theme again. If he disguised it as a treat for her to have dinner in the restaurant, where the new French chef was attracting rave reviews, she might be persuaded to talk to a masseuse during the evening. This would leave him with about fifteen minutes, more than enough time to do his work.

With this in mind, he decided to call into the club later in the week to book Mother an appointment to talk to the masseuse and to arrange for them to have dinner there. Saturday would probably be best; that would give him time to persuade Mother that he had her best interests at heart.

His choice of victim he would leave until later.

CHAPTER 13

She was used to preparing meals for her dad, but Eppie wanted this one to be special. It must convey everything she wanted to say to Matt. She knew there would be times when his job would have to come first, and she accepted this, since she loved him. In return, she hoped he would be able to listen to her concerns. She suspected that he might hold some old fashioned ideas about marriage. That is, if he had thought about it at all.

Eppie had chosen the Parma ham to remind him of Italy, a large slice of spinach quiche, his favourite, rocket salad, little new potatoes, cherry tomatoes, and two of the crusty rolls from the Italian delicatessen. As she covered the plate with cling film, she wondered if he would get home at all.

The murder had been highlighted on the local and national news and, although the details were not given, the grave police superintendent had stated that the victim was a young woman in her early twenties. Matt was on the front line and would have had to view her body. Eppie felt a surge of pride that he and his team would be the ones who would catch the murderer.

After tidying the kitchen, Eppie went into the living room where the new scatter cushions were attempting a brave fight against the dullness. She felt at a loss as to what to do for the rest of the evening. She had spent many evenings like this, marooned in some impersonal hotel room, waiting for her dad to reach port, but then she had been kept busy planning and smoothing the way for the next leg of his journey.

There were port authorities to be dealt with, supplies to be ordered. Sometimes the local dignitaries, together with the public and the press, would be gathering, wanting to meet and greet him as a great conqueror of the seas. They had no idea how hard Eppie had to work to get him to make port on time. Dad would become side tracked by a school of dolphins or a Sabine's gull and ignore Eppie's frantic messages.

She looked at him smiling down at her from the mantelpiece and felt a wave of nostalgia for those times, a sudden emptiness, which this new marriage hadn't yet expanded to fill. Eppie knew it would get better with time, unlike the time she and Mike were dumped on Aunt Sandra.

Auntie Sandra had been kind enough, taking payment in licence to rubbish Mum. Eppie found it difficult to listen to her criticisms, mostly because she knew they were spot on. Her Mum was both lazy and selfish. Life there was very different with its ordered routine, bed at nine thirty, sensible meals and clothes. Even the television was limited. Eppie could see that it was good for Mike who was engrossed in his A-levels, but it left her stuck with cousin Natalie, with whom she had to share a room.

At first, Natalie was kind, in a patronizing sort of way, but then she started the same party line as her Mother, such as that day when they were dressing to go to a school dance.

'You aren't going to wear that, are you?' Natalie sneered.

'Yes. Why not?'

'I think you should be careful.'

'Of what?'

'Well…of looking…too old.'

'You mean like my Mother?'

'Mum says she always used to flaunt herself.'

Eppie looked at her image in the mirror. The skirt and blouse had been bought on one of the good days, when Mum was in an indulgent mood. Maybe the skirt was a little too short, at the least four inches shorter than Natalie's. The bare midriff was all the rage and looked good on Eppie's slim figure. 'It's fine. Come on, let's go.'

Natalie's warning that her Mother wouldn't like it was correct and Eppie had been given the ultimatum to either change or stay in her room. Burning with hurt and fury she had elected to stay in.

At first, she threw herself on the bed and cried, and then when she had calmed down she had decided that she couldn't live here any longer. She still had the money her Mum had left in lieu of love. The money was the last contact with Mum. She counted it out, over two hundred pounds. Surely that would get her to where Dad was. Either she would persuade him to come home or she would stay with him.

Now, she was older and married to Matt, so it wasn't an option to run back to Dad. She had made her choice. And the timing had been right. Eppie had begun to feel a yearning restlessness, as if there had to be something other than the constant round of exotic ports, embassy parties, and the like.

She smiled at the thought of her dad coping with Isabella, the strong-minded young woman from Porto Rica, who had stepped into her shoes. Maybe it was good that he was only planning to finish this latest trip before hooking up with his old friend and former sailing partner, Howie Grace. Together they planned to open a yachting business on the island of Maui.

On an impulse, she picked up the phone, needing to hear her dad's voice, and trying to remember where he would be. If he had put to sea already, then he could be fighting stormy seas, sleeping, or busy making repairs; he could even be aloft.

But there was just a chance he might still be in Porto Rica picking up Isabella. Eppie started to dial without thinking, but then realised that this was Matt's landline. His, like everything else here. He wouldn't be very pleased to have an international call on the bill.

Eppie got out her mobile only to find it needed charging. Throwing it on the couch, she reached for the landline again. Damn Matt, he would have to put up with it.

'Dad?' Eppie could hardly hear the familiar voice due to the static and the amount of noise in the background. It sounded as if Dad was in the middle of a party.

'Hey. There's a surprise. How's the old married lady then? Hold on and I'll lose the racket.'

Eppie waited listening to the sounds. The music sounded live, and the beat of a drum stopped as someone called out.

'Pedro—do not go.'

She heard her Dad reply, 'back in a minute.'

She realised that that was all she was to him now—a brief interval in the real business of life. He had always thrown himself into getting to know the local people wherever he went. He enjoyed being part of their lives, joining in their celebrations and, at times, their sorrows, and although she found it interesting, she never had gained the easy rapport he immediately established. For a moment the sense of loss intensified.

'Don't tell me he's beating you already?'

'No, of course not.'

'I knew he wouldn't take my advice.'

'Dad.'

'Making a rod for his own back. I did warn him.'

Eppie didn't want to talk about Matt. 'Sounds like you're having fun.' She heard the longing in her voice even as she said it.

'Isabella's family is giving her a big send off. That's all.'

There was a pause as Eppie sought to say anything rather than how she was feeling. She was so used to being there at his side where communication was so easy and natural not at the end of a telephone.

'While you're in rainy old England with a strange man.'

Trust Dad to pick up on how she was feeling. 'It's sunny and, yes, it's strange getting used to Matt, especially after you.'

'Oh, blaming me are you?'

'Definitely.'

'It just takes time.'

'I know. He's on a murder case.'

'That's bad luck but it won't last forever, Lass.'

'I know. It's just this flat feels so…so his.'

'You didn't expect the poor man to put up frilly curtains in your honour did you?'

'Of course not. I hate frills.'

'You'll grow into it—change things gradually. Together.'

Eppie was thinking she didn't want to grow into it at all. And she wasn't sure Matt saw the need to change a thing, but before she could tell her dad, she heard someone calling him.

'Señor. The mamma she come.'

'Oh God. Eppie, can I call you back.'

'Yes of course. Dad, who is Mamma?'

'Isabella's grandmother. Apparently I have to be fully inspected and passed by her before the family will let Isabella come with me. She's sounds worse than the Godfather so wish me luck.'

'You'll be fine.'

'That's not all—if I survive the matriarch, tomorrow the whole village is turning out, led by the priest, to bless the Mary Lee. Can you imagine that—after all the storms she's weathered? I hope she doesn't take umbrage and bring us bad luck.'

Eppie laughed, not knowing quite how to say how much she missed him.

'It's not that glamorous, Epp. I'll be seasick before I start out in the morning with all the homemade grog they are forcing on me. And you know how I get on the morning after.'

'Rather Isabella than me then.'

'You should see her face. I shall probably be teetotal in a couple of weeks.'

'Good luck to her then.'

'Honestly, Epp, you've got a lot going for you there. Us blokes find it harder to change. Give him time.'

As she put down the phone Eppie knew he was right. Men resist changing what they see as working well for them. Matt would just expect her to fit in.

Feeling cold Eppie hunted for the central heating controls. They were in the airing cupboard, but she wasn't sure which buttons or dials to move. Giving up she decided to curl up in bed with her new Phillipa Gregory book and let herself be transported to medieval England.

Tomorrow she would talk to Matt and find out how to work the heating. And she would tell him about her job. Surely he would realise she couldn't stay cooped up in the flat forever.

CHAPTER 14

Back at headquarters, Matt watched as his tired team settled into the incident room for a summing up. He was proud of all of them, from the newest uniform police constable to Fluff and Sam. Each one had brought his or her own skill and dedication to the task that faced them.

Sam was already starting the Incident Board as Matt stepped to the front. 'I don't intend to keep you long. I'll just run through a brief outline of the information we have to date. And to say, although it has been a difficult day, I couldn't ask for a better team.'

He paused as Sam placed a smiling picture of Amy Metcalfe in the centre of the board.

'Amy Metcalfe, aged twenty-one. She worked at Timkins Solicitors as a clerk. Amy lived with her friend, Jodi Brown, who also works at Timkins. No known history of involvement with drugs, no steady boyfriend. Parents live in Leeds. They report, as far as they know, she lived an apparently normal life there. She had left home at nineteen to live with her college friend, Jodi, in Southam.'

Matt found the next piece of information upsetting as he imagined how her parents were feeling right now. 'Amy's visit to the spa was a twenty-first-birthday gift from her parents. Slim's initial diagnosis is that Amy was killed by pressure applied to the jugular and carotid arteries, the vagus nerves, at the same time, causing the heart to stop. So we have no blood trace to go on.'

He could see shock on the faces of some of the team and guessed Sam had put up photos of Amy's body in situ. For some it was their first murder case, and it was going to be a difficult one, unlike his, which had been sad and brutal, but which hadn't had the strange overtones of this one.

Matt was just starting to run through the forensic evidence when McRay slid into the back of the room. He hoped McRay could see the need to encourage rather than berate the team, and in an effort to keep him onside, Matt nodded towards him for permission to carry on. McRay nodded his assent.

'We think this is where the killer hid the items he used.' Matt indicated a photo of the heating panel. 'Unfortunately, Jason is pretty sure that he—and no, I haven't ruled out the ladies—wore gloves. In fact, it seems we are dealing with a very careful killer who plans well. We think he put the white robe Amy was wearing into the linen tub at the end of the corridor. This was taken away about twenty minutes later, and we were too late to stop it entering the laundry system.'

'Do we know yet what the killer was wearing, Sir?' Grant called out from the back.

Why did everything the man said sound insolent? Matt looked across to the dark, gaunt figure, standing with his arms crossed at the back of the room.

The DI had been foisted on them from another division two years ago. The rumours and gossip about him had been rife at the time. Matt tried not to let them get in the way of a working relationship, but he disliked the man. Being several years older than Matt he was inclined to question his decisions. Matt worked hard not to let the man's attitude affect him and, where possible, made sure he did not have to work directly with him. On a case like this, it would be difficult, since they needed everyone's input.

Matt ignored Grant's tone. 'We think the murderer will have made sure he blended in. Given the amount of white robes and other uniforms, he would find it easy to pass unnoticed. If, for instance, he wore a white therapist's suit, he could have placed it in the same laundry tub.' Matt waited for a moment in case there were any other questions before continuing. 'Amy's clothes were found in a locker in the day guest's area. These have been identified by Miss Brown and are with forensics. As are the white robes we collected from those guests who were in the immediate area.'

'So why the kooky kid's things, Guv?' Sam asked.

Matt looked at the board, then back at his team before replying. 'If we knew the answer to that one, we might be closer to catching our murderer.'

'Maybe he just likes them young,' Grant interrupted again.

'Except there appears to be no evidence of sexual activity.' Matt paused to see if Grant had a useful comment, but he was silent. 'As you can see, the victim was dressed like a young girl at a party. Also found with the body was a doll,' Matt said, pointing to a blown-up picture, 'a lollipop and, in the folds of the dress, a toy soldier.'

He heard a slight murmur ripple through the team and waited for it to end before continuing. 'All of these items are with forensics. Meanwhile, PC Harrison and her team, will be working hard to establish where these items came from.'

Wendy Harrison gave an embarrassed nod of acknowledgement and returned to her computer screen. Matt moved back to sit on the edge of a desk as Fluff went through those guests and staff who had been highlighted during questioning.

'So, at the moment, we have no suspects to add to the board. But it is likely that the murderer was posing as either a guest or a staff member at the club, and we will have interviewed him. These interviews will be analysed and cross checked by DI Grant.'

'As soon as I get them.'

The man's tone was belligerent and suggested that he was usually kept waiting for his information.

Fluff was not rising to his taunt and merely gave a brief nod in Grant's direction.

'I can get them to you within the hour, Inspector. Intending to work through the night are you?'

'Only if you will join me.'

There were a few wolf whistles from the men in the team. Fluff ignored them and Grant and finished what she had to say.

Matt could see that the team were finding it hard to concentrate, and stepped in to wrap it up for the day, reminding them all that it was going to be an early start tomorrow.

He was surprised and worried when McRay held up his hand to stop the exodus. Matt hoped that he wasn't going to cause upset at this time of night. He could almost feel the joint holding of breath in the room and was sure everyone was expecting the worst.

'You've all worked really hard today. Keep it up and we'll catch this bastard before he does it again.'

The relief was apparent as the team quickened their stride in an effort to get away before McRay could change his mind. Matt waited, knowing that he would have to give a first hand report to the man.

McRay spoke first. 'They respect you Matt.'

Matt was uncertain how to reply so hedged his bets. 'It's a good team, Sir.'

McRay nodded and went on to outline the support that had been granted on the case. Matt was grateful, until McRay said that he had made an appointment for Professor Meredith to come in to see Matt early tomorrow. Still, it felt good to have an echo of the old McRay back. It was just a shame that it took a murder to shake him out of his orgy of self-pity.

McRay was standing looking at the Incident Board shaking his head. 'Odd. Can't remember anything quite like this. We'll have to stop him before he gets the bit between his teeth, Matt.'

Matt realised that McRay was trying to make his way back, from the snarling bear he had become, to a functioning Chief Inspector, and sighing inwardly, he gave up the idea of heading home and prepared to talk through the case, as he used to do. He moved beside McRay to look at the photos of Amy.

'It gives me the shivers. He's trying to tell us something, Sir.'

'Why dress her up in such a way?' mused McRay. 'Any lead on the actual clothing?'

Matt shook his head. 'No. It looks like a pantomime costume—*Alice in Wonderland* or such. There shouldn't be too many places you can buy things like that.'

'Wendy is the best. If there is anything to be found, she is the one to do it,' McRay confirmed. 'But I can't see why the bugger would make it so hard for himself.'

'Showing us how clever he is?'

'Could be. He'll trip up somewhere. Meredith will have some ideas.'

Matt thought this was certain but kept his opinions to himself.

McRay moved towards the door then turned back to Matt. 'Get on home, Matt. It is going to be a tough one.'

Driving home around one in the morning, Matt found himself wondering how he should be with Eppie after their brief row. He needed her to understand that his work brought him into touch with the evil, dysfunctional, and dangerous people of this world. He had to know she was safe—kept separate from it all.

Aside from playing rugby, which was his safety valve, he had never before had to balance the job he loved with anything or anyone else. Now, Eppie was in his life, he was scared, deep down; in his gut he was scared. Having to worry about his wife could interfere with his ability to be single minded. This was how he worked best. But how did he fit Eppie into the equation? If he failed, it could mean the death of an innocent girl, and Matt didn't want another one like Gracie on his conscience.

He had been a detective inspector for just nine months, had solved his first murder case, and was no doubt feeling a little cocky, thinking he could carry on his life as normal. The first girl was nineteen, savagely raped and murdered. He had arrested her boyfriend and closed the case, eager to make the final game of the rugby season and the partying afterwards.

Gracie was found the next morning, just sixteen. And there was no doubt it was the same MO. Matt was still haunted by her. Could still hear her mother's screams as he broke the news. At Gracie's funeral, he made a pledge to her that he would do better in the future.

His interview with Gracie's killer was burned on his brain.

'So you followed Gracie Hawkes from school, intercepting her as she crossed the Alcester Road?'

'Yes.'

'Why did you choose to kidnap Gracie?'

'She looked as if she had a bit more go in her. Not like the other silly cow. Hardly touched her and she fainted—didn't last two minutes. No fun in that is there? You need 'em to put up a fight. It's hours of fun that way, especially if you let 'em think you just might let them go if they let you do the things you want. You can spin it out then, give yourself a full evening of fun.'

There was silence in the interview room as Matt fought both his need to batter the smug, self-satisfied face before him or be sick. McRay coughed and Matt pulled himself together.

'So, this is all about you having fun, Mr Fraser?'

'Of course. Although, believe me, they enjoy my Charlie boy despite all that moaning and begging.' Fraser rubbed his crotch suggestively.

'And Gracie?'

'One of me best was Gracie. I can tell you her young—'

'Have you done this before, Mr Fraser?'

Fraser grinned. 'Can't stop. Far too much fun.'

'So there have been other women, Mr Fraser?'

Fraser paused and was suddenly wary. 'A few.'

Sickening though it was to hear, Matt knew they needed to get as much information from Fraser in this interview as possible. The psychiatrist was on the way, and it was almost certain that he would find Fraser mad. This might be their only chance to find out the fate of the other women he had murdered.

'But not in this area?'

Fraser seemed relieved. 'Down home till a few years ago. It wasn't as much fun then as I didn't do them.'

'You didn't kill them?'

'Nope. Just let Charlie boy lose. They loved it.'

'So when did you first kill a women, Mr Fraser?'

'Dunno. No, no, wait. I do remember. About eight years ago. Lovely bit of stuff, dark hair. She served me at the pub, gave me that look. So I waited for her, said I'd walk her home, but she wasn't having any of it. Got all snooty, so I made her take a detour onto the cricket pitch. What she wanted all along. Soon had her knickers off and all ready for me boy but the bitch goes and kicks out at him. Decided to make her pay for that, I did. I was sad when it was all over, wanted to do it again.'

McRay, aware that Matt was working on controlling his anger, spoke for the first time.

'You have an excellent memory, Mr Fraser. I bet you can even remember the name of the pub and where it is?'

'Golden Horseshoe. Bristol.'

'That's very good. I wonder if you can remember any of your other triumphs.'

Soon the list had reached possibly eighteen women murdered and at least six rapes. If Fraser hadn't moved about the country, he might have been caught earlier. Fraser had shown no remorse, just a flat expectation that his needs were the only ones ever to be considered.

It was a relief in a way when he was declared mentally unfit to plead, as it meant he would not be released until he was considered safe to be let into the community. Matt hoped that would be never and that some well meaning, but deluded, psychiatrist would not let him loose to kill again.

McRay, aware that Matt was blaming himself for Gracie's death, had called him into the office soon after Fraser had been taken away.

'Sit down, Matt.'

Matt was certain this was the end of his police career. 'I will be resigning, Sir.'

'Like hell you will. That would be a luxury this station can't afford. No. We go through this case, learn what we could have done differently.'

'What I should have done you mean.'

'Yes. OK. What you, as the officer in charge, could have done.'

'Not been so bloody eager to lock up the wrong man for one.'

'Did he seem like the right man at the time?'

'Yes, but—'

'Then there are no buts, Matt. You did what you thought was right at the time. That's all you can do.'

'I needed it to be him. Needed the case closed.'

McRay waited while Matt tried to put his anguish into words. It felt almost like a confessional, but in the end, it was cathartic. Matt had to accept that he wasn't infallible, that he wouldn't always get it right, although he made a promise to Gracie that he would always try.

And this time, Matt didn't need Professor Meredith to tell him that, now that this killer had tasted blood, he would kill again and fast.

He was physically and mentally tired, desperate for some quiet time so his brain could assimilate all the information from the day. He found himself hoping Eppie was asleep, but then he felt an immediate rush of guilt. It was rotten luck that he had a murder case so soon into the marriage. Matt wondered if the pressure of the job had caused McRay's wife to leave and if his own marriage was doomed before it had started. Then, realising that it was the tiredness talking, he shut the thought out of his mind.

As he entered the flat, Matt was relieved to find everything in darkness except for a low light in the kitchen. Near the light was a note from Eppie saying a meal was in the fridge if he was hungry. Hunger was not something he thought about much when he was on a case; the team lived on pizzas and sandwiches eaten on the go and barely tasted.

As he removed the cling film and saw the care that Eppie had given to prepare his favourites, he was transported back to school days and lunch boxes, always with a treat lovingly prepared by his mother. Maybe there was something to this marriage lark after all.

Matt split the rolls and filled them with the Parma ham, adding just a little of the salad and, grabbing a beer, went into the lounge. Sprawled in his favourite chair and devouring the meal, he felt the tension drain away.

CHAPTER 14

It was just as he was drifting into a relaxed, almost meditative state, when the facts of the case could begin to organise themselves, that he became aware that something was different.

Instantly alert and standing, he looked about him. The first thing he saw was his favourite rugby trophy sitting on the bookcase, and he grasped it as if it were a lost child before letting his eyes wander to the mantelpiece. It just sat there, the silver frame glittering in the low light, the tanned, unkempt man grinning out at him.

Still clutching his precious trophy, Matt sank back down in his chair, realising that not everything in marriage was going to be easy. His flat, his space, was not just his now; it had to be shared with someone else. Although he loved Eppie, she was almost a stranger.

A soft kiss woke him, and he sleepily reached out to encircle his arms around Eppie, pulling her down onto his lap. It was only when she yelped slightly that he realised he was still holding the trophy. It didn't seem important now next to his need for her love and warmth, and he dropped it beside the chair to indulge himself in the softness of her body, all too aware that the day would stampede in soon enough.

CHAPTER 15

As the shrill demand of the alarm clock woke him at seven, Clive could feel the tiredness behind his eyes and the tension in his muscles. Finalizing his plans and the sense of power they infused had kept him up late.

His dreams had been of Ben. Not the soft, longing dreams he used to have, but one that shot brittle shafts of danger between them as Clive fought through an unfamiliar landscape of foggy, cobbled streets trying to reach him.

As he showered, he reasoned with himself that all he had of Ben were dreams. Did he want to give up the intense excitement and feeling of importance for this slight friendship, which might come to nothing?

However, being with Ben brought its own excitement in a softer, gentler way, awaking alien thoughts of loving and of being loved. No one had loved him since Lizzie gurgled her way into his life. Could Ben love him? All his old feelings of being unlovable surfaced.

Whereas, committing murder gave Clive an intense sense of power; he alone could choose who should live or die, like a Roman Emperor deciding someone's fate with a flick of his thumb. Surely, for such a powerful man there would be a million Bens. Maybe Clive didn't need him after all.

He pulled himself back to the present, reminded that he must keep up a very normal routine; nothing should stand out as different. Clive took up Mother's breakfast tray and then went to watch the news in the kitchen. Too excited to eat, he chewed on a cereal bar.

The murder was still headline news on the local channel, but on the national news, some new international atrocity had pushed it to the place before the weather report, in the spot usually reserved for children needing a bone-marrow transplant and the like. The added interest was a grey haired professor, lapping up the limelight like a budding rock star. He had nothing of great importance to say but still managed to make it sound as weighty as one of the Shakespearean tragedies.

Mother seemed more tired than usual, and Clive wondered if having Emily once a week could be wearing her out. He made a mental note to use this to curtail the visits by expressing his concern to Margaret over the state of Mother's health. That way he could regain some control and banish the infiltrator for good from his immaculate home.

Before leaving for work, he removed Mother's breakfast tray and helped her move with difficulty from the bed into the chair. Sensing the perfect opportunity, he sat on the edge of the bed and in his most concerned voice, leant towards her.

'I'd like you to think about having a few massages, Mother. I'm sure it would help with this stiffness.'

She was too distracted trying to get her sparse grey hair into some sort of respectable order before Mrs Sinclair arrived, to take in what he was saying and merely nodded. He had learnt that she was at her most vulnerable first thing in the morning, before those skinny limbs had eased off the night cramps and became used to moving again.

He pressed on. 'I thought we might have dinner at the spa one night soon. Their new French chef is getting rave reviews. Then I could arrange for you to chat to someone—ask if a massage would help?'

'Yes, yes,' she replied wanting to be rid of him.

Clive smiled with satisfaction and rose. 'I'll arrange it Mother,' he said, bending to plant the required kiss on her forehead.

Thoroughly pleased with himself, he manoeuvred the car into the midst of the morning rush hour traffic inching its way to work. His plans were laid and, as he went over them, he couldn't see anything he had missed. He was determined not to make the slightest mistake this time. With each outing, he would get better and better until nothing could stop him.

While waiting for yet another traffic light, he compared his precarious feelings for Ben to this wonderful new feeling of power coursing through his body, making him feel like a god. By the time he reached work, he was convinced he did not need Ben and had resolved to avoid him as much as possible.

It was only at the end of a long and boring meeting that he allowed himself to do more than glance at Ben. Ben was in profile, talking to Mr Phelps, the accountant, and the light from the window highlighted his curly hair, reminding Clive of a statue of a Greek god he had seen on a trip to Rome. He had an impulse to go over and join in the conversation but stopped himself and made his way to the door instead. Ben wasn't for him.

As he reached the door he sensed, rather than saw, that Ben was following him out.

Ben spoke before he could think of what to say. 'Could hardly keep from nodding off. How about you?'

'It was pretty dense wasn't it?' He tried to keep his voice light, although his heart was starting to thud so loudly he couldn't hear his own words.

Ben stopped by the secretary's desk and turned to face him. 'Well, I'm sure going to need a drink after that. Meet up later?'

Despite everything inside trembling, Clive managed a quick 'Yes,' together with a brief smile. This seemed to satisfy Ben as he nodded and turned away after favouring Clive with that warm, vivid grin. Was it his imagination or did it seem different? The smile had reached Ben's brown eyes, causing them to crinkle in the corners. That wasn't a mere courtesy smile carelessly bestowed on a colleague.

For Clive, time seemed to stop, and he wasn't aware that he had come to a halt until Phelps's accounts ledger file dug him sharply in the back.

'Come on, out of the way. Work to do, work to do,' grumbled Phelps.

He tried hard to keep calm but the good intentions in his head seemed to be at war with his body. It was only a couple of mates having a drink after work, nothing heavy, nothing out of the ordinary. But he wanted more than that, longed for a physical closeness with Ben that he had never desired with anyone. Questions raced around his head. Should he forget about his plans and put all his energy into developing a relationship with Ben?

Suddenly, Clive was angry. Why had this come now when he had decided—was set on a course of action? Why was this traitorous heart sending out lies to confound and confuse him? He had managed twenty-nine years without the useless organ and had been happy. Hadn't he?

He felt the need to strike out at someone, something. The nearest object was the waste bin beside the coffee machine, so he kicked out hard. His reward was the attention of every pair of eyes in the office. Clive tried to smile and pretend that he had knocked it over by accident, while acutely aware that hot, unfamiliar tears were welling up.

He crouched down to pick up the debris and to hide his display of emotion. Someone knelt besides him and he realised with horror that it was Anne.

'Oh, Clive, you are a silly one. Here let me help.'

As she bent beside him, he wanted to scream at her to leave him alone. The urge to push her head into the waste bin was so strong, he knew he had to get away before the desire overcame his normal caution.

Using the excuse of coffee dregs on his hands, Clive stumbled, rather than walked, from the room to find solace in the washroom.

As he washed his hands and face, he became calmer. Leaving all thoughts of Ben aside, he realised that it was time to face the fact that Anne was becoming more than a nuisance.

Ever since the conference in Harrogate, she had simply assumed they were a pair and had begun leading the whole office into believing her. He wished he could shout at her, loudly and brutally, in front of them all that she repelled him so much that he would rather go out with a dead cod. However, for the moment, Anne had the upper hand due to accidently seeing the costumes in the boot of his car.

Getting the right costumes to highlight his statements had been his hardest task, and for days he racked his brains while crossing out idea after idea. It was really only by accident as he glanced through one of the papers left scattered about the staff room, that he spotted an advert in the event's section for a huge sale of ex theatrical costumes in Birmingham. Taking care not to draw attention to himself, he scribbled down the details.

The sale was on the same day as the Harrogate conference and Clive began to see how he could make this work to his advantage. If he left early in the morning, as he had been planning to do anyway, it would take him less than an hour to get to Birmingham where he would have to wait another hour until the sale opened. Clive could make his selection and then head straight to Harrogate. He would only miss the opening rigmarole, which he knew was usually a waste of time anyway with all that concentration on getting to know your fellow attendees, whom you were not going to see or meet, hopefully, ever again.

On the day, as he waited for the sale to open, Clive debated whether to ring ahead to say he was stuck on the motorway. In this day of constant snarl-ups, it was always a valid excuse. Or, should he arrive late and only bring out his explanation if asked. If he arrived just before the coffee break and slid into the back, acting like he'd been there all the time, no one would probably take any notice. The delegates would all be dying for a coffee and a fag by then anyway. On balance, he decided against the call in case the police traced it or that someone remembered him calling.

Clive had parked the car around the corner from the sale and put on an old jacket and a flat checked cap his father had once worn, which, for some reason, his mother had decided to keep.

The cover story was that he was the producer of some amateur theatrical company and the next show in the village hall was going to require several of the chorus to look like little girls at a party.

Clive had invented the name of the village and show, which he thought should be written by their own local playwright, Randolph de Winter, of course. However, despite his elaborate preparations, no one really listened or appeared interested.

A sullen young man served him ungraciously with a martyred air. Clive got the impression the young man felt he was acting beneath himself and that he was only filling in time until called to portray Romeo for The Royal Shakespeare Company. Though he was glad to take the cash Clive offered him for the several costumes he had managed to find from the numerous rails haphazardly crammed into the huge warehouse.

It had taken him a long time sort out what he needed and, as he rushed back to the car with his booty, he realised that he would have to drive at some speed to get to Harrogate before the coffee break. Clive consoled himself by thinking that it might be better to arrive at coffee time and slide quietly in, and by the fact that the costumes seemed perfect for his purpose.

He smiled at the merry dance he would be leading the police. They would be dashing off in more than one direction, unaware that he had been extremely careful with every prop used, leaving them nothing that led back to him.

The only niggling worry was dear Anne, but Clive thought he had that situation under control. Anne believed she was in love with Clive and he found that giving her a little taste of what she wanted seemed to work. This wasn't an unusual situation in the office. Clive usually managed to offer the ladies his charmed attention and then use Mother as an excuse to keep his distance.

Anne started at En Jay's some months before and had shown such determination in her pursuit of Clive that she was becoming something of a nuisance. At first, he was his most charming self and expected the silly girl to fall into place like the others. But the little thank you cards for a job well done, flowers or chocolates for her birthday, Clive could now see only served to give her false hope, although he had treated her no different than all the other female staff.

Perhaps she was inexperienced, and she certainly wasn't attractive, or rather, she didn't make the effort to gild the lily like the other females. Her skin had a pale, sallow dullness that she could have enlivened by the usual makeup tricks. While her hair was straight in the prevailing fashion, it did not suit her thin features and only served to accent her long face.

However, it was her manner he found most difficult. She had become proprietary when around him, and it was obvious that she had begun to believe there was something between them, and she became intent on letting everyone know.

Even though Clive watched the other girls in the office shaking their heads and quietly giving her advice, she persisted. That was her main trait—her persistence—and he had the feeling that it would get her or him into trouble, especially now that she had something to hold over him.

Clive arrived at the Harrogate conference just as the coffee break had finished and the delegates were shuffling unwillingly back to the conference room. Pleading motorway problems, he opted for sympathy, giving the woman instructor his most apologetic smile. She patted him on the arm, said he could take five minutes, get himself a cup of coffee, and recover from his ordeal before joining the rest of the group. He was just about to thank her when he heard *her* whiny voice.

'Oh, Clive, thank goodness you have arrived safely. I was so worried in case you had had an accident. I told them it wasn't like you at all. That you are the most utterly reliable person.'

He turned to face Anne while trying to wipe the shock from his face, aware that the instructor was only a couple of yards away. Anne came towards him and before he could stop her, she gave him a hug in thankfulness that he was safe. Clive was aware that this was Anne's way of telling the instructor that she should keep her hands off, and it seemed to have the desired effect.

'I'll leave you in Anne's capable hands then. See you in five.'

As the instructor left, he fought to compose his features into something resembling pleasure that he was going to have Anne's company for the entire day.

'This is a pleasant surprise. What on earth are you doing here?'

'I talked Mr Hill into letting me come. I knew you would rather have company. It's such a long way to come on your own. And, well, I thought it would be rather lovely if we had dinner on the way home. I've checked out some places and marked them on a map. Shall I show you at lunchtime?'

'How did you get here?' He tried to keep the roughness out of his voice, knowing it held dread that she was expecting Clive to drive her home. Her reply confirmed his fears.

'I came by train. I did ring you several times last night but got no answer.'

She wouldn't have reached him, even though she had managed to acquire his mobile number, since he always ignored her calls. He had to think fast.

'I always go to *silent* in the evening. Mother thinks mobile phones are the work of the devil, sorry.'

'I thought that might be it.'

'Anyway, you are here now and it will be good sharing the day with you,' Clive said, back on track. He would have to play her game today but he could see that she was becoming a problem.

Even with his late start, the day dragged endlessly on and he didn't remember anything of the content. Anne insisted on sitting next to him, even when the instructor tried to divide everyone into different groups.

Lunch was a nightmare with Anne chattering on incessantly, enjoying her belief, and parading it front of everyone, that they were an item.

Clive was dreading the journey home and wondered if he could bring out his usual excuse of needing to get home to Mother. However, as they walked to the car, he realised that Anne was way ahead of him.

'Will someone be with your Mother today?'

'Yes, I have a housekeeper. Well, a sort of companion really for Mother.'

'It must be a great comfort to have her there when you are away, like today.'

'Yes.'

'And to know you don't have to rush back. I mean, after that terrible journey this morning you need to relax.'

He may have imagined it but she seemed to emphasise the words 'terrible journey' and he had the feeling she hadn't believed him from the start. She had it all worked out, and he had to give her credit.

Stifling his excuses, Clive realised it would be best to suffer her for a few more hours. He decided to put a brave face on it and play along with her, just for now.

'That's true. Let's enjoy our dinner. It will be such a nice change for me. Where would you like to go? You choose, Anne.'

He could tell this is what she wanted and she looked pleased as they made their way across the car park. As they approached the car, one of the men from the course stopped to talk to Clive. Anne had gone ahead to the car, so he clicked it open for her in case she didn't want to wait. Normally he would have opened the door for her. Mother always insisted on good manners.

Finishing his conversation, he turned towards the car to see Anne opening the boot intending to stow her briefcase. By the time he got to her, it was too late, and she was gazing down at the costumes.

'Oh.'

He closed the boot fast, grasping her arm to lead her around to the passenger side. He wanted to push her roughly inside, but instead waited patiently while she arranged herself, all the time thinking of how to explain the costumes, until he came up with, 'Some show of Lizzie's. I didn't have time to drop them off to her.'

'How exciting. What is the show and please say we can go and see it?'

'No way. It's just some scrappy thing they are doing at university.'

'But surely you will be taking your mother?'

'Not if I can help it. I've sat through too many of these things already. Mother fell asleep during the last one. Now where are we going?'

She dropped it then, intent on deciding where they should stop for dinner, but he knew she hadn't given up on the idea and was seeing herself taking his arm for what she imagined would be a family occasion.

During dinner, Clive acted the perfect gentleman, pulling out her chair and pouring her wine, even though the restaurant was not up to his usual standards. As he smiled at her across the table, his mind was racing, and he knew this couldn't go on. He would have to do something about Anne.

Now he was forever hearing her screechy voice saying things like, *'Clive and I drove down together,'* or *'Oh we had such a lovely dinner.'*

He tried confiding in his strongest ally in the office, the receptionist, Gloria. She was in her mid forties and treated him differently from the other girls. For one, she had no designs on him, due to her already running a hot affair with one of the town councillors under her husband's nose.

Gloria was the unofficial confidant for most of the girls in the office. In the past, when one of the girls became over enamoured and believed she was on the way to becoming Mrs Clive Draper, and he shuddered at the thought, he turned to Gloria.

Gloria would have a quiet word and the miscreant would fall back into the pool of rejects and cause him no further bother. Of course Clive was adept in not ruling out hope altogether, just to keep them in line. One never knew when someone might be useful.

Anne though was another matter. She and Gloria hadn't got on from the start. Anne tended to see Gloria as a mere receptionist and thought she was somehow better being one of the junior programmers. She refused to accept Gloria as the Mother Hen and would look down her sharp nose at Gloria and take no notice at all.

Yes, something would definitely have to be done about Anne.

CHAPTER 16

Matt hunted for a reasonably clean mug, and made himself a cup of instant coffee in the small kitchen, which doubled as a staff room. He wasn't looking forward to his meeting with Professor Derek Meredith at eight a.m. sharp. He had been told that, since the professor was such an important person, he should fit in the appointment to suit him.

As he stirred the coffee, he wondered again what so irritated him about the man. Maybe it was his arrogance. Or was it the way he dismissed the victims of a brutal murder? To the professor they were mere objects, to be coldly discussed and forgotten, the perpetrator being his main fascination.

It made Matt uncomfortable, as despite the need to keep a professional distance, he never allowed himself to forget the real people who were affected by violent crimes. Images of the victims, Gracie foremost, and those left behind, kept him going against the odds when everything seemed to be working against him.

Placing the mug beside the reports that were building into a precarious pile on his desk, he sat down and started to read.

It was only five minutes later that he was interrupted by a young uniformed constable who announced in a somewhat reverential tone that Professor Meredith had arrived for him. The PC then stood aside to usher the esteemed professor into the office. Matt could have sworn that the constable gave a slight bob of the head as the professor strode in, as if he were paying honour to a football hero.

With a glare, he dismissed the young man and rose to greet the professor, offering him a seat and coffee. With a glance at Matt's tatty mug, the professor declined the coffee.

To foster cooperation, Matt moved from behind his desk and joined the professor, sitting opposite him across the small coffee table, taking his notebook with him.

'Thank you for coming, Professor,' he said.

'My pleasure, my boy, my pleasure,' the professor purred.

I bet it is, thought Matt, *and so is the cheque at the end of it.* 'You have the briefing?' he continued, keeping his voice civil.

The professor took a folder out of his battered briefcase and nodded whilst opening it. 'Very interesting—this chap is making a bold statement, a very bold statement indeed.'

'So what is he saying?'

'Well...' the professor paused as if cogitating, 'Well, I would say that he is trying to tell us something about his childhood. He probably wasn't a very happy little boy, not happy at all. Probably felt he didn't belong.'

Great, thought Matt, any one of his team could have worked that one out, but he pressed on. 'So he was unhappy as a boy. But why has he started killing now?'

'Now this is most fascinating.'

Again, the maddening pause that Matt was sure he did for effect. He waited, trying not to let the impatience show on his face.

'Yes, intriguing. I believe there may have been some life event. Not necessarily catastrophic, but everyday, like death, birth, redundancy, a trauma say or the ending of a relationship. The sort of thing that happens to us all. However, in the case of this damaged individual it acted as a catalyst.'

Matt thought that any one of those events could push someone closer to the edge, but not into committing such a bizarre murder.

'Damaged in what way, Professor?'

The professor paused again, and this time, Matt was certain it was because he wasn't so sure of his ground.

'As I said, this person is damaged. He will probably have been coping, possibly coping well. However, some event has reawakened an inner turmoil and brought all the painful feelings to the surface, as it were. Killing may be the only way he can externalize these feelings. It may be a release. A most wonderful release.'

Matt felt as if the professor was contemplating some release of his own. 'So why choose a young woman?'

'He probably sees her as an ideal object upon which to express himself. Again, she could be related to his childhood.'

'He is trying to tell us something about his childhood?'

The professor nodded wisely, fingers together in the classical thinking pose.

'So what is he trying to say?'

The professor dropped his head onto his fingers before replying. 'Although it will be very clear to him, he will want us to work it out, to understand his pain. This will be part of his task, his enjoyment.'

'So we are looking for someone who is coping well in society, who wouldn't stand out? Who is clever and well organised and had a disturbed childhood? How the hell are we going to find him?'

'Ah, now that is your job, my dear boy, your job,' the professor intoned.

Matt wanted to shout at him.

'He will probably live alone.'

'I take it he is likely to kill again?' Matt asked, keeping his voice level.

'Oh yes, almost certainly. He will feel empowered by the process. Highly excited, like a hound that has tasted blood. He will want to recapture that feeling as soon as possible.'

'The victim. How will he select his victims?'

'I would assume that the chosen victim may be on the periphery of his acquaintances. In effect, they are standing in for those he would really like to kill but dare not.'

Matt felt his heart sink. If the professor was right, there would be no way to link this killer to his victim, or victims. With no obvious motive, it would be like looking for a needle in a haystack. If Matt and the team didn't move fast enough to stop him, he would kill again and again.

Although the professor continued, he gave Matt little insight into how they could catch this murderer, and Matt thanked him and brought the interview to a close.

With the interview out of the way, Matt hoped that the morning would bring in some good news, some progress on the many leads the night team had been working on. The murderer had provided enough evidence, so he was either a fool or confident his props wouldn't lead back to him. If it was the latter, then Matt had to hope that he would become too sure of his own power and eventually trip up.

As he joined the team, Sam was already half way through the briefing and had just asked Wendy to bring them up to date. Wendy hated speaking in front of everyone, so instead of going to the board, she stood by her desk. However, her report was concise and, as he listened, Matt blessed her for her thoroughness.

'I've made a comprehensive list of all known manufacturers of the type of dress Miss Metcalfe was found in, both made in this country and imported. Most of the imports come from China and can be found in fancy dress shops and on eBay. However, the material in this dress is from Yorkshire and is on sale all over the country. Likely sources for the made up dress would be theatre companies or, again, fancy dress shops.'

'Or they could be made to order?' Sam asked.

'Yes. Probably for a specific show.'

'I can't think of what show that would be, Guv.' Everyone knew Fluff was a theatre buff and loved going down to London on her days off.

'Some marketing companies buy up old theatrical, ex fancy dress shop stock and either sell on eBay, or if they are in need of space, they hold a sale. In addition, locally we have the Royal Shakespeare Company. They have their own costume department, and every few years they have a sale of their unwanted items, selling mainly to professional theatre companies. There was also a large sale in Birmingham earlier this year of the combined unwanted stock from several theatrical companies, including costumes from pantomimes.'

As Wendy concluded her report, Matt stood to thank her personally, causing her to flush as she eased her bulk down into her chair. 'I'd like you to follow up that Birmingham sale please, Wendy. Exact dates, who ran it, staff, stock, etc.'

She nodded her eager assent, and Matt indicated that Sam should continue. Sam said the dolls were made in China, with the main importer based in Leeds. They shipped to a variety of suppliers all over England, which included shops, both chains and private, some arcades, plus market stalls.

As far as the lollipops went, these were manufactured in Birmingham and shipped to several hundred suppliers in the country—mostly to seaside shops, theme parks, and again market stalls.

Matt realised, if he was going to keep McRay happy with the budget, they would never have the resources to cover all the possible outlets. If he was the murderer, he would have sourced all the items needed in a busy, jostling crowd where there was less likelihood of being noticed. Therefore, markets seemed the best bet. Even so, Matt knew it wouldn't be possible to do a manual check of every retailer of the dolls or lollipops in the country. If they just concentrated on the hundreds of markets it still left them with an almost impossible task. Their best bet would be to enlist the aid of the local police forces and maybe the association of market stallholders.

Sam seemed to be thinking along the same lines. 'It's not going to be easy, Guv.'

'No. Unless we go public with one of these items. The doll, for instance. It seems a bit out of date. Didn't we have those a few years back?' Matt asked.

Fluff spoke up. 'We had Cabbage Patch dolls—must be twenty or thirty years ago. A bit of a resurgence a few years ago. But this is more a Raggedy Ann and they have been around forever.'

None of the team seemed inclined to challenge Fluff's knowledge of dolls, so Matt asked, 'Would the doll be the best bet for a public appeal?'

'Surely the model soldier is the more unique item, inspector?'
DI Grant drawled from the back.

Matt hated the way he insisted on calling him Inspector in that
tone, but he kept his voice calm. 'Yes, definitely. But I would prefer
to keep our investigations with that item on a more private level.'

'Your call,' he said, somehow managing to imply that Matt was
wrong.

Matt let it go, as he was used to doing. However, he noticed
Fluff shoot a look of disgust towards Grant. He hoped she wasn't
going to make an issue out of it. Then Sam highlighted another
point.

'If we go public, who's going to take all the calls? You know
what it's like. We'll be fielding confessions from every nutter in
the country.'

It was a good point. Details about a murder would, under
normal circumstances, be kept under wraps for as long as possible.
Sifting through calls from the public, some trying to be helpful,
and others not, was going to be a costly business.

'Well, we do have the professor's esteemed opinion that our
murderer will kill again and soon. That should add some weight
to our request.'

Promising to ask for extra help, Matt ended the briefing and
sent most of the team back to the health club where the rest of
the maintenance men and some of the other staff were still to be
interviewed.

Matt was relieved that McRay seemed to have retained some
of the helpfulness of last night, as it meant they could discuss if it
would be wise to go to a public appeal with one of the items.

After working through the pros and cons Matt and McRay
thought it would be a good idea, and both agreed that the doll was
the most distinctive. Matt left McRay preparing to put the matter
before Superintendent Neal and headed back to the health club,
stopping only for a quick visit to the Royal Shakespeare Company's
costume department.

The building was made of corrugated iron, painted light grey
with yellow trimmings. It would have been easy to miss it except for

the large letters, RSC, on its side and two mega lorries, big enough to carry all the flats and equipment for the latest shows, parked outside. This seemed a far cry from the glamour of the theatre itself, set here on the small business park at the northern end of Stratford town.

After the brightness outside, the vast space seemed dim, and Matt could see very little for a moment. Mrs Mason, summoned by the outside bell, bustled up to receive him graciously enough, while reminding him that she was a busy lady, with a new production to costume. As if to emphasise, she pointed to two nearby rails hung with jewelled coloured velvet cloaks while a small golden puppet hung from one end next to a huge egg.

Matt raised his eyebrows at the interesting combination.'

'*Arabian Nights.* Christmas production.'

'Must get tickets and bring my wife.' It sounded strange saying 'my wife'. This was the first time he had used the phrase.

'I have received your fax, Inspector.' Mrs Mason retrieved the fax showing the dress Amy was found in from her apron pocket and spread it out onto the desk. Do you have a sample of the material?'

Matt handed her the small square of material Jason had allowed him to have and watched as Mrs Mason rubbed it between her thumb and forefinger.

'I am quite certain this is not one of our costumes. Apart from our Christmas productions, we would have no call for such items.'

'Can you give me any suggestions as to who might use such a dress?'

'Well, the fabric is very thin. I would think pantomimes or one of the more tatty costume hire shops.'

Mrs Mason was then distracted by a young man who approached carrying what looked like a peacock feather about fifteen feet long. Matt murmured his thanks and made for the door, receiving just a brief wave of the hand in dismissal. Mrs Mason had already moved onto the next problem.

Matt manoeuvred his way out of Stratford, dodging tourists crossing the road looking the wrong way and large parties of foreign students who felt it necessary to cross the road linked closely together, whenever and wherever they liked. Then out over the ancient Clopton Bridge, still bearing traffic over the River Avon after over five hundred years. Matt always liked to imagine Shakespeare crossing here on his way to London. As he squeezed slowly past a huge lorry, he wondered what Will would think if he were here today.

He arrived at the health spa to find Fluff exasperated.

'I'll swing for that bastard.'

Matt didn't need to ask who had caused her grief. 'OK what's he done now?'

'Upset Mrs Trowbridge. Admittedly, the CCTV tapes are useless, but he shouldn't have had a go at her. It's not her fault if they only cover the front entrance. Apparently, the Company feel it would be too intrusive of the guests' privacy to have them inside the building.'

'From what I have seen of Mrs Trowbridge, it would take more than Grant to upset her. Let's not waste our energy on him.'

'Sorry, Guv.'

'So where is everybody?'

'Jason's team are still working the murder scene and corridor. Oh, and the manager wants him to finish in the locker room ASAP, since he will need it for the day guests. So Jason is finishing off in there.'

Matt would have liked to keep day guests out of the club for at least another day, but the spa's owners had already started complaining that their business was being disrupted.

'Sam and Grant are interviewing. I'm making lists of everyone who came in and out yesterday. We've interviewed a lot of them already. There are a few delivery vans we'll need to chase though.'

'OK. I'll see if I can appease Mrs Trowbridge who might just be able to get us a nibble or two from the restaurant. Good chance for us all to have a catch up. Say half an hour.'

As Matt turned to walk away, Fluff called after him.

'Make sure there's no snails, Guv. You know they have a French chef.'

Laughing, he shouted back over his shoulder, 'will do.'

It was a long afternoon, and the entire team were kept busy going through all the debris left behind after a murder, in the hope that something or someone would give them a lead.

Matt had taken over interviewing and had sent Grant back to CID where he could work on cross checking the statements already taken. And it would get the man out of the way for a while. He hoped he hadn't made his own feelings clear about the man and influenced Fluff in any way, but lately the two seemed to argue all the time. He resolved to have a quiet word with Fluff when this was all over.

Late in the afternoon, McRay rang to say that Superintendent Neal had agreed to make a public appeal for information about the doll. The broadcast would go out on all news channels at six p.m. and be repeated at ten.

It had been a long day, so this was a good time for the team to stop for a coffee and sandwich to watch the chief superintendent, in full uniform, standing rather self-consciously, holding the doll.

Sam said it all. 'He'd look better with a teddy bear.'

Everyone laughed, releasing the tension.

CHAPTER 17

Clive composed himself and, back at his desk, tried to look as if he was working, when it struck him that maybe he could have it all. Why couldn't he have the power and pleasure of expressing his pain and Ben?

He allowed himself to fantasize about holding Ben, softly stroking his naked neck, and moving downwards to his chest and loins. Clive could feel his body responding and looked around, embarrassed as a schoolboy let down by pubescent hormones. Everyone else in the office appeared intent on their work, and he smiled, wondering if they, too, were locked into similar fantasies.

He wanted it all. It was simple. For the moment, he would keep his secret life separate. Then, when he had done enough to impress Ben, he would tell him. Ben would be excited and want to join in. Together they could experience the same exhilarating power, and it would fuse them together forever.

It was a call on his mobile that drew him back to the present. It was Lizzie, who blithely informed him that she was dropping Mother off at four-thirty for her shopping trip.

Lizzie saw Mother at the most once a fortnight, to take her to the library, and considered her duty done. Clive guessed that this was her way of getting rid of Mother early and escaping back to the world of academia. Not that Mother seemed to mind as, after all, Lizzie hadn't as yet produced any appalling babies, and so of course came lower in the lovable order than Margaret.

Lizzie gave him no chance to argue, merely stated what her plan was, and hung up. He was tempted to call her back, to say he had other plans, but he knew she never left any room for manoeuvre around her own needs and probably had Mother already strapped in her Mini.

Lizzie had always demanded her own way from the minute she was born. She tried to make his life hell when they were growing up, until he became clever and started to pretend he was the most caring brother.

The most difficult occasions were Margaret or Lizzie's birthday parties when hordes of giggling girls, all dressed in their best party frocks, arrived at the house to play silly games, while he was expected to hand around the sandwiches, move the chairs, and help blow up the balloons.

They hunted in a pack, led by Lizzie, and their sole aim was to torment him. They demanded kisses, made him hold their dolls, or even worse, dance with them.

On Lizzie's fifth birthday, she received one of those ugly Cabbage Patch dolls that were all the rage at the time. All afternoon she had been showing off to her friends, clutching the disgusting thing, which she had named Miss Molly. All of a sudden, she thrust it at Clive.

'You are to guard Miss Molly with your life, or I will tell Father. Do you hear?' she demanded before skipping off with a swish of her party frock to join in musical chairs.

All the little girls tittered as he stood there dangling Miss Molly by one arm, trying hard to look unconcerned while raging inside.

Clive waited until Lizzie was busy squealing with the others and then slipped out into the back garden. At first, he thought of drowning Miss Molly in the water-butt before deciding she might be too easy to find.

Instead, he climbed up to the tree house. This used to be his place, full of pirates and rogues, until Lizzie made her first foray up the small ladder. Since then, the pirates were vanquished in favour of tea parties with plastic cups and several dolls.

Ignoring his best clothes and with Miss Molly in his teeth, Clive inched his way along one of the strongest branches of the tree, until he could see down into the wilderness at the end of the garden. Taking careful aim, he flung the doll into the thickest part of an ancient blackberry bush. It fell straight into the heart, snagging its dress on the thorny twigs and came to rest balefully looking up at him. He rolled a great gob of spit and spat it down onto Miss Molly's face to see it land just below her right eye, so she looked as if she were crying. With a last quick look of triumph, he slithered backwards down the branch.

It wasn't long before Lizzie realised that Miss Molly was missing. Clive pretended innocence, something he was becoming an expert at. 'I put her there,' he said pointing at the garden swing. 'Just while I had a sausage roll. I didn't want to get her dress dirty,' he added for good measure.

With Lizzie's wailing turned into hysterics, father emerged from his study and Clive had to repeat his plea of innocence, while quaking under his long, suspicious stare. For a moment, he thought he wasn't going to be believed, that he would be dragged into the dreaded study for a telling off or worse. Father's eyes seem to bore right into his head, and Clive almost faltered under that gaze, but finally his father turned away to promise Lizzie another Miss Molly. Clive was glad to see she wasn't consoled, crying that she wanted the old Miss Molly.

Clive become more careful after the Miss Molly incident, and at least on the surface, was a most caring, thoughtful brother. He found this made it so much easier to get away with things. As for Miss Molly, she was never found, and he liked to think she was still there rotting away.

Clive gave a sigh and admitted to himself that Lizzie had managed to get one over on him, but he would make sure she paid for it.

Not being able to think of any legitimate reason to put off the promised trip again, Clive resigned himself to the inevitable shopping spree. He knew he would be trapped in Marks & Spencer's for well over an hour, trying not to lose his temper as Mother dithered between the merits of several pairs of plain cotton ladies knickers, all of which looked exactly the same to him.

He stood and moved across to tell Ben that their drink was off. Looking down at his dark, bent head, he noticed there were little curls at the base of his neck. Clive had to stifle a sudden impulse to reach out and run his fingers through them.

Ben seemed disappointed at the news but no alternate date was set. Clive consoled himself by thinking the delay gave him more time to be sure that a relationship with Ben was what he really wanted. However, being this close to him again he already knew the answer.

* * *

The local Marks & Spencer's stayed open until six. It was just as he had envisioned. The ladies lingerie department was crowded with women. Clive, as the only man, tried not to look as they held up, examined, or exclaimed over the intimate apparel that surrounded him.

Although Mother had become a whiz in her electronic wheelchair, she found the folding, portable one difficult, and he had to wheel her around. He was not averse to this, but advising on her underwear was way beyond his comfort zone.

As Mother indicated she wanted to go back, yet again, down the same aisles she had already been down twice, Clive could feel his helpful, caring-son persona running out fast. It was then he saw her. She was already homing in on them and, as she caught his eye, she waved. Eagle-eyed Mother had already noticed.

'A friend of yours, Clive?'

'Just a young lady from work, Mother.'

'Ah. You must introduce us.'

He could tell that Mother was already mentally assessing whether Anne was suitable marriage material. Did she look smart enough? Tick. Was she too tarty or normal? Tick. Did she look healthy and strong enough to have babies? Tick. Was she the right age? Tick.

By the time Anne had manoeuvred her way through the bra section to reach them, Mother almost certainly had them engaged.

Anne didn't waste any time on Clive but zoned in directly on Mother. 'So pleased to meet you at last, Mrs Draper. Clive talks about you all the time. I'm Anne. I'm sure Clive must have mentioned me.'

'No he hasn't. Although I can't imagine why not.'

Both Mother and Anne looked at him waiting for an explanation. He had to bring Anne to order, stop this nonsense before it went any further. 'Mother, the office is full of young ladies; I can't possible mention them all.'

Anne laughed and put a hand on Mother's arm. 'Oh, he's so shy. That is so sweet and just what I love about him.'

Clive squirmed as Mother looked up at him in surprise, seeking confirmation of this supposed loving shyness. There must be a way out of this. Looking at his watch, he reminded Mother that the store was due to close in thirty-five minutes. For emphasis, he pushed the wheelchair forward, causing Anne to take a step back.

'Then I really must make my choices. So nice to meet you, Anne. You must come to tea.'

Before he could begin to move, Anne, who wasn't ready to take this minor setback, squeezed him out of the way and inserted herself behind the wheelchair.

'Let me help, Mrs Draper. I would really like to.'

Without waiting for an answer, Anne wheeled Mother away leaving him fuming. Clive moved away to the safety of the men's clothing area from where he could keep an eye on them both.

He could see Anne chatting away, filling Mother's head with all sorts of nonsense, no doubt about their blossoming relationship.

One minute from closing, Anne returned Mother. Mother had several packages and looked happy.

'There, Mrs Draper, I hope I managed to help just a little bit.'

'Most assuredly, my dear. Such a pleasant experience.'

Anne smiled down at Mother before looking up at Clive. He could see triumph in her eyes.

'I enjoyed it. I look forward to seeing you at Lizzie's show.'

'Yes. Clive, you must tell me more about this show of Lizzie's. The costumes sound ridiculous.'

'It's nothing, Mother.'

'Well, as her family, we will go and support her. And Anne will be very happy to join us.'

He began to wheel Mother away, horrified at what he was hearing.

'Oh, and I want you to invite this young lady to lunch. No more of this silly shyness. I never heard of such a thing. As I have always said, Clive, finish what you start.'

Anne was becoming a clear, escalating danger to his plans. He needed time to plan what to do about her.

Unable to bear the thought of Mother going on about Anne, once they arrived home, he abandoned her to Mrs Sinclair with the excuse that he needed to fetch something from the office. Anne presented Clive with a delicate problem, but if she were to be despatched, everyone in the office would be a suspect, including himself. He would need to be very clever about how she was disposed of.

To cheer himself up, he decided to take a run out to DI Turrell's flat. Once he had the flat's number, he would be able to send the DI a little message.

CHAPTER 18

Eppie wished she had been able to tell Matt about starting her new job before he left, but he had showered and gone all within ten minutes, saying he would get a coffee at work. She was already asleep when he arrived home the night before, so there had been no chance then.

Now, as she brushed her hair, Eppie realised something had made her hold back. She had not wanted to lose the warmth and closeness of the night, needing to be reassured of his love, of his need for her.

Matt's anger of Monday had shaken her more than she had realised. It wasn't that she was afraid of him. And, although she tried to tell herself she didn't want to bother him while he was on a case, the truth was, once she had started work at the health club, he would have to accept it. Eppie felt she had to make Matt understand that he couldn't have everything the way he wanted. Their life together would have to be built on compromise. Despite this, she hoped that she wouldn't have to face him on her first day.

Eppie was nervous as she presented herself to Mrs Trowbridge, but this was soon forgotten when she was introduced to Sandi, one of the receptionists, whom she was to shadow for the next few days. Sandi was bubbly and helpful, and Eppie took an immediate liking to her. All the staff were busier than usual trying to reassure the guests who were alarmed at the continued police presence and questioning. Staff had been told to say that everything would be back to normal soon and that they were in no danger.

Sandi thought it was nice to have so many men about the place, especially the ones in uniform and was inclined to flirt with them. Eppie knew she would have to tell her at some point that her husband was in charge of the case but decided against it for the moment.

During the few quiet moments, Sandi began showing Eppie where everything was kept. When Eppie said she had only just got married, Sandi became excited.

'Oh, I'm getting married in six months. You must tell me all about it. I'm having such a hard time deciding on colours, the bouquet...well everything. Tom's no help at all.'

'Ours was rather sudden.'

'But that's dead romantic. We've been engaged for over a year. I think it must be easier your way. But we've got family coming from all over, even Australia and Canada. The guest list keeps multiplying, so everything has to be perfect.'

Listening to all Sandi's plans, Eppie was glad she and Matt had had a whirlwind romance and that her father, bless him, had taken care of most of the details of the wedding. She couldn't imagine having the event hanging around her neck forever. But Sandi had been trying to decide colours, flowers, dress, etc., for well over a year and seemed to be relishing the whole thing.

At one point during the morning, Eppie had seen the young man and woman who worked with Matt. She remembered them vaguely from the evening reception and thought the woman had a funny nickname, one that she couldn't recall. Neither of them had come to the desk nor seemed to recognise her, and Eppie was glad to leave it that way. She kept her fingers crossed that Matt was working somewhere else.

She decided to stop worrying about Matt and threw herself into work, learning everything she could from Sandi. With guests starting to gather in the lobby for the dining room to open for lunch, she and Sandi had become busy, so Sandi was unable to press her with any more questions about Matt or talk about weddings.

Eppie found herself dealing with guests on her own and was enjoying the variety of their requests, many she could already answer.

It was also good to see a familiar face in the polite young man from Monday. He smiled as he approached, and she tried to remember his name. He saved her by announcing himself.

'Clive. From Monday.'

'Oh, yes, of course.'

'So, did you manage to calm the angry husband?'

'Just about. But I haven't told him yet about the job.'

'So, see you back in the deli later then.'

Eppie laughed with him. Looking at him as he stood there, tall and straight, good looking in a slightly too neat sort of way, she guessed he would never be untidy or spontaneous but always controlled and careful.

'I want to arrange for my mother to talk to someone. See if maybe a massage could help her. She gets these dreadful cramps in her legs.'

'How thoughtful. Trouble is I don't yet know where to find the list of therapists or how to book one. I'm sorry but we'll need Sandi's help. Are you alright to wait a moment?'

'Of course.'

It seemed rude to turn away from him, even though Sandi had given her some forms to file. Plus he seemed to want to prolong the conversation.

'It must be nice working with people.'

'So far so good. I didn't want to be shut up in an office.'

'Is that what you did before?'

'No. I worked with my dad. So every day was different.'

'Working with my father would be my idea of hell.'

She laughed. 'It couldn't be that bad?'

'Not if you like square bashing.'

'Oh, I see, the army. So what do you do, instead?' Eppie picked up the slight hesitation before he replied.

'Oh, working with figures all day—very boring.'

Just then, Sandi came over to see how she could help. She took down the book with the details of all the therapists and Eppie made a mental note to remember where it was kept.

Eppie watched as Sandi ran down the list. Clive leaned right over the counter to view the details for himself, even though Sandi was pointing out possibilities. She read out the details of some, only to dismiss them as too young or too new, until Clive decided that a mature therapist, Mrs Mooney, would suit his Mother.

After thanking both of them, Clive turned to leave, then turned back to the desk.

'I've just had a thought. Would it be possible to fit us in for dinner on Saturday night? I've heard the French chef is very good and it would be such a treat for Mother.'

'Eppie, would you like to take care of this? It will be good practice.'

Eppie nodded and picked up the restaurant book, surprised that she remembered all that Sandi had taught her.

Talking about Clive afterwards, Sandi explained that Clive had taken his mother in after his father had died and from all accounts was a very caring son. He was a day member at the spa, coming in for a few sessions after work or on the occasional day.

It was not until nearly two o'clock as she returned from her lunch break that Eppie had to face Matt. As she rounded the corner from the staff canteen, there he was at Reception, talking to Sandi. Sandi had her flirty smile on as she looked up at him, and Eppie could see that he was appreciative, although he was maintaining his authority.

Eppie had the instinct to go back around the corner, but Matt looked up and saw her before she could move. At first, Eppie found it amusing as she watched the mixture of expressions cross his face, until it settled into a cold, controlled anger.

She tried a welcoming smile as she approached. 'Hello, Matt.' For a moment she thought he was going to ignore her and move away, but he made a conscious effort to turn to face her.

'Eppie,' was all he managed.

'I—I have a job. Here,' she said, feeling as if she were an underage teen caught in a nightclub. She could tell that he was shocked when he averted his eyes.

'I see. Well, I had better let you get on then.' With a brief nod to Sandi, he turned and walked away.

Eppie had never felt quite so shut out and alone even though Sandi was all agog.

'Oh, Eppie. Tell me that's not him! He's simply gorgeous.'

'And as mad as hell.'

For the rest of the day, Eppie tried hard to field Sandi's questions, none of which she felt like answering. This stern coldness was a side of Matt that she had never seen, and she would have preferred a stand up row.

Was she putting Matt in an impossible position? This was a murder scene, and he had to have authority and control. But then, how could her presence here make any difference? She had no intention of interfering or approaching him when he was busy. So why couldn't he afford her the same courtesy.

He could behave as normal with Sandi, so why not with her? Matt would just have to realise that she was simply doing a job. Eppie began to feel angry and was determined to hold her ground.

After all, this must be the safest place to be. With all the police about, no one would be stupid enough to attempt another murder here.

CHAPTER 19

Clive had arrived at the office early, hoping that Ben might be there and they could have a word without Anne's prying eyes.

Wherever he happened to be in the office, he could feel Anne watching him. She would bring him coffee and be inclined to stay and chat, all the time glancing around, intent on making sure that the whole office was aware of their supposed friendship.

If he went anywhere near Ben, she was there using a variety of ways to attract his attention. These were usually work related and Clive couldn't ignore her in the middle of the office but was forced to walk away and sort out her problem. Since Ben and he had begun getting closer, as he liked to think, he noticed that she had directed one or two sharp glances towards them. Whatever else he could say about Anne, he had to admit she was clever. She had picked up on his feelings for Ben and was jealous.

Anne had the power to make what could be private and beautiful into grotesque fodder for the office gossip machine. So far, Clive had managed to keep a delicate balance with her, but after her performance in Marks & Spencer's last night he doubted he could keep it up.

Today, Anne would be feeling powerful and there was no foretelling how she would be. Mother's approval would no doubt give her courage, and he shuddered at the thought of having to endure both her and Mother together. Anne would be certain to remind him that Mother had suggested she come to lunch.

Clive wondered what his life would be like without Mother. Commanding her full attention over the last two years had been enjoyable, but it hardly made up for her abandonment of earlier. Ben now complicated and coloured his life, and he didn't want to wait until she died to experience that love.

Today, it felt as if they had their own special wavelength, for Clive had barely seated himself at his desk when Ben arrived. He stood to welcome him.

'Sorry about yesterday. I just couldn't let Mother down.' Clive moved around his desk as Ben approached.

'Sure. Don't worry. I'm sure there will be other opportunities.'

Ben was standing right next to him now, and although the words sounded innocent, he had put the emphasis on 'opportunities.' They both knew exactly what he meant. He heard himself reply in a low voice. 'I certainly hope so.' He leaned towards Ben automatically reaching out his hand. What he wanted was to pull Ben forward and fasten their lips together. However, before they could even touch fingers tips a strident voice rang across the office.

'Good morning. You two are early. Lovely day isn't it? Shall I get us all a coffee?'

Ben recovered first, turning to acknowledge Anne. 'Great. Two sugars, hold the milk.' With a slight shrug of his shoulders, he moved away from Clive back to his own desk in the outer office.

With a satisfied smile on her face, Anne disappeared into the small hallway that served as a cloakroom to hang up her coat. She returned and moved over to the coffee machine, humming as she sorted out the three coffees.

Clive watched as she deliberately plonked Ben's coffee down on his desk so that some of the hot liquid tipped onto his desk and his leg.

'Oh, I'm so very sorry, Ben.'

'No problem.'

As Ben sought out a tissue to mop up, Anne smirked and came towards Clive, placing his coffee on a coaster before moving back to shut the door on the outer office. She turned to look at him with a concerned look on her face.

'I wonder if I could have a brief word, Clive.'

It was the last thing he wanted. There was a churning pool of anger deep in his stomach blocking any civilized reply, so he nodded instead and sat down resigned.

'It was so lovely to meet your mother last night. She's such a genteel lady.'

At least Clive could agree with that even though to him genteel meant pseudo posh and stuck up. 'Yes, she certainly is that.'

'I thought we got on rather well.'

He could see immediately where this was going. She was intending to use Mother as her ally to bring them together. With his anger fighting to explode, Clive applied his usual device of clamping it down and turning it into ice. This way, he could remain in control, could plan what had to be done with this stupid bitch who dared to imagine for one moment that he would ever wish to have anything to do with her. It was important that she continued to think she had the upper hand while he decided how to get rid of her.

'Yes. Mother did say what a pleasant young lady you were. She said I should invite you to tea.'

'Oh how lovely,' Anne simpered, 'but I thought it was lunch?'

'You're right. I'm looking forward to it.' Lying was so easy. You simply told someone what they wanted to hear, just like the politicians. He watched as she preened, putting up her hand to check her hair while glancing slyly around to see if Ben was watching. 'I'll check with Mother as to a time.' He stopped himself saying 'date' deliberately, not wanting to give her too much satisfaction.

Now she should be satisfied and could leave. Clive rose, intending to act the gentleman and open the door for her, but she remained seated, dropping her eyes demurely. He waited.

'There is something else, Clive. It is a little delicate and I only speak because I do not want your mother to be upset.'

'Then you must tell me, of course.'

'Please forgive me, but I am just a little concerned.'

The damn cheek of her. Was she going to tell him how to look after his own Mother? 'Anne you know you can tell me anything.'

110

'Of course, it is none of my business…'

She was certainly right there.

'And you do a simply marvellous job of looking after her.'

Would she ever stop rambling?

She took a deep breath. 'I'm just a little worried that your Mother would be upset if she knew of your friendship with Ben.'

Clive was so aghast he just stared at her. The little cat had sharp claws. If the outer office had been empty, she would have been dead at his feet. But several people had now arrived and there was a noisy buzz as they greeted each other and settled into work. Dead she certainly would be, but he would choose the how and when. Right now he had to play her game. Let her think she had the upper hand.

'My friendship with Ben?'

'It is becoming rather noticeable.'

He went over the few weeks since their first drink together and could recall nothing in his behaviour or Ben's to warrant Anne's ravings. 'Why should having a drink with a colleague be a problem for anyone, let alone my Mother?'

'Oh, Clive. You are such an innocent. Ben is not—he is an American. You mustn't let him lead you astray. Once he knows we are together, he will leave you alone. Then your Mother or anyone else will never need to know.'

God, how desperate must she be. To get her own way, she was willing to highlight his and Ben's flowering friendship, to his Mother and the entire office. She was now no longer just a nuisance but an imminent danger, one that needed sorting and fast. He needed time to think. Clive switched back into caring mode.

'Oh, Anne. It is you who are the little innocent. Why I hardly notice anyone else when you are in the office.'

Her dull face lit up for a moment with a brilliant smile. She thought she had won. She thought she had him where she wanted. She would learn differently.

He walked around the desk and, taking her hand, led her towards the door. 'Let's get together soon and chat about it. How about I sort out a time and come back to you?' He opened the door for her to pass triumphantly out. Her triumph wouldn't last long. He would make sure of that.

Sitting down at his desk, he began thinking of how he could get rid of her for good. Until, having ruled out a variety of ideas, he gave up and, forgoing his lunch, drove up to the health spa, past the bored uniformed officers sitting in their panda car at the end of the drive to keep the few hopeful journalists at bay, whilst letting him through with hardly a glance.

News coverage on his first statement was fading, but the reporters shouldn't worry as he intended to provide them with more headlines soon.

He was pleased to see both the new Mrs Turrell and the always-cheerful Sandi on duty. Clive waited until Sandi was dealing with a guest before he moved towards the reception desk so he could renew his acquaintance with Eppie. He smiled what he knew was his rather boyish smile and stepped forward to explain mother's problem. The perfect son, concerned for his mother's welfare.

He chatted with Eppie and made her laugh. If he was going to use her to get to DI Turrell, he needed her relaxed and friendly. While they waited for Sandi's advice, he let his gaze wander to the entrance of the dining room.

A small group of people had gathered waiting for the doors to be flung open ceremoniously by Anton the Maitre D'. They had that anxious look of smokers, eager to get the basics over with and go back to their first love. Clive had relied on that, since he needed to place his props in the smoker's tent, and this would be the best time.

He turned back to Eppie as Sandi joined her. Soon, it was all arranged. Mother would see Mrs Mooney, who apparently was a kindly, middle-aged woman who would be very sensitive with dear Mother. More importantly, he made a mental note of the hours the new therapists worked.

Sandi said she would leave a little note for Mrs Mooney to say they would be calling in. Then he wondered aloud if he should bring Mother to dinner that evening to give her a treat to combine with meeting Mrs Mooney. Both Sandi and Eppie thought this would be a lovely idea, and they were duly booked in for dinner on Saturday at seven.

He made to walk away, and then stopped to check his watch before heading towards the toilet. He wanted it to look as if he had decided to freshen up before leaving for an important business meeting. Rather pleased with himself, he allowed a small smile of satisfaction to reach his face. He had the distinct impression that his halo was very firmly in place.

Leaving from the side door, it only took him a minute to take the props from his briefcase and stow them safely in position.

He had also decided who was to have the honour of being the centrepiece in his next statement.

CHAPTER 20

Matt walked away blinded by anger. He wished he was on the rugby field and could find release in pure and cathartic action, but that wasn't an option. *Damn Eppie.* Why couldn't she understand that having her at the scene of his murder enquiry would distract him? He couldn't bear to think of her in danger, and until this killer was locked up, every woman would be, including Eppie. Matt was very tempted to go back and order Eppie to go home.

Before he had a chance to move, Fluff caught up with him.

'That's the last of them, Guv.'

'Anything?'

'No. Strange really, no one seems to be hiding anything. There's usually one or two pinching the towels or something. But not a tweet of guilt.'

Before Matt could reply, Sam arrived.

'There's one maintenance bloke, Pat O'Neil. He's in Ireland for his sister's wedding. Off from Tuesday and not back till Saturday. Be a good knees up I guess.' Sam sounded wistful.

'His background?'

'Nothing on the radar. Solid family man according to his mates.'

'Right. If there are no special concerns about him, we'll check him out Saturday. We're starting to get some earache about us being here.'

'Disrupting guests so I've heard,' Fluff interrupted. 'I would have thought it would be an advantage to have all you good-looking men about. Sam excepted of course.'

Matt stepped in before Sam could retaliate. 'Not as Management sees it. Jason still needs to be here, but let's head back to the office. Round up the others, Sam.'

Sam nodded and moved away.

Fluff looked at Matt. 'Prof still getting to you?'

Matt realised that he couldn't hide his feelings from Fluff. Her antenna was too finely tuned. One of the reasons she made such an excellent detective. He knew he had too many questions about himself and Eppie to externalise any of them at this point so he fobbed Fluff off.

'He was full of his own self-importance as usual. But I'm used to it by now.'

Fluff nodded and accepted what he said, but Matt knew she had put one of her mental ticks against it and would not let it go until she had worked it out. At least for now she had backed off.

* * *

Back at the office, Matt sighed at the pile of reports waiting for him. He had already been verbally given most of the information. He selected a file from the forensic team and skimmed through it. Jason had caught up with him earlier to say that the model soldier—Matt had duly noted the word *model* and not toy—was made in England by Frederick Smith and Sons about sixty years before. It looked very much as if it was part of a collection.

Sam came in just as he finished reading, and Matt pushed the file across the desk towards him. 'If he's trying to make us understand what he went through, why a soldier? Was he in the army?'

Sam looked up from the file. 'If it's this old, wouldn't it belong to his granddad, or even dad I suppose? Could be one of those obsessive sorts who meet up and re-stage battles and things. They take it really seriously too.'

Matt rose and started to pace the room. 'What sort of person,' he paused searching for another word but gave up in the end, 'plays with these damn things?' Matt held up the evidence bag in which the soldier was ensconced.

'Silly, old balding blokes,' Fluff answered as she entered the room, qualifying her answer due to the look from Matt. 'Military men? Ones who can't do the real thing anymore?'

Sam frowned. 'You think in the past they might have been in the forces?'

'Yes.'

'They're more likely to be your clever, nerdy type now. They re-enact all the old battles. Dunno why. Doesn't make sense if you know who won anyway, does it?'

Fluff had moved forward to the desk and was scanning the report. 'But these are ancient.'

'So they could have been passed down, father to son, or grandson. And according to the amount of dust on this little fellow, it's now owned by someone who isn't interested,' Matt said.

'So our murderer has either a military figure or a nerdy type in his family. Doesn't help us much, does it?' Fluff summarised.

Matt was aware that he held dozens of strings in his hands like reins. He needed to decide which reins to tighten, which to drop. Choose the wrong lead to follow and someone else might die. The decisions he made were vital, and he was aware that he was working against the clock if he was to stop a further murder. Unless the murderer had placed the model soldier on the body to send them down a blind alley, it had to be important.

'Sam,' Matt said, making up his mind, 'see what you can find out about this little fellow.' He passed the bag containing the soldier over to Sam. 'Re-enactment societies, where you would buy, collections, etc. The works.'

Taking the bag, Sam held it up and tried for an American drawl. 'OK little fellow you're coming with me. And no arguments—OK buddy?'

It was nearly five p.m. as Matt watched his team wearily settle into place for a briefing. Even the usually effervescent Sam had dark circles under his eyes. Matt knew every member of the team was working flat out and guessed they were looking forward to a few hours at home with the family or a pint down the local with time to catch up with all the latest football news.

Down time was the oil that helped to keep the team working the long hours they ungrudgingly put in on a case like this. He knew he would need to keep them motivated and focused. It was his job to stop them getting dispirited when the long, hard slog seemed to be getting them nowhere. Matt was probably the only one who wasn't looking forward to going home—the pull of his favourite chair and an hour or two of rugby on the box was negated by uncertainty on how to be with Eppie.

As Sam finished, Matt straightened up and moved to stand in front of the incident board. He made sure he stood tall with his shoulders back in an effort to create an air of confidence he was far from feeling, glad at least that they'd had some response from the TV appeal.

'Thanks for all the hard work.' Matt made sure his gaze included everyone in the room. 'This murderer thinks he is clever. He plans everything carefully. However, as we know, there will always be something he has overlooked, a small mistake. For example, we are already getting calls from the public in the doll appeal. And while there is nothing yet to take us forward, I am confident it will come. We can and will find that mistake before he can kill again.'

CHAPTER 21

By the time Clive arrived back to the office, he was still trying to work out how to rid himself permanently of dear Anne. He knew he couldn't use her in one of his statements. Her demise needed to look like an accident or suicide, and he must be sure he provided himself with a foolproof alibi. He didn't fancy facing that smart DS again unless he had completely covered his tracks.

As he entered the office, it was strangely quiet. Gloria was a lone sentry keeping the world at bay.

'Thank goodness. I'm dying to go to the loo.'

'Off you go then.'

'Thanks. Aren't you going to the do?'

'Do?'

'Artie's. He's treating everyone to lunch at Pizza Express. His way of making up for being one of the most miserable bosses ever.'

'No. I've got a deadline on the Foster account. I'll hold the fort if you want to go.'

'Clive, you are my hero. I'd really hate to miss a free lunch, especially off that old bugger. He owes me.'

She leant across and planted a kiss on his cheek, before snatching her coat and heading for the loo.

Clive moved into the main office and stood besides Anne's desk looking for inspiration and aware that a plan was beginning to form in his mind. Hearing the ladies toilet door open, he moved away.

'Thanks, Clive.'

With a cheery wave of her hand, she was gone, and it was then he noticed Anne's shoulder bag was still in its usual position, slung across the back of her chair. Clive felt a flush of excitement race through him. If she had left her credit cards behind, then he had found the perfect way to get rid of her. He would give her what she wanted, a date with him. But the date would be deadly and she would never return.

Seating himself at the desk, he opened her bag. With trembling fingers and an ear attuned for sound of anyone returning, he searched through it. There were two credit cards in a small zipped side pocket. He selected one and laid it in front of the computer.

The RSC website was easy to find. The Royal Shakespeare Company was busy rebuilding the main theatre, so their temporary Courtyard theatre would have to do. It was just past the Dirty Duck pub on Waterside.

He crossed his fingers and hoped there would be tickets to see *Twelfth Night* tomorrow. It was not one of his favourites, but it didn't matter. At last the site confirmed that there were some tickets available, the most expensive of course, and he booked two without hesitation, giving all of Anne's details and using her credit card. Just as he was finishing, the soft whine of the lift told him the workers were returning. He slid the cards into in Anne's bag and moved back to his office.

Clive just had time to seat himself at his desk when several cheerful staff poured out of the lift. A free lunch was a rare treat and worthwhile, even if they had had to put up with Artie to get it. Anne wasn't amongst them, and he hoped her computer would go back to screen saver before she arrived. If not, he would have to distract her.

She was one of the last to return and, by then, her computer was back to normal. Clive congratulated himself that the gods were truly on his side. Anne paused to give him a little wave before she sat down, so he indicated that he wanted to talk to her. She was at the office door even before he could rise to open it for her.

'Did you have a good lunch?'

'It would have been more fun if you had been there.'

'Sorry. Holding the fort so Gloria could get off.'

'How like you, Clive.'

She sat down and rearranged her skirt while Clive sat on the side of the desk and leaned towards her. 'Anne, I've had a word with Mrs Sinclair and she can stay late with Mother tomorrow. I was really hoping, if you are free, that we could meet up for a drink, have that chat.'

Her face lit up so that, for a moment, she almost looked pretty. He wondered what she would look like when he had finished with her.

'Oh, Clive, that would be so lovely.'

'Let's keep it quiet at this point, shall we? It will be our own little secret.'

'Of course.'

Then it was a simple matter to arrange a place and time and she left the office blissfully happy. It wouldn't last of course, and he wanted to laugh aloud at the thought of tomorrow, but stifled the rising merriment, turning it instead into a big smile. Anne looked back and returned his smile.

Thoroughly pleased with himself, he settled down to work for the rest of the afternoon, while contemplating what a wonderful day it was turning out to be. Everything was going his way.

Finding it was difficult to concentrate, Clive decided to take advantage of the gods being on his side to take care of a couple of other tasks.

For one, he wanted to prepare his little message to the Inspector. And two, if that cocky little Constable had thought she had got away with trying to trip him up, she would soon find out otherwise.

CHAPTER 22

Making her way home, Eppie began thinking about her and Matt. She had never experienced such cold anger before and wasn't sure how to deal with it. Would it be gone by the time he came home? Dad seldom got angry, and when he did, it was over in a hot flash. Anger she could deal with, but if Matt withdrew from her…Eppie pushed the thought to the back of her mind and started to prepare the vegetables for dinner.

With everything prepared, Eppie had just picked up her book when Matt came in. Letting it drop, she stood trying to assess his mood, holding herself back from rushing forward and throwing her arms around his neck. He looked tired, but as he walked towards her, she was glad to see the coldness was gone from his eyes.

Matt seemed to hesitate so she moved towards him. They could talk later; right now she needed to feel his arms around her. She had the sense that that was what he wanted too, for he was quick to enfold her and she snuggled into his embrace.

Eppie buried her face in his chest, enjoying his masculine smell that was mingled with sweat and pizza. It felt as if there was nowhere safer in the world. She thought about saying 'sorry.' It would be so easy, but she couldn't bring herself to spoil the moment.

Matt showered and changed as Eppie finished preparing dinner. Despite the surface harmony, she had the sense of a blockage between them. She was reluctant to bring up the issue, although she knew they would have to talk about her working at the spa.

Matt came into the kitchen to get the cutlery to lay the small table. 'Eppie.' He broke the silence as he turned to face her.

Eppie almost jumped but tried for casualness, 'Yes?' She knew what was coming and tried to stave it off by opening the fridge and examining its contents. 'Is there anything you would like for dinner tomorrow? I could do…'

Matt stopped her by turning her towards him and closing the fridge door. 'We have to talk about this. You must understand the position you are putting me in, Eppie. I can't have you on the scene of an enquiry, especially a murder enquiry.'

'But, Matt—'

'No buts, none at all. My main aim is to catch this murderer, protect the public, and you, my wife. I can't be juggling everything and worrying about you, Eppie, I just can't. Surely you can see that?'

Eppie was slow to reply as she tried to choose her words. 'I love you for wanting to protect me, Matt, I really do, but I'm in no more danger than anyone else. You aren't stopping any of the other women working at the health club, are you?'

'I'm not married to any of them, am I?' There was now an edge creeping into Matt's voice.

Finding it difficult to stay calm, Eppie replied, 'So because I'm *your* wife, I'm the only one who can't go out in the big bad world?'

'Now you are being completely ridiculous.'

The anger in Matt's voice was sparking Eppie's hot temper, and although she tried to control it, she knew she was becoming determined to make her point and at any cost. 'Ridiculous am I? You forget I have been in countless dangerous situations and dealt with hundreds of awkward officials.'

'But no one wanted to harm you. None of them were murderers I take it?'

'Now, you are being ridiculous.' Eppie turned back to the sink in disgust.

Matt moved swiftly to grasp her arm and spin her around. Eppie could see that coldness coming over his face again. 'I don't want you there.'

'Tough, because I work there.' Eppie pushed her way past him aware that her face was flushed in stark contrast to his. Making her way to the bathroom she slammed the door shut and sat on the edge of the bath trying, without much success, to stop the angry tears.

And Matt was wrong. She had faced those who intended her harm and in the worst possible way.

Seven months after Mum had walked out on them, Eppie, unable to put up with cousin Natalie and Aunt Sarah's constant criticism of her Mother, had decided to run away to join Dad.

On the railway station, she had queued for hot chocolate and a doughnut. She wasn't a seasoned traveller like the rest of the crowd and, as she struggled to find the right change, she could hear their sighs and impatient mutterings behind her. With the coins in her hand, she had glanced up to see the woman in the kiosk glaring at her, and in her hurry most of the money dropped from her hand to scatter across the marble floor.

The youth had stopped one of the coins from rolling away by putting his foot on it, and while she stooped to retrieve them all, he had stepped past her, placing a ten-pound note on the counter.

'A coffee please and take it all out of that.' He nodded towards Eppie.

The woman had favoured him with a smile of relief.

Eppie had managed to retrieve most of the coins and had stood to find the youth waiting, holding the drinks and her doughnut. She was embarrassed as he motioned to one of the brightly coloured steel seats, and as soon as they sat down, she tried to tip all her change into his hand. A couple of the coins rolled away under the seat.

'You're very good at this, aren't you? I bet you come from some little village where coin rolling is the main sport.'

'No,' she laughed. Besides, he had a nice smile and was not much older than her brother Mike. Everyone else on the station was dressed in suits with briefcases, even the women, and all seemed in a dreadful hurry, as if they were going to be late for some important meeting.

'On your way to somewhere nice?' he asked.

Eppie hesitated, aware that she had to be careful and so chose a variation of the truth. 'Meeting my dad.'

'Good. Not a place to be hanging about.' He finished his coffee and stood. 'Must go and check on my Mum's train. Take care.'

When he had gone, Eppie had felt lonely. She had a little time to wait for her train to Gatwick so she wandered into the bookshop, idly glancing through the magazines before going back to sit on the bench. There were few people about now. She couldn't see the youth anywhere so guessed his mother must have arrived.

Putting her rucksack on the bench beside her, she tried to relax, thinking of what her dad would say when she turned up. Had Aunt Sarah missed her yet? She was supposed to be in school, so Natalie would know she was missing and take delight in telling everyone if only to get her into trouble. Well, she had made up her mind she wasn't going back there.

A sudden wrench and her rucksack was whisked away. She hadn't even realised that anyone had approached. She turned towards the pounding footsteps ready to give chase, but the hooded figure was already yards away. Then she heard someone shout, 'Let me.'

The youth who had helped her in the coffee queue was racing after the thief. Eppie followed on after him until she caught up with him at the station entrance. He was bent over getting his breath back.

'Sorry. He jumped on a bus over there.'

'Oh, no. Should I tell the police?'

'Probably a good idea. They won't catch him now, though. It might be best to wait until your dad gets here.'

Eppie felt very alone at that moment. Everything she needed to get her to Hawaii and Dad was in that rucksack. With no passport or money she was lost, would have to ring Aunt Sarah and have the shame of going back to Natalie's smirking. She was trying to hold back the tears.

The youth put a brotherly arm around her shoulders. 'Hey. Cheer up. It can't be that bad. What's a few old clothes?'

Eppie felt the tears burst through.

The youth let her cry, even looked a little embarrassed.

'I'm sorry.'

'Don't be. Look my Mum's train is delayed. What don't you come home to mine, have some lunch? Mum won't mind. Sean by the way.'

'Eppie.'

It sounded so normal and domestic and she needed a haven. Eppie nodded.

The house was different than she expected and in a run down terrace not far from the station. Some of the houses in the street were boarded up and one had tattered curtains that looked like they had been in place for fifty years. Eppie hesitated but the youth encouraged her forward.

'Know it's not much but better inside.' He led the way to a house with a solid door and drawn curtains.

He opened the door for her to go in first. Inside, it was gloomy and Eppie hesitated only to feel a swift push on her back that caused her to stumble forward and fall to her knees. She heard him lock the door before pulling her roughly to her feet. His face now looked older and was set with a scowl as he manhandled her into the first room off the corridor.

The first thing she saw was her rucksack. The youth, she guessed the one who had stolen it, was tipping her belongings onto a rickety coffee table.

'Very worthwhile,' he grinned, holding up her passport and money.

Eppie moved forward to retrieve them from his grasp but felt herself pushed into a tattered chair, forced to watch as both the youths picked through her clothes. The first one lingered over her underpants, while looking at her and licking his lips.

'Daddy's little girl, ah?'

'That's what Mel pays us for, so you ain't having any,' Sean snapped.

'How's the sod gonna know then?'

'Don't be bloody stupid. The fresh ones, untouched by grubby hands like yours, fetch the best price and that's what he is getting.'

Sean walked across to her and touched her hair. She wanted to scream, to wake up from this nightmare, but all she could do was cower farther back in the chair. There would be no way she could fight these two; they were both too strong. She used to play wrestle with Mike when she was much younger, and he sometimes let her win, but this wasn't like that. Later, big brother like, he had told her what to do if a boy was too insistent. She must think back and remember everything he said.

The sulky youth was stuffing everything back into her rucksack. Sean moved towards the door.

'I'll fetch Mel. Don't soil the goods.'

Eppie heard the front door bang behind him. She was being sold on like a cow at market. This might be her only opportunity to get away. Sizing up the remaining youth, she thought he looked lighter than Sean. He came towards her, kneeling in front of her, reaching forward to slide his hands up her thighs.

'So. Are you really Miss Innocent? Never ever had it?'

She was too afraid to answer him.

'Now I wouldn't mind a little taste of that.'

Backing into the chair only made him come nearer. Now his hands had reached her small breasts and his mouth was leering towards hers. *Remember what Mike said. Remember.* She had never hurt anyone but she gathered her strength in her stomach and kicked out hard catching him in the crotch. He fell backwards with a surprised look on his face.

Eppie made for the door, flung it open and raced down the dark corridor to the front door. Fiddling with the lock was difficult as her fingers were trembling too much.

'Little bitch.'

He was hobbling towards her holding himself. The look of hate on his face was something she would never forget. Forcing herself to concentrate she opened the lock, stumbling out into the street just as he caught up with her. She avoided his grasp and ran fast along the street hoping that her kick would continue to slow him down.

There was no one around and she raced on hoping to see someone, anyone but Sean. She could see traffic on the intersection ahead and headed towards it. Where there were cars, there would be people. She would stop a car if she had to. Turning around she could see him running awkwardly. She offered up silent thanks to Mike.

The road was a busy little shopping area full of shoppers. Everything seemed normal. And there was a chemist shop. Chemists could be trusted; they were almost like doctors and were there to help. She would be safe now.

So, yes, Matt, I have faced someone who wanted to harm me, she thought. *And in the worst way.* Not that she could tell him. She had never felt able to talk to anyone about what really happened that day. Not even the kindly policeman who had put her on the train back to Aunt Sarah's. She had just told him her rucksack had been stolen.

Meeting her from the train, Aunt Sarah was too busy berating her, while Natalie just looked down her nose. Eppie had locked the nightmare tightly away in her mind.

CHAPTER 23

Mother had already eased herself out of bed when Clive took up her breakfast tray. She seemed grumpier than usual and snapped as he went to put the tray on the bed.

'Don't put it there, Clive. You can clearly see that I have already risen.'

'Sorry, Mother.' He moved to put the tray on the little table by her chair, knowing he had some news that would shake her out of her grumpiness. 'Mother, I've asked Mrs Sinclair if she could stay a bit later today.'

'Oh, Clive. It is my favourite programme tonight and you know how she chatters on all the time. Where are you going anyway?'

'Out with Anne.'

'Good. I thought that young lady would bring you up to scratch. It's about time someone did.'

'I won't be late.'

'Just treat her right, Clive. You should be married by now. It would be so pleasant to have another woman around the house.'

'I will treat her exactly as she deserves, Mother, don't you worry.' A laugh was building up inside at the thought of just how perfectly he was going to deal with Anne, so he left and gave vent to it in the kitchen, only forcing himself to calm down when Mrs Sinclair arrived.

She was early, which was good, because Clive wanted to leave nothing to chance and intended to drive over to Stratford to check out the route for the evening. He needed to find a place where he could be alone with Anne.

Clive decided that his visit to Stratford would be the perfect opportunity to post his message to DI Turrell. He looked at the padded envelope, sitting ready on the car seat beside him and went over the precautions he had taken, from gently lifting the model soldier from its fellows before placing it carefully inside the padded envelope. The stamp was in the required position, making sure it wasn't too far to the right, or the left. He didn't want to give the ardent professor any further clues to his personality. Before removing his gloves, he closed the self-sealing envelope, hesitating for a moment to wonder if he gave anything away by using a computer printed label, before reassuring himself that if the police were accessing his home computer they would be onto him, and he wasn't going to allow that to happen.

He had bought the envelope for cash over the counter at an office supply chain store. He had checked that at least another chain also carried the brand, and it was a popular size. With luck, it would catch the last post and arrive first thing in the morning. He felt a glow inside at the panic it would cause. Not that DI Turrell was one to show panic, but Clive knew it would hit him in his most vulnerable spot.

Clive realised with mild surprise that not only had Mr Thompson's history lessons sunk in, but also his father's descriptions of military tactics must have taken root. That would make the old man happy he was sure.

Next, it would be DC Meadows's turn. He had been surprised when he followed her home last night to find she lived in a big house overlooking St Nicholas Church in Kenilworth. He guessed it had been made into flats.

It was gone nine by the time he reached the office and most of the staff had already arrived. Gloria pulled a face at him as he came out of the lift.

'Tut, tut.'

'You've heard then?'

'She couldn't wait to tell me and everyone else by the look of it.' Gloria nodded to the office behind her and Clive could see Anne talking animatedly with two colleagues.

'This hardly fits in with 'keeping her at bay' does it? Or have you had a change of heart?'

'No. No it's not like that. I wanted to talk to her, away from this place. Let her down gently.'

'Well good luck with it. But I think you're making a big mistake. She'll be telling me to collect for a wedding present by tomorrow.'

'No way. Trust me.'

'It's your funeral, Clive.'

No, not his funeral but Anne's, he thought. First, they would have to find her body and he was hoping that wouldn't be for several weeks, if at all.

When he entered the main office, he guessed Ben had heard the news, as he was quiet, and simply raised his eyebrows in a question. Before Clive had a chance to say anything, Anne came towards him. He thought for one horrified moment she was going to kiss him on the cheek, but she just stationed herself between him and Ben.

'Good morning, Clive. I'll get your coffee.'

'Thank you, Anne.'

Once she had moved away, he turned to Ben. Before Ben lowered his eyes, Clive thought he detected a hint of disappointment. Damn the woman, he would make her suffer for this. He took a step closer.

'It's not what you think, Ben. I just want to talk to her—away from here—get her to understand that I'm not interested.'

'I don't think she sees it like that.' Ben turned back to concentrate on his computer screen.

'She will after I have talked to her, I promise.'

'We'll see.'

Before Clive could answer, Anne had arrived with his coffee, and he followed her into his office.

'Thank you.'

'It's no trouble, Clive. You know how I would do anything for you.'

'There is something, Anne.'

'Yes?'

'I think it might be better if you kept the details of where we are meeting to yourself. I hate to admit it, but I think you might be right about Ben. I wouldn't want him turning up and spoiling our evening together.'

'Of course, Dear. I'm so glad you have seen for yourself how right I am.'

He told her where they were meeting then spent the rest of the day, trying to avoid her, Gloria, or Ben, reassuring himself that his planning was impeccable and he would soon be rid of Anne.

By the time Clive arrived at the Courtyard Theatre, he had the details fixed firmly in his mind. It was a quarter to seven, so the lobby was not yet crowded for the seven-fifteen start. This was an important time, as he had to make sure people would recognise him and remember that he was waiting for a friend. He would be playing a role, rather like when he was in the school play. But, then, he had been hiding behind a mask most his life.

He ordered two glasses of wine and then two more for the interval. Sipping out of the one glass, he went towards the main entrance and found a small shelf where he put Anne's glass down so he could make a display of looking at his watch and of searching eagerly through the trickle of people arriving.

As the first of the coaches arrived to empty their excited punters into the lobby, he began to move through the crowd, both drinks in hand, starting to look a little anxious.

By five past seven, his drink finished, Clive put the other on the edge of the bar and got out his mobile. The tricky part had been deciding which number to call. He couldn't call Anne, as that would give him away, even though he intended to make sure her mobile phone went to the same destination as her. Instead, he called his direct line at work. That way he could erase the messages first thing tomorrow morning.

'Anne, are you nearly here. I'm wondering if I should pick up the tickets, since you won't have much time.' As he said 'Anne,' Clive stepped backwards, making sure he banged into a lady behind him. This was easy since the excited crowd hemmed him in on all sides.

'Oh, I am so very sorry.'

'That's all right. No harm done.'

'It's Anne. Think she would be late for her own funeral.'

The couple dutifully laughed but moved away, no doubt not wanting to be trodden on again. Clive hoped that they would remember him and his friend Anne.

People had already begun to go into the auditorium. The barman began collecting glasses.

'Have you finished with this, Sir?'

'Oh, yes. My friend is running late, and she won't have time to drink it now.' He gave the man a worried half smile and hoped he had a good memory. It was time to approach the box office and explain the situation.

'Excuse me.'

'Yes, Sir, how can I help?'

'My friend must be delayed, and since the tickets are in her name, I am wondering what I should do. Can I pick one up and go on in or will I have to wait for her?'

'What name are they under Sir?'

'Anne Clarke.'

'Here they are. If I could have your name please.'

'Clive Draper. We work together.' He made sure he looked around a few times, as if hoping Anne might still arrive in time.

'Right, Mr Draper, here is your ticket and I will hold onto the other and watch for your friend to arrive. We will do our best to get her seated, but she may have to stand at the back until an opportune moment. I would hurry if I were you, Sir. The performance is about to start.'

Clive took the ticket and moved towards the auditorium noting that one of the doors was already closed and the usher on the other was hurrying him forward.

As soon as he had settled into his seat, the lights dimmed. He didn't even attempt to concentrate on the performance of Twelfth Night, although the people around him appeared engrossed. His mind was racing with excitement. Soon the obnoxious Anne would be gone forever.

The first half seemed to last for ages and he could feel himself getting restless. Finally, the interval came and Clive made sure he was one of the first out to enquire of the staff if there had been any sign of his friend. As the answer was negative, he collected the two glasses of interval wine and went out to the courtyard space in front of the theatre, heading for the small wall with its miniature box hedging near the road.

He had made a note of this spot earlier. Clive deposited the two glasses of wine on the small wall, close to the hedge, and took out his mobile to dial his work number, talking loudly whilst moving amongst the crowd.

'Anne. Anne, where are you? I'm getting really worried now. Please let me know what's happening. It's the interval so I will leave my phone on for about twenty minutes.' He clicked off the phone and spoke to the group of people nearest.

'My friend. She hasn't turned up yet. I hope she hasn't had an accident.'

'I'm sure she will be all right. Shame, though, as she is missing a great performance.'

Musing on how kind people were, he hurried to the roadway and looked up and down, fully aware that some of the group were still watching him, before turning left down Waterside towards Stratford.

CHAPTER 24

Matt woke early missing both Eppie and his bed. He regretted losing his temper last night as it meant he had forfeited the opportunity to explain how much he loved her and wanted to keep her safe. The pressures of the case were immense on their own without having to worry about his wife.

This wasn't just any murder. The killer now had the taste for killing, according to the professor, and would be certain to strike again, unless they could stop him. It was now four days since the murder at the spa. Was the killer already becoming anxious to satisfy his need? Matt was acutely aware that if he and the team missed anything, another woman could lose her life.

But already there were rumours that the spa owners were badgering the Chief Superintendent to let everything go back to normal, profits being of more value than a human life. Matt wondered how long the Chief would be able to withstand the pressure.

After a quick shower, he tiptoed into the bedroom, half wishing Eppie was awake, so that he could at least begin to mend some of the damage. Maybe she was right, the spa could be the safest place for her. The murderer would be a fool if he struck there again with the police already on the scene.

Eppie was fast asleep and, as he looked down at her, he could see that her eyes were still puffy from last night's tears. Feeling a complete heel, he planted a gentle kiss on her forehead and left for work, cursing the job. This was no way to start a marriage.

Matt decided to take some time catching up with the information and reports, which were piling up on his desk. The team were busy following up different leads and continuing to gather information at the spa. Besides, he didn't want to risk seeing Eppie at the reception desk in case it provoked him into losing his temper again.

Matt was making good headway, until McRay put his head around the door.

'Got a minute, Matt?'

Matt put aside Wendy's follow-up on the distribution of the lollipops and stood. 'Of course, Sir.'

McRay sank into a chair beside the coffee table, so Matt joined him and waited for him to speak.

'I'm getting a rollicking from above. And the Super is being leaned on. I tell you, Matt, these men who own the spa are too rich for their own good. The sods think it can buy them whatever they want.'

'And they want us out of there?'

'Hole in one,' sighed McRay.

Matt was silent, thinking of the pros and cons of pulling all police presence from the crime scene. In a normal one-off murder case, if there was such a thing, it might be possible, but this was different and, besides, Eppie was there. He knew his worries about her shouldn't influence his judgement, but he couldn't stop his need for her safety surfacing.

'This one is different, Matt.'

'Yes, Sir. If Professor Meredith is right, this murderer will kill again, and soon. And while it is unlikely that he will kill in the same place, we haven't yet ruled out all the staff or guests. Also, we do not know the motive for this killing. It is possible that the killer has a grudge against the spa, which would put all the guests and staff at risk. I strongly feel we should maintain at least a uniform presence at the spa once the interviews are concluded.'

'I agree. Let me have a word, see what I can do. Keep me up to date by the minute, Matt.'

'Of course, Sir. And thank you.' Matt stood as McRay left. It was good to have him back on form, supporting the frontline troops.

The rest of the day passed in a whirl. Matt had little time to think of anything but of assessing the reports in front of him. By the time the tired team started drifting back to the office, Matt was glad he had some good news to tell them and called a briefing.

Matt held up the small batch of reports. 'Some of our hard work could be paying off at last. This is just the beginning of the response to the doll appeal.'

'Anything useful, Guv?' Fluff called out from the back.

Matt looked down at the papers in his hand and separated the top few. 'The usual kooks and these four. This one needs following up tonight so if anyone fancies a bit more overtime...' he said. There was silence from the team.

'I'm up for that. Help me save for those thigh-high boots,' Fluff said, amid a backdrop of wolf whistles.

To Matt, like most of the men on the team, the image of Fluff's long shapely legs encased in thigh-high boots was a tantalizing one. He pushed it to the back of his mind. 'Thanks. We'll need to leave as soon as possible. This lucky man we're interviewing heads off to Spain later tonight.'

* * *

Matt filled Fluff in as soon as they were on their way. They were heading for a small outdoor market near Hampstead. It could be a wild goose chase, but the trader had remembered a suspicious man who bought some dolls from his stall.

For a short time, the talk was easy as they discussed the case. Then they were silent until half way down the M40. Fluff glanced at Matt.

'Everything OK, Matt?' she asked.

He knew it was no good trying to fob her off so opted for a version of the truth. 'Too long on my own,' he replied.

'Can't be easy. Even without the case.'

Matt nodded, silent, as he manoeuvred his way through the rush-hour traffic spilling out onto the M40 around Oxford. He wondered what Eppie was doing and wished he could be with her, even if it did mean a row.

Now that the anger had gone, he felt confused. Surely, it was a husband's role to keep his wife safe. Was that old fashioned and out of date? He knew it probably was. The shock of seeing her there in the danger zone—that was what had thrown him.

'Give it time Matt,' Fluff said, interrupting his thoughts. 'It's a very different life for her.'

'Thanks. I'm sure we'll work it out.'

Matt risked a quick glance at her, realising the wisdom of her words. She was right. Eppie was used to travel and excitement; he couldn't realistically expect her to settle happily in a small market town, in his tiny flat. It wasn't as if she had any friends or family nearby. He imagined her there now, waiting for him to come home. He'd better let her know he may not get home until late, if at all.

Passing his mobile to Fluff he asked her to call Eppie. He was aware that Fluff hesitated for a moment, as if she wanted to say something, but he gave her no option, and she rang Eppie, without making any comment.

Matt felt bad knowing he should have been the one to make the call and visualising how upset Eppie would be, but he couldn't afford the time to pull off the motorway, so he shrugged off the image and returned to professional mode.

As they left the M40 and onto the A40 further conversation was ruled out as Matt concentrated on the heavy traffic.

Parking was easy, since most people were heading home. Matt and Fluff entered a square filled with shops on three sides and littered with market stalls. Most had closed for the night, although one or two traders were still packing away.

The wind whistled through the small alleyways off the square, causing the leaves to gather into swirling piles of orange. In one corner, a skip was overflowing with cardboard boxes and a bored looking youth was aimlessly driving a noisy machine, a cross between a lawnmower and a vacuum cleaner, amidst the people and stalls.

Facing them, The Gay Dog pub looked warm and inviting with the glow from its frosted windows spreading out over the darkening square.

Matt led the way across to the pub held the door for Fluff, unprepared for the wall of noise that burst out at them. He guessed that this was where most of the market traders came for a pint at the end of the day. Fluff led the way through the heaving crowd towards the bar. The crowd parted good-naturedly for her where Matt guessed they wouldn't have done so for him.

Matt was just wondering how they were going to find Archie Smith in this hubbub, when he felt a tug on his sleeve and turned to find a small, thin-faced man beside him.

'This way, Guv.' He turned and led the way through the crush to a large table in the window where several men and two women sat. 'Shove up, Pammy, let the lady sit down.'

Pammy, deep in some sort of argument with a large man farther down the table, moved along without a glance. Archie ushered Fluff into the space and squeezed in beside her. Just as Matt thought he would have to stand, the man opposite Fluff drained his pint and stood. Giving a brief wave to everyone else, he indicated his seat for Matt.

In this situation, Matt wanted to keep fairly low key, even though he was certain most of the crowd would have guessed by now who they were. 'Archie Smith?' he queried.

'The one and only.'

Matt allowed Fluff to do the introduction as she was closer to Archie, and he was finding it difficult not to shout above the noise of the several different conversations around him.

Archie waved his hand to stop Fluff taking out her warrant card. 'No need for that, Love. Clocked you a mile off. Now about your bloke. Judging the punters is what it's all about in this game. If they're time wasters, or the like, you move along to the next one pretty smartish, or the buggers will go next door. This one was odd, sort of hesitant, looked around him before buying. Now I wouldn't have thought about it twice, but then he puts on this smarmy act, says he wants the dolls for his dear nieces, and I thinks, well, as long as he's got the readies, I've got the goods.'

The word dolls had immediately hit Matt but Fluff was ahead of him.

'How many dolls did he buy, Mr. Smith?' Fluff asked.

'Archie, Love, call me Archie. Three. And it's not even Christmas yet. I suppose they could all have birthdays, but you know what I thought. I thought he was one of them—you know—them dirty buggers that interfere with kiddies.'

Matt felt his heart plummet. Three dolls. The murderer had prepared for at least two more murders. Matt tried to tune in again as Archie continued.

'I probably wouldn't have thought twice about the bugger, but just as he was walking away, this little kid, fuzzy sort of hair, races round the corner and bumps straight into him. I thought he was going to hit her. I was ready I can tell you. He wouldn't have got away with it.'

Matt was sure he was right.

'What happened next, Archie?' Fluff intervened.

'Well then, the kid's mother came round the corner, and all of a sudden he was all smarmy again. Patted the kid on the head and smiled at the mother. I thought then he was one of them that'll charm you with one hand and cut your throat, or worse, with the other.'

'This is very helpful,' Fluff said. 'Can you describe this man?'

'Phew—you see so many, you know.'

'It would really be a great help,' Fluff encouraged.

'Well, he looked like he'd come in from the country, but pale with it. Yes, one of them flat caps but it didn't sit easy—more for show than keeping your head warm I'd say.' Archie thought for a moment. 'Say he was late twenties, could be thirties. Had a jacket to match—that didn't fit either. Can't think of anything else— sorry.' Archie looked at his watch. 'Blimey, if that's the time, I'd better be off or the missus will be off to Spain without me. Hope that's helped, Love.'

Fluff gave Archie a card and the usual spiel and stood aside as he waved cheerio to his mates. Matt nodded towards the door, and he and Fluff followed Archie out.

Outside, the chill in the air, tainted with the smell of fried onions, made Matt realise he was hungry. He wondered what Eppie had prepared for supper. If he walked in now, she would probably throw it at him, and he couldn't blame her. Suddenly, he wanted to be there with her, to talk and hold her. Like Fluff said, they would work it out.

However, neither he nor Fluff had eaten since lunchtime, and he was about to suggest they get something to eat before heading back when his mobile rang.

Wendy had come up trumps yet again and had tracked down someone who had worked both days of the costume sale in Birmingham. He was a young actor called Anthony Mellor who had been resting at the time. Since then, his luck had changed, and he was now working with a touring company presently performing at a small theatre in Ruislip. Wendy had even found out the starting times of the play.

Looking at his watch, Matt calculated that they might just be able to have a word with Mr Mellor before the evening performance, although it meant no food and a late night. He relayed the information to Fluff.

'So, are you up for it? Treat you to a hamburger afterwards.'

'How could I refuse that offer?'

Matt wondered if it was his imagination or had Fluff seemed just that little bit too pleased at the prospect of spending the next few hours with him.

CHAPTER 25

She was waiting just where he had told her to—a few yards away from the entrance to the Dirty Duck. The pub was always busy, since it was just a little way along Waterside from The Swan and The Royal Shakespeare's main theatre. The Duck had a reputation for being the place where actors went to relax after a performance. One room, aptly called the Actor's Bar, was lined with signed portraits of distinguished actors, some long dead.

Clive told Anne that he would be coming along Waterside from the Holy Trinity Church end, and she saw him immediately, waving in an immature fashion.

'Oh, I thought maybe you weren't coming.'

'As if I would let you down.' It was an awkward moment, as she seemed to want to hug him. Clive moved swiftly to forestall any emotion and placed his arm under her elbow, moving her quickly away from the lighted area and across the road towards the old chain ferry. He needed to get her to the chosen spot.

'I thought we could have a quiet chat before going for a drink. I've wanted to talk to you alone for so long, Anne. We have no chance at work.' She giggled in response.

'That would be lovely.'

'Let's take the path along the river. It will be quieter there. Not that I would want you walking this way on your own in the dark, mind.' He put his arm around her shoulder for good measure, and she snuggled in to him, placing her arm around his waist. Clive wasn't comfortable, and her hair smelled like Mother's when she had just come home from the hairdresser's. But it was important that she didn't feel the tension in his muscles, and he tried to concentrate on something else. Across the dark space of grass and trees to his right he could hear the buzz of the theatre crowd. He had to finish this before the bell rang for the second half.

'How long have you been at En Jay's?'

'It's nearly eleven months now.'

'I thought it was about that. I have noticed you. It's just that En Jay doesn't go along with office romances. I had only just started there when two people were fired. It makes you very cautious.'

'I thought you and Ben...?'

'Two men having a drink—that's not frowned on. And it was great for me to get out a bit. As you know, I can't do that very often.'

'Because of your Mother?'

Clive nodded sadly. Anne tightened her arm around his waist and put her head on his chest. His main thought was that she might leave traces of hair but he controlled his impulse to push her away and patted her shoulder gently with his free hand.

They had passed the Brass Rubbing Centre now. It was dark, and there was no sign of anyone, but just in case, Clive kept his head titled downwards towards her so that, at a passing glance, they would look like a courting couple.

Only a yard or two to go. He could see the small tree he had chosen. Its branches were strong and drooped close to the ground over the water.

'Yes. I love my Mother and she is very good, but I don't like to leave her alone for too long.'

'I think that is what I love about you, Clive.'

She turned her face up, bringing her hands to pull his head down towards hers. Her eyes were closed and her mouth was expecting a kiss. He looked down at her with revulsion, but then he heard footsteps coming along the path. A couple were coming towards them, going towards Stratford. He mustn't let them see his face. He bent his head and let his mouth find hers. Her thin lips tasted of lipstick and mouthwash. Clive thought of the passionate kisses he longed to share with Ben. This was like kissing a toilet seat, and all his senses were screaming to pull away.

The couple were moving slowly. Anne was pressing her lips into his, and he could feel her tongue searching for an opening. He wouldn't open his lips but pressed harder needing to prolong the agony, until the couple had passed so they wouldn't see his face.

'Leave something for breakfast, Mate.'

The couple laughed and moved on. He unclipped his lips from Anne and glared after them.

'Ohhhh. I always knew you felt the same as me, Clive.'

It was time to show her just how he felt. He grabbed her roughly by the arm and almost dragged her the few steps to the tree, looking around to make sure no one else was coming, letting her think his passion had been awakened. She was looking up at him with wide eyes, eagerly awaiting an attack on her virtue.

'I want to tell you how I feel about you, Anne.' She gave that annoying giggle again and tried to do the Diana look, glancing up at him under her lashes. At that moment, he hated her but, fighting to hide his hatred, he managed a smile.

'I…well it's difficult to put into words. Come down here where we won't be disturbed, and I'll try to explain.' He manoeuvred himself easily down the small slope towards the water while holding onto the branches of the tree.

'Oh, Clive. I think you are trying to seduce me.'

This was something he couldn't do, even if his life depended on it. Clive moved to the edge of the water and held out his hand to her.

The river was high, swollen with the early morning rain, and the current was swift and taking all with it. It suited his purpose exactly as, hopefully, it would carry dear Anne far away down river. Or should that be up? But it didn't make a difference as long as she was gone forever. He forced himself to smile up at her.

'I just want you to myself. Are you brave enough to come to me, dear Anne?'

Clive put as much warmth as he could into those last two words, and she smiled at him shyly, while reaching out to grasp his hand. Once he had her hand in his, he would pull hard and she would go straight past him into the river. If needed, he would hold her head down for a minute and that would be it. Goodbye Anne.

Her hand was in his. Clive grasped it firmly and pulled. Anne shot down the small slope towards the water, and he saw the look of panic on her face. Putting out her other hand, she managed to grasp his jacket almost taking them both into the water. He hung on tightly to the branch to save himself, and unwillingly, her, as she clung to him.

She found her footing and held tightly onto him with both hands.

'I thought...thought for a moment I was going into the water. If you hadn't been here.'

'You are going for a swim, Anne.'

'Don't be silly. I can't swim, especially not in that.'

'That's what I am banking on.'

'Don't, Clive. You're scaring me.'

'They say it doesn't take long—less if you take a deep breath— let your lungs fill with water.'

'You're crazy. Let me go.'

He let her go and watched for an enjoyable moment as she began a frantic bid to escape up the small bank. With her heels she couldn't get a grip. Clive laughed at her efforts and reached out to grasp the hem of her coat, pulling her back towards him, swinging her round to face him. A position a little while ago she had desired but now found terrifying as she struggled to break free.

'Please, please. I'll do whatever you want.'

'Oh, I know you will, Anne, and you will do it most beautifully.' He could see what she was expecting and how she was preparing herself for the inevitable rape. The power was all his. If he wished, he could strip her naked and savagely rape her right here. They say that most women have that fantasy anyway.

Should he force her to face that reality? Clive could be as violent and cruel as he liked, make her degrade herself. It would feel good to hurt her for the trouble she had caused him. Then the faint sound of the first interval bell reached them, restoring his self-control and making him remember he couldn't afford to leave any evidence on her body. He should finish this now before the final bell prompted them to return to their seats. People would already be drifting back in the auditorium.

'Clive. Please stop this, please.'

Clive turned around suddenly so that Anne had her back to the dark water. She knew immediately what he was going to do and struggled frantically to renew her grasp on his jacket. He hooked one foot around one of the branches to free both hands.

'No.'

It was almost a scream, and he quickly clamped a hand over her mouth while working to ease her desperate hold. She kicked out violently but the kick went wild and merely caused her to slip so that both her feet ended up in the water.

She tried to scream again, shaking her head vigorously to escape his hand. He knew she was fighting for her life and this added to her strength. He hadn't wanted to put a mark on her in case it led back to him but this couldn't go on.

He released his hand from her mouth. She looked at him in surprise, maybe still wondering if this was a dream. Clive brought his hands to her neck.

'Goodbye, Anne.' He whispered it softly as he increased the pressure, knowing he had to control his instinct to finish the job. He needed the river to do that. Death by drowning—a tragic suicide.

Her eyes closed and he felt her muscles go slack. Time to slip her into the water. For a while, the bubbles rose from those thin lips. Leaves that were racing along in the water lodged themselves against her sharp little nose and made him want to laugh. As the bubbles ceased, he let go and watched as the river carried her away.

He glanced around to see if anything had been dropped. She still had her shoulder bag on when she went into the water and he hoped it would stay with her for a while so as not to alert the police of her place of embarkation.

Then he strode straight towards the road, easily jumping the small wall and getting out his mobile, dialled while retrieving the two glasses of wine as he made his way into the foyer.

It was nearly empty; the last few stragglers were being hurried into the auditorium by the staff. In the bright light, Clive realised his right hand sleeve was wet. Before anyone could notice, he tipped Anne's glass over that arm just as one of the staff came towards him eager to hurry him into the auditorium. Seeing his predicament, the man diverted briefly to reach beneath the booking counter, coming up with a hand full of paper tissues, which he practically threw at Clive whilst hurrying him into the theatre just as the lights were lowering. The usher guided him to his seat, indicating that he turn his mobile phone off. Clive slipped into his seat. The job was done.

CHAPTER 26

The theatre was about fifteen miles away in Ruislip. Traffic was much lighter now, and Matt began to think about Eppie. He knew he was avoiding facing the cracks of reality that were creeping into what, a few days before, was the most beautiful and perfect thing in the world. He wondered if all married couples went through this. Was it just a settling in period? Or maybe he just wasn't ready for marriage. Having jumped into marriage so joyfully in love, he just expected their life to follow the same pattern as his parents, with Dad the main breadwinner and Mum the fully supporting act. But maybe the old pattern was out of date and things had to be different now. He just wished there was a manual of some kind.

Matt and Fluff were led backstage by the scruffy security guard who gave his name as Trev. Trev was intrigued to know why they wished to speak to one of the actors, although he implied that it didn't really surprise him. He also seemed to think that his position entitled him to know why they wished to speak to a member of the cast and tried for the 'all mates' together act in an effort to persuade them to give him information.

Fluff already had his number and calmly repeated their request to speak to Mr Mellor on a matter that was private. Trev gave in and shuffled his way along a dingy corridor until they came to a room smelling of stale sweat and deodorant and from which several male voices emanated.

Trev moved to place himself fully in the doorway before Matt or Fluff could enter. 'Police Inspector for Anthony Mellor,' he bellowed so that the whole theatre must have heard, causing Matt to think Trev might have trodden the boards himself at one time.

All the men in the room turned to look at Trev, who seemed to be so enjoying this dramatic moment that Matt had to shoulder him aside to enter. Behind him, he thought he heard a grunt of pain from Trev and guessed that Fluff had 'accidentally' stood on his foot.

While their attention was focused, Matt introduced himself and Fluff and held up his warrant card. Then, as if as one, all eyes turned to look at a skinny youth who seemed to be in the middle of placing a curly blonde wig over his own dull, lank hair. Matt moved forward and addressed the youth. 'Mr Mellor?'

Mr Mellor looked back at his fellow actors reflected through the mirrors before taking a gulp, as he scraped his chair along the stone floor and stood turning to face Matt.

'Yes,' he replied.

'We think you may have some vital information about a case we are currently working on, Mr Mellor. Are you able to spare us a few moments, Sir?' Matt noted the relief on the actor's face and guessed that he had a misplaced fear of the drug squad paying any attention to his petty misdemeanours. Once this fear had been laid to rest it was apparent that Mr Mellor enjoyed the idea that he might be important to the enquiry.

'Of course, Officer, I shall be glad to help.'

Matt suspected that the actor might have felt that he was playing a role in one of those popular crime series on television.

Fluff led the way out of the dressing room and down to the end of the corridor, since there seemed nowhere else to go. Matt was sure that Trev would be lurking and listening somewhere, but they needed to carry on, so he nodded at Fluff to begin.

'Mr Mellor, we understand that you helped out at a costume sale in Birmingham on the tenth and eleventh of July this year?'

The actor thought for a moment in an obvious effort to make believe that his social and work calendar was so full that he couldn't quite remember.

'That's right. Just a little side job my agent came up with, still connected to the theatre of course. I wouldn't consider anything else. Ended up I only did the Thursday. Then I was called to audition. This role was just made for me,' he preened.

Before he could continue, Matt intervened, throwing in a dose of flattery for good measure. 'As an actor, you must have a very good memory. Can you possibly remember anyone buying several little girl party dresses, ones which would fit adults?'

Mr Mellor thought for a long moment. 'No, I don't think so. Besides, what on earth would anyone do with such things?'

Matt sighed and tried again. 'Like I said, Mr Mellor, this is really important and could possibly save someone's life.'

The youth put his head on one side in a portrayal of a character thinking while both Matt and Fluff held their breath.

'Wait a minute, wait a minute. There was a silly old bloke, not that he was old, but he was dressed that way, if you know what I mean?'

Fluff had her notebook out and nodded encouragingly. 'Very astute. So do you think he was trying to make himself look old?'

'Yes, that's it,' the youth replied, aiming to look wise.

Fluff wrote this down in her notebook before continuing. 'So, how did he do that? Could you possibly describe what he was wearing?'

'Well, he looked a bit like a country gentleman, all tweed cap and jacket. Like you would see in one of the old farces. The sort that gets locked in a cupboard or runs around without his trousers on. You know?'

Neither Matt nor Fluff knew, but they nodded anyway.

'And this man bought several dresses? Did he say what he wanted them for?' Fluff kept up the pressure.

Infuriatingly, they were treated to the thinking pose again, and they waited patiently, hardly daring to hope that this might be a real lead.

'Yes. Although I wasn't really interested, I remember now, he rambled on about some village show. Written by some local show off. You know the sort of ghastly thing they have on the village hall

149

circuit. Whatever turns you on, I guess. I'm just thankful I've left that all behind. Well behind,' he finished on a flourish indicating the peeling paintwork around him as if it were the Palladium.

'Did he say which village?' Fluff questioned.

'No, or if he did I can't remember. It was not one I recognized anyway.'

'Was there anything about him, way of walking, hair, anything which would help you recognise this man again,' Matt cut in.

'No, I'm sorry, I don't think so. Although, maybe if he were dressed in the same costume then I might have a chance.'

'Did he have an accent at all, Mr Mellor?' Fluff asked.

Matt inwardly congratulated her on choosing such an ideal question to ask the actor.

This time there was no hesitation. 'Midlands. South of Birmingham so definitely not Brummie—more refined, almost posh. I did voice with Cecily at the RSC,' he boasted. 'So I do know my accents.' The youth's voice dropped slightly, and it was obvious he was remembering his expert tutoring.

'How many costumes did he buy, Mr Mellor?'

Matt was aware that both he and Fluff were holding their breath as they waited for the answer. It represented how many young women might lose their lives.

'Oh several I think.'

'How did he pay?'

'The whole sale was cash and carry only.'

There seemed nothing left to do but thank Mr Mellor for his invaluable help and give him the usual spiel about getting in touch if he remembered anything else. They wished him good luck with the play, refusing the offer of free tickets, and turned back along the corridor. Neither of them was surprised when Trev appeared as if from nowhere to lead them off the premises.

As they headed back up the motorway, Fluff went over the information they had obtained.

'He sounds local and we know he's used the same disguise at least twice to obtain his props.'

'Well, he can't be that clever then, as he just seems to have drawn attention to himself.'

'At least we can circulate an artist's impression to other forces. Not that it will do much good if he has already stocked up on what he needs.'

Both were silent, remembering that if this was their killer, then he had at least two dolls left and had bought several costumes. He could have already murdered again. Matt broke the silence as the motorway services loomed into sight.

'Time for that hamburger?'

Fluff nodded and Matt swung out of the fast line slowing his speed ready to move over to the slip road.

The food was expensive and barely adequate but both were too tired to care and, together with a strong cup of coffee, it gave Matt the energy to continue on up the motorway.

The closer he got to home, the more Matt thought of Eppie. He knew he didn't want to face her tonight. Telling himself there was too much going on with the case, he decided to stay in the office, on McRay's couch. Once he had had some sleep, things would look better in the morning.

At the sight of McRay's couch, a sudden heaviness came over him. He needed to rest. Even the cold leather seemed to invite, and he was just happy to stretch out. He kicked off his shoes and loosened his tie and was about to lie down when Fluff came in with a mug of hot chocolate. Under her arm she had a blanket and a pillow.

She put the steamy mug down on the coffee table and moved closer to place the pillow at one end of the couch. Matt felt her hair flick across his face and put out a hand to brush it away, irritated at the memories it aroused of their brief affair, when she would tease him with that silky long hair, and he would reach up to run his fingers through it before pulling her down to him.

Fluff paused above him, and Matt wondered if this was what she wanted. It would be so easy to accept the comfort after such a long, gruelling day. Too easy.

CHAPTER 27

E ppie wondered if Matt would be home early. She hadn't seen him since their row last night, and he had left for work before she was awake. Part of her was longing to see him, as long as he wasn't in that icy, controlled mood. Some of that coldness remained trapped inside her, bleeding like a tiny icicle. It would be far better if he were angry; then, at least, they could have an honest interchange, with the chance of making up afterwards. Eppie kicked herself for resorting to tears and locking herself away.

As she began preparing dinner, she thought about their marriage. From the first moment they had met, she had loved him. But they had never sat down and discussed any of the practical details of their life together. Eppie needed to explain to Matt that he couldn't treat her as a small child to be protected and cosseted.

No one had looked after her in that way for so long, and her Dad, although the most loving and caring father was, in reality, more of a child than she. She couldn't change into a kept woman, given money for the housekeeping and resorting to watching daytime TV. And she definitely refused to be treated as some sort of liability.

However, neither did she want to entrench herself into an unmovable position. Matt was under enormous pressure right now, and she could only try to imagine what he had to face each day. It was touching, if old fashioned, that he wanted to protect her. Matt certainly had the physical strength, and she smiled at the thought of his strong, toned body. She felt a softening towards him for loving her so much and vowed to try to be more understanding.

Since it was getting late, Eppie had decided that she would eat without Matt and had just settled herself on the sofa with a tray when the phone rang. She reached for it while precariously balancing the tray on the edge of the bookcase, hopeful it would be Matt.

'Hello.' She was disappointed when a female voice answered.

'Mrs Turrell?'

'Yes.'

'This is DC Meadows.'

For a moment, she had difficulty visualizing DC Meadows until she remembered it must be the young woman with the long fair hair. The one Matt always referred to as Fluff.

'The Inspector has asked me to call. Just to say he will be very late due to on-going investigations.'

Eppie tried to keep her voice from faltering. 'Right. Thank you for letting me know.' It felt as if she had been shut out completely, but she wasn't going to let this woman hear how dismayed she was.

They were there together, doing something important. While she was here alone in this dismal flat.

Why hadn't Matt made the call himself? Just who was this DC Meadow's who did her husband's bidding? And why was she called Fluff? A bit of Fluff—an object of sexual desire?

Her food had become unappetizing, and Eppie opted for her favourite ice cream. Finishing her second dish, this time with chocolate grated on the top, she realised that she was letting her mind travel down a dangerous path. She had never envisioned herself as a suspicious, jealous wife unable to trust. It brought up images of her mother ranting at her father before she walked out.

She was so horrified that she might become anything like that screeching mother who had gone rapidly from marriage to marriage. She didn't want that.

Jumping up, she thought it best to keep herself busy. Before she could decide what to do, the doorbell rang. She wasn't expecting anyone. Maybe it was a friend of Matt's.

Even before she opened the door, the smell of baking drifted in. In the hallway was a neat, elderly lady holding a plate, on which sat a fruitcake.

'I hope I'm not disturbing you. But I wanted to welcome you. I am sure you and Matt will be very happy, my dear.' She held out the plate to Eppie.

'Oh. Thank you.'

'Careful it's hot from the oven. Dear, dear, look at me forgetting to tell you who I am. Mrs Davis from number twenty five.'

Eppie took the cake and held it up to let the aroma drift up her nose. 'That smells delicious. Please, come in.'

'Well, I will for just a minute. No doubt Matt will be home shortly.'

'No.'

'Oh. I hope I haven't said the wrong thing. John is always telling me to think before I speak.'

'Matt's working late on a case.'

Eppie led the way into the living room, pausing only to put the cake on the kitchen counter. Mrs Davis stood and looked at the new scatter cushions.

'Now that looks brighter already. I said to John that you would liven this place up. All those dark colours. They would still be living in caves without us, wouldn't they?'

Eppie laughed and agreed before offering Mrs Davis a cup of tea.

'No. No I don't want to hold you up. There was something else though. I was putting the rubbish out last night. John should do it but he was watching his football, and there was this young man. I asked if I could help him and he said he was looking for you. Said he wanted to send you a card to congratulate you. I said why didn't he come up, but he didn't want to disturb you, just send a card.'

'He wanted me, not Matt?'

'Yes. He definitely said Mrs Turrell.'

'I can't think who that would be. What did he look like?

'Well, he was tall. But then he would be to me. I'm only a smidgen, like you. I hadn't got my glasses on, so I can't tell you anything else.'

After Mrs Davis had left, Eppie still couldn't think of who the man might be. But it was probably nothing to worry about. Still she wished she could run it by Matt.

CHAPTER 28

Matt woke, slowly realising that he wasn't in his own bed. The space was too small for him, and as he began to stretch out his limbs felt cramped. In his dreams, he had been in a cave searching for Eppie down the many different passages but only catching glimpses of her every now and again. He was glad to be awake, although he still felt tired and wrung out.

Fully awake he sat up remembering that he was in McRay's office. Memories of last night and Fluff flooded back. He realised with a shock that he was glad it happened.

As he had flicked Fluff's hair from his eyes she had paused. He hadn't responded and Fluff had moved to place the blanket at the other end of the couch. Matt touched her arm.

'I'm sorry.'

Fluff sat down next to the blanket. 'For what?'

Matt felt awkward. 'I couldn't...Eppie.'

'Don't worry. It wasn't on offer.'

Matt tried to gauge her voice to determine if she was angry or hurt but couldn't detect anything. He realised he was a little disappointed. 'Oh, my mistake, I thought—'

'That's well in the past.' Fluff looked at her watch. 'And someone will be wondering where I am.' Fluff rose and made her way to the door turning only to say, 'Drink your cocoa while it's hot.'

Matt did as he was told before lying down on the couch. Fluff always played her cards close to her chest, and he wondered who she was seeing. If it had been just an act then it had been pretty convincing.

Matt wondered how Eppie would be this morning and if she would speak to him after last night. Most wives would be a bit miffed, and he wished now he had called her himself. Berating himself for being a coward, he reached for his mobile, suddenly needing to hear her voice and to make sure everything was right between them.

No one answered and, looking at the time, Matt guessed she could be in the shower. Disappointed, he left a brief message that didn't relay any of the things he really wanted to say.

Although McRay wouldn't be in this early, he needed to move himself and any evidence that he had been sleeping here. Matt scooped up his shoes, the mug, pillow and blanket, rescued and restored the two mini cushions to their rightful place at each end of the couch, and with a final satisfied look around, he closed the door. McRay would never know he had been there.

As he showered in the locker room, Matt thought again of Fluff. He had surprised himself in not wanting her. He realised with some satisfaction that he had said no, that he didn't want anyone but Eppie. But he couldn't help wondering if, at that moment when their heads were so close, had he drawn her mouth down to his, would she have responded?

He still wasn't sure about her story of someone waiting, and as he shaved, he ran through all her possible suitors within the CID team. He couldn't think of any single men, except Sam or Grant. Sam wasn't Fluff's type and she, like everyone else, certainly didn't get on with Grant. Of course, it could be a married man, but that sort of thing couldn't be kept quiet for long. Matt suddenly realised with a shock that he was a little jealous. Laughing at the irony of it, he told himself sternly that it was, after all, none of his business.

Refreshed by the shower, he decided to get an early start and catch up before the rest of the team arrived, but as he entered

CID, he found Wendy already busy at her computer. She seemed so engrossed, he merely nodded a good morning and went straight to his office. Then, just as he was settling himself at his desk, Fluff breezed in.

'Thought you might be hungry, Guv.'

Matt studied her as she placed the bacon bap on the desk in front of him. There was nothing he could detect that said she was the least bit upset about his rejection last night. Surmising that she was telling the truth about someone waiting for her, he gave in to the pangs of hunger that surfaced as the smell of bacon wafted upwards.

'Thanks.' Showing his appreciation, Matt took a huge bite out of the bap, delighted as the sharpness of the brown sauce hit his tongue. Fluff certainly knew his likes and dislikes. He quickly polished off this unexpected breakfast as Fluff went to update the incident board.

The next job would be to get hold of the police artist. He was sure McRay would okay the funding. A picture of how the man appeared when buying his props could then be sent out to all forces, so that it could be shown at the local markets.

The team straggled slowly in. By the time most of them had arrived, Matt felt like he had already done a full day. Sam came in with a long face.

'Told Pete that we're not likely to make the practice tonight and even less likely to make the match tomorrow.'

'I can imagine what he said.'

'Not repeatable. Never heard some of those words before.'

'Pete could write a dictionary of swear words.' Secretly, Matt was relieved. If he did get any time away from the case he wanted to make things right with Eppie.

To take Sam's mind off it, Matt asked him about the model soldier. Sam cheered up immediately.

'I couldn't believe it, Guv. There's a shop in London where all they sell are model soldiers, well, and all the bits and pieces, like the guns and stuff. The man there was helpful. Apparently, all sorts of people buy these things, even Lords and past Prime ministers. In fact, I couldn't shut him up.'

CHAPTER 28

Matt thought that must have been difficult once Sam was on a roll but said nothing as he continued.

'He even invited me down there to have a look around.'

Something in Matt's look told Sam he was losing his audience, and he got down to the facts.

'They do keep lists of customers going way back. Most are not computerised, but we are welcome to have a gander, if we get a warrant.' Sam consulted his notebook. 'He also gave me the details of two locals clubs. They meet regularly. To enact battles I suppose. Thought I might take a look?' Sam said, ending on a question.

'That could be worthwhile. Good work, Sam. Now, let's get on with the briefing.' Matt rose and led the way to the outer office.

Calling the team together, he let Sam outline what was happening with the model soldier before Fluff took over to give details of their London visit, ending with the fact that the possible murderer had bought three dolls.

'If this was our man, then he is obviously planning at least two other murders, possibly more.'

'So he's way ahead of us, then?' Grant said.

It was inevitable that Grant would have something to say and Matt sighed. He had no patience for the man today. He answered before Fluff could snap back.

'Yes.' Seeing the concerned faces in front of him, Matt forced himself to put forward the positive facts, even though, at this point, he felt tired and discouraged. 'That is exactly what it means. However, we are building up a picture of how this man works and have every chance to catch him before he can kill again.'

Matt paused as Grant mumbled something. He was sure he had heard 'Fat chance,' but he chose to ignore it and carried on. 'Just look at the evidence. We know how he tries to disguise himself.'

'But how is that going to help us, Sir, if he has already bought all the gear he needs?' Grant asked.

There was a murmur from the team at Grant's latest interruption. Fluff spoke for them. 'Shut up Grant and listen to what the Guv is saying.'

159

Matt knew they daren't waste time arguing amongst themselves. 'No. Grant has asked a valid question. I'll do my best to answer it. For a start, we now have reason to believe the killer is a local man. We know he has the props to carry out at least two more murders, maybe more. The source of dresses has been identified, and we are expecting more information shortly from the company. This will give us more idea what he is planning. There is also the possibility that we may pick up CCTV footage in the area of that sale. We are working on several angles.' Matt indicated the incident board. 'This man thinks he is clever, but he has already made some serious mistakes. We can and will catch him.' Matt didn't add that he hoped it would be before he killed again. He knew that worry was already there in the minds of the team.

They seemed encouraged as they dispersed back to work, but Matt knew that they were as worried and tired as he was. No one, least of all himself, wanted to fail.

Now he had better get McRay onboard regarding the artist. McRay grunted as Matt entered his office, and Matt sensed that some of his grumpiness had returned. Matt decided to put a positive spin on the findings from yesterday until McRay stopped him.

'I'll OK the artist.'

Matt sensed that McRay had something else on his mind.

'Sit down, Matt.'

Matt did as he was bid and waited until McRay looked up at him.

'We need to clear the site, Matt. The owners of the spa are putting pressure on us. I can see their point. It's hardly conducive to health and well-being to be constantly reminded that a murder took place on the premises, is it?'

'No, Sir. But—'

McRay held up his hand to stop Matt continuing. 'No buts, Matt. The Super is leaning on me. The lawyers are getting involved. Unless we have a strong reason to be there, we'll have to back off.' McRay watched as Matt compiled his argument against this move.

'I know that Jason still has some elimination prints to process, Sir. And we have a couple of staff to interview.'

'Couldn't these be done off site?'

'Yes, as long as those people are willing to cooperate.'

'Good.'

Matt could see that McRay considered the matter resolved and knew he had to have his say, even if it did provoke anger.

'With respect, Sir, I do feel we need to maintain a presence there. This is no ordinary, one-off killing. We know this killer will be on a high right now. He'll want to repeat the experience and show off just how clever he is. I feel he will do that by killing again in the same place.'

Matt paused to gauge McRay's reaction before continuing. 'There is now evidence that he has purchased at least three of the dolls and several of the dresses, so he obviously intends to continue.'

McRay was silent for a moment. 'Matt, we both know that you could have a hundred officers on the scene, and it wouldn't stop a crazy killer like this one.'

'No, Sir, but it might put him off for a while. Give us time to catch him. We do have a description now and evidence that he is local.'

Matt filled McRay in on the findings from yesterday and waited. The old McRay would have no problem doing what he felt was right.

'Right. There is to be no overt police presence. If you or the forensic team need to go there, you will keep a low profile and not go around upsetting the guests by acting like Inspector Morse.'

'Could we at least have a patrol car on the drive? It would be a good deterrent, plus the guests would be reassured.'

'Oh, alright, but only if there is nothing else for them to do, mind.'

He nodded, knowing he had to be content with half winning the battle. Matt knew how these things worked. He stood and began making his way to the door.

'How's that new wife of yours, Matt?'

'Fine. Thank you, Sir.' Matt would have been happy to leave it at that, but McRay followed him to the door.

'Damn bad luck, dealing with all this right now, lad. Look after her.' McRay gave Matt's shoulder a pat before turning back to his desk.

Matt detected a glimmer of wistfulness in McRay's voice. Did he regret what had happened with his marriage? For the first time, Matt felt some understanding for the man. McRay used to have a life outside of work, a wife and family. He hadn't always been this grumpy, aging man.

Was this what lay ahead for him? There seemed little chance that he would be able to get home early tonight. So he would have no opportunity to heal the rift with Eppie.

CHAPTER 29

Walking into the office knowing he would never hear Anne's shrill voice again was such a pleasure. Clive's first task was to erase all the phone calls he had made. He thought the police could possibly trace calls from his mobile, but they would have to suspect him first. Anne's mobile would be filled with muddy water by now, like her mouth and every other orifice of her skinny body. The thought pleased him and he almost giggled aloud.

Gloria arrived and, without waiting to take her coat off, came across to his office. Clive knew he had to be careful how he played this.

'Well. Did you set her straight? Or do I start collecting?'

He shook his head as if puzzled. 'She didn't show.'

'Get away.'

'Did you know she had booked theatre tickets?'

'Really?'

'RSC. I kept calling her from there, but there was no answer.'

'She's changed her mind. You're losing your touch, Clive. It won't be long before you will have to give old Gloria a run for her money.'

He dutifully laughed. Some of the office staff were arriving so Gloria turned to leave. 'It will be interesting to hear what she has to say today.'

'Bet she won't want to show her face. She'll take a sickie, you see.'

With the matter of Anne finally concluded, it was time to turn his attention to his next venture. Everything was now in place for the next statement, the last detail carefully planned. The timings would be tricky, but as long as dear Mother played the part he had mapped out for her, Clive was confident he would be able to present DI Turrell with another little problem.

If only it was as simple to sort out his muddled feelings about Ben. Clive couldn't even walk by him without the accompaniment of what felt like a brass band beating in his chest. All day, Ben had been avoiding eye contact and there had been no opportunity to talk to him alone.

The outer office was rapidly emptying, as it always did on a Friday afternoon. He glanced across to where Ben was sitting, head down, as if concentrating. He was usually the first to leave on a Friday, and Clive suspected he had many friends and a lively social life. He wouldn't want Clive asking him out for a drink, even if he could find the courage. He decided to put Ben out of his mind and go home to recheck the details for Saturday night. It was also important to keep Mother happy and on line for Saturday, or all his preparation would come to nothing.

It had been a busy week. Aside from his debut murder and the drowning of dear Anne, he had just finished a contract for the prestigious Governor Hotel. The software had been fully tested and delivered to the client, tested again on the client's premises, and signed off. That was the end of his responsibilities; it was now over to the service engineers.

With a sigh, Clive turned his back on Ben and began fastening his briefcase ready to leave. But before he could make it out of the office, the phone rang. He could choose to ignore it and pretend he had already left. Everyone dreaded that Friday afternoon call. He hesitated, then put his briefcase back on the desk and picked up the phone.

Mr Norris, manager of the Governor Hotel, sounded agitated. During the installation of the new software, it had become obvious that he was a worrier, always expecting things to go wrong. Now he was panicking, saying he had piles of bookings that could not be inputted. His area manager was visiting tomorrow and his job could be on the line.

After running through the usual suggestions, none of which worked, Clive said he would book one of the support engineers to call on him as soon as possible. However, Mr Norris had already been down this route only to be told that there was no engineer available. En Jay's had three support engineers to take care of just this sort of problem, but Clive knew one was off sick and the other two were already out working on other emergencies.

Looking around the office in case anyone might like some overtime, he found most had left, and the rest were studiously avoiding his eyes and hurrying their preparations to escape. Only Ben was still at his desk, eyes down and seemingly busy.

Giving in to Mr Norris's urgent plea, Clive resigned himself to making a visit to the hotel on the way home.

Ben looked up as he passed.

'Problems?'

'Only a complete computer nerd climbing up the wall.'

Ben nodded his understanding. He had helped on the programme and had met the computer illiterate Mr Norris.

'Mr Norris.' He guessed. 'Want me to give you a hand?'

The suggestion was so casual, Ben wasn't even looking at him, but Clive felt his heart begin its now familiar tremor of excitement.

* * *

Clive tried to relax, not easy while negotiating the Friday night traffic jams and with Ben beside him. He began thinking of something interesting to say, but found he was ruling everything out before it could reach his lips. In the end, he left most of the talking to Ben.

'Did you give her the brush off, then?'

'She didn't show. I think she must have realised she had no chance.'

'So, that's why she didn't come in today. She seemed so determined.'

'Yes. I thought it a bit strange too. Maybe Gloria got through to her at last.'

They both laughed and, as Ben chattered on, Clive was delighted to find out they shared the same taste in films, while their musical tastes differed widely. He wasn't even sure what the term 'soul music' covered but was inclined to think he wouldn't like it at all.

The Governor Hotel was small but luxurious and well known for its cuisine. Mr Norris rushed to meet them in a flap overlaid with profuse thanks that they had arrived so promptly.

To Mr Norris's relief the problem was quickly solved. As they started to leave, Clive began wondering if he dare ask Ben out for a drink. It was then that Mr Norris scurried up to offer them dinner in the hotel's award-winning Rose restaurant, by way of a thank you for solving the problem.

It only took a nod of agreement from Ben, a quick call to Mrs Sinclair, who explained that she couldn't stay on, but that she would make sure Mother had everything she needed and she would settle her in front of the television with a tray.

Mr Norris led them through an elegant panelled dining room to a table for two, situated in the large bay windows overlooking the rose garden. One or two roses were still in bloom despite the autumn frosts and matched the one that graced the centre of the table.

As they sat, Mr Norris snapped his fingers towards a black-clad waiter standing like a sentry at the edge of the room. The waiter adjusted the white cloth over his arm and strode towards them.

'Justin, these are my guests and are to have whatever they wish, including a selection from the wine list.'

It was obvious that here Mr Norris was in complete command as the waiter bowed over them.

In no time at all, they were enjoying a rack of lamb with all the trimmings complemented by a rather robust French red.

As he sat across from Ben, Clive tried to work out why he was so attracted to him. In some ways, they were exact opposites. Ben was always so cheerful and outgoing, whereas Clive had learnt early to be cautious and careful. Maybe that was it—Ben released that part of him stifled years ago, if there ever was such a part. The trembling inside was settling down, helped by the wine. He smiled at Ben across the table.

'More?' Clive asked holding up the wine bottle.

'Why not?' Ben replied, holding out his glass. 'And hey, we could always get a taxi home.'

Clive laughed. It had sounded like an invitation and, if he was free, free of that alien Mother at home, he could casually invite Ben home for a coffee, hoping all the time it would lead to more. He wanted Ben all to himself, away from everyone, wanted to be his in every way.

The waiter delivered their coffee and petit fours while Clive wondered whether he should be brave enough to suggest that they repeat this wonderful experience of dining out.

Ben had pounced on the petit fours. Clive had already realised that he had a sweet tooth from watching him devour the dessert and was happy to leave them all to him, content to watch the way he placed each one carefully in his mouth, withdrawing it partly before half closing his eyes as if in ecstasy while chewing slowly.

There was something very sensual about his actions. Clive began to feel an aching need, a need he knew only Ben could satisfy.

'This has been fun. We should do this again.' Once he managed to get the words out, they seemed to hang in the air, and he found himself holding his breath.

Ben had just put a petit four in his mouth but managed a huge grin that caused a little chocolate to dribble out of the corner of his mouth. He swallowed quickly and leant forward to place his hand on Clive's. 'I'd love to.'

It was such a light touch, but it seared into his skin and told him everything he needed to know. Ben wanted to be with him. Fireworks were going off around the room, and Clive could have sworn the waiters were dancing like in some silly commercial. Ben felt the same, could even love him. The warmth spread through his entire body and he savoured it fully before turning over his hand to grasp Ben's, matching his smile. 'How about lunch Sunday?'

'Sounds good,' he replied still grinning.

'We could go to Mario's…or,' Clive paused wondering whether to take a chance. He didn't care a jot about the food, just relief for the tension building in his loins. 'My place if you like?'

He waited, thinking he had overstepped the mark. Ben's brown eyes widened. Clive felt as if he were assessing his seriousness.

'If you are sure that is what you want,' Ben said, removing his hand to take another petit four that he put slowly into his mouth in the most suggestive way. 'Only I won't be responsible for what might happen.'

Clive felt a shiver as several sensual waves travelled through his body. That look told him Ben wanted him, loved him. Could something this precious really be his?

CHAPTER 30

It was now two days since Eppie had talked to Matt face to face. She had woken up the night before when she felt his warmth beside her. Thinking they might talk, she'd raised herself on one elbow to look down at him, but he looked exhausted, and she hadn't the heart to wake him.

On the way to work, Eppie thought again of Matt's phone message of the previous morning. The words sounded so formal, like a receptionist reminding you of a dental appointment. If she hadn't been in the shower, and they could have spoken, it might have been different, but even her message back sounded stilted and functional.

Eppie was disappointed to find that Sandi's shift didn't start until one p.m. and although Nina, the morning receptionist, was helpful, she just didn't feel as relaxed as she was with Sandi.

Eppie decided to put all thoughts of Matt out of her head, and though the morning went quickly enough, she was relieved to return from lunch to find Sandi behind the desk.

It was halfway through the afternoon when there was a lull in guests needing their attention that Sandi asked Eppie what was wrong.

'Come on, tell me. How was he?'

'Fine.' Eppie tried to fob Sandi off.

'Oh, come on. It must be hard getting used to living twenty-four hours a day with a man.'

Eppie laughed at her astuteness. 'It's even harder when you haven't seen him since Wednesday. And then he was blazing mad.'

'Oh, you mustn't read anything into that,' Sandi advised. 'My Tom doesn't even think to ring me if they have a big shout on. That's the way they work, believe me. Can't juggle two things at a time. I guess it's the same for your lovely Matt, especially as he's in charge.'

Eppie thought for a moment about what she had said. Who would want the responsibility of catching a murderer, never mind one so close to home? 'Yes, that's true,' she said while wondering what Matt was doing. Maybe he was wrapping up the case right now, and this stumbling start to their life together would be over.

The rest of the afternoon sped by as they laughed over Sandi's insights into men and how they worked. Eppie would never have thought that Sandi, who was so engrossed in the petty details of her wedding, would also have such a sensible, down-to-earth attitude to the male species. Some of the stories about Tom had Eppie in stitches, which she had to stifle whenever a guest came to the counter.

There was the first time Sandi had taken Tom home to meet Mum and Dad. 'My Mum was so nervous, she'd cleaned the house from top to bottom, as if the Queen was coming to tea, but she wasn't a patch on Tom. I've never seen him like that. I think he would have rather gone into a raging inferno. And it nearly ended up that way.'

'What on earth happened?'

'My dad had decided, as it was such a lovely day, to have a barbeque. Now understand, Dad didn't believe in wasting money on one of those new fangled barbeques, so it was a grill and an old oil drum.'

'Sounds feasible.'

'Not what Tom thought. I could tell he was horrified the minute he saw it.'

'Did he say anything?'

'Not at first. It was so funny to watch him trying to be terribly polite, while squirming as he watched Dad light the coals. Then he suddenly jumped up and offered to help, suggesting that the whole thing might be better away from the fence, and safer resting on something non flammable.'

'How did your dad take that?'

'He sort of gulped and agreed. Mum and me nearly fell about laughing, especially when they began to move it. Tom had suggested they put the coals out first, but Dad wasn't having any of that. So there they were, Dad with the barbeque gloves and Tom with the oven gloves, staggering across the garden.'

'Sounds dangerous.'

'Oh it was. Dad tripped over the rhubarb and the coals went everywhere. We all jumped up, worried that he or Tom had been burnt, so we didn't notice at first that the shed was on fire. Seems like some of the coals had rolled over that way.'

'What an introduction to the family.' Eppie could imagine Sandi telling her grandchildren that story.

* * *

At home, after putting the kettle on and kicking off her shoes, Eppie picked up the post, idly turning over the only interesting envelope to see who it was from. The back was blank, but the small padded packet had an unusual bump in the middle. Despite giving it a prod or two, Eppie couldn't guess what it contained, so she stopped poking in case it broke and placed it with the rest of Matt's post. The pile was growing, as he hadn't looked at it for days.

There was little chance that Matt would be home early, so Eppie decided not to start dinner. Instead, she would empty her remaining suitcase and find room for her stuff. Not having any space to put her belongings was like being back at Aunt Sandra's, and she didn't want to feel like that again.

She started on the wardrobe, removing several old shoes and a pair of rugby boots. Then, reaching far into the back, she found a shoebox.

The box held assorted cards, an old watch, a withered corsage, and a few photos. The photos showed a family wedding, then one of Matt with his arm around one of the bridesmaids. They were smiling up at each other. Eppie thought they would both be about eighteen. She was very pretty. This must have been his first love, one that meant a lot to him as he has kept these mementoes.

Eppie wondered what her name was and why Matt hadn't mentioned her. But the subject of old lovers had never come up. Picking up the pile of cards, Eppie opened the top one. *'Aug 2011. Happy Birthday, All my love, Jo.'*

So this wasn't some long past affair but someone who was still in his life, still sending him messages of love. Eppie knelt holding the cards in her hands trying hard not to allow the significance of them to bleed into and colour her view of the love she and Matt had.

Her past affairs were over, finished. No mementoes, just memories. Not like these objects, which were still alive, still demanding a place in Matt's life, a place in his heart. Somehow, that must dilute the love Matt held for her. Jo had known Matt for much longer; they would have shared countless occasions. Their love must be special for Matt to keep these things.

CHAPTER 31

He woke early, too excited to sleep. Images of Ben and his smile replayed in Clive's head to remind him it was real. Ben had actually agreed to come to lunch tomorrow.

Slipping into his robe, Clive went down to the kitchen to start the coffee percolating, before turning on the kitchen television, eager to view more of his publicity. He was disappointed to find little that was new.

The newscaster just recapped what was known already and linked into the old interview with the police superintendent requesting information about the doll. Clive thought how ridiculous such an authority figure looked holding a cheap doll and consoled himself with the knowledge that tomorrow he would be top billing again.

Having watched their efforts, he thought that it was very unlikely that anything could be traced back to him. He had been careful to disguise himself and had never bought more than three dolls at a time, from any one market.

Markets were bustling, busy places, and the turnover was quick and mostly anonymous, unless you were a regular when you might be greeted with a cheery *'Hello, my love, couldn't your mum come today, then?'* or such, guaranteed to earn a girlish chuckle from some grey-haired pensioner who happily played along with the joke.

Clive switched off the television, his thoughts returning to Ben and that soft, brief touch. Ben had given him the courage. True, it was only lunch tomorrow, but he could think of no better way to celebrate his success of this evening. Tomorrow, Mother would be on her weekly visit to Margaret's to coo over Emily. This would be his only chance.

Was it too soon to ask Ben to the house? Would he see it as a ploy to further the relationship in the ways Clive remembered from his brief affairs with girls, when it was the done thing to ask if they wanted to come in for a coffee, while meaning 'let's fuck.'

He had never really liked that word but supposed it adequately described those relationships where sex was the main object. Now, he couldn't remember any of the girls and had retained no fond memories of that time. He was simply testing the waters to see what everyone else seemed to find so absorbing.

Since meeting Ben, Clive understood why. It wasn't just to do with bodily functions or making love, because until now he had never considered any love was involved in the sexual act. With Ben, there was a deep desire. Clive wanted to hold him, feel him, smell the scent of him, press his naked body tightly against his own and let nature take its course.

He was preparing Mother's breakfast tray when the local paper arrived. The headlines caught his eye. 'Professor Meredith says the killer will strike again,' it proclaimed, and underneath was a long article in which the esteemed professor gave his view of Clive's personality.

Clive gave the professor six out of ten, admitting that the man had managed to get some aspects of his life right. He had lived alone until Mother arrived and could be considered a loner, although he hoped that would change soon. Of course, he was intelligent and able to give attention to detail; that came with his job as a programmer. He could go along with the disturbed childhood, although he was sure it hadn't seemed that way to anyone else and most definitely not to his family.

Mother's feeble voice jerked him back to the kitchen. She would want her breakfast, which was already late. Clive couldn't afford to upset her today, in case she cried off dinner tonight. He needed her for cover, if his plan was to succeed.

Dutifully, he assembled the tray and took it up, alert for any signs that she might not come up to scratch. Thankfully, she seemed to be in her normal morning grumpy state, and he strove to be extra helpful and seemingly caring.

'Good morning, Mother. It's a lovely morning.'

'It will be cold.'

'Till the sun warms everything up. Then it will be crisp. Just as you like it.'

'Do not assume to tell me what I like, Clive.'

'No, Mother.'

He placed the tray on her lap, but she seemed uninterested in the food. He could tell she had something on her mind.

'What you can tell me about is your evening with Anne. Especially as I have met the girl.'

Clive decided to risk a version of the truth while looking a little sad. 'I am ashamed to say that she didn't show up.'

'Did she say why?'

'No. She didn't show up for work yesterday. I did try ringing her but there was no answer.'

'Then the girl must be ill or have been called away. You must try again later, Clive.'

'I will, Mother.'

Mother turned her attention to her breakfast while he decided to go through her wardrobe to help her decide what she wanted to wear tonight. Clive knew he risked her becoming awkward if he made too much of a thing about it, so he carefully selected the patterned woollen dress she had selected from Marks & Spencer's on their recent shopping trip, plus another, duller one from last year. He watched her eyes and guessing that Mother was looking forward to an excuse to wear the new dress, hung it on the outside of the wardrobe door before going downstairs while she finished breakfast.

Relieved that Mother was on board, he returned to the kitchen, wondering how DI Turrell was feeling this morning. By now, the little solider had surely arrived unannounced in their little love nest. The significance of Clive's gift was guaranteed to shock and unsettle the man. He would realise that Clive could visit anytime. Maybe while he was out wasting time in useless efforts to catch Clive, the Inspector would know he could be visiting the lovely Eppie.

Pouring himself another coffee, he went over the rest of his plans one more time. The required items were already in place within the smoker's tent. The ornate vases had proven hollow, and it was easy to slip everything he needed into the space beneath them at lunchtime yesterday. He had even carefully chosen the dress, thinking of his model's colouring. She would want to look her best, given the amount of photos that would be taken of her in this, her final scene in life.

CHAPTER 32

Matt had crept into bed not wanting to wake her, still thinking of what McRay had said. He knew Eppie was the best thing he would ever have in his life. He had to make sure that his marriage didn't end up the same way as McRay's.

But catching this murderer before he could kill again must take priority. He wasn't about to risk someone's life for his own selfish ends. It was a balancing act he—and Eppie—would have to learn to deal with.

He woke early, slipping out of bed without waking her. This should have been their first Saturday at home together. Matt had been looking forward to taking Eppie places and showing off his guiding knowledge. But there would be other weekends and, right now, he couldn't cope with sorting out the complex emotions between them. She would probably be going to work anyway.

Reaching the office, he consoled himself with a call to Eppie's mobile. When it went to voice mail, he was disappointed. He left a short message simply stating that he wasn't sure what time he would get home and that she should eat without him. The *'Miss you'* at the end he substituted for all he really wanted to say.

With so much information coming in, all needing to be assessed for possible follow-up action, Matt's attention was fully occupied all day. The pattern of the day had echoed the previous one with reports and information piling in. People like Wendy dealt with much of the information, finally coming to Matt when a further decision had to be made.

It was only when Sam plonked the remaining half of a sandwich pack in front of him that he realised the day had sped past.

Through a full mouth Sam mumbled, 'You're gonna need that if you intend to stay all night, Guv. But I warn you, you'll be in deep trouble with the Missus.'

Matt stretched and looked at his watch. 'Didn't realise that was the time. Thanks, Sam. You finish that.' He pushed the unappetising carton back across his desk. 'Eppie might have saved me something.'

It was late afternoon, so Eppie would be home by now and this might be a good time for them to talk.

He was surprised as he entered the flat that there was no inviting smell of cooking. When he had asked Eppie to marry him, he didn't know or care if Eppie could cook or not. But the few meals she had prepared had been delicious, and he had begun to look forward to them.

Maybe she was still cross with him. The kitchen was tidy and silent; in fact, the whole flat seemed still. Had he pushed her too far already? With an urgent need to find her, he crossed the living room in a few strides.

She was sitting on the floor of the bedroom with the shoebox, the contents spilled out in front of her and Jo's latest card in her hands. She hadn't heard him come in but when she looked up he saw the pain in her eyes.

'I'm sorry, I was trying to—'

'It doesn't matter.' He knelt in front of her, taking the card out of her hands to let it drop carelessly on the floor, with the other useless mementoes.

'I should have told you.' He pulled her towards him holding her head in both hands while he wiped the tears from her eyes with his thumbs.

'I just wanted some space.'

'It will be all right.' He had never seen this vulnerability in her before. His Eppie was strong, even feisty. His Eppie uncertain and upset made him want to protect her, hold her in his arms, and keep her from all hurt. He reached out to her.

'I didn't mean—'

He shut her up by drawing her close and fastening his mouth on hers, a long and passionate kiss that released the emotions in both of them. Feeling her relax against his chest, Matt shifted his arms to lift her effortlessly onto the bed.

Making love to Eppie had always been easy, but now there was a feeling of desperation—the only way to wipe away what had come between them, all the silly things didn't matter. Everything would be all right if they could just get back to the basic expression of their love.

Eppie murmured one word: 'Work.'

'Can wait,' Matt whispered back, while nibbling her ear and undoing her blouse.

Afterwards, it was easy to talk.

'I wasn't prying, just wanted to finish unpacking, find a home for my stuff.'

'My beautiful wife shall have a whole wardrobe all to herself.' Matt made to jump off the bed as if to see to it immediately. Eppie laughed and put her arms around his neck to stop him leaving. Seeing her smiling face, Matt kissed her again and sank back beside her.

'At Aunt Sandra's, there was no room for my things. Or for me really.'

'I didn't mean for it to be like this. I thought there would be time to sort it out together.'

'I know.'

'This bloody case.'

'It's not your fault,' Eppie assured him. 'Just what you do.'

'Eppie, I want more than anything for you, us, to be happy. To have a good life together.'

'Hey, we will.'

'If you had seen McRay. He pretends to hate all women, but it's because he is hurting so much. He let the job take over.'

'I won't let that happen to you.'

'Not easy. There are times when it has to.'

'But it won't always be this bad, will it?'

As they lay in each other's arms, he knew he would have to explain. 'I should have told you about Jo.'

'No.'

'Yes.' Matt paused. 'She, Jo, well, we were there for each other through some good and bad times. For me, when Granddad was suspended and after he died.'

'Matt, you don't have to.'

'I need—want to, Eppie.'

Memories of that time shadowed across his face. Eppie lay still and waited.

'It sort of fizzled out. No great fireworks. Jo was becoming a doctor while I was making a hell of a mess being an Inspector.'

'I don't believe that.'

'I thought I knew it all back then. Then…then after Gracie died, I realised I knew nothing.'

'Gracie?'

'She was sixteen. If I had locked up the right man, she would still be alive. But I was careless, in a hurry. Soon after that Jo stopped coming home.'

'She blamed you?'

'Not really. There was no room for that. I hated myself too much.'

'You loved her?'

Matt turned to look at her. 'Yes. She was my first. But I'm damn glad she wasn't my last.'

CHAPTER 33

The call came early and Matt was instantly awake, aware that it could only be bad news at this time in the morning. As he struggled to get out of the crumpled duvet, he hoped the call hadn't woken Eppie. He took the call in the kitchen. Matt had feared that he was dealing with a killer who wouldn't stop at one victim, and he took no pleasure in being proved right.

Matt drove fast through the deserted streets with the blue light throwing back a thousand reflections from the windows of dark buildings and shops before passing on down the hill and past the brooding ruins of Kenilworth castle.

Although he was trying to keep his mind on the horror of a second murder and all he needed to do, he found it slipping back to Eppie. Even though they were close again, neither of them had brought up the cause of their row. Matt still wanted to keep her safe.

The news of this second murder at the health spa this morning helped to justify his stance, but he knew she was right—he couldn't expect to protect her from all the evil in the world no matter how much he wanted to.

He switched off the blue light as he turned into the driveway of the health spa. No sense in having the murder scene cluttered up with startled guests before it was necessary. Far better to let them sleep peacefully in their beds for a while longer, even though one of them might turn out to be the murderer.

There was a peaceful stillness to the early autumn morning as the first rays of the sun slid across the damp grass. As a crime scene, Matt realised it was going to be a difficult one. The grass had already been flattened by just the vital and well-trained officers who were quietly going about their work.

Slim, the police surgeon met him at the outer cordon with a sad shake of his head.

'I'd say the same MO, Matt. Bloody, bloody waste.' Slim shook his head and paused while Matt remembered that Slim had three daughters of his own and always keenly felt any case involving a young woman. 'We've got a real problem on our hands now, haven't we?' Slim continued.

There wasn't really anything Matt could say, so he nodded and put a hand of condolence on the man's shoulder. After putting on his forensic suit and signing in, Matt steeled himself to move towards where the officers were preparing to erect a tent over the body.

No murder was ever pleasant to look at, yet Matt felt a sense of rage as he looked down at what could be a scene from some romantic old movie with the heroine gracefully reclining on a swing waiting for her prince to claim her. Except that there would be no prince for this young girl, and her clothing was more that of a child going off to a party. A party she would never reach.

As Matt stood looking down at the pathetic sight, the rising sun dappled through the trees for a moment to highlight a lock of her hair to a soft ripe wheat colour. Matt looked quickly around to see if the arc lights were ready and motioned for the officer to turn them on.

There was no mistaking it; this was young Sandi from Reception. The girl who was showing Eppie the ropes and had been so kind and happy. Matt suddenly felt sick at the thought of his Eppie coming so close to the mad bastard who could do this. It could have been her lying there. He had let her and Sandi down. Images of Gracie crossed his mind. However, berating himself wouldn't help and with an effort, he pulled himself back to act as the professional he was.

Knowing that the forensics team, under the highly capable Jason, were on the scene, Matt had a brief word with him to discuss the possible routes the murderer might have taken before leaving him the space and the peace to get on with his job. Jason's team were the experts, and the crime scene was in their charge. Matt left them to it and walked towards Reception.

Harold Foster, or Harry, as he insisted Matt call him was becoming anxious to see so many policemen arriving yet again at the club. Harry was the night porter who had been on duty from ten the previous night. He was an ex-military man and Matt guessed he would take his duties seriously, no flirting with the staff or guests while he was minding the shop.

Matt was just about to ask him for the senior management's telephone numbers when a bustling Mrs Trowbridge came through from the grounds. Despite wearing her dressing gown, hairnet, and slippers, she retained her air of grandeur, which reminded Matt so much of a hospital matron.

'Perhaps you would like to explain what is going on, young man,' she demanded as if she held Matt personally responsible.

Matt wished that Fluff and Sam had arrived. There was nothing he could do but tell her the full truth and try to gain her utmost cooperation. Aside from having access to the official records and rosters, she was the type of person who would make it her duty to find out everything she could about her staff and could therefore be invaluable. Matt decided that it would be best to be blunt with her, but it was impossible to tell how someone would react to the news of a murder.

'I need to have a word in private, Mrs Trowbridge.' Matt led her away from the reception desk and Harry.

Mrs Trowbridge took a moment to take in the seriousness in his face before replying. 'Come to my office then.'

Mrs Trowbridge seated herself behind the desk, and Matt had the feeling that she was using the desk as a prop to distance herself from what he was going to say. As soon as he was seated, she spoke abruptly. 'It's another one isn't it?'

Matt could see that she was mentally preparing herself for another murder, but he wondered how the shock of finding out that the victim was one of her own staff would hit her.

He didn't have the time to tread carefully, and he assessed that Mrs Trowbridge was made of stern stuff. 'Yes,' he said softly. He saw the pain in her eyes before he continued. 'One of the staff. The reception staff.' He watched and, for a moment, thought her face was about to crumble into tears before she pulled herself up.

'Who?'

'I think her name is Sandi. She had beautiful sandy-coloured hair.'

Mrs Trowbridge stood and turned to look out of the window. 'Oh my God.'

Matt knew he would have to give her time to digest the information, but she surprised him when she turned towards him.

'How can I help? What do you need from me?' she asked in a strong, stern voice.

In a short time, everything was under control. The manager was on his way in. Matt had the full name and address of Sandi Tomlinson who had lived at home and of her fiancé, Tom Graham, whom she had been planning to marry in six months.

Fluff and Sam had both arrived, and Sam was interviewing Harry while Fluff was arranging with Mrs Trowbridge the best way to handle the in-house guests. It was decided that they should be kept away from the left side of the house, since it gave easy access to the murder scene. This meant that part of the dining room would be sectioned off, the café would be out of bounds, and the dedicated group of smokers would have a temporary shelter at the rear of the house, even if this meant upsetting the other guests.

It was lucky that the guests took their pre-ordered breakfasts in their rooms and the first classes or treatments did not start until nine-thirty. Matt calculated that gave them at least three hours head start. There was no way that the news could be kept from the guests, but if the spa could run as normal, it would keep them busy at least until the team had a chance to question them. Day guests would be turned away at the end of the driveway and advised to ring before returning.

Matt had just stopped to take a bite of the bacon sandwich that the excellent Mrs Trowbridge, still in her dressing gown, had rustled up for the team. The team had come in straight from their beds at the call so were very grateful. Not that Matt could taste a thing except the extremely drinkable coffee that was on offer. It was now eight thirty, the guests would be awake, and the team was gearing up to question all of them. Fluff came up to him with a clipboard.

'Guv?' She sounded hesitant.

Matt smiled inwardly at her use of the phrase most beloved of cop shows but one she insisted on using if the lower ranks were around, even though he had asked her not to.

'Yes?' he mumbled through the bacon sandwich.

'Do you want to interview the receptionist who was on duty with Miss Tomlinson yesterday afternoon?'

For a moment, Matt couldn't understand why she was bothering him with such a question, until it struck him that Eppie had been on duty yesterday, Eppie, who was already thinking of Sandi as a friend. Eppie, who could have come face to face with her killer.

Matt put down the half-finished bacon sandwich and wiped his mouth with the paper napkin, to give him time to think. He had to be the one to tell his wife that the girl she worked with yesterday had been brutally murdered; there was no way he could get out of that. Common sense then took over, and he knew it would be best if he left the formal interview to Fluff and Sam.

'I'll see her first, tell her about Sandi. Then it would be best if you and Sam took over.'

Fluff nodded, pleased with his decision.

'Let me know when she arrives.'

'Will do.'

As Fluff left, Matt put aside his half-finished sandwich and returned to the immediate problems.

CHAPTER 34

Clive made sure he was up early. This was easy considering that he was bursting with excitement following his success of the night before and the thought of Ben coming to lunch.

Torn between needing Mother to be ready for Margaret at eleven and seeing what publicity his latest effort was bringing in, Clive decided to get Mother up and moving first.

He thought again about how much easier it would be if she didn't live with him. True, Clive enjoyed his power over her, although it didn't begin to make up for her dismissal of him as an infant, but now it would be good if she would just die and be out of his way. He wondered briefly about helping the process along, but decided that it would draw attention to himself, and it would be best to leave it, for the moment.

Taking up her breakfast tray, he was dismayed to find that she wasn't even stirring. Putting on a cheerful air, he pulled back the curtains and let the autumn sunlight flood into the room. Mother grunted and turned away. Clive stood looking at her hunched shoulder, fighting the desire to stride to the bed and pull her physically from it.

'Good morning, Mother. It is going to be a lovely day for taking little Emily to feed the ducks.' He watched as she emerged from the covers.

'I'm tired,' she grumbled sitting up. 'I would never have gone out last night if I had known how late we would be.'

CHAPTER 34

Given she was home and in bed by ten-thirty, he didn't feel the complaint was justified, but decided it was best not to argue with her. 'It was later than I'd planned. Sorry about that, Mother.'

She nodded and gave a grunt of agreement as he helped her ease out of the bed and carefully into the bedside chair. As soon as she had started on her breakfast, he made his way back to the kitchen, and too excited to pour himself another coffee, turned on the television.

Clive was disappointed to find that *BBC News* was in the middle of highlighting all the upcoming sports fixtures. His fingers trembled as he flipped to *Sky News*. They too were in the middle of their sports section, although what sports had to do with a news programme he could never understand. Realising he would have to wait until the news headlines on the hour, he poured himself a bowl of muesli.

Of course, it could be that his message hadn't been discovered yet or that the news hounds hadn't got wind of the event. He thought this was unlikely as he had placed her close to the smoker's tent, and they were bound to be up early and heading straight out for the first puff.

Then there it was, featured on the main news. The grave police superintendent stating that a young woman had been found murdered this morning. It was too early to say whether this murder was connected to one a few days ago, he continued. The flashbulbs highlighted his strong features as he turned, ignoring the barrage of questions about serial killers and police incompetence to move back into the safety of the station.

The police were baffled, that was easy to see, and Clive was the only one who knew exactly what had happened. He had them running in circles, was way ahead of them, and while they were sorting out what happened to Sandi, he already had chosen another girl to repeat the process. He didn't intend to give them time to catch up but would hit them again, when and where they least expected it.

He wished he could see DI Turrell's face this morning. Young Sandi had been working with his wife, and he would realise that

187

Clive was moving closer and closer to her. The Inspector was powerless to stop him.

The press, true to form, were already making suggestions of failure and once one started baying, the rest would follow. He wondered again if the DI had opened the package yet. Maybe he would drive by the Turrell's flat later this afternoon, on the way back from picking up Mother's tablets. Just to see if there was any sign of life.

Until then, he wanted to concentrate on preparing a simple lunch for Ben, although he sincerely hoped there would be something completely different on the menu.

It took him a long time to get Mother up and dressed, and then he began to get anxious, as Margaret was late. Mother noticed his anxiety.

'For goodness sake, Clive, stop going back and forth to the window. Anyone would think you can't wait to be rid of me.'

'Don't be silly, Mother, I wouldn't like you to miss seeing little Emily. I know how important she is to you.'

'You don't want me here when your colleague arrives more like. You still haven't told me who it is.'

'No one you would know, Mother.'

'Have you made it up with young Anne?'

'I haven't heard from her.'

'Well, you could do worse, and it is about time you had a woman to keep you in order, Clive.'

He couldn't resist replying. 'I thought I had you to do that, Mother.'

'Well, I won't be here forever, will I?'

Clive wanted to say, '*No you won't, and if I have anything to do with it your demise, it will be sooner rather than later,*' but instead he forced himself to sit down, pick up the Sunday paper, and appear to relax while fuming inside. He spent the time making plans for his third outing and almost forgot about the clock, until Margaret arrived fifteen minutes late with the lame excuse of Emily teething.

As soon as Mother was out of the house, Clive set about preparing a simple pasta for lunch. He was still not sure that Ben's feelings matched his own and didn't want any embarrassment, should he believe only lunch was on offer. He tossed a green salad with balsamic vinegar and oil dressing and went to set the dining room table, carefully choosing the spring green napkins and adding a small vase of burnt orange chrysanthemums to complement the china.

Standing back, he was pleased at his efforts. He had invited no one to the house since Mother had arrived. By now, Mother and Margaret would be busy planning his wedding, and he smiled as he thought of what they would say if they knew the truth.

CHAPTER 35

Sandi had been on the late evening shift, which started at one p.m. This shift was fairly quiet after about eight when most of the day visitors had gone.

During the evening, the in-house guests were usually dining, relaxing in their rooms, or in the hydro centre that stayed open until seven in the evening. Also, some therapists continued to provide treatments until nine. Occasionally, the spa would put on a talk or a film, but these usually finished around eight-thirty.

Harry was sitting, looking old and weary, the military bearing and sense of purpose gone as the news of Sandi's murder had sunk in. He looked up as Matt entered. His eyes looked watery. Matt sat down beside him.

'She never goes off without asking me. I should have checked. I should have checked.' Harry shook his head in despair.

'It was already too late. There was nothing you could do.'

'She shouldn't have been out there on her own all night. I could have done that much for her.'

Matt needed to get Harry out of his orgy of self-pity if he was going to be of any help. Knowing Harry's army background, Matt tried for command, rather than letting him go any further into his self-blaming. 'The only thing you can do for her now is to help me find out who did this. I need you to take me through everything, very carefully, from the moment you arrived at work last night.' Matt watched as Harry straightened in his seat.

'Well, I got here at twenty-one-thirty hours, as usual. If it's Sandi, then we have a chat, see how the wedding plans are going on…Oh dear, oh dear.'

Matt brought him back. 'Then?'

'I, err, I go round and make sure all the doors are locked.'

'How long does that take?'

'Eight minutes.' Harry thought for a moment then added, 'Unless Poll, the cat, has sneaked in. She's not allowed in at night you see and some nights she leads me a right merry dance, trying to hide away in some nice warm spot.'

'And last night?'

'No sign of her.'

'So by twenty-one-thirty-eight you were back at the front desk?'

'Yes. No, wait a minute; I helped a lady with her wheelchair.'

'So it was later?'

'It only took me a minute or two, Sir. Her son had gone to get the car.'

Matt felt Harry might have been about to add a salute. 'What happens then?'

'I check the phones have all been switched through and move my chair, so I can see the front door.'

'Is that when the receptionist usually leaves?'

'Well, I usually tell 'em to hop off. Most of them anyway. Some just want to take advantage and would be through them doors as soon as they see your shadow without even a by your leave. Can't even get myself organised. I don't like that. But Sandi always asked, never took it as a right. I should have known something was wrong. I should have known.'

Before Matt could continue, there was a knock on the door and Fluff came in.

'Sorry, Guv, but thought you might like to see this.'

She handed Matt a list of people who had eaten in the dining room last night. Highlighted half way down the list was Clive Draper and guest. Matt looked up at Fluff for explanation.

'Day guest from Wednesday. We interviewed him twice.'

Matt nodded his understanding. Fluff left and he turned to Harry.

'Harry, is the dining room still open when you arrive?'

'Sometimes. If his nibs, St James, can't get rid of the stragglers. But they have their ways. I've watched 'em at it.'

'And last night?'

'Closed. I could see them setting up the tables for lunchtime.'

'Did you see a man called Clive Draper? I think he is a day member here.'

'Yes. That was her, his mother. In the wheelchair.'

'Oh. I see.' Matt was disappointed. It hardly seemed likely that the killer would saddle himself with his mother on a killing spree.

'And you were with this lady for how long.'

'No longer than a minute or two. I pushed her to the car, and her son was very grateful.'

'Thank you, Harry. You have been a great help.'

Matt ended the interview and gave Harry his card. The old man left looking defeated, and Matt felt for him.

Once Harry had left, Matt knew he would soon have to face Eppie and tell her that Sandi had been murdered. He had all the training and knew how to give someone bad news, but this was his wife. More than ever he wanted her out of here, wanted her safe. The murder of Sandi had proved his point. Eppie could be in danger. But he didn't want to cause another row between them. He had never thought marriage would be this hard, and he wondered how he could support her through this and remain professional.

He turned as the door opened to see Eppie's bewildered face as Fluff ushered her into the room. She came towards him, and he enfolded her in his arms. Eppie pulled back first to look up at him with a question on her face. Matt led her to a chair and sat beside her still holding her hand.

'Eppie, there has been another murder.' He waited for a moment for her to digest this before continuing. 'It was someone you knew.' Mat could see her frantically searching the list of family and friends in her head, wondering who it could be, so he carried on quickly. 'I'm sorry, but it was Sandi.'

She looked at him in amazement for a moment before replying. 'But, but I was with her yesterday. She is getting married. I…I… she helped me. I…' she stuttered to a stop in shock. Matt knew he couldn't tell Eppie any of the details of Sandi's death, so he moved quickly back into the usual pattern when talking to a witness.

'Since you were with her yesterday afternoon, we have to interview you officially.' He waited and watched her fight to stop the decline into tears before adding. 'It could help us catch whoever did this. Anything you remember, no matter how small, may give us a lead.'

Eppie nodded, and Matt stood up ready to hand her over to Sam and Fluff. Eppie seemed surprised that he was leaving, so he stopped at the door to explain. 'It wouldn't be right for me to do this, so Sergeant Withers will be with you shortly.'

From the stricken look on her face, Matt felt like he was abandoning her to a firing squad, so he tried to lighten the mood with humour as he opened the door. 'Don't worry, he doesn't bite.' As soon as he had said it he knew it was wrong. This wasn't a colleague he could joke with, but a member of the public who had just been told of a death. To try to make up for it, he gave a big 'I'm sorry' grimace and closed the door behind him.

CHAPTER 36

Eppie watched the door shut behind Matt, feeling lost and trapped. It was illogical, she knew, as she wasn't in a police station and could probably leave at any time. Her mind turned back to who would want to murder Sandi? Then memories of her kindness yesterday came flooding back, and Eppie couldn't stop the tears.

It was only when a fair-haired woman handed her a tissue that Eppie realised that anyone had come into the room. The man with her announced that he was Detective Sergeant Withers and indicated the woman as Detective Constable Meadows. He paused and waited for her to blow her nose and wipe at her eyes.

'Sorry. I hadn't known her long but she was such a lovely person. Getting married soon...'

'Mrs Turrell, since you worked with Miss Tomlinson during the afternoon, you could have specific information that could help us catch this killer.'

Eppie liked the young man with his earnest face. The woman had remained silent, but Eppie was certain she was the one Matt referred to as Fluff, the one who had rung her the other night. 'I'll give you all the help I can.'

'We'd like you to think about yesterday afternoon. Did Sandi react to anyone who came to the desk? Was there anyone she seemed to have a relationship with, both good and bad?'

'No.'

'Or was there anyone who Sandi seemed unhappy or afraid to see?'

'No. But Sandi wouldn't let it show. She would smile and be kind to everyone.'

'And nothing else happened during the afternoon that caused you concern, that seemed out of place in any way?'

Eppie thought. They had been busy, yes, but it had been fun, and they had laughed together so much. Now someone had brutally killed Sandi. It didn't make sense. 'No we got on well, had a laugh. Will you catch who did this?'

'We are doing everything we can. But we need the help of people like you who may have seen the killer.'

'I'll do anything.'

Finally, Fluff spoke, her voice confirming that she was the person who rang Thursday evening. The night that Matt hadn't come home.

'Think really hard, and if there is the slightest thing, please give us a call. It may not seem much to you, but it could just be the one piece of information that completes the jigsaw and helps us put this murderer where he belongs.'

She sounded quite passionate about catching Sandi's murderer, and Eppie warmed to her. Eppie felt that she wasn't much help at all and apologised. The Sergeant, Sam, reassured her and gave her a card to call him if she remembered anything. Eppie wanted to say she could just tell Matt, but it didn't seem right somehow.

Afterwards, Eppie was glad that the interview had been conducted in a formal way. Her mind was racing, trying hard to remember, so by the time she was let out of the room, she felt weak and sick.

Matt was talking to a bald-headed gentleman in Reception. He put his arm out to stop the man in full flow and came towards her. 'Eppie. I'm so sorry. Are you alright?'

Matt touched her arm, and it was almost a stroke. Eppie wanted more than anything to feel safe in his strong arms, but she wouldn't do that to him, not here where he was the one in charge of trying to find out who killed Sandi. Eppie thought suddenly of Tom, Sandi's fiancé.

'I'm fine. What about Tom? Have you told him yet?'

'That comes next.'

Eppie could tell from his face that he wasn't looking forward to being the one to tell Tom that he wouldn't be getting married, and he would never see Sandi alive again. She wanted to hug him, to let him know she understood. Instead, she said lamely, 'Poor Tom. Poor you.'

Then Mrs Trowbridge bustled up and led her away to have a restoring cup of tea. Eppie always thought tea was overrated but guessed the very act of preparing and drinking it gave one something to do in times of emergency. She guessed that Mrs Trowbridge needed the anchor more than she. Although the girls talked about how strict she was, they also acknowledged that she was like a surrogate mother with genuine concern for each of them. The death of Sandi must have really upset her.

Eppie was sure anyone who had known Sandi would find it hard to think of her life being taken in such a callous way. She couldn't bear to think of how Tom would feel. Eppie hoped she hadn't suffered or been too afraid in those last few minutes, and she shivered at the thought.

If Sandi and Tom's last words towards each other had been angry ones, it would make it so much harder to bear. She resolved to try harder not to row with Matt. He was under great pressure right now.

Mrs Trowbridge insisted on sending Eppie home, although she would have much preferred to stay and work. That way, at least she could feel she was doing something and could be near Matt for a little longer. Also, being behind the desk might help her to recall something. Instead, she would go over each minute of the time she had spent with Sandi yesterday.

CHAPTER 37

Since Fluff had elected to take on the task of informing Sandi's parents of their loss, Matt took Sam with him to interview Tom Graham.

According to Wendy, Tom was a fireman currently working a shift at Leamington fire station. This meant that he would be surrounded by a tight circle of friends used to helping each other through any situation. They would be there to pick up the pieces if Tom broke down.

Ordinarily, Tom would be top of the suspect list, but in this case, unless of course Tom was playing a very clever game, Matt was pretty sure he wouldn't be the man they were looking for.

The fire station was a fairly modern brick building with the familiar glass folding doors behind which stood two gleaming fire engines. Matt felt a surge of excitement as he looked at the red giants. They brought back memories of clambering aboard one as an eight-year-old, and the thrill had never quite left him.

As they went through the small side door, Matt was surprised in what he had perceived to be a masculine reserve, to be met by a stern looking young woman in uniform who demanded to know their business. Matt left Sam to give their details and identity and simply held up his warrant card at the required moment. It wasn't long before the young woman led them upstairs to the common room where several men had just finished a meal. Two were clearing the table while others lounged in front of the television.

'Big fellow—going bald, although I didn't say that, mind.' The woman indicated the two men playing pool at the far end of the room.

Although no one looked directly at them, Matt could feel that everyone in the room was noting their progress as they moved towards the pool table. The players continued with their game, until Sam coughed to gain their attention and asked for Tom Graham. Before he could continue the smaller man spoke.

'What's he done this time, then, run off with the Mayor's wife or dented the boss's car again?' he joked.

It was obvious that the whole room was aware that they were the police and although everyone appeared relaxed, an air of wary anticipation hovered like a cloud among them. Sam gave the spiel and Matt felt the cloud thicken, as one or two of the men stood ready to protect their own. This was good, since Tom Graham was going to need all the support he could get when they had done their job and devastated his world with their vile news.

Matt stepped forward. 'Could we have a word in private, please, Mr. Graham? It concerns Miss Tomlinson.' Whatever Tom was expecting it certainly wasn't this. Matt watched the big man look from him to Sam searching for some evidence that this wasn't as serious as Matt's voice suggested and mentally crossed him off the suspect list. Fear replaced the hope in Tom as he nodded, holding onto the pool table for support, his strong, tall body seemingly withered into itself in the dread of what was to come.

The smaller man was the first to react, as he placed a hand firmly on Tom's shoulder before moving to herd the other men from the room. Matt and Sam moved around the pool table and indicated some chairs nearby.

Tom allowed them to lead him. 'What has happened? Has there been an accident?' he blurted out unable to wait any longer.

Sam looked at Matt almost willing him to be the one to break the bad news.

'I'm very sorry to say that Miss Tomlinson has died, Mr Graham.' Matt always found it best to give out bad news in stages.

Tom was looking at them incredulously. 'But we had lunch together, just yesterday. And she called me from work,' he said, as if Matt must be wrong.

Matt found this a common reaction as the person tried to cling onto the vivid memories of their loved one alive and well with no hint or reason for them to be now beyond their touch and protection.

'She didn't suffer at all.'

Tom looked at him uncomprehending. 'Then how…why?' Tom broke off and Matt was aware that the truth was now hitting home. However, worse was to come, and Matt steeled himself to carry on.

'I'm so sorry to say she was murdered, Mr Graham.'

Tom glared at Matt, as if he had personally killed Sandi and moved forward in his seat. Matt didn't move but was aware that Sam had readied himself for action.

'We believe she may have been the second victim of a murderer who killed earlier this week at the health spa,' Matt continued, bracing himself for the anger that sometimes follows such news. It didn't come immediately, but then Tom sprang to his feet with his fists clenched.

'My God, you've let that bugger run around free. Free to kill again. You did nothing to stop him killing my Sandi…my Sandi.'

Matt had put a hand out to keep Sam seated, aware that this anger would be quick to play itself out, and he was proved right as Tom collapsed back onto his seat with his head in his hands.

Matt knew that there was important information they must gain from Tom, and they couldn't yet let him have the luxury of descent into despair.

'Tom, you could help us catch this murderer before he kills again.' Matt waited a moment for Tom's head to rise and he was sure Tom was listening before continuing. 'Anything you can tell us may help, no matter how small. Right now, we need to know what time Sandi called you last night. And it would really help if we could analyse the call.'

Matt waited for what seemed a long time before Tom rose like a very old man to get a jacket from the back of one of the dining room chairs. Fishing in one of the pockets, he brought out his mobile phone but held onto it for a moment, aware that this was his last precious contact with Sandi.

'I'll personally guarantee that you will get your mobile back and that the phone call will be intact, Mr Graham,' Matt promised.

Tom moved forward slowly and placed the phone in Matt's hands. 'I usually call Sandi at about eight thirty, but we were on a shout. She called me—left a message.'

'Thank you.' Matt handed the phone to Sam who had the evidence bag waiting. 'We also need to know where you went to lunch yesterday and at what time.' Since Tom looked somewhat baffled at this request, Matt clarified. 'In case anyone followed Sandi from there.'

Tom nodded before replying, 'About twelve. Penny's Pizza's two doors down. Sandi was working the one to ten shift. She often did on a Saturday, and we'd both try to rota off for Sunday night, so we could go out—pictures or the like. Sunday is our night.' Tom stopped, as the awful emptiness of his life without Sandi began to evolve into reality.

Matt was thinking that it might be a good time to stop for the moment, since they had some leads to follow. He nodded to Sam to present the card with their phone numbers to Tom and explain that he was to call them day or night if he thought of anything else that would help. Also that they would want to see him again.

As they stood, the door opened as if by radar, and the smaller man who had been playing pool with Tom came through, followed by the woman in uniform. The woman came to sit at Tom's side, while the man reached into a cupboard to get a bottle of whisky and a glass. Matt moved away, knowing that Tom would be in safe hands.

It was as they drew away from the fire station that Sam echoed Matt's thoughts. 'Phew, that was hard going. Poor bugger didn't know what had hit him.'

Matt nodded, aware that the interview had affected him more than usual. He had had to face many families and tell them their loved one wouldn't be coming home, but Tom Graham's pain had channelled into his worries about Eppie and his need to keep her from danger. He couldn't begin to imagine how he would feel if he were ever placed in Tom's position, and so pushed the idea to the back of his mind before it stopped him concentrating.

CHAPTER 38

The ringing of the doorbell set off shivers of excitement, and Clive paused to take a sip of wine to fortify himself before moving to let Ben in.

He opened the door to Ben's back as he clicked his key towards his old hatchback parked in the circular driveway. Ben turned with that now familiar smile.

Almost shaking, Clive stood aside to usher him in. 'Please come in,' he said. The words sounded so formal, and he sought to add something lighter. 'It's great to have you.' Then, realising that the words had accurately stated his desire, he blushed in embarrassment and tried to retrace. 'Oh, I didn't mean—'

Ben interrupted him by putting a hand on his arm. 'I know. Don't stress.' Then he moved into the hallway, looking around to the carefully selected and placed modern art statue and the Perry Wellman picture that graced the wall.

'Wow.'

Clive wasn't sure this was the reaction he expected, but it would do for now. At last he was here.

'This is some place,' Ben said, moving forward into the lounge.

Clive moved after him, anxious that Ben like his home.

'Love the uncluttered look. However, remind me never to invite you to my place,' he added with a laugh.

Clive wanted to leave showing him the rest of the house until after lunch, fearing that he might not be able to keep his feelings from showing once they reached the bedroom. 'Can I get you a glass of wine?' he asked, leading the way down the hall towards the dining room.

Ben enjoyed his food, but lunch to Clive took an eternity, as he watched Ben carefully place each morsel suggestively in his mouth, until finally, they both declined dessert, and Clive offered to show him around. Ben gave him that assessing look again.

'I'm dying to see what an Englishman's castle is like.'

He felt unable to reply and simply turned to lead the way out of the dining room. Ben's hand brushed against his as they made their way up the stairs, and he took the opportunity to grasp Clive's hand, pulling him closer.

'If you are sure?' he whispered his face inches away.

In answer, Clive leant towards him until their mouths met in one long exchange of pent up passion. No further words were needed then, and he opened the door to his bedroom, pausing on the threshold to turn back to Ben for confirmation.

The sight of his large double bed with its elegant white counterpane and matching cushions, waiting there, made him hesitate. It was Ben, who, taking hold of his hand, led him forward.

He paused and looked steadily at Clive, as if checking that this was what he wanted. Clive willed him to continue until Ben placed a hand behind his head and drew him towards him.

The taste of Ben's mouth spread excitement through the whole of Clive's body and he could already feel himself responding. Clive put his arm around Ben's neck, eager to feel the soft curly hairs he had longed to touch. With desire overwhelming him and firing down into his loins, he felt his fingers tighten and pull savagely at the hairs, cruelly signalling his urgent need. Ben pushed him backwards onto the bed.

Then it was as if his entire body was trying to become one with Ben's. They ripped their clothes away until they strove against each other naked and free, hands and lips eager to experience each other's bodies as they writhed in passion.

He could feel Ben's penis pressed against his loins and his own hardness rising. Clive's passion was now becoming desperate for its climax.

In perfect tune with his need, Ben spun him face downwards on the bed and began to thrust vigorously into him. For a moment, the pain cut through the ecstasy, but then, as Ben drove deeper and deeper, Clive gave himself up to the pure pleasure, which was only heightened when Ben's hands slid around his hips to grasp him with expert hands. Then Clive gave himself up to the intense joy, letting wave after wave of complete fulfilment overcome him.

It was afterwards, as they lay sated with their arms around each other, that Clive felt for the very first time really happy and loved. This was so different than when he had stumbled his way to an uneasy and purely physical satisfaction with some loose and stupid girl. He felt Ben looking at him and turned to meet his eyes. They kissed, this time without the hungry desire but with a tender, soft loving.

Clive lay in Ben's arms, slowly allowing the love to absorb itself into his very being. Ben was part of him now, and he wanted to share everything with him.

He turned to see Ben's face in profile. His eyes were now closed, one arm flung carelessly above his head.

Should Clive tell him of his other absorbing passion? He wanted more than anything for him to be part of it, to experience with him the power and excitement.

CHAPTER 39

As Matt called the team together, he could see they were flagging. This exhaustion was not surprising since most of them had been working non-stop since before six this morning. There was not much information he could give them as they waited on an interim forensic report from Jason, and there would be no hope of more than a preliminary path report until at least tomorrow.

'Thanks for all your hard work today, everyone,' Matt said to the team. 'It seems fairly certain that we are on the way to having a serial killer on our hands. Professor Meredith had indicated that the killer would want to kill again, at shorter and shorter intervals.' He paused to look around the room at their serious faces.

'As you can see,' Matt indicated the picture of Sandi that Sam had just placed on the board, 'the details look the same. Ditto for the MO, although we should have more on that from Slim tomorrow. He is looking at time of death between nine and twelve p.m.'

'Were the same objects found with the victim, Sir,' asked Wendy.

'Yes, exactly. These are with Jason. The victim is Sandi Tomlinson, aged twenty-three, lived with her parents in Warwick, and engaged to be married next April to Tom Graham, a fireman. They have been engaged for eight months. We have interviewed Tom and ruled him out of the enquiry. The last time he saw Miss Tomlinson was at lunchtime on Saturday. That was at...'

'Penny's Pizzas, Guv,' Sam said.

'Thanks, Sam. Penny Rigby couldn't recall anything or anyone suspicious from Saturday lunchtime, although she did remember Sandi and Tom sitting at their usual table. She says all the regulars knew of their forthcoming wedding, and Sandi would update them on the details. Penny says it was almost as if she was part of the family. Fluff?'

Fluff stood to take over. 'Sandi's body was found by an Amanda Pearson, who was on a two-night pre-wedding package. The bride is a fitness fanatic and, as matron of honour, Amanda had agreed to give up smoking while undertaking her duties. However, the temptation was too great and, at five-thirty, she slipped out to go to the smoker's tent.'

'I bet she's given up now.'

Everyone ignored Grant's flippant remark and Fluff carried on. There was nothing to report from her visit to the grief-stricken parents, except they seemed normal, loving parents. Matt thought of the ripples that spread out and engulfed those close to a murder victim.

Sam gave a brief outline of their interview with Tom Graham before self-consciously reading out the phone message Sandi had left for Tom at twenty-forty-seven last night:

'*Hi love.*'

'That's Sandi,' Sam said.

Matt indicated for him just to read the transcript.

'*Have you been busy or is the engine gleaming? I know you don't like it too quiet.*'

Sam coughed and Matt indicated for him to hurry up.

'*Busy here. Demanding bride with millions of hens. I won't be like that—promise.*'

'*Anyway, I'm guessing you're out saving babies and little old ladies. Love you. See you tomorrow. Love you.*'

Listening to Sam reading out the last loving message to Tom, in a rather flat voice, only emphasised the sadness of it all. Matt still had a vivid picture of Tom as they had left him, a broken man. Could a man ever recover from the sudden, tragic loss of the love of his life? He supposed thousands did so every day. His thoughts went to Eppie, and he wondered how she was feeling.

Sam's voice brought him back. 'Towards the end part of the tape there is something in the background. It sounds a bit like a squeak but we should have more on that in the morning when the audio guy has had a look, or a listen.'

'No chance of us having a listen then, Sir?' Grant drawled from the back.

'We have had our hands full all day, so I thought it best to leave it to the experts, although it would be a good idea if you have a few hours to spend this evening,' Matt added, as the team grinned, always happy when Grant had been knocked back.

Matt knew he would never like the man. He had been difficult from the start, even though Matt had made every effort to help him integrate into the team, Grant held back, giving off an aura of amused superiority.

'It can't be that you have something else to do, can it, Grant?' Fluff called out without looking around to face the man.

Matt saw Grant's face darken. Fluff would be wiser to leave him alone.

'Not like you then, DS Meadows,' he snapped.

Fluff flushed amid the whistles from the team, and Matt stepped in to suggest they take a break ready for an early start in the morning. The new shift of uniform officers would take over some of the mind-numbing sifting of information coming in about the dolls, lollipops, dresses, materials, soldiers, to mention just a few of the leads the team were following.

DS William Oldham would supervise, although he hadn't been too happy to be awakened from his post Sunday-lunch doze in front of the TV with a request to turn out. Old Bill, his nickname, was the oldest member of the team and approaching retirement, but Matt was confident that he would do a good job in keeping everything on track now he was here.

Fluff came up to Matt as the rest of the team began to leave. 'Going to take a break yourself? I would think Eppie could do with five minutes of your company after this morning.'

Matt knew she was right; besides a sudden tiredness was washing over him, and he had had the niggling worry of Eppie in the back of his mind all day. Still, he felt he needed to keep on top of everything.

It was as if Fluff could read his mind. 'Come on, Old Bill will be fine. You know he will call you if anyone as much as sneezes,' she teased.

Matt grinned at her accurate description of Bill, who, with his pension firmly in view, took no risks whatsoever and, come to think of it, probably never had. 'OK. You're right, and I give in gracefully,' Matt laughed as he gave her a mock bow.

Fluff turned to leave, but Matt called her back and pushed shut his office door. 'My turn to give advice now,' he said. 'Best not to cross Grant. I don't know what he is capable of, but I just can't trust the man.'

Fluff didn't answer straight away. 'I do know exactly what he is capable of. That's the problem.'

Matt was surprised at the contained anger in her face. 'Anything I should know about?'

'No. I'll deal with it, Matt.' Giving him no chance to question her further, Fluff opened the office door. She turned before she left and, in an obvious attempt to lighten the mood, she said, 'Go home to Eppie. I'll be fine.'

Matt had to be content with that, so after a brief word with Old Bill, just to make sure he would call him if anything came up, Matt left.

He decided to go home his favourite way, along the Myton Road and over the bridge into Warwick. Although slightly longer, this route took him past Warwick Castle.

Seeing the Castle standing there so firm and solid after all these years always gave Matt a sense of proportion, no matter what problems he was facing. In his tour-guide years, it was one of his favourite places, very different from the ruins of Kenilworth, but all ages seemed able to enjoy what was on offer. He was dying to show Eppie all around the area, but there had been no chance yet. Resolving to remedy this as soon as the case was over, Matt headed on through Warwick and home.

As he let himself into the flat, the wonderful smell of roast beef drifted out to meet him, and he realised how hungry he was. Eppie was in the kitchen washing dishes and singing along to a CD. She seemed happy and unaffected about Sandi's death, which left Matt puzzled, as he had visions of her still sitting crying. She turned, sensing his presence and came immediately to kiss him, putting her wet, soapy hands around his neck to pull his face down to her level.

'Oh, I'm so very glad you're home. Can you stay? I've cooked just in case,' Eppie indicated the rib roast steaming fresh from the oven, as she tried to wipe the soap from Matt's neck with the tea towel.

'Are you all right? I thought—'

Eppie put the tea towel down. 'At first all I wanted to do was cry. It's too dreadful to think about. Poor Tom and her family. Then I thought, the best thing I could do was feed the man in charge, help him catch Sandi's killer. It's helped block it out for a while.'

Eppie stopped, noticing how tired Matt looked. 'But you can't do that, can you?' Eppie took hold of Matt's hand and led him to his favourite chair. 'Right now you're going to sit there and let me wait on you. Everything is nearly ready. Wine or beer?'

Matt opted for a beer and, taking a deep breath, he sat relaxing for the first time that day. The wonderful smell of a Sunday roast had circulated every corner of the flat and took Matt back to those family dinners at home when he and Megs, his sister, would pester their dad for the first, slightly burnt, cut of the meat.

Living alone he had never bothered with roasts and hardly ever slipped a pork chop or steak under the grill. He was looking forward to this dinner, and his flat seemed like a real home at last.

As Eppie brought him the beer, she put a pile of post at his side. 'Only if you feel up to it; otherwise it will wait, I'm sure.'

Matt looked idly through the top of the pile and, as these were uninteresting, he concentrated instead on his beer and contemplation of the meal to come.

It was after his appetite had been satisfied, and he was sitting congratulating himself on marrying such an excellent cook while waiting for Eppie to bring out the apple crumble that she called from the kitchen.

'What was in that padded envelope? It was such a funny shape, I tried poking it but thought it might burst.'

Matt moved lazily from the table to collect the pile of post that he had left on the little table beside his chair. Selecting the only padded envelope, he slit it open to let the contents fall onto the table just as Eppie was about to place the bubbling apple crumble in the middle.

He stood looking down at the little soldier in complete horror. The wonderful sense of home and comfort was shattered. The evil he was fighting had reached into the very centre of his life. It was here in the midst of his home beside his wife. She wasn't safe here. A thousand questions began firing off in his head.

Eppie gasped at his reaction and almost dropped the crumble but managed to recover and moved forward again.

'Don't touch it', Matt commanded.

Shocked, Eppie took the crumble back into the kitchen and, still wearing the oven gloves, returned to stare from Matt to the little soldier.

'Is it dangerous?' she ventured.

For a moment, Matt was inactive, then he took an evidence bag from his pocket and, hooking the end of his pen through the arm of the model, lifted it carefully into the bag before doing the same for the envelope and placing it into a separate bag. Returning to his training and taking the required action had cleared his mind, and he knew what he had to do. He looked up at Eppie.

'Very dangerous. It means that the vile bastard who killed those girls knows where I live. Probably also that I am married. That puts you in danger. If he is set on getting at me, he'll use any means he can. He wouldn't think twice about harming you, and I want you out of here, now. Go pack a bag.'

For a second, Matt thought she was going to argue as she waved her still gloved hand towards the kitchen and the remains of the meal, but then, after looking up at his grave face, she gave in and, leaving the oven gloves on her chair, she moved towards the bedroom.

Matt already had the phone in his hand, but he pulled her to him as she went past. They clung to each other, and before the phone was answered, Matt managed to whisper, 'Sorry,' and plant a kiss on her forehead.

* * *

Eppie left him as he began giving orders. She was used to travelling light, and it took her only a couple of minutes to pack enough for a few days and to pick up her book before returning to the living room.

Matt was still on the phone, so she left her bag in the hallway and went into the kitchen to put away the rest of the beef and wash the meat pan. The crumble was too hot to go into the fridge, so she placed it in the oven instead. She had no idea when they would be able to return, and somehow she wondered if it would ever feel the same. Eppie had read about how people who had been burgled had found it difficult to go back into their own homes. This must be similar or even worse, for the person who had sent the soldier had murdered Sandi and that other poor girl.

She found herself looking out of the little kitchen window at the cars parked in the road. Was the murderer out there watching? Had he followed her or Matt home? He could be any one of those seemingly normal people she and Sandi had spoken to, tried to help, or joked with. It didn't seem possible that someone who could commit such awful crimes would be able to conceal it so well. She would have thought such depraved wickedness would at least show in the eyes. For the first time, Eppie felt a shudder of fear run through her.

Matt was dealing with this on a twenty-four-hour basis, trying to catch the murderer before he could kill again. The second murder would have already given him a sense of failure, and now he would be worried about her. She was just wondering where they would go, or if she would have to stay somewhere on her own when Matt called.

'Eppie, any chance of staying with Amy or Mo? Failing that it might mean a hotel room with a police guard,' Matt gestured helplessly at the choice.

'I'll ring them,' she replied, moving to get her mobile from a pocket of the packed bag.

Matt nodded and continued his calls, pausing only to open the door to a uniformed officer to whom he handed the two evidence bags.

Eppie could get no answer from Amy, either on her landline or mobile, and vaguely remembered her mentioning something about a holiday to America. Mo answered the phone just as Eppie was thinking of hanging up. She sounded harassed and breathless. In the background, Eppie could hear little Liam crying fretfully.

Mo apologised and explained that Liam had chicken pox and was irritated by it, so she was spending all day and most of the night, putting lotion on the pustules. Wishing Liam a speedy recovery, Eppie hung up after promising to call back for a chat in a few days.

Moving across to Matt, who was still on the phone, she put both arms around him as he opened his free arm to hug her. This was maybe the last time they would be this close until the murderer was caught, and Eppie wanted to imprint the smell and feel of him deep into her memory.

As he finished the call, he put the phone down and held her tight before drawing back to look at her, as if he too wanted to remember every detail of her. A knock on the door broke the spell, but before moving to answer, Matt bent to kiss Eppie, who returned his passion so that only a second knock broke them apart. With a last look into his face, she let Matt answer the door.

This time it was Sam, and Matt led him into the room. 'Sam is going to take you to the station. It will be easier to take you from there to where you will be safe.'

'In case anyone is following,' she surmised.

'Yes.'

He hadn't elaborated, and Eppie guessed he didn't want to spell out the dangers ahead.

'Any luck with Amy or Mo?' he said in a lighter tone.

Eppie shook her head, knowing that this left no option but a cold hotel room with a series of unknown police officers to babysit her. As she picked up her bag, she comforted herself that it wouldn't be for long and that she could make friends with some of Matt's colleagues and maybe even finish her book.

Pausing only to give a brief final hug to Matt, she followed Sam down the back stairs to where an unmarked police car with a plain-clothed driver was waiting.

CHAPTER 40

Clive lay beside Ben, trying to find the right words to tell him about his wonderful secret. Then the phone rang. Ben shifted his sleepy head and gave a little moan of annoyance, reaching out his arm to keep Clive beside him. Clive heard the answer phone kick in and was content to leave it.

However, it had spoiled his peace. Clive received few calls, so the likelihood was that it would be Margaret. What if Mother was returning early? It would be just like her to ruin everything. This would be a ploy for her and Margaret to get a look at his supposed bride.

He had no intention of introducing Ben to the family or of enduring their endless reproaches. Not that he could ever tell them the full extent of their friendship. This love was his alone.

Ben sighed and sat up.

'You'd better get that. You know you want to.'

He was right. Clive needed to know if Mother and Margaret were on their way.

'Sorry. Mother might be ill or something.' He slipped on his dressing gown and went downstairs.

It was as he thought. Mother was feeling tired after being out so late last night, and Margaret was returning her home. He cursed them both and returned upstairs to alert Ben.

He was already out of bed and Clive stood in the doorway for a moment looking at him as he reached for his clothes.

'Momma is on her way. Right?'

Clive nodded as he moved across to him, needing to hold him one more time. Their kiss reawakened the desire in both of them, but it was Ben who pulled away first.

'Look, I'm out of here. Too soon to be playing happy families. OK?'

'Yes, of course.'

'We'll do this again soon. I promise.'

'And I'll see you at work.'

'Sure.'

Clive had to be content with that and, within five minutes, Ben was gone, leaving him with fifteen minutes to have a shower and tidy up. By the time Mother arrived, he was sitting in the living room calmly doing the crossword.

As they came in, he could see Mother's sharp little eyes move around the room, seeking any evidence of his guest. Margaret even grinned at him as if there was some conspiracy between them.

'Sorry. I did my best, but you know what she is like.'

'I understand. Thanks.'

'I was a little worried about her pain tablets too. We turned her bag out and couldn't find them.'

He knew exactly where the tablets were, having removed them from her bag himself at dinner last night. It had only taken a moment to roll them under the radiator next to their table. He had insisted they sit there out of consideration for Mother who, he explained, felt the cold.

After making an extensive pretend search, Clive came up with the suggestion that maybe she lost them while they were at the spa last night. Mother thought it unlikely, but he insisted on ringing in case they had been handed in.

For this sort of occasion, his persona of a caring son really paid off, and his worried and concerned approach instituted a search on the site by several staff, one of whom soon discovered the little bottle just where he had placed it. Clive gallantly insisted on driving out there to collect it.

He needed to time his visit to coincide with the arrival for work of the one he had chosen. She was to be the centrepiece of his next communication, and he needed to know what car she drove and from which direction she came.

After Margaret left, he forced himself to listen to Mother twitter on about Emily's latest achievements, none of which interested him in the slightest. It felt as if Mother, here in his house, where Ben had been just an hour before, defiled the memory. He found he couldn't bear to be there with her, so after fixing her a light tea, he headed out for the spa, going by way of the DI's flat.

The small block of flats seemed to be on fire as the windows caught the rays of the late afternoon sun. He drove slowly, glancing at what he guessed would be DI Turrell's windows. There was no sign of life but then the little soldier must have started his rout by now. His only disappointment was not being there when the DI opened his gift. Clive tried to imagine the shock on his face while consoling himself that it was nothing compared to his plans for Tuesday. He had never believed in not hitting a man when he was down; instead, he found it the best time—when you have the advantage.

Mika was her name, and he guessed she would have some Oriental blood that should make her easy to spot. Clive had chosen her from the rota when he had booked the masseuse for Mother. She was new and therefore wouldn't know him at all. Plus, she worked from six to nine p.m., Friday until Tuesday, which was perfect for his purpose.

As he waited in the guest's car park, he went through his plans again. Clive's main worry was that public outcry would cause the health spa to be closed. That granite like superintendent was already calling for such action. After Clive's next endeavour, he would probably have his way.

He thought with a shock that he would have to find a new field of operation and ran over the possibilities. Warwick University was his favourite. There would be ample raw material there, and he began to be quite excited at the opportunities and had to pull himself back to concentrate on the immediate plan.

Precisely at five-forty-five, a black and white Mini drove through the car park and made its way to the staff parking lot beyond. It was darker there and he had already checked out that the CCTV cameras didn't extend to the area.

Clive waited thirty seconds before he got out of his car to follow her into the club. No one else had arrived, so this had to be her. She was small and slim, carrying herself with an easy grace. He made sure he was right behind her and heard the receptionist greet her by name.

He could feel his body tensing, as if preparing for war, excited and scared all at the same time. He wanted to do it now, tonight. His fingers craved to go around a warm neck, to squeeze and squeeze harder until the eyes glazed over and the body fell limply into his arms to become the basic material for his work. Forcing himself to concentrate, he managed to hold down his mounting excitement. He couldn't afford to make the slightest mistake but had to hold himself in check until Tuesday. Then he would be making national headlines again, maybe even international.

Clive hoped Mika used these last two nights well, since they would be her last.

CHAPTER 41

Before Matt left the flat, he glanced around, trying to recall the comfortable, happy feeling of home he had been experiencing with Eppie just an hour earlier. They seemed to be past their argument of the other day, and he knew their marriage was right and they would make it work.

He wished he had the bastard who had spoilt it all in front of him. But whoever delivered the model soldier had far greater crimes to answer for, and it was his job to catch him. Making a vow to himself that he would do just that, he locked the door and went to his car. As he drew out of the parking lot, the patrol car across the street pulled in behind him. Matt felt this was a bit over the top but McRay had insisted.

As soon as he entered the office, he had the sense that something wasn't right. Sam seemed to be hovering, almost waiting for Matt to step through the door.

'Guv,' he said hesitantly. 'There's someone here.'

Matt continued to stride forward with Sam walking backwards in front of him, physically trying to slow him down. When this failed, he put a hand on Matt's arm.

'Someone from division.' Sam was apologetic as he nodded towards McRay's office.

Through the frosted glass, Matt could see the back of a woman wearing a dark suit. She was standing next to McRay and another more burly figure that he guessed belonged to Professor Meredith.

'Thanks, Sam,' he said, moving past Sam towards the office. He had half expected this. McRay would consider him personally involved and therefore liable to compromise the investigation. Matt had hoped he would give him the benefit of the doubt but he may have received orders from above.

McRay saw him walking towards the office and opened the door to usher him inside. 'Matt, come in. This is DI Hadden from division,' he said indicating the woman. 'You will realise that we have no option but to take the case away from you, given what has happened.'

Matt turned towards the woman, automatically holding out his hand. He tried to keep the shock from his face as she returned the brief handshake, giving no indication that they had ever met before.

There was little trace of the fun-loving Jenny from nine years ago. She had retained her trim figure but her face now held lines of hardness. Even now, it was difficult for a woman to make her way in the police force, and he guessed she had had to make some hard decisions along the way.

McRay continued, 'And Professor Meredith kindly offered to come to help us shed light on what is happening. Perhaps you would all like to take a seat.' McRay waved to the couch and chairs opposite, and Matt couldn't help thinking of the night he had slept there. It seemed a long time ago.

With an effort, Matt brought his mind back to the present and prepared himself to listen to one of the professor's rambling lectures. He was surprised that the professor seemed genuinely concerned for his and Eppie's safety, pointing out the possible motives for the murderer sending one of his props to Matt's home address.

'This clearly shows that he sees you as his personal adversary, Inspector.'

'Why did he send it to the inspector's home?' Jenny asked.

'I would suspect that he was striking where the inspector is the most vulnerable, at his family.'

It was only a flicker of the eyes, but Matt was sure that McRay hadn't yet fully advised Jenny of all the details, including the fact that he was married and that Eppie was at risk.

She concealed it well. 'And where are the family now?' was all she asked.

McRay replied. 'We have had to compromise, given the cost of maintaining around-the-clock watch on a hotel room and have placed Mrs. Turrell with one of our female officers. It is not the ideal solution, I agree, but the best we could do at short notice.'

Jenny nodded in agreement. 'So this killer is a risk taker. Does he want to be caught, Professor? He leaves items with the victim, any one of which could lead us back to him, and now he chooses to add to that risk by singling out Inspector Turrell?'

'There may be a deeply buried element of that. However, I believe he is showing us how clever he is, taunting us. He also wants us to feel his pain, so we can be aware of why he has set out on this course.'

Jenny nodded before continuing. 'So why Inspector Turrell? Is it just because he is—was—in charge?'

Matt noted how she had corrected herself, and the truth hit home. He had held all the threads in his hands, but now he was to be left stranded and redundant. He forced himself to listen to the professor.

'Well, I would suspect that the inspector reminds the murderer of someone in his past, someone he did not get on with or with whom he feels he has a score to settle. One thing is for certain, he is a clever, cunning individual and should not be underestimated. I would recommend the inspector should also have protection.'

Matt felt quite touched that the professor should think about his safety, even though he was sure he could handle himself against the killer and would relish the chance to come face to face with him.

'We'll take good care of him,' McRay answered, as the professor stood to leave. 'Don't you worry.'

Jenny was still reading the case notes but looked up as the professor was about to move away. 'Just one more question, Professor?'

He nodded.

'Why a model soldier? He is dressing these women up to look like young girls at a party, so it hardly seems to fit, does it?'

The professor sat down opposite Jenny and leant forward. 'Exactly. I find this most interesting. I don't think the little fellows ever represented a form of play for him, although they probably do come from his childhood. He seems to have attached some sort of hate to them, so I would suspect they belonged to someone in authority over him, like a father or grandfather.'

'And now someone like DI Turrell?' Jenny asked.

'Well, yes, like DI Turrell,' the professor nodded.

'So, it follows that the murderer must have met DI Turrell, either because of this case or before?'

There was silence in the room, as they all digested the implications of this. McRay spoke first. 'We'll need to go over everyone we've already interviewed. Matt think of your old cases. Anyone with a grudge.'

Matt didn't want to waste his time going through old case notes. In his experience, there would always be some perp who resented being stopped in his career. He'd had the same amount of threats as any other DI who was doing a good job. But he was now side lined, and it was all in Jenny's hands, now, so he gave a reluctant, 'Yes, Sir.'

'Thank you for coming, Professor.' McRay moved to open the door.

Jenny half rose and shook hands. The professor stood ready to leave.

Matt stood and thanked him too, and this time the feeling was genuine. Jenny had returned her attention to looking through the main notes of the case. Matt glanced at her profile, thinking that she was still attractive, except for a certain coldness. She looked up at him, as if she was aware of his scrutiny, and he went to sit beside her, deciding to play along with her obvious need to keep their past affair secret. There would be time enough later to catch up with old times. Stopping this murderer was more important.

She was efficient, and Matt admired her thoroughness as she identified the main points. He paused in his run-through of the leads they were following, and she used the opportunity to speak to McRay.

'I would like Inspector Turrell to continue to work with me on this case, Chief Inspector. The team have been working well, and it would be a shame to upset that. And, once I get up to speed, if our murderer still sees the inspector as a personal target, well maybe we could use that to our advantage.'

McRay glanced at Matt, gauging his reaction to this suggestion. Matt nodded his agreement, glad to still be of some use. Although he did wonder what Jenny had in mind when she considered using him to catch the killer. He thought he would let that one pass for the moment. He supposed he would have to clear out his office, but if it were just for this one case, it was going to be a nuisance. Here was another of his quiet thinking places gone. He had always been able to alternate between home and office to ponder any case, but now both options were compromised.

'There are one or two things I would like to set in motion before the morning briefing, Chief Inspector,' Jenny said.

McRay nodded as Jenny continued. Matt recognised the well-cultivated tone of authority in her voice. Like him, she had learnt of the need to take full control.

'I would like all those interviewed after the first murder to be cross referenced with those who have been or will be interviewed after this second murder. Many will be staff, I know, but it would be useful to highlight those who were at the health spa when both murders took place.'

Matt could see her reasoning but wondered if they had the resources. The hard-working backup team, seconded from uniform, were already working flat out.

Jenny didn't give Matt or McRay any chance to argue. 'I will need the report on Miss Tomlinson's phone call to…' She paused to check the papers. 'A Mr Graham, as soon as it is analysed.'

'I'm…we're…hoping to have that back by the morning,' Matt paused, uncertain how to address her. McRay stepped in.

'The interviews are collated and checked by DI Grant who will be back in tomorrow,' McRay explained.

Matt was looking at Jenny when McRay mentioned DI Grant. Although she covered it pretty well, he watched her face pale, together with a slight tightening of the jaw. So she and Grant had a history, and Matt would guess that it wasn't a pleasant one. Jenny as well as Fluff. So the man preyed on women. He made a note to watch him.

Her demands for the moment satisfied, Matt suggested he show her the way to his office. Jenny rose and followed him, after loading him up with several files. As soon as they were inside Matt's office, Jenny spoke.

'So, a wife, ah?'

Matt had expected that she would want to keep up the pretence that they did not know each other and was shocked at this sudden change. 'Yes, of nearly three weeks.'

'Oh, bad luck getting this lot so soon into wedded bliss,' she sympathised.

'Yes, it's not easy,' Matt confirmed, while opening the top drawer of his desk and beginning to pull out all files there.

Still standing beside the desk, Jenny seemed to hesitate. 'Look, stop. I think it is silly you moving everything. How about if we shove a small desk or a table in here? That would do for me. After all, I'm not going to be here forever, am I?'

She turned and walked back into the main office. Matt straightened. He felt a bit bewildered by her sudden change from the cold, in-charge DI Hadden, to someone resembling the Jenny he had known before. As he followed her, he supposed it was how she had survived. He would need to be a buffer between her and the team. For a start, it would be a good idea to find out what he should call her.

Jenny had pounced on a small table, which was piled high with box files. Signalling Sam to help her, she started to put the boxes onto the floor. Matt could see that Sam looked sulky and reluctant to help, so he moved forward to encourage him. With the table cleared, he and Sam carried it into the office, and under Jenny's directions, they placed it opposite Matt's.

'OK, Guv?' Sam asked, emphasising the *Guv* and clearly stating his loyalty to Matt.

'Yes. Thanks,' Matt replied, moving Sam towards the door, while trying to signal for him to calm down. 'And for now, I'm not your Guv,' he said close to Sam's ear as he pushed him through the door and closed it behind him. He turned to face Jenny. 'So, what should I call you?'

'In here "Jenny" and out there...well, we had better not use "Guv," had we?' she said, nodding towards Sam. 'How about "Ma'am" just for out there in front of the troops?'

'Sam's a good sergeant.'

'I'm sure he is,' she said dismissively, busy arranging the files in order on her desk. 'Let's see the phone call from the victim...'

'Miss Sandi Tomlinson,' Matt couldn't help interjecting.

Jenny favoured him with a cold stare, which told him not to interfere when she was speaking. 'To her boyfriend, Tom Graham,' she continued.

Remembering Tom's grief, Matt wanted to interrupt her again and say that Tom was Sandi's fiancé and that they had been planning their wedding for the last six months, and he wasn't just a boyfriend but that Tom and Sandi were fully committed to each other. As Jenny continued, he decided against it.

'Time of murder?'

'She had been there all night. Slim thinks probably between nine and midnight. Most likely the earlier. He'll give us more in the morning.'

'Time of phone call?'

'Eight forty seven.'

'So we can assume that she made the call to Mr Graham, and almost straight away became victim number two. What time did her shift finish?'

'Ten. She sometimes left early, if Harry, the night porter, had arrived. However, he said she had never left without asking him first.'

'And he didn't see her?'

Matt nodded. It was good to go over the details of the case with someone from the outside, someone with a new eye who might spot something they had missed.

Jenny snapped the file shut and stood up. 'We need that phone call analysed. You took down a transcript before sending it to audio, I take it?' she demanded.

'Sam did, but it's not typed up yet.'

'Right, tell him I need that now. I'll get hold of the sound guys.'

Matt left her dialling the switchboard. He didn't stop to tell her that he had already checked, and Nick Forest, the audio expert, wasn't due in until tomorrow, having only arrived back from a holiday in America early this morning. Sam, who shouldn't even be here, was talking to Old Bill. He turned as Matt approached.

'How is it going, Matt? If you want me to deck her I will.' Sam punched the air in an imitation of a boxer.

'No, it's good,' he said, trying for a lightness he didn't really feel. 'Let's work with her; otherwise, we'll just be giving the murderer more chances.'

'OK, if you say so.'

Matt knew the rest of the team would follow Sam and fall into place. 'Yes, I do. Thanks,' he replied, giving Sam's shoulder a pat. 'Right now, I need the transcript of Sandi's phone call to Tom.'

Sam turned to his jacket, which was over the back of his chair, to extract his notebook. 'This is a bit rough I'm afraid,' he said, flipping through the book until he came to the relevant page. We both listened to it. Nothing there, except for that squeaky sound, which could have been anything. So what does she think she is going to find?'

'She's trying to get Nick to come in tonight.'

Sam laughed. 'Well good luck to her there.'

Matt wasn't going to stay and argue. 'In the meantime, can you type that up for me? Please,' he added, seeing Sam baulk at the idea. He was relieved when Sam nodded and sat down at his computer. 'Thanks,' he said, heading back to his office.

As he opened the door, Jenny was in the middle of a phone call. Her tone was strident.

'And I want you to imagine turning on your television tomorrow morning to hear there is another victim. If that happens, you will know that it was all down to you. Nevertheless, if you think it is more important to sit there with your feet up, then you get on with it.' Jenny slammed the phone down. 'Poncy bloody idiot.'

Matt thought she was being somewhat unfair and was about to say so when she turned on him.

'As soon as those names are compiled in the morning, I want them interviewed.'

Matt said nothing, still getting used to having orders barked at him. He hoped this wasn't how he sounded.

Jenny looked up, wondering why he hadn't acquiesced to her plan.

'Understand?'

'Yes, Ma'am.' It was a minefield, trying to figure out which Jenny was speaking, the friendly version or the bossy harridan, and Matt knew he would have to tread carefully until this case was over.

CHAPTER 42

Eppie was surprised when the unmarked police car stopped at a substantial looking older house, overlooking the ruined Abbey in Kenilworth. The house looked too big for one person.

The driver, a plain clothed policeman, lifted a hand to stop Eppie opening the passenger door, and they waited as another car came alongside them. Eppie found she was almost holding her breath until the car had gone past. Two cheeky youngsters were fighting in the back seat and the driver was a harassed looking young mother.

With a final look around, the man signalled her to go, and Eppie scrambled out pausing only to say thank you. The policeman seemed annoyed at this and indicated for her to go quickly up the pathway.

Eppie felt like a schoolgirl but did as she was told. As she approached the front door, it opened and the woman known as Fluff ushered her in. Inside the hallway it was dim, but as her eyes became accustomed to the lack of light, Eppie noticed the wonderful pattern of what must be the original flagstones.

Fluff led the way upstairs to the first floor, turning right at the top of the stairs towards the front of the house. It was much lighter here, and the landing was wide and carpeted. Eppie guessed the house was divided into flats. Fluff opened a white door marked 'Four' and stepped aside for Eppie to enter.

Eppie was struck by the amount of light that flooded into the room from the street lamps. Combined with the light-coloured sofas and the small table lamps, it gave the room a glowing, cheerful feeling. Eppie moved instinctively to look out of the large bay widow.

'Sorry, but it will be best if you stay away from the windows,' Fluff said, moving beside her to close the floor to ceiling curtains.

Eppie stepped back. 'Oh, I didn't think.' She realised with a shock how serious this was. How long would she have to stay here? And when would she see Matt? Suppose they never caught the murderer? She didn't want to be here with a strange woman who knew more about her husband than she did.

'I'll show you your room and then put the kettle on.'

Eppie guessed she was trying to lighten the situation. 'Thanks. I didn't bring much, so it won't take me long to unpack. Sorry to be fostered on you like this.'

'Part of the job,' Fluff said.

From the way she said it, Eppie thought it sounded as if it was the very last thing she wanted. She couldn't think of anything to say to make the situation easier, so she followed meekly along behind her.

'Bathroom,' Fluff indicated, pushing open the door to a large modern bathroom, white and gleaming, complete with bath and shower. 'And here is your room.'

Eppie moved past Fluff into the room. This room was light, too, but the window was much smaller. The room had the same basic colours of the living room except for the bedspread, which was of a multi-coloured patchwork design that added a comfortable cheerfulness to the room. As she put her bag on the bed, Eppie knew she could survive happily here and turned to thank Fluff, only to find she had gone.

As she unpacked, Eppie wondered what she was supposed to call Fluff, as that was her nickname at work. As she put a few things away, she began a guessing game in her head as to what Fluff's real name was.

'Tea or coffee?' Fluff called from the kitchen.

Instead of calling back, Eppie made her way to the kitchen. Now this was more like it. Although it was modern, the room had a warm homey feeling that Eppie had been longing for. It was very spacious after Matt's tiny flat, and there was even room for a wooden table with four chairs.

The heart of the house, Eppie thought, remembering those days at her Gran's when she had made her first biscuits with little, somewhat grubby, hands and waited as the smell wafted through the kitchen for them to be taken from the oven. She had been so proud as Granddad, who said he was the official taster, had taken the first one and declared that they were the best biscuits he had ever eaten.

As if reading her mind, Fluff produced a tin of biscuits and placed it in the centre of the table. 'Not homemade I'm afraid. Have a seat. Did you say tea?'

'Yes, please. I love your kitchen—the whole flat. Matt's...ours is so small.' Eppie had the feeling that she was being disloyal to Matt but Fluff seemed to understand.

'They don't need the space we do,' she said, handing Eppie a mug of tea.

As Eppie sipped, Fluff pushed the biscuit tin towards her.

'Help yourself. They're kept in that cupboard. Below, tea and coffee and then cereals,' Fluff pointed to the right. 'Have a potter through and you'll soon find where everything is.'

'You won't be here?' Eppie couldn't stop herself asking.

'I'll be working as normal, but you will be fine,' she added. 'Don't answer the door to anyone—or the phone. Downstairs left, Jake. Some sort of writer; you'll probably never see him. Right, lovely Mary. Used to be a nurse. She'd do anything for you. But remember she is eighty. Opposite, Tilly and Don, both work in a bank. Haven't been here long and keep themselves to themselves.'

'It's a beautiful place to live.'

'We'll call you by mobile if we need to. Stay in and mind the windows. A patrol will go past every hour, and if you are worried just call the station.'

'Oh, I just thought—'

'Super's just taking precautions, as you're one of our own.'

Eppie had never thought that by marrying Matt she would gain an adoptive family, and at first it seemed quite nice, but then, thinking about it, somewhat controlling as she had had no say in any of the arrangements. She felt a bit like a parcel that was being passed around. She had a thousand questions but decided to keep the conversation light. 'Have you had to babysit anyone before?'

Fluff put down her mug and shook her head. 'Not at home, only a hotel and once at a safe house.'

'Do you think it will take long?'

'Impossible to say. This murderer is clever. It may take a while before he slips up. Our only hope is if he begins to think he is omniscient. That no one can catch him. That will be our chance.'

Eppie felt daunted. In the rush, she had never really thought that she would be away for long. There was the apple crumble waiting in the oven. She must remind Matt it was there. Then she realised how silly she was being. Matt had far more important things to worry about. She told herself she would have to get on with it, make sure that she didn't add to his burden. 'Please call me "Eppie," and what should I call you? "Fluff" is for work isn't it?'

Fluff laughed. 'Yes. My name is Jane. All my friends outside of work call me that.'

Eppie felt privileged to be included in the friend's group and started to relax. It wouldn't be so bad and she and Fluff—Jane— could get to know each other a lot better. Maybe then she wouldn't feel so separate and shut off from Matt's work life.

'Have you eaten?'

The thought of the lovely meal she had prepared made Eppie feel sad. 'Yes, thanks. We were in the middle of roast beef dinner when all this kicked off.'

'Hey, stop. You are making me hungry just thinking about it.'

'Haven't you eaten?'

Fluff grimaced. 'Was on for a promise of pasta and a bottle of wine. But it all hinged on how the case was going anyway.'

'I've really messed up your evening, haven't I?'

'Not really. Think I would have been asleep in five minutes to tell the truth.'

'Tell him it was my fault.'

'*Her*,' Fluff emphasised.

For a moment Eppie wondered if she had heard right. 'Oh I see. Well she will probably be more understanding.'

'Yes. She'll be fine.'

There was quiet for a moment. Eppie realised this meant Fluff wasn't a threat to her and Matt. She had been silly to think about it. She broke the silence. 'You'll need something to eat.'

'Don't worry. I'll have a slice of toast or something.'

'I've messed up your date, so let me throw something together while you relax and have a shower. It's the least I can do.'

'You really enjoy this cooking lark don't you?'

'Yes. Yes, I think I do. Wasn't sure at first, but I like it.'

'The ideal wife. You will be giving the rest of us a bad name,' Fluff laughed.

'Hardly. And I'm sure Matt wouldn't agree.'

'Not upsetting him already are you?'

'He's a bit old fashioned I suppose.'

'Aren't they all? What they really want is a replacement mother.'

'I hope not,' said Eppie, appalled at the thought.

Fluff laughed at the face Eppie was pulling before saying, 'If you're sure, think I might grab that shower.'

While Fluff was showering, Eppie opened every drawer in the kitchen. It was well equipped but needed stocking up on grocery items. She had a hard time deciding what to prepare but in the end opted for simple pasta with a sauce made from limp mushrooms and squashy tomatoes, topped with grated cheddar from which she had scraped off the mould. By the time Fluff joined her, the meal was waiting and smelt really appetising.

'Now I could get used to this,' Fluff said, as she sat down at the kitchen table.

It wasn't much later that Eppie opted for turning in. Jane was on the phone to her partner and Eppie felt a pang of guilt for upsetting their plans. As she got ready for bed, she realised how tired she was. All the tension of the day was taking its toll.

Placing her mobile on the bedside table, she lay wondering if she should call Matt but decided against it as he could still be working. Then, just as she was drifting into a troubled sleep, the phone rang and she was talking to Matt. His voice sounded tired, but lightened as they exchanged brief words of love.

CHAPTER 43

The flat seemed darker and emptier than ever before. Matt wandered from room to room, as if hoping to find Eppie, but also knowing that he needed to check to see if it was safe. Not that this type of murderer was going to put himself face-to-face with anyone who would be a match for him, just unsuspecting young women. Was McRay right? Did this man know him? His first thought was that it must be something to do with Gracie, but he soon ruled this out. Gracie's Mother had died just two years after her daughter, and her father had remarried. So it must be something to do with this case. Someone they had interviewed already. They had interviewed so many people, and he began reviewing them all in his head while moving through the flat.

After checking everywhere, he went into the kitchen. The faint aroma of apple brought back vivid memories of what had happened earlier. Matt opened the oven and took the crumble out. Always his favourite, it was still slightly warm and made him feel close to Eppie.

He had arrived home many times late at night, but never before had it felt as if there was something missing—a warmth and loving. Three weeks living with Eppie, and she had only been gone a few hours, leaving him feeling lost and lonely.

Matt thought again of Tom Graham and wondered if he was alone tonight. He and Sandi would never be together again, never have their wedding or the chance of a life together.

He had the sudden impulse to call Eppie, to hear her voice. She sounded sleepy.

'I didn't wake you, did I?'

'No. Just dozing. It's hard in a strange bed. Besides, I miss you.'

'Me too. I'm just about to tuck into the crumble. Made me think of you,' Matt said wistfully.

'So it's all cupboard love then?'

'Damn. You've sussed me out. Fluff looking after you?'

'Yes. I like her,' Eppie said, her voice sounding light.

'That's not hard.'

'It is when she works with your husband. How about you? Where are you?'

'At home.'

'Is that safe?'

'Yes,' Matt assured her. 'Believe me, this sort of pervert wouldn't want to face me, not unless he was backed into a corner.'

'I hope you're right. Please take care, Matt.'

'You too. Do everything Fluff says.'

'Will do. Love you.'

'Sleep well, Love.'

It was a brief call, but it made him feel better. When it was over, he loaded a dish with apple crumble and took it into the living room. Seated in his chair, he enjoyed the crumble and then sat back to let the details of the case wash over him, together with relaxing tiredness. In this half-asleep state, he began thinking of Sandi's last phone call to Tom. Beyond the pathetic last words, was there anything there that would help him to catch her murderer?

As he drifted into a half sleep he began thinking of the squeak in the background and began running through all things he could remember that squeaked. Doors squeaked, cars sometimes developed an annoying squeak, pens, chalk on blackboards, and the lid of the photocopier. He had a bike once that squeaked, until his Granddad had showed him how to use an oilcan. A bike, now that might be it.

Matt sat upright. Could the murderer have come and gone by bike? Excited by the idea, Matt felt full of energy. He needed to do something now. Jumping to his feet, he reached for the phone. If Harry was on duty tonight, he would go and see him. Harry could tell him if any of the staff came or went by bike around that time of night.

Matt rang Harry, who said of course he could come round, he would be glad of the company. The policemen in the patrol car circling the grounds were not very talkative, although Harry had offered them a coffee.

Matt drove fast, needing to put on the blue light only in the built-up areas to ease his way through the few night owls. He drove past the dark bulk of Kenilworth Castle with its ruined towers reaching high into the night sky.

Harry was waiting to unlock as Matt drew up. He swung back the double doors and led Matt to the comfortable chairs near the desk, where two cups of coffee waited. Matt took a grateful sip. 'Thanks, Harry. I needed that.'

'It's been a long, sad day, Sir. She was a lovely girl. I don't know who would want to do that.' Harry shook his head.

'Harry, do many of the staff come to work by bike?' Matt broke in before Harry could get into reminisces about Sandi. It seemed a little hard, but he had come for a reason.

'Why, yes. I do myself, always have. Keeps me fit, it does,' he said proudly. 'Is that important, Sir?'

'Well, it could be. Does your bike have a squeak, Harry?'

'I should think not. I keep all my equipment in good order. Why my old sergeant would have me up on a charge…that he would. Here, you can see for yourself.' Harry rose and moved to open the folding door of a room marked 'Luggage Room' to the left of Reception.

Matt could see that it was empty, except for a bike and what looked like an old wheelchair in the far corner. Harry paraded his bike before Matt.

'There you go. Perfect working order. Wouldn't have it any other way.'

Before Harry could get even more indignant, Matt clarified his thinking. 'No one is saying it was yours, Harry. Sandi called her fiancée just before she was killed. In the background we can just about make out a squeak. Now, if we could find out what made that squeak, it could lead us to whoever murdered Sandi.'

'That's what I want right enough.'

'So who else comes to work by bike?'

Harry wheeled his bike back into the luggage room and closed the doors before answering. 'Fred. Over in maintenance. But he'll only do one week of nights out of five, and there's no way I'd let him bring his bike in here, that's for sure. Then there was one of the early morning chefs. Used to have to tell him off for whistling. Guests come here for a rest not to be woken up by his flaming racket.'

'And the day staff?'

'There'll be quite a few of them, from the village, but I don't see most of them, as I'm off home and straight to bed.' Harry had a sudden thought. 'There're the bikes for the guests. They are here all the time.'

'Where are they kept, Harry?' Matt began to feel excited.

'By the duck pond, in a special shelter. Locked up tighter than the CO's wife.'

'Can I see them?'

'Well you can look from the small studio, but I can't take you out there. All the alarms are on now. Besides, you couldn't even move them an inch, not with the steel bar running through to keep em safe. Best wait till morning.'

Matt realised the sense in what Harry was saying but wondered if they had the luxury of waiting. Still, he couldn't really go clomping around the grounds disturbing the remaining guests, those who had decided to be brave and chance their visit against the murderer striking again. Thanking Harry for his time, he gave him his card and said he would probably see him in the morning.

* * *

The double bed offered no comfort without Eppie, and Matt tossed and turned all night. By the time morning came, he was glad to be up and eager to get to work. The sooner the murderer was caught, the sooner he would have his Eppie back.

CHAPTER 44

It was early when Matt arrived, and only a few of the overnight team remained in CID. He was glad he was still working from his office and silently thanked Jenny for being so accommodating. She was already hard at work but looked up as he entered.

'Morning, Ma'am,' Matt couldn't help teasing her. Her mind was on the job, and she didn't acknowledge the joke. 'Have you been here all night?'

'More or less. Got the audio jerk to come in early so thought I had better be here too.'

Matt felt empathy with Nick in being bullied by this women, who one minute seemed to be the old Jenny and the next a cross between Margaret Thatcher and Attila the Hun. But she did look tired, and Matt could see how she had acquired those hard lines. Any good detectives pushed themselves hard during a case, and he wondered if his face also bore the brunt of the strain.

'Did Nick come up with anything?' Matt was wondering how to tell her that he went to see Harry last night.

'As a starter, he thinks the noise probably came from a wheeled vehicle, but he is still working on it.'

'Huh.'

She looked up abruptly and waited for him to continue.

'I was thinking about a bike I had, as a kid. I kept riding it through every puddle I could find and it developed a squeak.'

Jenny was giving him the 'get on with it' look. 'I kept thinking about it. Couldn't sleep so went to see Harry, the night porter.'

'And?'

Matt liked her directness. 'He and one of the night maintenance men come in by bike. Several of the day staff too. No squeak on Harry's. Maintenance works a rota so they do one week of nights out of every five. There are also bikes for the use of guests. They were under lock and key for the night.'

'Well done. Except,' she paused, looking up at him before turning away and continuing. 'Don't forget that this killer is targeting you, Matt. I'd prefer it if you had another member of the team with you from now on.'

'I would have relished meeting this bastard.'

'Thought you were more the cerebral type, Matt. Marriage made you go all macho?'

He decided to ignore her dig. 'I'd like to check the rest of the bikes out this morning.'

'We can get one of the foot soldiers to do that. I have been having a look at these interviews Grant was analysing.' She reached forward to bring up a screen on the computer.

Matt wondered what Grant would say when he realised she had picked up his work midstream. Whatever their history, she wasn't going to pussyfoot around him.

'These people were at the scene of both murders. I want them all interviewed again. Today,' she added, as Matt picked up the printout. 'Twenty-nine names, twenty-five of them are staff. So one team at spa and one to chase up the other four.'

'We still haven't finished all the interviews at the spa.' Matt hesitated, thinking of a diplomatic way to say he didn't think that was the best way forward. Jenny sensed his unease.

'Say it,' she commanded, sitting back in her chair and looking up at him.

'If we had the manpower, I'd agree with this plan, but it does mean taking some of the team away from working on other leads. Could I make a suggestion?'

She nodded.

'We already have a team on site, catching up with those people we didn't interview yesterday. Could we add these names to their list?'

'OK. But put these people at the top of the list. You and DC Meadows can hit the other four. And I'll add any more that come up during the day.'

Matt thought about arguing, making his case for some time for revision of the evidence and catching up with reports, but realised that was her job now, and he didn't have a leg to stand on. He nodded and turned to leave the room when she spoke again.

'We'll have the briefing first.' Matt opened the door for her and she led the way to stand in front of the incident board.

The chatter stopped as everyone turned towards her. Matt knew what it was like standing there in front of the team with everyone expecting you to be more intelligent, to lead, and show them the way. He had tried to make them realise that the DI's job was only a small part of the whole, that it was everyone adding his or her skills together that made the difference. All were of equal value. She hadn't asked him to introduce her but waited confidently for their full attention.

'Thank you. You probably all know by now that the murderer has targeted DI Turrell and he and his wife are at risk. Therefore, I am taking over this enquiry. My name is DI Hadden.'

'What about DI Turrell?' Sam called out.

'DI Turrell will remain working on the case.'

Matt detected a small ripple of relief run through the room. It was nice to know that he had good support within the team, but the main thing now was catching the killer. He hoped Jenny would be able to harness the team's different talents to full advantage and that she wouldn't use too much of the harsh bullying he had heard last night.

She got straight down to business. 'I have spoken to the pathologist who confirms that death was between eight p.m. and midnight last night and that the MO looks exactly the same as for the previous victim. He will give us more later. We have also received the preliminary audio report on the phone call made from the victim to her boyfriend at twenty-forty-seven hours on Sunday. It is believed the sound heard in the background is most likely from a wheeled object, such as a bike.'

Matt watched her as she ran the briefing effortlessly. It was strange to stand back, to watch and digest the information in another way. He didn't have to allocate tasks, decide where the effort should go.

He felt himself tense involuntarily as Grant ambled in from the staff room with a mug of coffee, late as usual. Jenny waited as he stopped dead, looking from Matt to Jenny in shock. Then he shook his head as if bemused.

'I have taken the work you were doing on the interviews, DI Grant,' Jenny informed him as he reached his desk.

Grant put down his mug and looked up at her. 'That's all right, Sir,' he replied emphasising the *Sir*.

Matt moved a step closer to Jenny who seemed to have frozen.

Grant pretended to realise his mistake and drawled. 'Oh, sorry. How should I address you, DI Hadden?'

Jenny recovered and snapped. 'DI Hadden will do fine, thank you.'

Whatever secrets their past held, it was obvious that it had affected Jenny badly. Matt watched as Grant sat down, shrugging his shoulders and grinning at those closest to him. The man acted as if he had won that round. Matt would have liked to know what he held over Jenny; that way he could forestall trouble, but it would be best if she felt able to come to him, and he resolved not to push her at this point.

He would have liked to work with Grant today, so he could keep an eye on him, but Jenny had decided Grant should head up the team at the spa with Sam. Sam would go to the Post Mortem on Sandi when Slim rang. That left him with Fluff.

At least Fluff would be able to fill him in on how Eppie was really coping. She had seemed cheerful on the phone, but Matt guessed that was because she didn't want to add to his worries.

As Matt followed Fluff out of the room, they passed Grant's desk. Grant smirked at Fluff.

'You'll be all right now. Be putting in for your sergeant's exam I suppose?' Grant sneered.

'And why would that be any of your business?' Fluff retorted.

Grant raised his hands as if backing off. 'Just wanted to wish you luck, that's all.' He waited until they had just passed him before adding in a carrying voice. 'Not that you would need it.'

Fluff went to turn back towards him, but Matt took her arm and propelled her towards the door. She shook his arm free in the corridor.

'Whatever is going on, Fluff, we can't waste time on it now. For a start, he isn't worth the bother.'

Fluff nodded but remained tight-lipped.

She remained unusually quiet as they set out. He wondered if her altercation with Grant had upset her, but it wasn't like Fluff. He'd seen her handle even McRay's attempts at bullying with ease.

He left the silence sitting uneasily between them as they drove through Warwick and past the ancient Lord Leycester hospital. Its leaning, half-timbered walls had seen centuries go by and gave out a warm, comfortable sense of permanence. It was after they passed the Westgate that she broke the silence.

'Matt, there is something you should know,' she said, as if it had taken her a lot of effort to get the words out.

Matt couldn't second-guess what was coming, so he gave a non-committal, 'Yes?'

'I know DI Hadden.'

The traffic was light, so Matt risked a quick glance at her face. It was flushed.

'So do I, although I haven't seen her for a long while.'

'Yes, she told me.'

'Told you?' Matt wondered how much Jenny had told his Constable. Surely, she wouldn't undermine his authority by talking about their brief affair.

'Everything,' Fluff said, keeping her eyes on her lap.

Matt was shocked. He needed to know more. Pulling the car into a convenient parking space in front of the nondescript church where Tolkien was married, he switched off the engine and turned to face Fluff. 'Why would she do that? It was so long ago and doesn't have any bearing on the present.'

Fluff still didn't look at him. Matt began to feel that there was something else. This wasn't about him. He looked away and spoke softly. 'You can tell me, Fluff. Whatever else we have been, we've always stayed friends.'

'Because…because we are an item.'

'An item?' Matt refused to believe what he was hearing. 'How can you two, I mean…Oh.' The sudden rush of understanding left Matt stammering for words. Jenny was Fluff's significant other. The one who was waiting the other night. Wow, how wrong he had it. Fluff was looking at him now and he sensed she was waiting for his approval. 'Some detective I am, hey?' Matt said turning to grin at her.

She smiled in return and sighed. 'It's only been a few weeks. I've wanted to tell you, but then Jenny turning up here sort of forced the issue.'

'Yes. I can see it might be a bit awkward.'

'Tell me about it,' Fluff said with a sigh.

Suddenly everything fitted together. 'Grant knows?' Matt guessed.

'Yes. He made life hell for Jenny at Division. Thought it his duty to tell everyone. She would have left if her Guv hadn't stepped in and told Grant it wasn't on. That's when he got moved.'

'Now he's trying it all over again.'

'Yes. He seems to have the idea that there are lesbian conspiracies everywhere stopping him from advancing.'

'When, of course, his own delightful personality has nothing to do with it.'

'Exactly.'

'I'll talk to him,' Matt offered.

'No. I'd rather you didn't. It will only make him more determined to cause upset.'

'OK, but if he gets out of line, I will deal with him.' Matt started the engine and pulled out into traffic, silent for a while as they left Warwick, past the romantically named Tournament Fields

Business Park. Maybe not such a strange name, as all business in the present economic climate was a battle.

'So we—' Matt stopped, still trying to get his head around Fluff and Jenny.

Fluff turned to look at him.

'Our affair?' Matt asked.

'Was delicious,' Fluff replied.

'Then how...why?'

'It just happened.'

'Oh God. Was it me...did I...?' Matt stuttered.

Fluff laughed. 'Turn us both into lesbians? Don't be silly. It was nothing to do with you. Big head.'

'Well I hope not, or Eppie is not going to be happy.'

CHAPTER 45

Clive was excited as the lift rose upwards. He was squashed behind two young women giggling about some party and the boys they had fancied. He didn't like the way one of them kept glancing in his direction, so he pretended not to notice. There was no way he was going to encourage them. He couldn't risk another Anne.

It was a relief when the lift emptied. He looked towards Ben's desk, but he, as usual, hadn't arrived yet. Feeling unsettled, Clive tried to get down to work while looking up at every opening of the lift doors. The last time they had been in the office together, it had been as mere colleagues. Now that they were lovers, would everyone immediately be aware of their relationship?

He had just started to concentrate on his work, when a call came through saying one of his clients, whom he had been due to see tomorrow, wanted to change the meeting to today. Having nothing specific in his diary, there was little Clive could do but accept.

Mrs Angelo, of Angelo's Foods was one of those awkward clients who hired an expert and then refused to let them do their job. By the end of the morning, Clive would have gladly added her to his victim list, if it weren't for her inbuilt protection in the form of mounds of flesh, which wobbled like a jelly every time she emphasised a point.

Maybe she enjoyed sampling the goods, and he doubted that even his strong hands could force their way through such a formidable barrier. Clive was already in a state of contained excitement, trying to appear normal, while every inch of him was flooded with adrenalin, preparing for what he intended to do tomorrow. He found himself switching off from her rampant voice and, instead, went over his plans for the umpteenth time.

He had determined yesterday evening that Mika would arrive around five-forty-five and drive her black and white mini into the staff car park. This meant he would have to be in position at least fifteen minutes earlier to be sure he didn't miss her. Mika would be very glad, he was sure, to have a police escort from the end of the driveway and into the spa. Except that she would never reach the spa.

Posing as Detective Inspector Browning, Clive had decided to put himself on an equal footing to DI Turrell; he would direct her to the darkest corner of the staff car park. Then it would be only a matter of seconds before she was ready to become his third statement. The palms of his hands were burning at the thought and, although he longed to use them around Mrs Angelo's fat neck, he reasoned that it would be such a waste to use his talents on her.

A shudder as Mrs Angelo banged on the table to emphasise a point brought him back to the present, and he had to give her his full attention. The sooner he was out of here the better, so he pretended agreement and resolved to work out the programme in his own way. Then, when it was completed and presented to her, Clive would compliment her on her foresight and excellent planning abilities. He had worked with clients like her before, and it was by far the best way to deal with the situation.

Towards the end of the meeting, his phone rang. Grateful for the interruption and pleading a possible emergency, he rose and stepped out of the room into the open-plan office. The sound of Ben's voice brought the familiar quickness to his breath.

'So what have you been up to, then?'

Clive searched his mind, examining the past twenty-four hours since Ben and he became as one, to see if he had given himself away, but could come up with nothing, except his desire to tell Ben everything, to have him join in the excitement. Noticing his hesitation, Ben laughed.

'Am I going to be seeing you on Crime Watch?'

Clive finally stammered a reply. 'Why would you say that?'

'Well, a rather dishy detective came here looking for you. Seems you were present at the scene of a murder last Saturday. Now, if he had been looking for me, I would have given myself up straight away. He could have taken me away, handcuffs and all,' Ben teased.

Clive reasoned with himself that this must have been a routine visit, so he joined in the joking. 'Oh yes, while having dinner with my mother, I might have committed the odd murder or two,' he laughed.

'Oh great. Now you tell me,' Ben kidded.

'I needed to impress you first.'

'Oh you have. You certainly have,' Ben sighed in his sexiest voice.

Clive found it embarrassing that his body was reacting to the sound of Ben's voice and the memories of yesterday it was evoking. One or two of the workers had already looked up at the word murder. He sought to cut it short before he became carried away.

'Look, I'll have to get back to my client.'

'OK. I get it. The tasty detective is coming back later. I'm definitely going to be here. See you then. Love you.' The last few words were almost whispered and Clive was frustrated that he couldn't return them but, instead, had to be content with, 'Yes, me too.' Besides, a little part of him was jealous of Ben finding DI Turrell dishy. True, he was only kidding, but it wasn't what Clive wanted to hear. 'See you then.'

He could tell Ben was laughing at him trying to sound business like and formal but forgave him when he suggested meeting for lunch near the office.

After escaping from the Angelo woman, Clive drove towards the office, and the first qualms began to cross his mind. Was the police visit routine? They would certainly want to interview anyone who was at the spa, like before. Memories of that last time when he had let that silly woman constable get the better of him, made him wary.

Maybe he should avoid going back to work for a while. Alternatively, should he go back now, have lunch with Ben, and then get called out again? That way, it wouldn't look as if he was avoiding the inspector. That seemed the best plan.

The route back to the office took him past the Inspector's flat and he parked opposite the block, pretending to look through his briefcase but watching for any signs of life. There was none, and he was tempted to go and ring the flat's buzzer before ruling this out as an unnecessary risk. He began to wish he had not sent the little soldier to the inspector, since, by now, the inspector would have his wife hidden away, safely out of danger and his clutches.

Clive visualised how wonderful it would be to have the inspector's wife, Eppie, as his next centrepiece. The more he thought about it the more he wanted it. It was perfect. The DI would have to admit Clive's superiority over him and spend the rest of his lonely life going over all the mistakes that led to his wife's death.

But how would Clive find her? Police had safe houses or used hotels to hide people away. Where would they put Turrell's wife? Would the one little soldier warrant a posh hotel? Unlikely. She would be staying with friends or family out of town. Unless she was being put up by one of his colleagues? If this were so, then it would probably be a female or one with a wife.

He thought of the annoying young DC and realised she would fit the bill exactly. He had followed his instinct, as fate guided him, so he knew where she lived. It would be worth keeping an eye on her flat.

Ben had chosen a trendy place for lunch. The wooden floors, bright red metal seats, and the occasional print offered just the right obeisance to the young professional type and allowed, Clive was sure, an extra charge on the basic lunchtime fare of salads and sandwiches.

It was a popular place and, at first, he couldn't spot Ben amongst the chattering throng. Then, from a high stool set at a table around a pillar, Ben waved. Just the sight of his cheerful face caused a warm flush to colour Clive's face, so that walking towards him, he felt like a beacon the other diners couldn't fail to notice.

Clive was both embarrassed and thrilled when Ben jumped up to greet him with a kiss. If anyone noticed, they would know he was loved, someone special, a significant other, and he revelled in the feeling.

'I've ordered for you.'

'Oh. Thanks.'

'Thought it would save time. Knew you wouldn't want to be late for your meeting with the sexy DI.'

'No way.' Although he laughed with Ben and went along with the joke, the worries remained to spoil the occasion.

He walked back to the office with Ben, only taking his fake phone call as he reached the middle of the main office. He gave a good show of annoyance, declaring he would swing for Mrs Angelo, before leaving to supposedly sort her out.

As he passed Gloria, she handed him a note from her message pad. 'So no Anne again. You have given her the hump.'

'Me. I didn't do a thing.'

'Well, I will keep your secret as it has been very peaceful here.'

Clive gave her a smile while thinking if only she knew.

Waiting until he was alone in the lift, he read Gloria's note. It said *'Mrs Sinclair phoned. The police had called at the house and had disturbed Mother, who was now in a foul mood. Please ring her.'*

CHAPTER 46

Matt was quiet, thinking about Fluff and Jenny.

'Of course this does mean we won't be able to go off piste. I can't expect you to lie to her.'

'You want to go to see Harry and the bikes?'

'It feels very important.'

'Then we'll call it something else, like forgetting to mention, rather than lying. If she asks outright then we come clean.'

'I'll take the flak anyway. You can always say I ordered you.'

Fluff laughed. 'Yes, Guv.'

While Fluff phoned the spa to ask Harry to wait for them, Matt drove out through Warwick towards the bottleneck of the Warwick Island, thinking that in days gone by they would have been on horseback. And Fluff would be called Lady Jane, destined to spend her time within the castle walls, growing herbs and doing embroidery. He couldn't imagine her, or Eppie, fitting in with that regime. But at least there wouldn't be the morning traffic jams.

He hit the blue light, scaring all the motorists around him, as they wondered if it was intended for them. Easing out to the edge of the traffic, the other cars grudgingly gave way and they were soon free and heading towards the spa.

Harry was deadheading the last of the autumn roses as they drove up. He looked tired, and Matt was suddenly struck by how old he was and how much the death of Sandi had affected him.

He had felt personally responsible for not being able to save her. Harry looked up as they got out of the car.

'It is really good of you to wait, Harry. I know we are keeping you from your bed.'

'Glad to do it, Guv. Glad to do anything that helps,' Harry said, rolling the de-headed roses in his hand. 'I've got the keys to the guest bikes, and I've made a list of everyone I can think of who comes to work by bike. There.' He handed Matt a page torn from a reporter's notebook, which contained several names written in a careful but scrawny hand.

'Thank you, Harry, these will be invaluable, and we'll check all of them out.'

Matt handed the list to Fluff as Harry led them through the building to one of the rear entrances and out into a small courtyard at the side of the building. It took the three of them less than ten minutes to come to the conclusion that all of the bikes were well maintained and none squeaked. Disappointed, Matt looked towards the staff bike rack. It was too early yet for a lot of the day staff to have arrived, and there were only two bikes there. Both were locked but could be moved a small distance proving that neither was what they were looking for.

After thanking Harry again for his help, Matt had to admit defeat. The rest of the bikes arriving with day staff would be checked as per Jenny's orders by uniform. It was time that he got back to what he was supposed to be doing.

The first two visits were routine, two middle-aged businessmen making sure they made full use of their corporate membership. This apparently included dinner on a Saturday night. One had said he was with his wife and the other was entertaining a lady client.

Matt wasn't interested in their white lies. That both had been dining with a woman on Saturday night, wife or otherwise, meant they had other things on their minds. While one gave his wife's name, the other hesitated, leading Matt to promise that his companion would only be contacted in the unlikely event that they charged him with murder. At this, the man gulped and almost whispered the lady's name.

As they left this last visit, Fluff agreed that neither man appeared to be their murderer, although she had carefully noted down everything they said.

Their next visit was to a software company, where they needed to talk to a Clive Draper. He had been dining at the spa on Saturday evening with his mother, so he was also an unlikely suspect, although as Fluff had pointed out, Clive had also been on the scene of the first murder and had been interviewed twice.

They were received graciously and directed to the second floor to be greeted by a middle-aged woman, who rose from her desk facing the lift. Gloria's job as receptionist doubled as a guardian to stop unauthorized folk wandering about the offices. Matt smiled at her and produced his warrant card.

'We need to have a quick word with Clive Draper.'

'Certainly, Inspector. I believe Mr. Draper is out at a client's, but I will just check for you.'

They waited while Gloria rang through and asked the question.

'I'm so sorry, Mr Draper is indeed out. One of his assistants is coming to have a word with you. If you would like to take a seat...' She indicated a small, IKEA-type sofa in the corner. He will be with you in a moment, Sir.'

Fluff led the way to the sofa. It was not big enough for two people, so both elected to stand. A young man joined them almost immediately. His smile and dark good looks were set to charm. He offered Matt his hand.

'Ben Henderson. How can I help, Officer?'

Matt noted the American accent. 'We wanted to have a word with Mr Draper. I understand you are his assistant?'

'Yes. And I'm sorry but he has been called out to see a client. It is hard to say when he will be back. The lady he has gone to see has a reputation for being difficult. But I would think it will be around lunchtime. Is this about that dreadful murder at the spa? He was very upset about the poor girl.'

Ben seemed to be only talking to Matt, so Fluff interjected.

'Name of client?'

'Angelo Foods.'

'Shall I get him to call you, Officer?'

'No need. We'll be back.' Fluff enjoyed telling him as she handed over her card.

'Sure.'

She waited until they were in the lift.

'Little toady. Yes, Officer; no, Officer.'

'Just my natural superiority.'

'He fancies you.'

'Jealousy, jealousy.'

Both were grinning as they left the building.

CHAPTER 47

Sam paused before pushing open the door to the path lab, getting his warrant card ready to show Babs, the super-efficient secretary who guarded the office. No one ever got past her. Sam was sure she would make her own mother sign in and show her ID.

Today, Babs was nowhere to be seen. In her place was a young woman, fair-haired and very pretty.

'DS Withers. Sam,' he added, holding out his warrant card and smiling. She smiled back before checking a list on the desk.

'Oh, I don't seem to have you on this list.'

'Probably not. Slim only rang an hour ago.'

'I'm sorry. I'm just filling in. It's Babs's birthday. They're having a bit of a party, you see. I'll just go and check, if you don't mind.'

Sam didn't mind at all, as he watched her uncoil her long legs from behind Babs's desk.

'Not at all.' Sam found himself running his fingers through his hair in an effort to tidy it, even though it always looked untidy no matter what he did. Maybe he should sit on the edge of the desk, one leg dangling like they did in detective movies. That always looked sexy. His deliberations were interrupted by Slim's voice and the young lady, as she held open the door to the inner office.

'Sergeant Withers, come in,' Slim shouted.

She held open the door for him so that he had to pass close.

'I'm Kim,' she said when he was directly opposite.

'Sam.' He offered his hand and she took it and smiled up at him.

The moment was broken by Babs who appeared at his side with a huge slice of chocolate cake that she pushed towards him. 'Put the student down you letch and have some cake.'

Reluctantly taking the cake, Sam let the door swing shut but not before he watched Kim glide back to her desk. 'Thanks and a very happy birthday.'

'Big one. Bet you can't guess which.'

'No and I'm not going to try.'

'Coward.'

Slim whispered in Sam's ear. 'Tricky one, try forty, as it's fifty.'

Sam nodded his thanks and nibbled at his cake. Cake was the last thing he needed before viewing Sandi's body. But to the lab personnel it seemed to present no problem, since the desk, doubling as a buffet, was piled high with food, and everyone was tucking in. Sam supposed they had to get used to dealing with the dead or they would never eat at all.

Moving towards the small table that held the soft drinks, he poured himself a Coke and managed to leave the cake tucked behind the orange juice cartons.

He had only taken a sip of his drink when Slim came towards him. 'Come on. Let's get back to work, Sergeant.'

As Slim led the way, conflicting emotions battled within Sam. The first sight of the bodies lying on the slabs, cold and alone, always made him feel sick. But as soon as Slim started to explain the workings and what he looked for within all the gore, Sam had to admit it was fascinating. If he could liken it to anything, it would be like working on his first car, when he would take bits out and learn from his dad what they did.

'Here we are.' Slim removed the sheet from the nearest table to uncover Sandi.

Sam thought how pathetic she looked and was glad that the autopsy was already over.

'All finished. Same MO as before. Full findings and photos are ready in the office.'

'Thanks.' Sam made to turn away. Maybe he would have time to chat up the lovely Kim.

'But there is something here I would like you to see.' Slim took Sam's arm and led him to another covered body.

Sam took a step back. Even the sophisticated air conditioning system couldn't carry away the smell of decaying flesh, which permeated the air from the bloated corpse that lay there.

'Drowning. I thought suicide at first. But come here.'

He tried not to breathe as Slim encouraged him closer, pointing at the neck of the girl.

'Fairly faint, nearly missed it, but there is also internal damage.'

'A bruise?'

'Yes, same place as the other two. So maybe not suicide at all. She could have had help from our chap.'

'My God. Then why didn't he—?'

'Dress her up? Slim interrupted him. Who knows? That's for you to find out. And I wish you would hurry up. I don't like this place filling up with young women. They ought to be out enjoying themselves.' Slim went to cover the girl.

'Any ID?'

'Pretty soggy. We passed it all over to uniform. They might be able to make sense of it.'

'Good. Let's hope they have got somewhere.'

Sam thanked Slim. After wishing Babs a happy fortieth birthday, which made her giggle, he stopped by the office to pick up the paperwork on both the women. He was still puzzling about where the second body fitted in when he left, so he failed to catch the special smile bestowed upon him by Kim.

Torn between ringing Jenny or Matt, Sam gave in to his immediate instinct to ring Matt.

'Hi, Guv. Just been to the PM. Slim says same MO.'

'No surprise there then.'

'There is one—he has another young woman there with similar bruises on her neck. Found in the River Avon near Welford-on-Avon Sunday night. Drowned. It looked like a suicide till Slim found the bruises.'

'ID?'

'With uniform in Stratford.'

'Get over there pronto, Sam. Hang on…what does Jenny say?'

There was an awkward pause as Sam thought how to tell Matt that he hadn't told Jenny yet.

'Sam. Don't play silly buggers. Tell her now.'

'Will do, Boss.'

'I'm sure she will come to the same conclusion. But if not, maybe you could lead her gently in the right direction.'

'You are kidding, aren't you?'

'She's good—just give her a chance.'

'OK.'

CHAPTER 18

A rather flustered, middle-aged woman responded to Fluff's enthusiastic pressing of the buzzer. She wiped her hands on a small flowered apron. On notification that they were police officers, Matt thought she might need a chair.

'Oh dear. It's not Mr Clive is it?' She paused and seemed to be running through all the family in her head. 'Or Margaret, Elizabeth? Not little Emily?'

Fluff moved forward to reassure her that their visit was merely a routine follow-up concerning those people who had been at the health spa at the time of Saturday's murder. Relieved that the shadow of death was not visiting the house, she explained, as she led them into the hall, that Mrs Draper was having her lunch.

'We do understand, Mrs…?'

'Sinclair. Marjory Sinclair.'

'We understand that it will be extremely inconvenient for Mrs Draper, but it is vital that we talk to her. She may have noticed something that no one else has. That something could help us catch this killer before he strikes again.'

Mrs Sinclair gave a gulp and, without a word, turned back down the hall. Fluff raised her eyebrows to Matt.

'Well done,' he said.' What do you think of that?' Matt nodded towards the picture hanging in the small lobby.

Fluff gave it a quick glance. 'Not my cup of tea. But I bet they are worth a bit. He must be doing alright.'

Mrs Sinclair returned and indicated that they should follow her. She led the way to a pleasant dining room towards the rear of the house. The glass doors opened onto a patio, bright with colour from several potted chrysanthemums.

Mrs Draper sat at a glass table and was halfway through a chicken salad. She indicated for Mrs Sinclair to bring over the electronic wheelchair, which was parked in a corner of the room. Once the chair was alongside hers, she stood and made the two steps towards it on her own. Matt had moved forward ready to help but backed off at a signal from Mrs Sinclair.

'Shall I save this for you, Mrs Draper?'

'No thank you, Mrs Sinclair,' she replied, manoeuvring herself easily from the room and along the hallway towards the front of the house, causing Fluff to flatten herself against the wall. 'Come along then, Inspector.'

Once they were seated in the sparse living room, she opened the conversation. 'I expect you are here because of that dreadful murder on Saturday night. If there is anything we can do to help, of course we will.'

'We are checking with everyone who was at the health spa that evening. I understand that you and your son, Clive, dined there that night,' Matt asked. 'May I ask what time you left?'

'Certainly. It was gone nine. It meant I was late going to bed in fact,' she added grumpily.

Matt thought she must be a difficult woman to live with. 'Were you with your son all evening, Mrs Draper?'

'Of course, we had gone there to dine together,' she snapped, her eyes suddenly wary.

Fluff pretended consulting her notebook. 'Did you see a Mrs Mooney about having a course of massages?' she asked in all innocence.

'Oh that. Clive thought it might help. With the aches and pains,' she replied, indicating her legs.

'And Clive was with you during the consultation?' Fluff persisted.

Again the slight sense of wariness and this time a hesitation. 'No, he was not, but I was with the women for a very short time.'

'So would you say it was five, ten, fifteen minutes, or longer, Mrs Draper?'

'I don't know. About ten minutes, maybe a little longer. What are you suggesting?'

Matt stepped in. 'We are simply trying to establish where everyone was at around the time of the murder, Mrs Draper. Did you notice anything or anyone suspicious during the evening?' He smoothly distracted her away from concentrating on her son. She had already told them what they needed to know. She didn't trust him.

She looked as if she was making her own connections, and she answered automatically. 'No, nothing.'

Matt rose as if satisfied and Fluff followed. 'Thank you very much, Mrs Draper. It was good of you to see us.' She nodded as they began walking towards the door. Matt turned, as if on an impulse. 'Oh, do you happen to know where we could find your son at the moment?'

'He will be at work, Inspector,' she replied, turning her chair away from them in an obvious dismissal.

Mrs Sinclair was hovering and showed them out. As soon as the door closed behind them, Fluff expressed what they were both thinking. 'She doesn't trust her son.'

'And, although that doesn't automatically make him a murderer, we need to find him as soon as possible. Give his work a ring, see if he's got back there yet.'

'Would you take your mother along if you were going to commit a murder, though?' Fluff asked as she dialled.

'It would be a brilliant cover.'

'Yes, but it ties him into that very tight time frame, doesn't it.'

'Maybe he got a kick from having his mother on the scene.'

'It could be something simple. Like she doesn't like a girl he is seeing?'

'Possible.'

Fluff snapped her fingers. 'Or…now this is more likely, he can't tell her he is having it off with his fawning assistant Ben.'

Matt had to admit it was a possibility. Still, whatever the reason for Mrs Draper's mistrust of her son, he was aware of a tiny quiver deep within. Was Clive Draper their murderer?

He was disappointed when Fluff shook her head.

'Seems he was called out again.'

CHAPTER 49

Although the bed was comfortable, Eppie had managed to get little sleep. She had already become accustomed to Matt's warmth beside her, so the empty space loomed large, reminding her constantly that he was out there alone and possibly in danger.

Her dreams of Matt were interspersed with Sandi and hundreds of model soldiers, which marched relentlessly on towards them. Eppie kept kicking them out of the way, but they came on and on like an army of ants, until she woke in a cold sweat.

In the darkened room, she couldn't remember where she was for a moment, until she felt the patchwork bedspread, and it all rushed back. Had the dream meant something? Was Matt in danger? Eppie had been upset when he told her that he had gone back to the flat, although he had tried to make light of it. Why did she have to be protected and hidden away while he was putting himself at the mercy of the killer?

Matt had tried to reassure her, explaining that the murderer was targeting young women not fit young men. It was a logic that Eppie found hard to dispute, but it didn't help her feeling of helplessness and the hidden feeling of guilt. By ignoring Matt's pleas to stay away from the health spa, she had given the killer an opportunity to invade, not only their home, but their lives. Although she hadn't yet accepted the little flat as home, now that it was threatened, it seemed very precious.

Far worse was the thought that she had put Matt in danger. She knew that there were times in his work when he was at risk, but this killer was taking a delight in targeting him. If only she hadn't insisted on having her own way. Marriage was so much harder than she thought it would be.

She did know that if she lost Matt now, like Tom had lost Sandi, she didn't know whether she would want to go on. A wash of anger swept over Eppie. How could one person devastate so many lives? This man may be mad, but he was astute enough to hide behind an ordinary life, every day pretending, so that he could emerge to kill again and again.

Eppie sat up in bed, going over in her head all the people that she and Sandi had welcomed and helped at the front desk. All had seemed so normal. Well, except maybe for Mr Spires, who couldn't seem to remember his way to the changing rooms and complained that the notices were too small. Had that been a front? No, Eppie decided that, unless he was acting a very clever part, he was too dumb to carry out the murders.

It would take someone with intelligence. She started thinking of possible suspects she had encountered and, after searching in her bag for her notebook, she turned on the bedside light and began writing them down. By the time she had finished, the light was starting to slide into the room past the edge of the curtain. She had six possibilities. None of them stood out as the murdering kind, but that was the point, really.

There was Ken, who came in after work every day. Sandi said he was training for the London Marathon, so surely he had other things on his mind. Ross and Stuart came in Saturday morning to tone up for their game with the local football club. The team had won their away match Saturday, so they must have been busy celebrating their win over in Kettering, so that let them out.

That left an older man whose name she didn't know, that nice Clive who came in on Friday about his mother, and a dark-haired man of about thirty, who only wanted to speak to Sandi. Could he be the one? Should she tell Matt or ring the sergeant who had interviewed her. Where was the card he had given her? She found the card tucked in beside a damp tissue and put it on the bedside table. There were sounds of Jane moving about the flat, and Eppie wondered if she should discuss these suspicions with her.

However, by the time she had slipped on her robe and moved into the hallway, she heard a click as the front door shut. Jane had left a note on the kitchen table, reminding her to help herself to anything she needed and saying that she didn't know when she would be home. Half-heartedly, Eppie made herself a cup of instant coffee. She would return to her list after she had had a shower.

Jane had opened the curtains in the living room, and the sunlight was streaming in. Eppie edged as close as she dared and looked out as she drank her coffee. Across the road, the sun was catching the spire of St Nicholas Church. Matt had told her there used to be an abbey next to the church, and she could just make out a portion of ruined wall.

Kenilworth Castle was one of the places she had always wanted to visit. She had read in the local paper that the Castle had opened an Elizabethan Garden, recreating the one built by Robert Dudley to impress Queen Elizabeth I. Promising herself that she and Matt would see the garden next summer in all its glory, she went for her shower.

It was well past lunchtime when Eppie had refined her list of suspects for the tenth time, writing down everything she could remember, no matter how small, so that each suspect now filled two pages. Well, except Mr Squires who she couldn't imagine being able to tie his own shoelaces, never mind murdering anyone. At least it had given her something to do, something that might help solve the case before anyone else became a victim.

She had been pouring over her list for too long, so standing and stretching, she enjoyed the warmth of the sun pouring into the room. She longed to go for a walk in the fresh air. How long would she have to stay cooped up like this? She had even finished her book, and the flat contained little reading matter to interest her. Matt had promised to send a couple of books via Fluff, but she couldn't really hold him to that as he would be busy.

Instead she decided to get lunch, and this was an adventure in itself. Although Fluff had the perfect kitchen, her interest in cooking was no match for it. Besides the nearly full tin of biscuits, Fluff's staple diet, there were two slices of dry bread, no milk, and some out-of-date eggs, a squashy banana, and an apple. Eppie tried the cupboards that yielded only two tins of soup, several tins of corn, an obvious favourite, but little else.

Not feeling imaginative, Eppie settled on the soup, with toast and an apple to follow. She wanted to get back to her list of suspects. She would have loved to stock the kitchen with food, but that was out of the question. There would be no chance of preparing a meal for when Fluff came home, which was a pity, since she would have enjoyed working in that kitchen.

With lunch out of the way, Eppie returned to her list, visualising each of her suspects in turn and trying to imagine them committing cold-blooded murder. No one stood out, so she began enlarging on their actions, writing down what each of them had said or done until she started to get a headache. Feeling the need to move, she was doing some stretching exercises when Fluff came in.

She looked tired and, throwing her small shoulder bag on the couch, had disappeared into the kitchen with nothing more than a grunt, returning with the open biscuit tin from which she was selecting all the jammy dodgers, munching as if she hadn't eaten all day.

Eppie thought it was the wrong time to mention her list.

'Bad day?'

Fluff nodded and sank down on the sofa, kicking her shoes off with a sigh.

'Fancy a brew?'

Spitting out small biscuits crumbs, she answered. 'Please.'

By the time she had made the strong tea Fluff liked and brought it through, Fluff had slowed down on the biscuits. Eppie wondered how to bring up her ideas. She watched as Fluff took a great gulp of the tea.

'That's better. Thanks.'

'You haven't got any nearer to catching him?'

'No. And I should still be out there damn it.'

'Oh.' Eppie realised that Fluff would still be with the team, with Matt, if it wasn't for her. 'I'm sorry.'

'Not your fault. Matt will work better knowing you have something to eat. He's worried I'm starving you to death.'

Eppie felt like a traitor for joking with Matt that she was living on bread and water.

'Thought I'd pick up a curry. Is that OK with you?'

Although she liked most hot spicy foods, curry wasn't one of Eppie's favourites but she was grateful for the offer. 'Yes, that would be great. Let me give you some money.'

'No need. Oh, and if you write out a grocery list for tomorrow, I'll try and pick up some stuff.'

'You think I'm going to be here for a while?'

'No way of knowing. We're all working flat out to catch the bastard. If he thinks he is on a roll and can't be stopped, that's when we stand a chance.'

She held out her list. 'I was going through everyone who came to the desk on those few days I worked with Sandi. Do you want…'

Fluff took the notebook with some reluctance. Eppie felt she didn't really want to be bothered.

'I've made a note of anything suspicious.'

'Great.'

Eppie watched as Fluff put the notebook beside her on the sofa while she drained the mug of tea.

'Another?' Eppie asked, somewhat disappointed that Fluff hadn't even glanced at her list.

'I'll just nip out to the takeaway first.'

Eppie had the feeling that if she looked at the list at all it would just be to humour her.

At least the curry was good and Fluff had remembered to pick up some milk and bread. Plus Matt called and it was good to hear his voice, although he sounded tired.

'Hi, Love. How's the prison? I did make your warder promise to feed you.'

'I appreciate that and it was great. A nice change from biscuits and stale bread.'

'Hey, don't knock it. Fluff might put you in solitary.'

'She's in the shower. Matt it's lonely here. And I miss you.'

'I know, Love. Miss you too but hopefully it won't be for long. I'll get you something to read—haven't forgotten.'

'Matt, I've started a list of all the people who came to the reception desk.'

'Great. Show it to Fluff. Sorry, have to go. Love you.'

Eppie only had a second to add that she loved him too and Matt was gone.

The notebook lay where Fluff had tossed it. No one was interested.

CHAPTER 50

The house had a stillness over it as he let himself in. For a moment, he couldn't make out what was wrong, then he realised there was no cheerful bustle of Mrs Sinclair, no welcoming offer to put the kettle on, or singing in the kitchen.

Mother was sitting in the living room, her wheelchair facing the door, hands folded in her lap. There was something serene and accepting about her. Clive sensed immediately that she knew. How, it didn't matter. He was aware that her cold eyes followed him as he moved to sit opposite her. She waited until he sat. Her voice was calm.

'Why, Clive? Why?'

He had always imagined this moment. All those mornings as he helped her out of bed, the evenings as they sat across from each other when he made her listen to the boring details of his day. He had enjoyed the control he had over her these last couple of years. But the last two years had never made up for what she had denied him as an infant. He doubted anything could. Clive used to imagine himself explaining how bereft, shut out, he had felt.

But now, well, it didn't seem to matter. She didn't matter any longer. He was no longer striving for her love or attention.

'Surely you know?'

'No. I want you to explain, Clive.'

'And I can't be bothered.'

'You owe me that at least.'

'Owe you? Oh no. I owe you nothing. Nothing at all, Mother.'
The last word was bitter on his tongue, and he spat it at her. She
recoiled slightly before rallying.

'Then indulge me.'

He looked at her sitting there, regal and calm. She must be
aware of what he was capable of. Of what was to come. Suddenly
he wanted, needed to tell her. She should know after all the cause
lay with her.

Clive walked slowly around her chair. Her eyes didn't follow
him but flickered, as if wondering what he might be about to do.
'Very well, Mother, I will explain.' He sat down again, taking his
usual evening position across from her. But this was no cosy chat.
He sought for the best way to begin. She sat waiting. 'I was how old
when Lizzie was born?'

She seemed surprised but answered. 'Sixteen months. Why?'

'Still a baby then?'

She hesitated. 'No, not really, although you were still in nappies.
It was time for you to start growing up.'

'To be a man, like father?'

'Well, yes.'

He could feel the anger rising but fought to control it. He
wanted to remain calm and rational. She must understand.

'A baby still. Thrust from your arms. Not able to understand
why you didn't want me, didn't love me anymore.'

'Now you are being melodramatic. And it doesn't suit you,
Clive.'

He could see the scorn in her eyes. 'Melodramatic am I?'

Clive rose and walked away from her trying to get his memories
in order. He had to make her understand how it was for him. He
turned back to find her looking at him. She waited with such calm.
He admired her courage.

'You flung me from the nursery into the care of my idiot
father who could only think of turning me into a homage to
himself. Parading his stupid soldiers and his manly values. As if
I cared a jot about protecting the sister who had stolen you away
from me.'

268

She turned her head away in disgust. Clive moved to kneel in front of her, determined now that she should hear everything. She refused to look at him, so he reached forward and grasped her face roughly in his hand, forcing her to look into his eyes. 'Do you know how much I wanted to kill the vile intruder? Wanted to place my hands around that tiny, pink neck and squeeze, and keep squeezing?'

He brought up his other hand and let both hands move downwards to her scrawny throat to emphasise his point. She seemed to be holding her breath but she was now looking fully at him. 'Wanted to feel the life slowly leave, the gurgles, cooing, crying and her control stopped forever.' His hands tightened around her throat.

'You are mad.' She brought up her frail hands to push his away.

Clive let his hands fall and knelt there wanting above everything else to put his head in her lap. To have her gently stroke his hair and sing a lullaby. He could stop then and rest. It was as if she sensed his need. She put her hand up to gently touch his head.

'You always were a needy baby, Clive, crying if I left the room or didn't hold you.'

Her hand was now a caress and Clive dropped his head to her lap, letting everything go for a moment. A moment was all this could be. He knew that. Then she began to hum softly and he felt the deep, racking sobs begin to course through him. Clive felt her body recoil at his emotion. She moved her hand away as if he was contaminated.

'Stop it, Clive. You are a grown man now. Where is your self control?'

The familiar words brought him back to his senses, and he raised his head to look at her. The lips were tightly compressed causing all the ugly lines there to deepen. Clive jumped to his feet, ashamed that he had allowed his deepest needs to surface.

'Control? Oh yes, I have self-control. I learnt that early. It was the only way to get some satisfaction. But it was never enough,' he said, getting to his feet to stand above her. 'All the petty things I did could never, never make up for what was taken away from me.'

There was silence for a moment as he sank down into the chair, suddenly exhausted and wanting it to be over. She studied him, as if he were an alien being who had infiltrated her world.

'Now it is happening all over again.' He watched as his words hit her like a blow to the face.

'Oh, my God. Little Emily. You are jealous of a tiny baby.'

Finally she understood. He had to do it now, while he had the strength. Now that she knew why. Clive leaned forward, half standing and half crouching. His face was close to hers, his fingers encircling her skinny neck. 'Yes, Mother,' he said, as he watched the life drain from her. She didn't struggle and it was almost as if she welcomed it.

Afterwards, he carried her to her usual chair by the fire and stood back to gaze down at her. She looked awkward, so he placed a small cushion beside her head, which wanted to loll at an unusual angle. The fire wasn't lit, so he put her rug around her knees to keep off the draughts. Now she looked comfortable, even if she was asleep forever.

Then without a backwards glance, he left. He had to prepare for his next statement.

CHAPTER 51

The kitchen felt cold and empty with no Mrs Sinclair concocting those tempting dinner smells. Had Mother confided in her? He doubted it. Mother wouldn't like to wash her dirty linen in public, especially not this brand of dirty linen. A son who was a serial killer went against her concept of a proper family. If he was ever caught, it would reflect badly on her, and Clive laughed at how the newspapers would lay his misdemeanours at her door, saying he had a bad upbringing. After all it was always the parents fault wasn't it?

The more he thought about it, the more he began to realise he might enjoy the role of a troubled soul. There would be a kindly psychiatrist who would listen carefully to his every word. He would take notes and look very serious. He would be fascinated as to what prompted Clive to kill. Everyone would be intrigued, and he could tell them, even write a book about his life. That would be worth something. Not that he would be allowed the profits, but maybe he could give them to Ben. He would always remember Clive then.

Thinking of Ben made him realise that he wanted to be free to enjoy his love, be with him, share everything, not locked away. Maybe it wasn't such a good idea to get caught.

Now was the time. Clive should tell him, let him share the excitement, the sense of power. Together, they would be able to carry on forever. After each murder they would make violent, passionate love.

Clive needed to be with Ben right now.

Ben was laughing and breathless as he answered the phone and Clive could hear music in the background along with several other voices.

'Ben Holbrook's wedding services.'

More laughter from the chorus behind him that threw Clive into a turmoil of doubt and confusion. 'Hello, Ben. I was hoping we could meet up?'

'Clive. Great to hear from you. But, well, I'm a bit tied up tonight. It's Pete and Jazz's stag do. And as big chief organiser, I've got to stay around to insist they all have a great time.'

'Oh.' Clive couldn't keep disappointment out of his voice at the thought of Ben giving his time and attention to anyone else.

'Hey, why don't you come and join us? I'm sure Pete and Jazz won't mind and, anyway, they won't notice, given the amount of tequilas they are soaking up.'

Clive didn't want to share Ben with anyone.

'We're at Henry's. Do you know it?'

'No.'

'Go past The Brown Horse, and Henry's is in a little side street to the right.'

There was an explosion of noise from behind Ben. It didn't sound like the sort of place Clive wanted to be.

'Must go, Buff is climbing on the bar.'

With a click, he was gone leaving Clive undecided about what to do. If he wanted to be with Ben, he would have to suffer his drunken friends. A stag night—Pete and Jazz? Of course, he had forgotten that homosexuals could now go through a civil ceremony. Ben and he could be legally married. Everyone would then know Ben was his. Even Mother. Clive would ask him tonight.

Excited by the prospect, he set about making up a tray for Mother, who would have to be content with soup and toast. She didn't seem interested when he took it in to her, and he giggled as he remembered that he had made her go to sleep. Clive didn't have to try any longer to gain her love. She was asleep. He had the power to do that.

He placed the tray on the table beside her and stood looking down at her small and scrawny body, dwarfed by the high backed chair. She seemed to have shrunk into it. Clive bent to straighten the rug over her knees, pausing as he patted it into place over her lap.

'I could sit here now, Mother, and you wouldn't be able to stop me, no sharp words, no nasty push onto the floor. But I don't want to.' She took no notice.

'I am getting married, Mother. And no, it is not nosey, interfering Anne.' He felt the laughter bubbling up inside him at the memory of the muddy leaves piling up against Anne's sharp little nose. 'I will bring Ben here and he will hold me, as you never did.'

He had triumphed over them all; he was the powerful one. Closing the door behind him, he let the laughter loose to drift around the hallway and disappear up the stairs.

It was easy to find Henry's, since the noise was shooting out across the small alleyway. Clive went towards the flashing neon sign and past the bored doorman who nodded and held open the door for him. A mass of gyrating bodies, lit by occasional vivid flashes of red and green, was all he could see. Everyone seemed to be moving in unison to what sounded like a tribal drum.

Thinking he would never find Ben in this throng, he took a tentative step forward, just as the DJ slowed the pace. Most of the bodies moved to collapse into seats, and then he saw him and wished he hadn't.

Ben had his arm around a skinny youth who was leading him off the dance floor. Clive felt his heart tighten, as he watched the youth turn to kiss him on the mouth. Ben didn't appear to return the kiss but it was hard to tell. Clive took a step back just as Ben turned to see him. Before Clive could move Ben was at his side.

'Now this is great. I need someone sane. You'll be able to help me with this mad lot.'

He leant forward for a kiss, but Clive's face must have told him and he held back.

273

'Hey, you're not worried about Pete are you? He's getting married to Jazz, so there is no need. Come and meet them all. Mind you, they're not at their best.'

He took Clive's arm and led him through the few dancers smooching around the floor.

Although there were only four of them, they were generating most of the noise in the room. Clive was embarrassed to be part of the group. One was climbing onto a chair, glass in hand, and he guessed he must be Buff.

'Toast—that's it. To...to...'

The others were shouting at him to get down as he tottered. Ben moved towards him and Buff flung himself forward, arms tightly around Ben's neck.

'You're...the best...my Benny best...'

The others picked up the chant. 'My Benny best...Benny best,' as they crowded around to enclose Ben in a group hug.

Clive stood alone watching them, jealousy burning a hole in his heart, until he felt he would choke if he didn't get some air.

Out in the alley, the air was cold, but he knew it wouldn't cool how he felt inside. Ben's so-called friends, drunken and lewd, how could he bear to be with them?

Clive had to prove himself, show Ben that he was all-powerful; then he would want to be with Clive instead. Tomorrow's murder would go exactly as planned and that would impress Ben.

But what if he added something special, just for Ben. What if he laid the inspector's woman at his feet as a trophy, just like ancient warriors threw down the heads of their enemies at the feet of a queen. He knew just where she was hidden and could find a way past their silly security measures.

By the time he reached home, his plan was almost fully formed with just a few minor details to be worked out. He had just checked on Mother, who hadn't moved at all, when the doorbell rang.

'So who's the scaredy cat then?'

Clive couldn't hide the shock of seeing Ben standing there, but as he strode past him into the hallway, he was overcome with pleasure. 'Just not my scene, sorry.'

'Not mine either, but someone has to be the dedicated driver.'

'Have they finished?'

'Some chance. I've just dropped them at Gabriel's—they stay open till the last man standing. Pick them up later. They're too drunk to get into much trouble now. Except chucking up of course, and I'd rather not be there for that stage.'

'Can you stay for a drink? Oh, sorry. It could be tea or coffee.'

'Coffee would be great. Thanks. In here?'

Ben was about to push open the door to the living room. Should Clive let him see how clever he was in putting Mother to sleep, in stopping her interference in his life? But no, he wanted the whole package in place first, so he could present it to Ben as a magnificent token of his love.

'No. Shush. Mother is sleeping.' He managed to stop the giggle in his throat and turned it into a cough.

'In there?'

'More comfortable. For her legs, she says.' Clive moved down the hallway and encouraged Ben to follow him to the kitchen.

'Maybe we should check on the old lady. I'd like to meet her?'

'No.'

'Oh.'

'She gets a bit crabby if she doesn't have her sleep. I've just made sure she is comfortable.' *And sleeping forever*, he wanted to add. But he could tell him that tomorrow.

Clive wanted Ben to stay, wanted to experience the loving once more. Yet he knew Ben must be persuaded, honoured. Once he realised how clever and powerful Clive was, he would only want him, not his idiot drunken friends.

He wanted to touch him, to slide his hands over those powerful shoulders, down to his hips. But if Ben loved him now, he would be lost, unable to concentrate on what must be done to capture and prepare the trophies he must lay at his feet.

Ben lingered over his coffee and with the temptation growing in him, it was Clive who said he was going to turn in.

'And, I need to collect the revellers. I sure hope they've finished heaving.'

Clive experienced a flash of intense anger that he should be leaving him for those so unworthy. If he chose, he could be here with him forever, like Mother. But Mother was asleep. Hearing her lullaby in his head, he giggled and tried to stop as Ben looked sharply at him. Clive needed Ben awake, so he could be naked in his arms, could love and hold him.

Shutting out the thoughts of their lovemaking, he allowed Ben to kiss him, pulling back before the taste of him set fire to the smouldering within. He would allow him to go, so that he could stand triumphant before him tomorrow. Then he would never leave.

'Come round tomorrow?'

'OK. About seven?'

By then, Clive should have added Mrs Turrell and DC Meadows to his trophies, but he might still be engaged in his work with Mika, so it would have to be later. 'Make it eight.'

'Sure.'

With that, he was gone. Clive stood at the door and waved as Ben drove off before going in to tell Mother. He took delight in taunting her.

'Tomorrow, dear Mother, I will bring my Ben in to meet you. Two men together, think of it, Mother. You will die of shame. But, no, you can't do that can you?' His laughter rang about her. 'We will strip each other naked and make you watch, as we arouse each other. Then you will see me happy and loved at last.' He moved towards the door, turning only to add a final echoing, 'At last,' before skipping into the hall.

Aware that he was becoming over excited, Clive decided to take one of Mother's sleeping pills. She wouldn't need them anymore, and he needed to rest before battle.

* * *

In the morning, wonderfully refreshed and not having to prepare breakfast for Mother, he allowed himself the luxury of bacon and egg. Mother couldn't tolerate fats, so she hated even the smell. He decided to open the living room door so the aroma could drift in to her. Maybe he should eat his breakfast in front of her. But the sight of her was starting to offend him, so Clive shut the door and enjoyed his breakfast in the kitchen. It would be a long day, and he didn't know when he would be able to eat again.

Next, he checked the warrant card he had prepared for the evening. He had meant it to be shown outside in the dark, when a quick flash and an arrogant attitude would get him by. During the day, the showing would have to be less and the attitude more.

Gloria said she would pass on his message when he rang to say he was taking Mother out for the day. Next, Clive rang Mrs Sinclair and told her that he was going to spend the day with Mother so she could take a paid day off.

Having chosen the yellow dress for Mika, the deep rose for Eppie, and the blue one for DC Meadows, he laid them carefully in the boot, together with all the accessories he needed. He hoped they appreciated the trouble he was taking to make sure they were dressed in colours that suited them.

Time to say goodbye to Mother. She seemed to have shrunk even further into her chair, and he tried to make her more comfortable. As usual, she was unappreciative and Clive gave up in the end. 'Goodbye, Mother. I'm going to finish what I started.' She should be pleased at that, even if she couldn't show it. Not that she had ever seemed pleased with anything he did. But it didn't matter. He declined to kiss her forehead. There was no need now to go through the charade that she could ever love him.

Clive could see DC Meadow's house from the Abbey Fields car park. With the DC's car gone, Eppie Turrell would be alone just as he thought. Attending to Mrs Turrell was going to be easy. DC Meadows would be harder, but Clive was convinced that once he showed the gods he was worthy, she would be directed towards him.

Everything was on his side, as it was always meant to be. And soon the constable could have a go at solving her own murder. The thought amused him. Maybe after she was dead she would be able to whisper clues in the inspector's ear. That is, if he wasn't too devastated by his wife's death.

Laughter escaped, shocking Clive with its loudness. Something slinking through the undergrowth stopped still, green eyes turned towards him and made him realise he would need to suppress his joy and excitement.

CHAPTER 52

Sam came up to Matt as he locked his car. Matt was suspicious that Sam had been waiting for him.

'She wouldn't go for it, Guv. Said we were too busy to go chasing rainbows only not so politely as that.'

'Jane Doe from the river?'

'Yep.'

'Well, maybe she's right. Although I would at least like to find out who she was.'

'Want me to go undercover, Guv?'

Matt laughed at Sam's imagination.

'You've been watching Spooks again. Let's see if we can persuade her first.'

Jenny gave the briefing a textbook quality. She knew exactly what she wanted and expected, so interrupting the flow was not well received. She was about to wrap up, and Matt was surprised she hadn't mentioned the drowned woman. He could feel Sam looking at him.

'Can I just ask if we are following up on the woman in the river? DI Hadden,' he added for good measure.

'For what purpose?'

'That she has similar marks on her neck as our victims.'

'And drowned, Inspector Turrell. Drowned.'

'So the killer could have been disturbed.'

'Or she could have been indulging in some form of sex play. You are a big boy, so you do know the kind of things that go on, don't you, Inspector?'

Matt was tempted to retort but held back. It was not going to help to lose her cooperation. So, for the moment, he just nodded and smiled.

'And, Inspector, I need you back here for this stupid meeting with the owners of the spa. Four-thirty sharp.'

After Jenny had given the team their jobs for the day, Matt went over to Sam, trying to avoid Fluff with whom he had been paired for the day. Sam was to go back to the spa with Grant.

'That was low, Guv.'

'Don't worry. I've got a mate at Stratford. I'll give him a call, see if he can tell us anything. I'll call you later. Oh, and take your car just in case.'

Matt didn't want to put Fluff in an awkward position, since she would want to be loyal to Jenny. He had already compromised her over the bikes.

As they set out to conduct more interviews, one of them Mrs Mooney, she sighed. 'What are you up to?'

'Me?'

'Don't pretend, Matt. I saw you and Sam with your heads together.'

'Oh that.'

'It's the suicide isn't it?'

'Yes. I think we should follow it up.'

'I agree,' Fluff said.

'You do?'

'Not much we can do about it, though. Unless you had something in mind?'

'Not really. Thought I might ring Ned Collier at Stratford, that's all.'

'Well, get on with it.'

Matt laughed. He should have known he couldn't fool Fluff. Ned was on duty and promised to see what he could find out.

Meanwhile, their next stop was Mrs Moony, the masseur, who had been away on Sunday and Monday. It was disappointing that she was unable to give them any new information. She confirmed that Mrs Draper had been with her for about fifteen minutes and that Clive had not stayed with his Mother, adding, rather wistfully, that she wished her own son was as caring.

Their next stop was back at En Jay's, where Gloria told them that Mr Draper was taking his Mother out for the day and so wouldn't be in. When pressed as to whether the day off had been booked in advance, she was cagey and said she believed so.

'He charms them all, doesn't he? She was lying her socks off.' Fluff took her frustration out on the lift button.

'Evading the truth certainly.'

'How stupid can women be?'

'They fall for our natural charm of course.'

Matt dodged the expected blow from Fluff.

It was after they had stopped for a quick sandwich that Ned rang.

'Your young lady is, or was, Anne Clarke, of 5 Sandhill Close, Shipston. Her documents were pretty soggy but we think that's right. Mobile phone waterlogged. Uniform have been to that address today but there is no answer, so she could have lived alone. No luck with the neighbours, all working I guess. We're doing some further checking—see if she lives with anyone.'

'Thanks, Ned. I owe you.'

'Well, you could introduce me to that new wife of yours. Never thought you would go legal, not with all the young ladies who throw themselves in your direction.'

'I'm a changed man, Ned. Wait until you meet her, then you will understand. Let's meet up for a drink one day soon.'

As he put the phone down, Matt realised he was faced with a dilemma. He should go back to Jenny with this information. But she had been adamant this morning that they would be wasting their time, and he didn't fancy trying to change her mind.

Looking at the address, Matt could see that Sam was the nearest. He would be able to get there from the spa in five minutes, and Matt knew he would be up for it. Fluff made up his mind.

'Oh get on with it. You know he's dying to do something naughty.'

Matt laughed and dialled Sam but was disappointed to get put through to voice mail. He was wondering what to do next, when the phone rang.

'Hi, Guv. Grant was right beside me, so I thought it best to lose him. Do we have lift-off?'

'Not unless you are Biggles. We do have a name and address for the young lady, though. Uniform went there earlier, no answer. As it is close to you, thought you could give it a try.'

'Great. I'll think up a cover story for sour chops.'

'We'll text you the details.'

'Get back to you as soon as I can, Guv.'

'Good.'

The afternoon dragged on. No useful information was gained from the next two people interviewed. Matt looked at his watch; it was time to start heading back to CID for the meeting. He wasn't looking forward to being in a position where his opinion wouldn't pull any weight. That was down to Jenny now.

Why hadn't Sam called? Matt turned the car to go back to base, when his phone trilled. He stopped and put it on speaker for Fluff to hear.

'Guv. This is too much of a coincidence. She worked at En Jay's.'

'Good God.'

'I couldn't believe it either. She'll have to listen now.'

'I hope so, Sam. Bloody good work.'

'Grant thinks I've got the trots. Had to go back twice. Then her housemate came home from work. So bingo.'

'Must go, Sam. Well done again.'

Matt looked at Fluff.

'You will have to tell her, Matt.'

'I know. I'm just composing my argument.'
'Good luck.'

* * *

At least she didn't demand to know where he had got the information but she remained resolute that they didn't have enough information to pick up Clive Draper.

'It's all circumstantial. He was on the scene of both murders, yes. He also works at the same place as a suicide victim. We have no DNA or witness statements to link him to the crimes. What do you want me to do, Inspector, put out an APB? Suppose he is on a day out with his elderly Mother, and we surround him with cop cars and drag him off. We might just give her a heart attack? Have you thought of that?'

Matt was trying to stay calm. 'With respect, we risk him committing another murder, Ma'am.'

'I'll take that risk. Yes, we will question him again in the proper manner, even invite him to come down to the station. Right now, I need you here for this meeting. Understood?'

'Ma'am.'

Fluff patted his hand. 'She's doing what she thinks is right.'

'Doesn't make it any easier though. He could be out there now watching his next victim.'

'We've just got time to try Clive's house again.'

Matt was surprised. 'You sure you are up for it?'

'Yes, come on let's go.'

The journey was frustratingly slow, as the build up to rush hour had started. Then they arrived at Clive Draper's house to find that no one was home, so the whole exercise was disappointing.

Already late for the meeting, Matt drove back to CID knowing he would have to face Jenny's wrath.

Deciding to keep Fluff out of the line of fire, he gave her twenty pounds and suggested she pick up a book or two for Eppie on her way home.

CHAPTER 53

Once Eppie had dressed and showered, she let the sun flood in, pulling the curtains exactly as Jane had shown her. She couldn't resist a brief glance across the fields. Most of the leaves had fallen now, and the trees all had a deep ring of golden brown at their base. Eppie wished she could go out for a walk, since autumn was her favourite season. She loved the leafy, earthy smell that took her straight back to childhood. At this time of year, the excitement of Bonfire night would be looming, and she and Mike would be collecting wood and making a Guy.

With a sigh, she began the hunt for breakfast. The fare was slim, narrowing by the day, but at least Fluff had asked her to write a grocery list, so there might be hope of replenishment soon.

The morning dragged, so declining to be dragged into watching daytime TV, Eppie wrote down the most needed grocery items. So much was needed, but she didn't want to make it too expensive for Fluff—Jane, she reminded herself—since she wasn't sure what happened in these cases. Would Jane get expenses for having her here? She decided to keep to the basics.

Afterwards, she returned to her notebook and the list of suspects. Even if the professionals were not interested, at least she felt that she was doing something.

It took a while to reach Clive Draper, who was near the bottom of the list, one above Mr Squires as the most unlikely of suspects.

She tried to remember everything about him from whenever he had come to the desk.

He had been pleasant and chatty, seemed interested in why she had taken the job. Then he said something about not wanting to do the same job as his father and mentioned *square bashing*. Something soldiers did.

Soldiers.

The little model soldier had attacked them in their own flat. It was a slim link but it was a start. She shut her eyes and began to visualize every detail of Clive's visits.

On Friday, he had asked her about arranging a massage for his mother. She had been unable to help him; so, while waiting for Sandi, they had chatted briefly, although Eppie was ready to turn away. Looking back, it was as if he wanted to keep her talking.

When Sandi was free, she suggested that Eppie should stay to learn how to answer such a query. So Eppie had relaxed and watched as Sandi took a blue book from one of the pigeonholes behind her. At the thought of Sandi, Eppie felt her eyes filling up. She was such a lovely person to have in the world.

'Do you think your mother would prefer a male or a female therapist, Mr Draper?' Sandi asked.

'I'm sure she would be more comfortable with a lady.'

As Sandi ran down the list, Clive had leaned right over the counter following her as she suggested different therapists. Was there anyone he had given special attention to?

There were a couple of new therapists and, thinking about it, he had seemed quite interested in them. But when Sandi had said that one of them was a man, his attention had switched to the other. She had a funny name; Eppie tried but couldn't recall it, although she was sure it began with an M. All that Eppie could remember was that she worked from Friday to Tuesday evenings from six to nine.

Clive had made sure he read all M's details for himself including when she worked and the hours. Then he changed his mind and decided that his Mother would prefer an older woman and had settled on Mrs Mooney. Now, looking back, his behaviour seemed suspicious.

Bursting to discuss her ideas with someone else, she wondered if she should call Matt. Deciding against disturbing him and not wanting to appear silly, she took out the little card the Sergeant had given her, but there again, was this important information, or would she be wasting his time? She decided to wait until Fluff came home and put her notebook with the grocery list on the kitchen table, anchored down by the biscuit tin. Clive Draper was now marked with a red star.

Lunch was a glass of milk and a biscuit. Afterwards, feeling restless, she tried one of Fluff's exercise CDs before resorting to daytime television. It was only when the buzzer rang that she realised she had nodded off.

Under strict orders not to answer, she couldn't resist peeking through a tiny space at the edge of the curtain. A white delivery van was outside and, as she watched, the driver was walking back towards it. He had no parcel in his hands so someone, probably Mrs Williams, must have taken it in.

Eppie was longing to get out of the flat if only for a few moments. Surely, it couldn't hurt to go down and collect the parcel? Going to the front door, she listened. All was quiet, so she opened the door an inch; then, feeling a bit silly at being so cautious, she opened it farther and went out to the top of the stairs. Halfway down she stopped as Mrs Williams' door opened.

'Oh, there you are, Dear. Jane said she has a visitor. I was just going to bring this up. Would you like to take it?'

Mrs Williams was carrying a square box. Eppie hesitated, thoughts of bombs or poison running through her head. But the box looked light and innocent. Mrs Williams carried it with ease as she came up the stairs towards her. There was nothing Eppie could do but reach out and grasp it.

'Thank you for taking it in.'

'No trouble at all, Dear.'

The parcel was a box wrapped in brown paper. The printed label said Mrs E. Turrell at this address. It must be from Matt. Maybe he had sent her something to read. Bless him. Amidst all the things he was worrying about he had thought of her. She couldn't wait to see what his tastes would be. Tearing aside the wrapping, Eppie took the lid off the box inside.

Lying in the bottom of the box, staring innocently up at her, was a doll. Its cloth body was contorted to fit into the space giving it a tortured look. It didn't seem to have a neck, but then Eppie realised that around its neck a red ribbon was tied so tight it looked as if the head might drop off at any minute.

Eppie threw the box away from her, as if it were red hot. The abused doll fell out and landed at her feet. She jumped back and stood staring at it. *He* knew she was here. She was no longer safe. Could he see her now? Outside the window was a large Chestnut tree. Common sense told her that he wouldn't have climbed the tree, yet she dropped to her knees just in case. On the floor, she felt safer but knew it was a lie. She was trapped. He was coming to kill her.

Needing time to think, she crawled behind the sofa. Phone. She had to reach the phone that was on a small table near the door. Or get her mobile from the bedroom. That would mean she didn't have to pass the living room windows. She began a fast, awkward crawl down the corridor.

Her battery was low. Matt's line was busy, so was DS Withers. Fluff wasn't answering. All the other numbers Fluff had written down were by the landline. Should she dial 999?

The woman was calm and efficient although Eppie must have sounded crazy, as she tried to explain about the doll. It was only after mentioning Matt's name that everything moved fast. A reassuring man told her to stay where she was, to keep the door locked, and not let anyone in but the police. Someone would be with her ASAP.

It seemed like hours, but was probably only a minute, before the buzzer rang making her jump. By then Eppie had crawled to the front door, making a detour round the other side of the sofa so that she wouldn't have to look at or touch the doll again. Pressing herself against the wall, she stood to press the intercom.

'Mrs Turrell, this is Inspector Browning. I have been sent by DI Turrell.'

'Oh, thank you.'

'I understand we have a bit of a situation. The first thing we need to do is get you to a place of safety. There is no need to be frightened now. Just let me and my officers in please.'

'Of course.' Eppie pressed the open button and leaned against the wall. She would be safe now. She opened the door an inch.

'It's all right, Madame. If you would go back inside your flat we won't need to bother you.'

'Very well, Officer.'

She heard Mrs Williams's door close.

His voice was familiar. Eppie had met him recently. She tried to think where.

Footsteps started to climb up the stairs.

One set of footsteps. He had said *officers*.

Suddenly she knew. It was Clive Draper. The man with the red star against his name. If she stayed here, he would kill her.

But where could she go? Her only exit was down the stairs. She had to leave now.

Slipping out of the door, she ran towards the small planter under the window on the landing. Squeezing behind it she made herself as small as possible and hoped the small bushy plants would conceal her.

He was at the top of the stairs, turning towards her. Pressing her face into the foliage, she held her breath. He put his hand against the door to the flat. She saw him smile when it yielded to his touch.

This was her only chance. It would only be a minute before he realised she wasn't there. She shot from behind the planter and made for the stairs, taking them three at a time. At the door, she hesitated. Should she ask Mrs Williams for help, at least tell her to call the police? But it would take a while to explain, and if Clive caught up with her, he would kill the old lady as well.

Outside she felt safer but knew he could see her from the flat. Flattening herself against the rough bricks of the house, she moved along until she came to the hedge bordering the house next door. It was thick and thorny and offered no escape.

There was no way through to the back of the house. Her only chance was to head towards the road and across to the parking lot where there were bushes and trees.

He must have realised by now that she wasn't there. If she didn't take her chance now there might not be another. Even now, he might be looking out of the windows to see which way she had gone or thundering down the stairs towards her.

Taking a deep breath, Eppie ran. No cars were coming, and she shot across the road and ran behind the bushes that bordered the car park. Crouching down, she looked back towards the house.

He was there at the window. Had he seen her? Eppie knew she couldn't wait to find out and began making her way through the parked cars towards the church, crouching and running at the same time. Already, the light was fading, and darkness would help her.

From a small rise in the churchyard, Eppie crept behind a gravestone and watched as Clive came out of the house, across the road, and into the parking lot. In the distance, she heard sirens. The real police were on their way. But Clive was between her and them. He was still coming towards her through the car park. She turned and ran, stumbling amongst the uneven surface of the graves.

CHAPTER 54

Jenny was pacing up and down Matt's office as Matt walked through CID. Even from here, he could see her clenched fists and jaw. He was only halfway down the office when she flung open the door and marched out to meet him.

'I said four-thirty. How dare you keep me waiting? How dare you?' she spat.

Matt was unsure of the best way to handle her. This was shades of McRay at his worst. So he simply said, 'Sorry, Ma'am. But I think it is important we interview Clive Draper as soon as possible.'

'I will tell you what is important,' she snapped, already moving towards the stairs and the Superintendent's office. 'And right now it's trying to get some sense into these so-called important men.'

Matt found himself hurrying to keep up with her, certain that his time could be better spent, especially now that they had a possible suspect. He hoped the meeting wouldn't last long and he could get back to the important work.

Jenny strode up to the Superintendent's secretary and, looking down on her coldly, said. 'We are expected.'

Mrs Morris was an old faithful who knew how to deal with all comers. She wasn't going to be put down. 'Yes. Please go in, but knock first, as you are a little late and they may have started without you,' she said with a gracious smile.

Jenny turned to give Matt a glare that said, 'this is your fault,' before moving to knock on the Superintendent's door. McRay opened the door and ushered both to join the group around the table. The Superintendent nodded briefly before introducing them to the three other people.

Two were plump, important-looking men, used to getting their own way. The third was their lawyer, a smart, thirty-something young woman, who also looked as if she brooked no opposition.

She waited until they had sat down before continuing. 'My clients will certainly seek damages, should any attempt be made to close the premises down.'

The Superintendent made as if to speak, but with one look she silenced him and continued outlining her client's case. The argument moved back and forth, and Matt, finding himself not called upon to give any input, began mentally reviewing the case.

Clive Draper had been on the scene of both murders. Anne Clarke worked at En Jay's and she had been found with the similar bruising on her neck as the victims. There had to be a connection. But Clive Draper would have had very little time, in a public place, to murder Sandi. How could he have done that?

He wondered if uniform had found any bikes with a squeak. And even if they had, how did it help to explain how the murder was committed. And where was Clive Draper? What did they know about him? He worked as a programmer at En Jay's and lived with his mother who used a wheelchair.

It was obvious that Mrs Draper didn't fully trust her son, but why? Matt knew it could be for a variety of reasons, but now he couldn't think of any. His mind seemed to be sticking, going over and over the interview they had had with Mrs Draper.

She was reserved, polite, and appeared co-operative, but there was something wrong. True she was disabled and that might colour her behaviour. But she seemed to have adapted well. He thought of the speed that she had manoeuvred her wheelchair down the hallway, and how Fluff had flattened herself against the wall to stop her toes getting run over.

The idea shot into his head with such speed that he almost shouted it out. The wheelchair. Would Clive have taken his Mother's cumbersome electric wheelchair out on Saturday night or would he use a lighter one or even have borrowed one from the spa?

That essential quiver of excitement was so strong that Matt knew he must be on the right track. Matt recalled seeing a wheelchair in the corner of the luggage room when Harry had wheeled out his bike. What if Clive had used that and, come to think of it, that room could be their crime scene. There would be no reason for anyone to go in there outside of checking in and out times when it would be piled high with cases. He had to find out now.

Deciding to risk the wrath of everyone, he stood, interrupting one of the important men mid speech. 'I'm so very sorry, ladies and gentlemen, but I have to attend to something very urgent, directly concerned with the case,' he added for good measure.

Making his way to the door he could hear several voices and commands rising in the air behind him, but he ignored them all and kept going.

Reaching the CID office, he knew he had to stop, calm himself down to think, and work methodically. He needed to know if the spa's wheelchair had a squeak, if Clive carried an ordinary wheelchair in his car when taking his Mother out, if Harry remembered if that wheelchair had a squeak. And of utmost importance, he needed to know where Clive Draper was at this moment.

Opting to make the phone calls first, he was about to go into his office when Sam and Grant came in. Sam looked tired, and Matt guessed it hadn't been an easy day for him, having to work with Grant. Plus, he would have got a blasting from Grant for going to Anne's home. Now he was going to have to ask him to continue for just a little while longer.

'Grant and Sam, you've come just at the right time. I need you to pick up a Clive—'

'Can't do,' Grant intervened, before he could finish. 'Working on higher orders,' he grinned, enjoying Matt's position and plonking himself wearily down at his desk. 'Madam needs these interviews compiled, ASAP she said. And Sam is assigned to me.'

'In your dreams, crap head. What do you need, Guv?'

Matt looked down at Grant, decided not to waste time arguing with him, and turned to Sam instead. Sam had picked up on the signs that something important had come up and perked up at the prospect of catching the murderer.

'Sam, you have the address. He is Clive Draper—IC1 male, late twenties, fair hair, tall. Remember, you interviewed him after the first murder. He lives with his disabled mother at this address. Keep a watching brief until I get there, but let me know if he starts to move.'

'Right, Guv,' Sam said, already half way out of the office, eager to get started and all tiredness forgotten.

'She won't like it,' Grant intoned.

'She doesn't have to. You let me worry about that.' He did not intend to discuss his decision with Grant, so he turned and made his way to his office where he dialled the spa.

It seemed an age before he was put through to Mrs Trowbridge, but he thanked her quick intelligence as she went to do as he asked, promising to call him back straight away.

She also gave him Harry's number. Matt was about to dial it, when Jenny stormed into the room, banging the door so hard behind her that it bounced back open.

'What the fuck do you think you are doing?' she stormed, almost dancing with rage.

Matt hadn't the time to humour her. 'Making a phone call,' he said, continuing to dial. This was vitally important. Too important to be sidetracked by personalities or egos.

'You. Do you realise how stupid I looked in there? They think I have no control at all over the people under me.'

There was no answer from Harry's line, so Matt replaced the receiver. He would give Jenny one more chance to understand what he was doing.

'Look, sorry about cutting out. But it suddenly became clear. If I'm right, we could catch this killer, and you'll get all the glory. That is what you want, isn't it?' He watched as she fought her anger and was impressed when she managed to nod.

'Tell me. Make it fast and good,' she said, moving to sit at her desk.

'I think the squeak is from a wheelchair. The spa has its own wheelchair. It is kept in the luggage room, which is beside the reception area. The perfect killing room. Mrs Trowbridge is checking to see if it has a squeak at this minute. Also, Clive Draper took his mother to dinner there on Saturday night. She is in a wheelchair. Fluff and I both felt she was not being entirely truthful when we interviewed her yesterday. Now we know that an apparent suicide victim, with the same bruises as the other murder victims, worked at En Jay's with Clive Draper.'

Matt paused for breath, aware that he now had Jenny's full attention and that Grant was heading towards the office. 'Plus, we haven't been able to catch up with Mr Draper yet. We need to check that wheelchair too.'

She had taken it all in and wasted no time. 'Get round to the Draper household.'

Matt jumped in before she could rattle off any more commands. 'I have sent Sam, on a watching brief only.'

She raised her eyebrows but didn't slip back into anger. Matt admired her professionalism. 'Join him. If Mr Draper is there, bring him in. If not, ask the mother the questions left over from earlier. Then we'll put out a call for him. Picture?'

'Membership application,' Matt turned to the computer and brought up Clive Draper's picture on his spa-joining form.

'Doesn't look like a murderer, but then, they so rarely do,' she commented, reading Clive's details.

From the doorway, Grant coughed. 'Your lists, Ma'am.'

Jenny didn't bother to look up. 'Leave it for now.'

Matt didn't want Jenny distracted by anything and moved to shut the door on Grant, but Grant pushed past him to place a CD on Jenny's desk. She looked up at him, surprised that he was insisting. Matt saw the signs of her temper returning.

'What part of "not now" did you not understand DI Grant?'

'Yes, give us a five minutes, Grant,' Matt intervened.

For a moment, it looked as if Grant was going to leave, but then he turned at the door. 'You wouldn't be so happy to jump to this dyke's tune if you knew who she was screwing.'

Grant's voice was raised, and people in the general office were turning to look. Jenny stood, horrified that history was repeating itself. Matt put both hands on Grant's shoulders and propelled him from the room. He pulled the office door shut behind them as he tried to control his anger.

'Damn you. It so happens I do know. Although what it has to do with you or anyone else I can't guess.' Aware that he had more important matters to concentrate on, he turned to go back into the office.

Aware that he now had an audience, Grant shrugged and started making his way back to his desk. Matt had opened the office door when he heard, as he was supposed to hear, Grant's comment to the rest of the team.

'Wouldn't be surprised if he and his new missus aren't joining in.'

Grant was still grinning from his clever remark when Matt reached him, spinning him around, arm pulled back ready to deliver a right-hander. Suddenly, Matt felt himself held in a bear hug, both arms pinned to his side.

'That's enough, lad, I'll deal with this.'

Through his rage, Matt recognised McRay's voice. He had forgotten that McRay had been nicknamed Bruiser in his younger days and was surprised at the strength in his arms.

It only took a second before Matt regained his senses and his anger evaporated. He shook McRay's arms free and turned away from Grant, glad to see that he looked shaken. McRay nodded to Grant.

'My office, now.'

Matt headed back towards his office where Jenny was standing white faced in the doorway.

'Sorry,' he said, a little shamefaced.

She shrugged. 'It was inevitable that he would cause trouble. It's what he enjoys.'

'Mrs Trowbridge?'

'Not yet.'

Matt was disappointed.

'Join Sam. I'll ring you as soon as she comes through, or as soon as I can get hold of Harry.'

* * *

He drove fast, mostly thinking about Fluff and how she would react to Grant's petty comments. He wished he hadn't lost his temper, even if it was only for a moment, but it was the mention of Eppie that had sparked it. Thank God for McRay. If he hadn't intervened, Matt could be on a charge right now. This was the old McRay, back on form. He wouldn't let Grant get away with his trouble making.

CHAPTER 55

Eppie eased herself up from the cold grass. The smell of damp earth clung to her. Pressing her head against the rough tombstone, she risked a peek towards the parking lot. There were only a few cars there, and she couldn't see Clive.

Beyond the car park, she could see the house and the blue lights of the patrol car. Fluff's car was pulled up next to the patrol car. Help was so close. Eppie wondered if she should scream and run towards them.

As she watched, Fluff came out of the house and went towards her car. It was difficult to see but Eppie was sure she was holding the notebook. Thank God she had found it. M would be safe even if it gave her no help.

Which way should she go? A welcome light from the church porch was cutting across the gloom. But if she ran towards it would highlight her.

Then Eppie heard determined footsteps on the path. A thin beam of light hit the gravestone to the side of her. Before it could swing to reach her, she doubled up and ran towards the church.

The sound of a hymn greeted her. Stepping into the church Eppie stopped. This must be the junior choir. There were about twenty, ten- to twelve-year-old boys and girls. The choirmaster was a rotund woman of about fifty.

All of them together would be no match for Clive. Eppie knew she couldn't stay here and moved back into the porch, keeping close to the cold stone walls. She watched for any movement out there in the dark.

There was nothing. No torch, no footsteps, no movement. He could be waiting until she made a break for it. Or maybe he would think she had found help and wouldn't be expecting her to come out. As she waited, wondering what to do, she became aware of footsteps behind her. In a burst of laughter and chatter, the youngsters were leaving. Soon the lights would be turned off leaving her alone. Using this thought to give her courage, Eppie shot out into the dark, hidden amongst the crowd. The children turned left towards the car park, so she ran up a small path leading away from the car park and to the right.

No one reached out to grab her, but she knew she couldn't relax. Somehow she had to get to the spa. Fluff needed help to stop Clive killing M. With no money or phone, she wasn't sure how she could do this. The temperature was beginning to fall and she started to shiver.

The small path came out onto a street of small shops, all of which seemed to have shut up for the night. She turned left heading towards the houses and a sign, which said Kenilworth Castle.

Some of the houses had lights on promising warmth and safety. Would it be better to knock on someone's front door, or stop one of the cars rushing by? They might think she was mad, wandering about with no coat on in the cold, and race on by or shut the door in her face.

Eppie turned as a car slowed behind her, ever fearful that it would be Clive. But the driver was waiting while the car coming the other way passed a parked van. Relieved, she took a step forward, giving a wave, but the driver kept his eyes rigidly forward refusing to notice her.

Disappointed, she stepped back on the curb, only to jump forward again as a taxi slowed on the other side of the road. In response to her frantic waving the taxi stopped. Eppie ran across the road and scrabbled in to sink back relieved in the warmth.

'Where to?'

'Oh. Police station. No, Heath Stone Spa please.'

'You all right?'

'Yes...no.'

'Think we had better make it the Police Station then. That's unless they have shut up for the night. Think they're a bloody shop or something they do. Closed when the burglars and all the other buggers start work. Don't make sense does it?'

'No.'

'Here. How you gonna pay me? You've got no purse or coat.'

'I don't know. I just had to get out of there.'

'Oh like that is it. Can't abide a man who hits a woman. But it still don't pay my bill, Love, does it?'

'I'm sorry.' Eppie toyed with the idea of telling him everything and that a young girl was in danger, unless he took her to the spa, but he would probably think she was mad. Although she was now safe, M and possibly Fluff were still in danger. Maybe she could persuade him to ring the police on his radio, although it had been hard enough to get through last time. It would be best to go straight to the spa and warn M, just in case Fluff hadn't understood her notes.

The taxi waited at the traffic lights indicating to go right. Eppie realised that they were going to pass the parking lot and slumped down in her seat.

There he was. Pulling out in front of them. He couldn't have seen her, could he? Was he on his way to the spa?

The taxi stopped.

'Can't go on, Love, sorry and all that but need the money.'

Eppie knew she must do something. Inspiration struck and she leaned forward.

'Could you take my watch as security? Please.'

She handed it over. He put on the cab light and turned it over in his hand. She knew she had won when he put it in his pocket.

CHAPTER 56

Sam was parked about a hundred yards from the house when Matt joined him.

'Dead as a doornail here, Boss.'

A mental picture of Clive Draper's frail mother came to Matt. 'Don't say that, Sam.'

As always, Sam picked up the undercurrent. 'Why, you don't think…?'

Matt had just filled Sam in about Clive Draper when his mobile rang.

'Affirmative with the wheelchair. It has a squeak. Bring him in, Matt.' Jenny's voice sounded energised, almost excited.

'Any news from Harry yet?' Matt asked, trying to control the answering excitement he was feeling. This was it. At last they had a lead. Could take action.

'No. According to the redoubtable Mrs T, he goes to his daughters on a Monday. She is pulling his next of kin form, so we are working on that.'

'Good,' he said, eager now to be taking some action and already starting the car.

There was no answer as Sam rang the buzzer, just an echoing silence that set Matt's hairs on end. There was something wrong. Signalling Sam to keep ringing, he moved to look through the large bay windows. There were no lights on in the house, and at first it was difficult to see.

Eventually he could make out a figure near the fireplace. It was Mrs Draper but she appeared to be asleep. Matt was certain she didn't have a problem with her hearing yesterday. He knocked loudly on the glass but there was no movement. Now certain Mrs Draper was in trouble, he had the right to force an entry.

It wasn't easy, since the house was protected against burglars, but a plant pot through one of the panes of the kitchen door soon afforded them an entrance. As they entered the living room, Matt moved to Mrs Draper's side, lowering his voice in case she was asleep.

'Mrs Draper, it is Inspector Turrell. We met yesterday.' There was no response and now he could see she was dead. Her face had that certain dull whiteness which showed up the bruises around her thin neck.

Matt hardly needed to check but he followed the routine. She hadn't seemed a very pleasant woman, but even so, Matt felt a certain sadness, for she had died at the hands of her own son. No one deserved that.

Sam was already calling it in and soon this whole house would become a crime scene with Jason and his team taking over. Matt and Sam had a responsibility to make sure that Clive Draper wasn't still in the house, although Matt was sure he was long gone. It gave them the chance to find something that might tell them where he had gone. Jenny would be putting out the APB right now, but this killer was too clever to let himself be seen walking down the street. They needed something else.

Drawing on their forensic gloves, he and Sam began a quick search of the house, starting at the top. The house had three stories, and the top rooms were used for little more than storage. The light overlay of dust showed that nothing had been disturbed for a while.

They continued down to the main bedrooms on the second floor. The rooms were large. Matt was standing in the doorway of what was certainly Mrs Draper's room when Sam gave a shout.

The excited, 'Here, Guv,' was what Matt had been hoping for and he hurried to the large front room. It was a tasteful, if simply furnished, room. Sam was standing by the row of built in cupboards, which took up an entire wall. At one end, besides the immaculate suits, jackets, and shirts that hung in neatly arranged rows were three garment bags. One was open, showing five empty metal hangers. On the sixth was an oversized child's party dress in lilac with a deep purple sash. Matt heard Sam's intake of breath.

'Oh no. Guv, he's on his way to do another three.'

As Sam opened the other two garment bags to reveal more dresses, Matt was already on his mobile to Jenny. He could hear the response car's siren in the background and the conversation was difficult. She was on her way to join them but what he had to say couldn't wait.

Clive must have known that his mother would be discovered. Even if he had been rational when he had started out on his killing spree, he had just killed his own mother. Surely, that would tip him over the edge. And he wasn't the sort to leave the country. No, with nothing to lose, he would want to show off, show the world just how clever he was.

Matt thought back to what the professor had said. He wanted everyone to understand why he had been driven to take this action, or something like that. Maybe Clive wasn't thinking clearly at all, but really believed that he was invincible. Sam counted the dresses in the other two bags; each contained six dresses. So maybe Clive had accepted this might be his last killing spree. Matt was certain he would want to make it count, thumb his nose at them all.

But he had taken three dresses with him. Three women were in danger.

Thank God Eppie was safe. Matt had a sudden moment of doubt. Was there anyway Clive could have found out where she was this time? He consoled himself that Fluff would be home by now and she was no fool. The siren stopped, and he could hear Jenny clearly.

'Did I hear that right, Matt? You think he is about to commit another three?'

'Yes. Hold on.' Sam was trying to get his attention. Matt watched as Sam slid out a stout cardboard box from the bottom of the wardrobe and eased the lid upwards. Inside, thrown together in an untidy mess, were over a hundred model soldiers.

'Inspector,' Jenny demanded.

'Sorry. Sam has just found the soldiers. We believe Clive took three dresses with him, so have to assume that he intends to kill again, Ma'am.'

'Oh, God. Then we have got to stop him. I'm one minute away. Keep searching.'

Matt could hear the urgency in her voice and decided not to mention that they could be too late already.

Sam was pulling out other boxes that contained hair bows, lollipops, and dolls. Matt moved to go through the dressing table drawers but they yielded nothing interesting, so he continued to the bedside cabinet to pick up a small picture frame.

'Interesting.'

Sam came to join him. 'Good looking.'

'Work colleague of Clive's. Name of Ben. Looks like he thinks a lot of him.'

'Which could be why the girls weren't—'

'Molested. Yes, his interest lies elsewhere.'

By the time they had finished, Jason and then Jenny had arrived. Jason was in a hurry to secure his crime scene, so after signing them in, he banished them to hold a brief conference outside the front door.

'He will know we are onto him, but looking at his pattern, I think he will want to show us that he can still outsmart us. I think he will head back to the spa,' Matt said.

'Uniform are still there. I'll alert them. You and Sam go to the spa. I'll ring it in and arrange backup.'

Matt turned towards his car only to find it hemmed in by the forensic team's full complement of vehicles. Even if he went over the neat flowerbed, he couldn't see how he could manoeuvre it out of there in a hurry. It would have to be Sam's old banger, which was still parked on the road.

'Take the response car.' Jenny indicated for the uniformed officer to give up the keys. He was reluctant, until she clicked her fingers impatiently. Matt was already moving towards the car when she shouted after him. 'You've done the course?'

Matt nodded as he jumped into the driver's seat. He did not intend to tell her it was over six years ago.

CHAPTER 5 7

The light from Clive's torch hardly pieced the shadows. It was as if the memorials to the dead were ganging up to protect his quarry. He had always felt ill at ease when passing through graveyards and was finding it hard to force himself forward.

Then he saw her run towards the lighted church and hesitated. Her gods might give her temporary shelter, but his were more powerful. They would bring her to him at the right time. Clive would let her think she was safe for now, and then, when he had her husband and his team distracted by his next masterpiece, he would seek her out again. Eppie Turrell would keep until later. Besides, he had to attend to Mika.

* * *

He pulled into the lay-by and turned off the engine. It wouldn't be long now. The sun had lowered behind the trees and dusk was turning rapidly into night. The birds were in their nests, twittering to each other. Mother always sent them to bed when the birds were in their nests.

Mother was asleep now. Asleep like the birds. The thought made him smile. He had made sure she was warm, like a little bird in the nest. Except she had no one to cuddle. This made him laugh.

Even to his ears, the laugh sounded odd, as it reverberated around the parked car. Maybe he was going mad. No. No. This would mean that they had won. Father, Blake-Spencer, and all the others who had tried to bend him to their will, order him about, like DI Turrell.

Clive pulled back, forcing himself to concentrate. He ran his hands over the patterned leather of the steering wheel, the cold hardness of the side window, felt the smooth roundness of the gear leaver. She would be here soon, and he wanted it to be perfect. This one was for Ben. For their love. He imagined telling him what he had done in his honour. It would bind them together forever, and Ben would hold him and love him.

A car swished by, rocking his car and disturbing his thoughts. He glanced at the dashboard clock. It was time for him to become Detective Inspector Browning again and to get into position to meet her. He checked the 'warrant' card, sure that in the dark it would pass muster. She would feel it a privilege to be escorted into work, to be protected.

Clive locked the car door and hurried the five hundred yards to the place he had chosen, just a few feet from the main driveway to the spa. He had worked out that she would come from the left, so he concentrated on the road with only the occasional glance towards the right, just in case she had decided to come a different way.

Eight minutes to go if she was on time. What if she was sick or had swapped shifts? No, he wouldn't even think about it. This was meant to be. He had planned it all too carefully. He had proven that he could fool them all, that he was invincible. She had to come.

The deepening dusk was now infused with light swirls of fog that seemed perfect for his purpose. Even nature was working with him. She must come to take her role in destiny.

At last, headlights glanced off the hedges as a car approached. Soon the black and white mini was driving towards him, slowing down and indicating that it was turning into the spa drive. Clive stepped into the road and held up his hand. She braked but stayed in the car. He moved to the driver's window and performed the motion of winding it down while holding up his warrant card. She obeyed him without question.

'Detective Inspector Browning, Ma'am. We are taking no chances after the recent events here at the spa and are escorting all lone females into the building.' Clive made his voice sound serious and official, modelling it on DI Turrell. She gave a little giggle.

'Oh. How nice, Inspector. Thank you.'

'I will ride with you. It will be safer that way.' He moved around to the passenger side of the car and waited for her to click open the door. Then he was inside and indicated that she should proceed.

Clive glanced at her as they wound their way up the driveway towards the car park. She would fit into the yellow dress he had chosen, and it would highlight her dark hair. He wanted this statement to be perfect. The excitement was building within him. Eager to do their work, his hands itched and tingled. But he must be patient, must wait until they reached the darkest side of the staff car park, when the job could be done without fear of discovery. Where even the CCTV didn't reach.

The Mini's headlights swung around a curve in the drive and caught the patrol car full on. Two uniform officers, coffee in hand, turned momentarily towards them. Clive tried not to hold his breath and instead gave a brief nod. The Mini passed by and continued up the driveway, while Clive congratulated himself on his plan. It was obvious they would have stopped him if he had been a lone male but a couple would not pose a threat.

His confidence was shaken seconds later, however, as the patrol car sprung into action. Its siren shot through the stillness of the night and the blue light glanced repeatedly across the back of their heads. Was he found out?

As they listened, he was relieved to realise that the sound was moving away.

'Will it be him?' Mika asked, nervously.

'I wouldn't think so,' Clive assured her in a calm, but authoritative voice. 'Probably an accident or a domestic.'

She was looking scared, and he couldn't afford to have her getting skittish at this point.

'We still have a team on site,' he added. This seemed to reassure her and she drove through the main guest parking lot and into the smaller staff one beyond.

Clive directed her to park just where he wanted her, close to the hedge where he had hidden his props. She switched off the engine and turned to thank him. He reached out, as if to pat her shoulder, but instead grasped her around the neck and pulled her towards him.

By the time she had realised what was happening, he had brought up his left hand to enclose her neck. She was struggling frantically, fighting for her life. And she was strong. Her hands had found their way to his face and were scrabbling to reach his eyes. The confined space within the car was hampering his hold, and he could feel his grip loosening. He tried to move his head away from her probing fingers but felt a sharp scraping of nails across his right eye. His hands went instinctively to his face.

She used this moment to kick open her door, stagger from the car, and disappear into the dark of the car park.

Momentarily blinded and in pain, by the time Clive got out of the car, she was yards ahead of him, halfway across the staff parking lot and dangerously close to the well-lit guest parking area where the CCTV would pick them both up. She mustn't be allowed to get away, to spoil his plan.

Ignoring the pain in his eye, he began to run after her. She was running wildly, fuelled by terror. Clive made a supreme effort and closed the gap, but then she glanced back and added a desperate spurt.

She was his. This couldn't be happening. No one was allowed to refuse their place, their role in his statements.

Even Mother. Mother. Mother, who had let him place his head in her lap, had stroked his hair, sang to him. He should go home to Mother. But Mother wouldn't like it if he let this girl go. She would be cross. *'Always finish what you start, Clive.'* He could hear her voice echoing through his head.

He heard a twig snap. She was trying to take a short cut through the bushes that bordered the car park. Should he run through the parking lot and cut her off or follow her? Mother was silent. Maybe she didn't like him killing off her favourite ones. The ones she loved and cuddled. But she no longer had the power. He did.

The thought added renewed energy, and he dived into the bushes behind Mika, hearing her laboured gasps just ahead of him. He was catching up. Could reach out and grasp her.

She turned to lash out at him. He made his move to end her freedom but felt his arm held. Mother? Mother had come back to restrain him. As the girl stumbled out onto the forecourt of the spa, Clive realised it was just a thorn tearing into his jacket. The girl had almost reached the front entrance. He must stop her.

He raced after her, but she had gone inside as he approached. The light seemed blinding, painful to his eyes. *'Always finish what you start, Clive.'* Mother was right; he had to go on.

There she was in Reception. Clive moved towards her, but someone was blocking his way. The matron woman, solid and sure, feet rooted to the ground in front of his girl.

'Back off. I warn you, the police are on their way.'

Clive moved to the left in an attempt to get behind her, to the girl, his girl, but she turned again to face him, shielding his prize behind her.

'She's mine.'

'Not this time.'

'No, no, you can't stop this happening. You can't stop me.'

'We'll see about that.'

She altered her stance and brought up her hands as if she was going to box with him. This made Clive laugh, and he moved forward. The girl screamed. The Matron dropped her arms and looked behind him.

'Thank, God. You got here in time.'

He turned, expecting a regiment of police, and then sniggered as he recognised the little smart-ass police officer who had tried to trip him up.

She held up her warrant card and took a step towards Clive.

'Detective Constable Meadows. Clive Draper, I am arresting you for the murders of Sandi Tomlinson and Amy Metcalfe. You do not have to say anything.'

Exhilarated, he laughed again and heard it reverberate loudly around the lobby to bounce back at him in a thousand high-pitched shards. It was as if he had multiplied, become even more powerful, invincible. Fate had sent this woman into his hands. She was meant to pay for her crime. He could see that now.

'But it may harm your defence if you do not mention, when questioned, something which you later rely on in court.'

Clive moved towards her and she held her ground, although he saw she was positioning herself for his attack. Not that she had a chance.

'Anything you do say may be given as evidence.'

He was within two feet of her now and held out his hands, as if in supplication to her wishes, but she was wary. He stayed that way and waited. She looked at him hard and long before continuing.

There was a moment's silence. This was fun, letting her think she could have the slightest power over him. With fate and the gods on his side, she had no chance. She stepped forward.

'Turn around and put your hands behind your back.'

Clive half turned, as if to obey, waiting until she reached one hand back for the handcuffs. Then he swung round and struck hard, felling her with one blow to the side of the neck. He heard a cry from behind.

Given her colouring, the lilac dress would have been better, but the yellow would have to do. He must prepare her, take her to the car park. As he bent to lift her, he thought there was a slight flutter of her eyelids. He must finish the job.

A feeble blow caught him across the right shoulder. He turned to find the matron woman backing away armed with a hard file of some kind. She wasn't worth bothering with, and he only needed to wave his arms and shout 'boo,' to enjoy watching her as she scuttled back to the girl, nearly falling over in her hurry. The girl stepped forward to steady her.

Giggling to himself, he turned back to collect the Constable. Someone else stood in the doorway. His gods were rewarding him.

Mrs Eppie Turrell. They had presented her to him. He was truly blessed.

She paused to take in everything before rushing towards the Constable, kneeling at her side feeling for a pulse. And then she looked Clive directly in the eye. 'Leave her alone.'

Clive knelt and leant towards her. 'Oh I will. Now that you are here.' He reached across to take her warm neck into his tingling hands, but she was too fast and stood, aiming a kick at his head. Still half-kneeling, he caught her foot and twisted, hearing a crack, as she landed face down on the marble floor.

Then, aware that the Matron woman was approaching him, he moved to scoop his prize into his arms.

CHAPTER 58

There was silence between them, a heavy sense of urgency as Matt skilfully manoeuvred out of the driveway now crowded with police vehicles. It was as if they were both holding their breath.

Just as they were clear and ready to turn into the road Matt's phone rang. Matt hesitated, glancing down to check the caller. It was Fluff. His immediate thought was of Eppie, and he wondered if anything had happened to her. With a coldness spreading through him he answered the call, putting it on speaker.

'Fluff?'

'Guv. I have been trying to get you. I can't go into the details but there is a possibility that our man is a Clive Draper. He may be planning to attack again tonight at the spa. I'm almost there now.'

Burying the sense of guilt he felt at the relief that Eppie wasn't in danger, Matt replied. 'Spot on. He's just murdered his mother. We're on our way too.'

'Matt, that's not the only thing.'

'Fluff?' Something in her voice told him it was bad.

'Eppie is missing. Clive went to the flat and I think she must have escaped him. She had left me some notes about who Clive was going for next. There is a patrol car looking for her. I'm sure they will find her soon.'

A mixture of fear and anger shot through Matt. He couldn't deal with either right now. Had to carry on.

'Liaise with uniform when you get there.'

'OK, but I'm halfway up the driveway and there's no sign of the patrol car.'

'Shit.'

'Guv?'

'Hold off until backup arrives, that's an order. We'll be there in fifteen minutes, try to make it ten.'

'Something's going down here, Guv. Call you back.'

'Fluff? Fluff? Bugger and blast.'

Matt didn't waste anymore time but cleared the driveway, allowing the siren to scatter startled motorists out of his way.

'Sam, call Jenny. Tell her we need her to get backup to the spa ASAP. Tell her Fluff is there on her own, that will shift her.'

With a puzzled glance at Matt, Sam picked up the police radio.

'She has come to the same conclusion we have and is on the scene now, damn it.' Matt swerved to avoid a deaf and blind driver who was blocking the only chance they had of getting through the junction.

'Bloody moron.'

'Uniform should be there though, Guv.'

'Should be yes. But apparently not.'

While Matt concentrated on a minor busy patch, Sam rang Jenny. Matt heard him relay the message and ask about uniform before ending the call.

'Blimey, you were right. She's jumping into action, no questions or anything. What's going on then?'

'Tell you later, Sam, OK.'

As Sam nodded, accepting that the present situation was paramount, the radio buzzed into life. Sam picked it up.

'DS Withers.'

'Tell the boss that some taxi driver rang to say his wife is on her way to the spa, where she believes another murder is to take place.'

'Eppie? What the hell? When?'

Grant's voice crackled over the radio. 'About a minute ago, Sir.'

Matt ignored the snide Sir at the end. This was the wrong time to get riled by the man.

'Where was she when she called?'

'I'm afraid I don't know, Sir. I wasn't aware that it was part of my duties to keep track of your wife.'

Sam gave a sharp intake of breath as Matt scraped past a car that had pulled over only to pull out again just as they were even with him. By the time the way was clear, the radio had gone dead.

'Bastard.'

'Shall I get him back?'

'No. He will be no use. Try Fluff.'

'She'll be fine, Guv. You know what women are like.'

No, Matt thought, *I don't know*. Eppie was the first woman he had ever wanted to share his life with. And she was turning out to be an unknown quantity. He was learning fast that she would do what she thought was right and not as he wanted. Where did he ever get this stupid idea that a wife would be subservient to her husband anyway? It wasn't how it was in this day and age. He knew he was damn lucky that she had been willing to give it all up for him.

'Keep trying.' Matt couldn't keep the tension out of his voice. They had all been so busy with the murder of Mrs Draper. Surely to God, Eppie wouldn't be trying to stop Clive Draper on her own? At least Fluff was there now.

As he manoeuvred in and out of the now thinning traffic, Matt knew that it would be just what Eppie would do, and he knew he had to put it out of his head for the moment. Negotiating traffic at this speed, even with the lights and siren was dangerous enough, and he dared not give way to the panic he was feeling.

By his side, he heard Sam repeating the call to Fluff. But there was still no answer.

Matt felt a spike of anger. It was as if Eppie had no regard for his feelings, the pain that would devastate him if anything happened to her.

CHAPTER 59

The Inspector's woman was struggling to get to her feet when Clive reached her, but one leg was damaged and there was blood running down her forehead. This was a pity, since he wanted all his *statements* to be perfect. He took out his hankie and attempted to wipe away the blood.

She didn't seem to understand what Clive was trying to do and dragged herself backwards away from him, until she was against one of the pillars to the left. He stopped, facing her. Her eyes held no fear, just defiance.

She must go to sleep, like his Mother. He brought up his hands, allowing them to move towards her neck, savouring the thought of compressing that pink skin. It didn't matter if there were footsteps behind him. The foolish old woman couldn't stop him now.

Clive ignored the blue light flickering in the corners of his vision and the sirens slicing through the night, coming closer this time. He had to do it now. Make her his. He could see she was preparing to hit out, but that didn't matter, she couldn't stop the inevitable.

The blow when it came was from the side, catching Clive unawares and knocking him sideward. Regaining his balance, he spun to face his attacker, hands in defence position. Clive didn't recognize the man, but he had that certain solidity of a police officer. He had no time for this, but the man was already closing in. Obviously, he wasn't going to bother with the niceties, was only intent on stopping Clive.

'Get out of here,' the man shouted to Clive's prize.

She looked dazed but took his advice and began to hobble away up a corridor nearby. Clive noticed that the matron woman and the girl had retreated back behind the reception counter, although the woman still clutched the file to her ample bosom as if it were a shield.

The man lunged forward trying to grasp his arm, no doubt to spin him round and bring his arm up in restraint. Clive aimed a blow at the man's windpipe. Seeing the blow coming, the man moved his head, but the blow landed with sufficient force to cause him to double up, fighting for breath. Clive added a vicious kick to his side, and he sprawled on the floor, face turning red and beginning to froth at the mouth. There was no time to finish the job. He needed to recapture his prize. Nothing would matter then.

With a last look of contempt towards the two women behind the desk, Clive set off along the corridor after Mrs Turrell. She wouldn't have been able to move fast, and he was sure to catch up with her. When she became the centrepiece of his third statement, it would devastate DI Turrell and he would know forever that Clive was cleverer and more powerful.

Clive lifted his voice so that it bounced back off the walls of the corridor.

'Where are you Mrs Turrell? You know you can't escape me.'

CHAPTER 60

Eppie limped along the corridor, trying hard to remember where it headed. She had to find somewhere to hide before he caught up with her or she would be dead within seconds.

Was Fluff dead? She had looked so white.

Her head hurt, but it was the leg that was slowing her down. She forced herself on through the pain, moving as fast as she could.

She passed the multi-purpose gym; it offered no place to hide. She went on past linen and equipment stores to the end of the corridor, till the only option left to her was the double doors leading to the aqua complex.

Behind the swing doors was a wonderland of water. Bubbling hot pools were interspersed amongst twenty-foot palms; waterfalls cascaded over rocky outcrops, and splashed down into the large irregular shaped swimming pool. The whole area was larger than a football pitch.

Looking around, she realised this was a mistake, for although the area was huge she couldn't see anywhere to secrete herself. She started to turn back then froze as footsteps came towards her. He was calling to her.

'Where are you, Mrs Turrell? You know you can't escape me.'

A shudder ran through her. There must be somewhere. Would she be better in the water? Eppie was a strong swimmer and the pain from her leg would ease in the water.

'You are meant to be mine.'

Eppie could see the madman's outline behind the doors. She couldn't wait any longer. She limped to the edge of the pool and eased herself in. As he burst through the doors, she struck out towards the middle of the pool.

There was silence as he stood looking for her and Eppie slowed her pace to move through the water as quietly as possible.

'Mrs Turrell. The gods have brought you here to me. You are mine.'

Although the water had muffled his voice it had a booming quality, which made him sound nearer than he was. Eppie renewed her pace.

'I will show them all. I am the cleverest. Mother can tell you that. She is sleeping. *"Rock a bye baby in the tree top, when the wind blows, the cradle will rock."'*

Eppie slowed down, trying to judge where Clive was and if he had entered the water after her. She wondered at first if she was hearing things. Maybe the bang to her head was causing hallucinations. She stopped and listened. A lullaby spread out over the water followed by an inane laugh.

This was more frightening. There would be no reasoning with a madman, who was intent on killing her.

She could see him now. He was moving towards the edge of the pool, planning to follow her across the rocks. Eppie swam on past a large island and for a moment she thought she must be out of his view.

In front of her was a small island. This might be her chance. If she could clamber on it and hide amongst the rocks, he might miss her. It could give the police time to reach her. She thought of Fluff and prayed she would be all right.

Clambering awkwardly onto the island, she was about to crouch down and hide when the double doors flapped open. Clive had flattened himself against the wall.

Eppie screamed a warning.

CHAPTER 61

As they cleared the last bend in the drive, Matt could see the two police cars outside, the emergency lights flashing blue and red over the walls of the building and the grounds. At least Fluff had backup and that meant Eppie would be safe.

Even so, he skidded the car to a halt and ran for the entrance, bent low and ready for action with Sam beside him. Whatever he had expected, Matt was shocked at the scene. Two officers down.

Fluff was lying deathly still with Mrs Trowbridge kneeling at her side. She gave Matt a look of desperation as she glanced up. Nearby a dark haired young lady was trying to get Grant to sip water from a glass. He was coughing and choking. Matt was surprised to see him here.

As he ran towards Fluff, he barked the order, 'Officers down.' As Sam began calling for urgent medical and backup, Matt knelt beside Fluff, horrified to see how pale she was. Feeling for a pulse, he had trouble finding it at first, and then felt an immense relief as the slight, thready, life energy fluttered under his fingers.

'Come on, Fluff, come on. We're here now. You'll be OK. Stick with us, don't you dare…'

'Guv.'

Matt looked up. Sam was besides Grant. The man was trying to speak between fighting for breath.

'You should hear this.'

Something in Sam's eyes forced him to his feet and over to Grant. The man had a look of desperation that was nothing to do with his injuries, and was pointing towards the left. As he coughed and spluttered, all Matt could make out was the word woman. He was about to tell Sam to take a look when Mrs Trowbridge stood and took a step towards him.

'It's Eppie.'

Matt stared at her, part of him unwilling to hear what she had said.

'Eppie. He's following Eppie.'

The realization shot through him like cold steel, giving power to his muscles. He was halfway towards the corridor shouting over his shoulder to Sam. 'Stay with Fluff, order her to hang on.' Then he was pounding down the corridor, frantically checking every exit as he ran. At the entrance to the swimming pool he hesitated.

For a moment Matt stood, uncertain of which way to turn. He listened and tried to catch any sound above the water. He could hear nothing and wondered if there was another way out.

At that moment, his mobile rang. Before he could answer it, something hit him hard across the back of the head throwing him into the pool. As he hit the water, he thought he had heard someone shout out his name.

The next few seconds were hazy as the water closed over his head. The taste of chlorine mixed with blood rushed into his mouth. Dimly through the water, he could see a wavering figure standing at the edge of the pool. He kicked hard against the side to propel himself several feet away from the edge leaving a spreading trail of blood behind him.

He surfaced and wiped the water from his eyes. At last he was looking into the face of the man who had murdered at least three women, one of them his own mother. Matt didn't want to count Fluff, not yet, although she had lain so still. Eppie he couldn't even bear to think about. Had she called out to him?

It always surprised Matt over the years that evil didn't show on the face. There were no lines or marks, no demonic light pouring from the eyes. Clive had quite a pleasant face, even if now it was etched with desperation, a desperation he knew mirrored his own.

This killer was cornered, dangerous, and had nothing to lose. Matt cursed himself for letting him take first blood. Matt gave a shake to rid himself of the excess water and a stab of pain shot through his head. Ignoring this he moved towards Clive.

Clive glanced towards the door looking for a way of escape. He stopped and Matt was thankful to hear footsteps running towards them. There was no escape.

Matt pushed on through the water and saw Clive pause and look towards the small island. Matt followed his gaze although the pain in his head screamed. Through the blur he could see a figure. It must be Eppie. The figure waved and he heard her call.

'Matt. Let the others take him. Please.'

Behind him there was movement and he turned, causing his head to complain and his vision to blur even more. When he re-focused, he felt a mixture of fear and rage race through him, realising that Clive was starting to scramble across the rocks at the edge of the pool towards Eppie.

Matt knew he had to get to her first. He turned and began to swim across the pool to intercept Clive. He aimed for an area of sun loungers, set on a mock sandy beach, half way around the pool. He was glad his muscles were responding and his head began to clear as he ploughed forward reaching the sand at the same time as Clive.

Clive jumped to the left and nearly fell over a lounger. Matt followed, throwing the chairs aside before lunging forward in a rugby tackle, which brought them both crashing down. Clive was stronger than he looked, and Matt struggled to gain the upper hand.

As they fought, rolling over in the sand, it was an even match until Clive aimed a kick at Matt's stomach and staggered to his feet, pausing only to scoop up a handful of sand. Too late, Matt saw the thousands of grains flying towards him. Most of it went straight into his eyes and he floundered.

Clive used the advantage to clamber up the rocks—still heading towards Eppie. Matt ignored the sand even though it was stinging and scrambled almost blindly after him. It took him only a second to catch up.

Clive was on the edge of one of the small hot pools. Matt decided on brute force and heaved himself forward again. He caught Clive around the knees causing him to lose balance and throwing them both sideways into the bubbling whirlpool.

Sinking beneath the bubbles, they writhed against each other, tossed by the powerful water jets. Matt felt his eyes start to clear of the sand. He tried to get a stronger hold on Clive, but his fingers slipped and fumbled on the wet cloth. Clive kicked out viciously. Matt knew he had to stop this madman before he could get to Eppie.

As they both surfaced, he aimed a right-hander at Clive's head. Clive ducked sideways and managed to climb onto the next step where he turned and delivered a karate chop to Matt's neck. Matt moved his head just in time, catching the deadly stinging blow on his left ear.

Clive used the time gained to clamber out of the pool and on towards Eppie. Matt dragged himself out, weighted down by the water that streamed from his wet clothes, and staggered on after Clive.

Clive was slipping and sliding on the rocks ahead of him—wet feet finding no purchase. Matt could hear his laboured breathing just a few feet away, as he struggled to catch up with him and keep his own footing. All those muddy Saturdays on the rugby field were beginning to pay off.

Then the pace of the racing waters changed, the bubbling and frothing turned into a series of gurgles and trickles. Matt became aware that there were figures at the far edge of the pool. Help was on the way.

Spurred on, Matt closed in on Clive who turned and prepared to land another karate chop.

Matt was ready for him this time and dodged it easily bringing up his right fist in an upper cut to the jaw. Clive fell back and Matt moved in, ready to restrain him.

Help was close, but they had no chance of reaching Eppie in time, only he could do that. The blow had floored Clive, and he seemed groggy, but Matt didn't want to take any chances. He stood over Clive trying to assess if he was faking. Deciding he was feigning, Matt bent forward to haul him to his feet. Feeling Clive's muscles tense, he moved swiftly to put him into a restraining hold.

Clive kicked and struggled, as if he didn't feel the pain the hold must be bringing to his arm and shoulder.

'You can't win. She is mine, Inspector.'

'Not this time.'

Matt guessed at his determination and pushed Clive forward onto his knees. The pure physical effort of the fight and the blow to the head was beginning to take its toll, and Matt was unsure how much longer he could hold on.

'Sam hurry,' he called, hearing the fear in his voice.

'Hold on, Guv, nearly there.'

Matt had never been so glad to hear Sam's voice. He dared not look around but could hear footsteps clambering over the rocks; then, at last, Sam was at his side ready to take over.

Matt waited until Sam had a firm hold on Clive's arm, just below his and then eased his grip. It was the moment Clive had been waiting for, and it was as if he had been storing every ounce of energy to take one last spring. In one leap, he was three feet away and already into a long running stride, springing from rock to rock, the survival instinct now adding fuel to his muscles.

The suddenness of Clive's move had knocked Matt off balance, but Sam was already racing after him. Matt's first thought was of Eppie, but he saw with relief that other members of the team were moving towards her. Eppie was safe, and there was nowhere for Clive to go.

He must realise that, Matt thought, as he watched Clive reach one of the supporting girders at the far wall. Sam had stopped a few feet away. Matt had a sudden fear and shouted a warning. 'Sam, be careful. He's got a lethal karate chop.'

Matt watched as Sam stepped back. Clive gave a sudden smile before turning and began to climb the girder. Matt staggered to his feet. 'Stop him,' he ordered.

Sam made a move towards the girder and then hesitated as a female voice gave a command. 'Leave him, Sergeant. He can't go anywhere.'

Matt turned to see DI Hadden standing at the edge of the pool. Couldn't she see the risk? If Clive jumped, he would never have to face his victim's families in court.

CHAPTER 62

The growing sense of exhilaration gave him a surge of power. He had escaped the Inspector, as it was meant to be. Soon he would be well out of his reach, soaring high over his head, able to look down on him with contempt. Clive's wet shoes slid on the iron girder causing a sickening slide downwards. Despite his grazed shins, he forced himself on. He couldn't lose. Nothing could stop him.

At last, he reached the top. Pausing to regain his breath, he looked down upon Inspector Turrell. Even from this height, he looked battered, with blood caking the side of his face. Clive watched as the sergeant reached his side and he saw the DI gesture upwards.

Their voices seemed far away, drifting up to him only after first echoing around the complex. Clive tried out his own voice, delighted in its powerful flight around the domed roof before it sank to the ground for the enlightenment of the mere mortals.

'You can't beat me, Inspector. You can't beat me. You can't beat me.' He liked the repetitive beat. 'I've won, Inspector. I've won. I've won.'

'There is nowhere for you to go. Come down and we'll talk. I'll get you some help.'

Why did this useless inspector think he needed help? Clive was completely out of his reach.

With a tremendous effort, he hefted himself to sit astride one of the pillars that crossed the pool. High up and all powerful, like the gods, he would be able to fend off anyone trying to reach him with a swift kick or karate chop.

Below him, the area around the pool was filling up with other members of the DI's team.

'You. Come down immediately,' that woman's voice rang out again.

The sharpness of her voice sounded like his Mother. Had she come for him? She sounded cross.

Clive would sing her a lullaby and she would go back to sleep with the birds. He laughed at the thought and began to sing.

CHAPTER 63

All Matt wanted to do was go to Eppie and hold her. At least she was safe, and he could see uniform had just reached her. His head was throbbing, and he felt the urge to lie down. But it wasn't over yet. Although there was nowhere for this killer to go, he still wasn't in custody.

Clive had reached the top of the girder and had swung himself easily onto one of the metal beams crossing the pool. Maybe it was best not to put Sam at risk. His team had been devastated enough by this bastard. He wondered how Fluff was.

Sam looked reluctant but returned to join Matt. Matt felt himself sway with the effort of looking up. Sam put an arm out to steady him.

'You need help, Guv. He's not going anywhere.'

Matt knew he was right, but he wanted to see this through to the end. He sat down on a nearby rock to regain his balance. He could see Eppie limping towards the edge of her island with the encouragement of the uniformed officers.

Above them, Clive was also watching. He seemed to be laughing at his achievement. His voice boomed up into the domed roof before spiralling down to them.

'I've won, Inspector. I've won. I've won, won.'

The childlike words echoed like a mantra around the complex.

'Bloody hell. He's gone barmy,' Sam exclaimed.

'Probably always was. Just good at hiding it.' Matt thought they would need the white coat brigade to talk Clive down. Feeling stronger, he stood. He had a better idea, but before he could tell Sam, a paramedic came towards him.

'Matt, stand down.' Jenny nodded towards the paramedic.

Matt guessed she must be torn between dealing with this and being with Fluff. She took in what was happening and began giving orders.

'You. Come down, immediately.'

Her sharp voice seemed to fly straight up to Clive. He paused and looked down.

'Mother?'

As the paramedic reached his side, Matt reached out a hand for Sam, drawing him close and giving whispered instructions, before allowing himself to be tended to. Sam hurried away, already on his mobile, going around the back of Jenny so that she didn't notice him leaving.

'I'm not your mother. Come down.'

'Shush. Mother is sleeping.'

Clive started to softly sing a lullaby. *Rock a bye baby, in the tree top. When the wind blows the cradle will rock. When the bough breaks the cradle will fall. Down will come baby, cradle and all.*'

There was an eerie stillness as everyone listened. Matt felt a shiver creep down his spine as the lullaby became louder and louder. Jenny broke the spell.

'Oh God. He's playing the loony card.'

She turned in disgust to those closest to her. Matt wondered if she had forgotten all her negotiating training. This was the wrong way to handle him. Matt tried to stand, but found a firm hand held him in place.

'I wouldn't advise it, Sir. That's a nasty head wound, and I need to make sure you are stable before we can move you.'

Matt felt like telling the man that he had been doing a lot more than mere moving, but a part of him knew the man was right and was only doing his job. He sat back and during the man's administrations tried to see Eppie.

The other paramedic was wading across a small strip of water, bag held high to reach her. One of the uniformed officers was already with her. She would be safe now. Matt had to give up and let Jenny handle things her way, even if it wasn't right.

An enormous sense of tiredness came over him. He felt himself being manoeuvred gently into the recovery position on the rocky ground. From this angle he could see Clive inching along his beam. He seemed far away, like a circus dream from childhood.

'I am Detective Inspector Hadden, and I need you to return to the ground immediately, Mr Draper.'

Her words had no effect, and Matt watched as the singing grew louder and Clive continued to move forward. His eyes seemed to be fixed on something ahead but down to his left. Matt tried to move his head to look, but the man tending to him spoke sharply.

'Try to lie still, please.'

The paramedic had moved in front of Matt and was using a stethoscope to listen to his heart. There was nothing Matt could do but lie still; it was over for him.

But something was stopping him from drifting off, something important. Where was Sam? Had he been successful? Why didn't he come back?

In the background, Matt could hear Jenny's strident voice, laced with Clive's humming. The humming stopped. Suddenly, Matt knew exactly what Clive was planning to do.

He resisted the paramedic and sat up, pushing the man aside. Clive was much farther along on the beam and right above Eppie. He was going to jump on Eppie.

Wavering, Matt managed to stand and shout. 'Jenny.'

She turned, with one glance dismissing his usefulness. He had to get her attention. He took a step forward with the paramedic holding onto his arm.

'He's going to jump.' With great effort, Matt managed to get the words out at almost his normal volume. She turned towards him again and then back to Clive, assessing the situation. It seemed an age before she took action.

'Get everyone out from under him—now. Fast.'

Matt sank down exhausted onto the rock to watch as the uniformed officer, the other paramedic, and Eppie looked up, all aware for the first time of the danger they were in.

It was as if they were frozen, then they started to move. The officer picked up Eppie and was preparing to enter the water. On the other side of the small gap, the other officer was reaching out to receive her. The paramedic began gathering up his gear.

'Stop. Stop. Stop.'

Everyone looked up at Clive. He was directly above the group. Matt wondered how accurate his aim would be if he jumped now. It was difficult to say, but someone was likely to get hurt. They needed a negotiator. In this situation, it was one of the first things Matt would have done. He had learned that lesson the hard way.

'She is mine. Get away from her.'

Not one of the group moved an inch, and Matt was grateful for such brave men. Jenny tried to distract Clive.

'Mr Draper.'

He gave her only a cursory glance.

'Mr Draper, talk to me. We'll try and get you whatever you need.'

'I need nothing. *"Finish what you have started, Clive."* That's what you always say, Mother. '

Jenny moved closer to Clive.

'Clive, I want you to leave this now.'

Matt could see what she was trying to do, but she was treading a fine line and could antagonise him instead. Clive glanced in her direction again.

'Shush, Mother is asleep. Asleep with the birds.' Clive giggled at this. 'Shush.'

Jenny seemed at a loss. Below Clive the group looked as if they were preparing to move. Matt could see it was going to be difficult to move at any speed with an injured person between them. Clive had picked up on their intentions.

'No. You must not take her. She is mine.'

Clive had sat himself sideward on the beam. He looked about to throw himself off. It was hard to judge from where Matt was, but he seemed to be over Eppie. The island was small, leaving little option for her and the others. He wanted to shout out for Eppie to throw herself in the water. That would give her the best chance.

Jenny was pacing up and down. She looked angry.

'Right, I've had enough of this. We'll have to go up and get him.'

'Wrong move,' Matt muttered beside himself. The paramedic gave his arm a squeeze in sympathy. Matt heaved himself to his feet again and staggered towards Jenny. This time, the paramedic did not try to stop him.

There was a general gasp as Clive first crouched and then rose to his feet, balancing precariously on the narrow beam. Matt realised he would be able to take better aim from that position. It would be like diving.

Would Eppie, who was injured, be able to move out of his way fast enough? Matt doubted it, even if there was anywhere to go on the small rocky island. He needed to reach Jenny, tell her what to do.

'It's me he really wants to hurt. Let me distract him.'

Matt thought at first that Jenny was going to refuse but then she nodded ungraciously and Matt stepped forward. He was trying to recall the details of a basic course on negotiating, taken many years ago. Something about making friends with the hostage taker. He didn't think that was going to work with Clive. Aware that the paramedic was close behind him, he took a couple of deep breaths and stepped forward.

'Clive.'

Clive turned towards him. He tottered and went into a crouch in an effort to regain his balance.

'Detective Inspector Turrell. I thought I had dispatched you?' Clive said, giving Matt his attention for the moment.

'I have to admit, you certainly got the better of me, Clive.'

'That was a foregone conclusion, Inspector. You didn't have a chance. I am too clever.'

'Very clever. I can't begin to understand how you managed it all, right under my nose, too. I must be really stupid.'

Matt kept his gaze on Clive, although it hurt to keep his head at this angle. He dared not drop his eyes to Eppie for a moment, in case this drew Clive's attention to her. He hoped the group would realise what he was doing and manage to get away.

Clive was laughing out loud, a strange, almost manic laugh that bounced about until only the lingering echoes remained.

'You are very, very stupid, Inspector, if you think you can distract me from my task.'

Matt cursed as he watched Clive stand again. He sought for something to hold him.

'I really would like to know how you managed to outwit me. After all, you wouldn't want anyone else to take the credit; the fame belongs to you. There's always a copycat waiting, one who could take your glory away.'

Clive hesitated, and it was as if the room held its breath. Then he turned back towards Matt.

'No one will follow me. No one has the power.'

Matt watched as Clive lifted up his arms as if speaking to his disciples. The man was raving. Then he stopped, lowered his arms and, for a moment, Matt thought he might forget himself and take a step forward.

But Clive's attention was focused on something behind Matt. Matt turned to follow his gaze. Standing just inside the swimming pool was Sam. By his side was Ben.

Sending up a silent thanks to Sam, Matt prayed that the young man would agree to help them. Sam had obviously told Ben what was going on as he looked pale and frightened. Sam brought him across to Matt.

'Ben says he'll do his best, Guv.'

Matt nodded, feeling his strength fading. From nowhere, the paramedic had procured a folding chair for him to sit on, and he sank down thankfully onto it, nodding for Ben to come closer. The young man bent his head to listen to Matt's whispered instruction.

'Thanks for doing this. It won't be easy, but this could help us save the lives of the people over there. Clive is threatening to jump on them, and I don't fancy their chances if he jumps from that height. I need you to persuade him to come down to you. Say whatever you think he wants to hear. And remember, he is mentally unbalanced at the moment.'

Ben nodded and Matt was relieved he had caught on fast.

'Don't talk to that man, Ben. He is my enemy,' Clive shouted from above, his voice booming throughout the vast complex.

Ben took a large step away from Matt.

'I'm here for you. That's all.'

'I knew you would come. See, I have them all at my feet.'

'You sure do, Clive.'

'I have wanted to tell you all about my powers.'

'Ha, I already knew you're special. Come on, how could I forget Sunday?'

Despite being thrown into this bizarre situation, Ben was doing really well, lightening the situation and recalling good moments. Matt watched as Clive sat down on the beam. He was relaxing. That was good.

'I wanted to tell you all about it then, when you held me,' Clive said.

'I'll hold you now and you can tell me,' Ben replied.

'Like mother. Mother, where is mother?'

Clive was looking around and starting to get agitated. Matt whispered across to Ben. 'Tell him she is sleeping.'

'Mother is having a nap right now. Clive, come down so we can be together.'

'Shush. Mother is asleep.'

'Time for us now.'

'She wouldn't hold me.'

'I'll hold you.'

This needed to end and quickly. Matt could see Jenny, who had been joined by McRay, was getting restless. He whispered to Ben again.

'Move closer, but not too close. Encourage him to come down.'

Ben moved along the edge of the main pool. Matt could see Jenny shake her head and move to stop him, but McRay put a hand out to hold her back. Clive had gone quiet, hugging himself and thinking.

'Clive?'

'Is she warm enough?'

Matt thought Ben seemed unsure of what to say, and he was now too far away for Matt to coach him.

'Well, we could go together and check her out,' Ben said, which was precisely what Matt would have advised.

Clive giggled. 'She won't like that. She won't like it at all.'

'Let's go to my place, then. I just want to hold you, Clive.'

'Love me?'

'Love and hold you.'

Matt could imagine how hard it must be for Ben to be saying these things to a person he had just found out was a serial murderer. He had done very well, but now his words were starting to have a hollow ring to them. It might be time to take over, but he was sure it shouldn't be him.

Matt looked over to Jenny who seemed to have the same idea, and she was walking forward to stand besides Ben. He just hoped she could play it differently and keep the strident tone out of her voice.

'Clive, do you think it might be a good idea to come down now and join your friend? You have won, and he wants to congratulate you.'

Everyone waited. Then Ben had the inspired idea to hold up his hands to Clive, beginning a clap that was hesitantly picked up around the room. Soon, the whole room was clapping. Up on the beam Clive seemed stunned, then he began to laugh, a mad, fierce sound. The clapping slowed and then petered out. Jenny was prompting Ben.

'Clive. Please come down to me.'

Still laughing, Clive began moving along the crossbeam. As he reached the junction with the supporting pillar, he swung himself across, then paused, grasping on with one hand while holding the other aloft, a bit like an actor acknowledging his audience, before starting to climb downwards.

It was as if everyone in the area knew this was a crucial moment. No one moved. Clive must be safely on the ground and away from the pillar before he could be arrested.

Jenny was talking to Ben. Matt guessed she was asking if he would move towards Clive as if to greet him. Ben started to move forward, going around the side of the pool, while Jenny's hand held the others in check. Matt was holding his breath. Could this whole nightmare be over at last?

Clive slid the last few feet to the ground and held his arms out to Ben. Ben backed away in revulsion. Jenny gave a quick signal and Clive found both his arms held securely by two uniformed officers. His face twisted with pain at Ben's repulse, Clive was led away, screaming nonsense. There was no way he could be tried as a sane man.

CHAPTER 64

Matt couldn't remember too much of what happened straight afterwards. He vaguely recalled being moved to a trolley and of it speeding down the corridor to the lobby. The fluorescent lights whizzed by overhead and made his eyes hurt so much that he wanted to shut them, but he forced them to stay open. He needed to see for himself that Eppie was really safe.

The lobby seemed dizzyingly full of people. For a brief moment, he was aware of Mrs Trowbridge hovering over him, while the background was filled with police and paramedics.

He could see Jenny, halfway out the door, trying to get away from McRay. He wanted to ask how Fluff was but no one seemed to be taking any notice of him. He felt invisible, way below everyone's eyesight. They all seemed intent on their own tasks.

Matt could see an ambulance, drawn up at the entrance, doors open waiting to receive him. He tried to sit up, to protest, only to find that he was tied down in some way. He had to make someone listen to him. Then the trolley stopped and his own friendly paramedic crouched beside him.

'It's OK, mate. We've just fastened you in for the ride. You're going to be all right.'

'Eppie.' It was all Matt could manage. He was relieved to see the man stand and look around as if searching for her.

Then she was there beside him, smiling and reaching out from her wheelchair to hold his hand. He found himself squeezing her hand, unable to say any of the things he wanted to, like not wanting to face life without her, but it didn't matter right now.

Matt was annoyed when McRay's dark bulk bent over him, spoiling the moment.

'Well done, Matt.' McRay patted him gingerly on the shoulder, as if afraid he would break. Matt let go of Eppie's hand and forced himself to ask. 'Fluff, Grant?'

But from the look on McRay's face, he knew the news wasn't good.

'DC Meadows—touch and go, but she is getting the best care. DI Grant will be fine.'

Matt thought of the debt he owed to them both.

McRay had turned to Eppie.

Afterwards, Matt wasn't sure he had quite heard what was said, but it sounded like, 'I hear you played a big part in the apprehension of this murderer. Maybe you should think about joining the force, Mrs Turrell.'

Matt also hoped he had imagined the gleam in Eppie's' eye at this suggestion.

THE END

2096619R00172

Printed in Great Britain
by Amazon.co.uk, Ltd.,
Marston Gate.